Outstanding praise for Lisa Jackson!

"No one tells a story like Lisa Jackson. She's headed
straight for the top!"
—Debbie Macomber

"Lisa Jackson takes my breath away."
—Linda Lael Miller

Outstanding praise for Elizabeth Bass!

"Bass introduces wonderfully needy characters who
discover their untapped strength. The teens and their relationships are particularly well developed. Kristin Hannah
fans and readers attracted to Lisa Genova's novels will appreciate this novel. Definitely buy for readers who demand
character growth and relationships in their fiction."
—*Library Journal* on *Wherever Grace Is Needed*

"Bass's sparkling debut will inspire laughs and tears . . .
With bountiful grace and a real feeling for her characters,
Bass creates a three-hanky delight."
—*Publishers Weekly* on *Miss You Most of All*

Outstanding praise for Holly Chamberlin!

"A great summer read."
—*Fresh Fiction* on *Summer Friends*

"Explores questions about the meaning of home,
family dynamics and tolerance."
—*The Bangor Daily News* on *The Family Beach House*

Outstanding praise for Mary Carter!

"A marvelous combination of wit and heart and a reflection
of the way a couple can endure one another's faults for the
sake of love and devotion."
—*RT Book Reviews* on *The Things I Do for You*

"Gripping, entertaining and honest. This is a unique,
sincere story about the invisible, unbreakable bonds of
sisterhood that sustain us no matter how far they're buried."
—Cathy Lamb on *My Sister's Voice*

Books by Lisa Jackson

Stand-Alones

SEE HOW SHE DIES * FINAL SCREAM * RUNNING SCARED
WHISPERS * TWICE KISSED * UNSPOKEN * DEEP FREEZE
FATAL BURN * MOST LIKELY TO DIE * WICKED WAYS
SINISTER * WICKED GAME * WICKED LIES * SOMETHING
WICKED * WITHOUT MERCY * YOU DON'T WANT TO KNOW
CLOSE TO HOME * AFTER SHE'S GONE * REVENGE

Anthony Paterno/Cahill Family Novels

IF SHE ONLY KNEW * ALMOST DEAD

Rick Bentz/Reuben Montoya Novels

HOT BLOODED * COLD BLOODED * SHIVER
ABSOLUTE FEAR * LOST SOULS * MALICE * DEVIOUS
NEVER DIE ALONE

Pierce Reed/Nikki Gillette Novels

THE NIGHT BEFORE * THE MORNING AFTER
TELL ME

Selena Alvarez/Regan Pescoli Novels

LEFT TO DIE * CHOSEN TO DIE * BORN TO DIE
AFRAID TO DIE * READY TO DIE
DESERVES TO DIE

Books by Elizabeth Bass

MISS YOU MOST OF ALL * WHEREVER GRACE IS NEEDED
THE WAY BACK TO HAPPINESS * LIFE IS SWEET

Books by Holly Chamberlin

LIVING SINGLE * THE SUMMER OF US * BABYLAND * BACK
IN THE GAME * THE FRIENDS WE KEEP * TUSCAN HOLIDAY
ONE WEEK IN DECEMBER * THE FAMILY BEACH HOUSE
SUMMER FRIENDS * LAST SUMMER * THE SUMMER
EVERYTHING CHANGED * THE BEACH QUILT
SUMMER WITH MY SISTERS * SEASHELL SEASON

Books by Mary Carter

SHE'LL TAKE IT * ACCIDENTALLY ENGAGED * SUNNYSIDE
BLUES * MY SISTER'S VOICE * THE PUB ACROSS THE POND
THE THINGS I DO FOR YOU * THREE MONTHS IN FLORENCE
MEET ME IN BARCELONA * LONDON FROM MY WINDOWS
HOME WITH MY SISTERS

Published by Kensington Publishing Corporation

LISA JACKSON

Summer Days

ELIZABETH BASS
MARY CARTER
HOLLY CHAMBERLIN

ZEBRA BOOKS
Kensington Publishing Corp.
http://www.kensingtonbooks.com

ZEBRA BOOKS are published by

Kensington Publishing Corp.
119 West 40th Street
New York, NY 10018

All Kensington titles, imprints and distributed lines are available at
special quantity discounts for bulk purchases for sales promotion, pre-
miums, fund-raising, educational or institutional use.

Special book excerpts or customized printings can also be created to fit
specific needs. For details, write or phone the office of the Kensington
Sales Manager. Attn.: Sales Department. Kensington Publishing Corp.,
119 West 40th Street, New York, NY 10018. Phone: 1-800-221-2647.

Zebra and the Z logo Reg. U.S. Pat. & TM Off.

First Kensington Books Trade Paperback Printing: May 2014
First Zebra Books Mass-Market Paperback Printing: June 2016
ISBN-13: 978-1-4201-4148-1
ISBN-10: 1-4201-4148-1

eISBN-13: 978-1-4201-4441-3
eISBN-10: 1-4201-4441-3

10 9 8 7 6 5 4 3 2 1

Printed in the United States of America

CONTENTS

YOU AGAIN

Elizabeth Bass

CHAPTER 1

A glint of light made Meredith turn her head. *Was that Sam?*

No. Absolutely not. An airport, international flights, was the last place Sam Desmond would turn up. Sam was the guy who, when she'd once dreamed aloud of a getaway to Paris, had replied, "What's in Paris?"

Not a world traveler, Sam. At least he hadn't been when she had known him.

Still, in the moment before she got caught at the back of the security line, she'd glimpsed a man who looked like Sam on the other side of the Plexiglas barrier, his tall, trim figure disappearing around the corner. The man had been wearing glasses—no doubt the source of the glint—and he'd had short, brown hair. She'd always loved the way Sam's floppy cowlick had defied his efforts to maintain an über-orderly appearance.

She took a mental step back. *Let's see . . . tall, glasses, brown hair.* That only described about hundreds of thousands of guys in New York City, never mind the rest of the tristate area, as well as males from places the world over who might be connecting through JFK Airport today. "Stats and probabilities don't favor that scenario," Sam himself would have reminded her, eyeing her in that worried, pinched-brow way, as if trying to decide whether he'd made a huge error hooking up with someone who, in addition to never having gotten to the second level of The Legend of Zelda, had never taken calculus, and wasn't interested in string theory.

Which was part of the reason she'd broken up with Sam in the first place. Anyway, this probably wasn't him. She took a deep breath, stepped out of her shoes, and tossed them into a plastic tub.

Still, that glimpse had set off all kinds of ringing in her head, and try as she might to ignore the sound, the bells kept swinging. The clanging lasted through the X-ray and the wait for everyone's parade of almost-too-large carry-ons, laptops, and other paraphernalia to be scanned on the conveyer belt. As they were stepping back into their shoes, she turned to her sister. "Maybe this isn't such a good idea. My coming along, I mean."

Janie's big eyes widened. "What? Why?"

"Oh . . ." Mentioning a phantom sighting of Sam to Janie would be conversational suicide. Her sister would think she was losing her mind. It had been seven years, and from long experience Meredith knew the equation. *Janie + me voicing Sam regret = mental health lecture.* So Meredith reached for other equally valid reasons for not stepping on a flight to Peru with a bunch of people she barely knew, who all shared an interest in an activity she only halfheartedly participated in. "I don't really belong."

"Sure you do. You've been coming to the class . . . off and on."

Off and on, because she got an occasional guest pass at the yoga studio Janie belonged to. She appealed to Janie's frugal nature. "And the money . . ."

"The money has been spent," her sister said. "The time to back out of a trip is not after you've already cleared security."

So true. And she didn't want to back out—that is, she didn't want to bail on her sister, who was here for her sake. Janie was a reluctant traveler who usually needed to be blasted out of New York, but she'd known Machu Picchu was a place Meredith had always dreamed of going.

Meredith nodded and tried not to appear troubled as they moved down the open corridor toward their gate.

Obviously, she didn't succeed in hiding her angst, because Janie said, "If you're feeling mixed up, maybe the universe is trying to tell you something. It's trying to tell you that you need to take a break and stop worrying so much."

According to her sister, the universe was always trying to get through to people—and by some coincidence, its message always sounded as if it had been dictated by Janie.

And why not? The voice of Meredith's universe had always been Janie's. Meredith had been a late-life baby, seven years younger than her sister, and their mother had died before Meredith's second birthday. As far back as she could remember, Janie had been her lighthouse, telling her how to navigate life's rocky shores. Even after their dad married Christa—Clueless Christa, they'd called her—Janie's had continued to be the mom voice in Meredith's head: *"Sit up straight." "Don't put your mouth on that." "Do you* really *want to wear that to school?"* But Janie was still the big sister, so she was also saying things like *"If you don't stop singing that stupid song about waltzing bears I'll haul you to the zoo myself and feed you to the grizzlies."*

Janie was sending her that feed-you-to-the-grizzlies look right now.

"You're right," Meredith said, soldiering on toward the gate.

The gate, where Sam was honest-to-God standing, staring right at her. She smiled and even let out a laugh, as much at his comical shock as from the joy of making eye contact with him again after so long. Sam did not smile back.

Her gaze shifted to the woman next to him. *Gina?*

Meredith's smile froze. It *was* Gina. Janie's best frenemy.

Gina of the perfect bendy-stretchy yoga body, which, no matter what pose they did, was always flexible enough to enable her to turn and aim a superior smirk at Meredith's amateur efforts. She of the ice-blue eyes and blond hair with blonder highlights. Gina, who seemed to be one of those people put on the planet to intervene on the off chance that Meredith started to feel a little too self-confident.

Sam, evidently, was Gina's traveling companion. Her alternate yoga mat was slung over his shoulder.

Janie caught sight of Gina as they approached the gate. "Oh, look," she muttered to Meredith. "Gina brought Mr. Fabulous with her."

"Mr. Who?" Meredith squeaked, certain she had heard wrong. *Fabulous* was not a word her sister would ever have used to describe Sam. Ever.

"The boyfriend she's always blathering about," Janie said.

Meredith swallowed. "Do you see—?"

"Of course I see," Janie hissed under her breath. "Alviero Martini luggage for a trip into the Andes! She'll probably get us all kidnapped by Shining Path guerrillas, or whatever they have down there now. If some of us come back without ears, guess who will be to blame."

Gina and Janie eyed each other with the intensity of two friendly cobras facing off. Then, standing toe-to-toe, they both smiled, dropped their carry-on bags, and threw their arms around each other with gleeful squeals.

"Can you believe it?"

"We're finally on our way!"

Others from the yoga group lined up to take their turns greeting the new arrivals. They were a huggy bunch. Meredith said hello to Claudia, their instructor and group leader, and a few of the women Janie always dismissed as yoga mommies. Meredith had only been to the class three times, so she didn't really feel comfortable hugging anybody yet. Unfortunately, *not* hugging just made her feel more first-day-of-schoolish and alien.

She stood to the side and studiously avoided catching Sam's eye until she could be sure to do so without making an idiot out of herself. Heat rose in her cheeks even as she listened to her sister and Gina spewing compliments at each other.

"Look at you," Gina said. "Gorgeous even at seven a.m.!"

"You smell like mangoes. Is that your shampoo?"

Meredith cast a surreptitious glance at Sam. He was staring intently at his shoes.

What was he doing here? How had this happened?

Janie had never liked Sam, and as a result Sam had always resented the sway Janie held over Meredith. Even when she and Sam had been a couple, Meredith had tried to avoid get-togethers with the three of them. Now they were all unwittingly going on vacation together. The three of them . . . and Gina.

Gina finally pulled back from the lovefest and yanked Sam to her side. "Janie, this is—"

"Sam?" When at last Janie recognized the man with Gina, she stepped back, almost stumbling like an ingénue in a horror film scrambling to escape the zombie.

"Hello, Janie," he said without joy.

Gina's smile froze, and her gaze flicked anxiously between them. "You know each other?"

"We used to. That is, Meredith knew him."

At that point, there was nothing to do but look straight at Sam, who finally smiled back at her. "Hi, Meredith."

"Hi, Sam. I'm surprised to see you here."

Gina stepped forward, hooking a proprietary arm through his. "Why surprised? Sam was the one who insisted we come when he saw the brochure I brought home from the studio. He said it would be adventurous, and romantic."

Sam pulled Gina even closer and kissed the top of her head. Meredith's stomach did a drop and roll, and she could feel her eyebrows leaping into her forehead in unison with Janie's.

She shot a desperate glance at her sister. Was it still too

late to back out after you'd cleared security but before you'd stepped onto a South America–bound plane with the one-time love of your life and his horrid new girlfriend?

"I warned you the company would be dreary," Gina said.

Sam tensed. Not that Meredith and Janie would be able to hear them. They were three rows back, and the roar of the plane's engines during takeoff absorbed sound. But the others . . .

Who was he kidding—he didn't care about the others. Just Meredith. How had this happened?

While planning the trip, he hadn't given much thought to the other people on the tour, or anticipated feeling like an interloper. But among the group of nine women he was definitely the odd man out, even though a guy name Seth had appeared just before boarding. Seth was both bearded and bald, enthusiastically hugged everybody a few seconds longer than was comfortable, and lugged an acoustic guitar as his only carry-on item. He obviously considered himself part of the group, even though the others didn't seem ecstatic about his presence.

But Sam wasn't here for the other people. This trip was about him and Gina. He'd been bugging her to go somewhere together for months, but she hadn't wanted to leave New York and be "thrown off her stride." Whatever that meant. He'd guessed she didn't want to leave her routine—she was a busy person and he was too, so he could understand that reluctance. But he was determined not to make the mistakes with Gina that he'd made with past girlfriends. When he'd spotted the brochure about the trip to Machu Picchu, he'd leapt on it as the perfect solution. They could have a travel adventure, and Gina could take part of her routine with her—the yoga part.

But now it appeared he was inadvertently taking his romantic past with him too.

Gina plucked the in-flight magazine from the seat pocket in front of her. "You never mentioned you knew Janie. I know I've talked about her. We used to have coffee together all the time after class."

"I guess I heard you mention the name, but I never knew it was the same Janie."

"How many Janies are there in New York?"

He could never tell if she was just messing with his head when she asked questions like that. Because he was pretty sure she knew that in a city of eight million, there were a lot of Janies. "To be honest, I probably haven't thought about Janie in years. It was her sister I knew. Meredith and I attended the same college and ended up sharing an apartment in New York the summer after we graduated. It was a friend-of-a-friend arrangement, for a summer, just because we were both new in the city. And it was a lifetime ago." God, he needed to stop babbling. It made him sound guilty. Gina said nothing, so he added, "I barely recognized her just now," for good measure.

"Really?" Her brows soared in curiosity. "But she's in that commercial. Even I recognized her when Janie dragged her to class, and I don't even pay attention to diet food."

"Commercial?"

"Slim Delites brownies. You mean you know her and you never noticed?" Gina smiled, pleased. "She plays the fatty who decides to eat a Slim Delites brownie instead of a whole bag of Oreos. Though obviously in real life, Meredith does the opposite."

"She looks healthy to me." Just the same as she ever did.

"That's one way of putting it. She weighs 142." Gina enunciated the number as if dropping a bombshell with each syllable.

How did she know Meredith's weight?

"There's a digital scale at the studio," she replied, as if she had spyware in his brain. "And she actually gets on it. When other people are around." She licked the tip of her finger and flicked a page of her magazine. "Not. Very. Bright."

He remained silent, and then felt unchivalrous for not standing up for Meredith. A voice from a lifetime ago floated up from the recesses of his mind. *"Obviously, I expect a little more from you than you're willing to give."*

He bristled. Why should he stand up for someone who'd walked out on him?

And it had to be said, the gaping holes in Meredith's education had always stunned him. Not very bright? How could he argue with that? Once, when Meredith had been quizzing him for a graduate school entrance exam, it had become clear that she completely misunderstood the concept behind the word *binary*. God only knows what theater majors studied in college, but it was tragically apparent that budding thespians weren't getting past base-ten mathematics.

"We would have been better off having a stay-cay in the city," Gina said. "We should be hunting for an apartment, not traipsing around Peru with these characters."

They had decided to move in together, but both their apartments were too tiny to make a practical home for two, even in the short term. Her house-hunting vacation would have been more sensible, but he wasn't feeling sensible. If there was anything he'd learned from past romantic failures, it was that sensible sank relationships.

He had all sorts of romantic things planned for this trip. Activities lined up pleasantly in his mind, mirroring the to-do list app on his phone. First, the candlelit dinner in Cuzco at the special restaurant he'd found. Followed by a romantic journey into the Andes, topped off with a proposal at the top of the world, against the backdrop of the glorious ruins of Machu Picchu.

That last cost him a moment's worry. Sure, they *looked* glorious online, but were they? Also, the place would probably be crawling with tourists. It might be like popping the question in the middle of Time's Square, and if that was the case, what was the point of traveling all that way and spending so much money—?

No. That kind of thinking was very Old Sam. He was New Sam now. New Sam didn't do cost-benefit analysis when it came to marriage proposals.

A signal dinged throughout the cabin, and the flight attendant announced that the captain had okayed the use of electronic devices. Janie tossed her magazine into his lap and whipped out her iPad.

"What are you doing?"

"Checking messages." She tapped and scrolled, reabsorbed into the world they were flying away from.

Suppressing a sigh, he started reading a travel article on Wisconsin. The writer was attempting to move away from the cheese-and-beer angle and create some razzle-dazzle about his subject, but in the end he just focused on the expensive cheese, the high-end beer. Sam struggled to keep his mind from wandering.

He'd have to pick up a paperback at the Miami airport.

He wondered what Meredith read on long flights. In the old days, she'd always gone to the library and come back lugging armloads of stuff, more than anyone could read in the time the library permitted. Then she would forget the due dates, or a book would end up lost behind a couch cushion, and the delinquent fees would mount. Within three months of arriving in New York, she owed the library eighty-nine dollars—which seemed mathematically impossible. Short of hurling books into the East River, how did anyone end up owing that much? He'd set up an Excel file for her on her computer to keep track of what she borrowed. She forgot to use it.

The puzzling part was, Meredith had seemed to resent his giving her that spreadsheet. It was as if she thought that by trying to fix a problem for her, he was judging her, or criticizing her. When really it just pained him to see her tossing money away.

Money had been so tight that summer. Boxed-macaroni-and-cheese tight, sometimes. An aspiring actress, Meredith had limited herself to temp jobs to accommodate auditions she never got called for. And though he made okay money working in a bank, rent ate up over half their income, and the rest just seemed to dissolve after a couple of weeks of meeting friends at bars after work and for movies on weekends. Eventually it dawned on them that they weren't in college anymore. By the sultry end of August, he was saving for graduate school, and they passed most of their time in their tiny apartment, trying to economize. Video games and cards for entertainment, cheap wine from Trader Joe's, lazy sleeping-in weekends . . . The apartment had been cramped, the future completely precarious.

He'd never been so happy. He'd never been in love before. Really in love. All the goofy symptoms his friends had displayed back in high school—the vacant grins, the humming of mindless pop songs out loud without realizing it—he had exhibited for the first time at age twenty-three.

"Oh. My. God."

Gina's cheeks had turned a chalky white.

"What's wrong?" he asked.

"Another fish tank catastrophe in New Hampshire. The third one this week." She frantically tapped out a missive on the screen's keyboard. "An orthodontist's office this time. The Perfect Pride people are in a panic."

He frowned. This must have to do with an account she did PR for. "I thought Perfect Pride made dog food, cat food . . . stuff like that."

Her lips tightened. "Fish food would fall under the category 'stuff like that.' "

"Oh." He tilted his head. "I had some goldfish die when I was a kid. I forgot to put drops in the water or something."

"This isn't about *drops*. It's about Perfect Pride Fish Flakes. And these weren't crappy little feeder fish you win at a street fair; these were exquisite tropical fish that cost hundreds if not thousands of dollars. I can't believe this is happening—and now, of all times." She smiled tightly and took a sharp breath. "I need to draft a release, okay? Read your magazine and chill. I'll come up for air in a minute."

He was going to remind her that they were on vacation, but that might have pushed her over the edge. Instead, seeing his chance to stretch his legs before the drink cart came up, he stood and headed to the back of the plane. At Meredith's row, he noted the empty window seat. In the middle, Janie sat reading the article on Wisconsin. Looking up from a picture of a Holstein, she darted a quick, suspicious, accusatory glance at him.

He hurried on.

A short line snaked away from the washrooms in the back of the plane, jamming the aisle. Sam considered going straight back to his seat, but Gina would still be working, he still wouldn't have a book, and now the drink cart was pulling even with his row. He stood hunched, ignoring the irritated glances from the people sitting in the aisle seats. Nearby, a baby started wailing. Was it any wonder he avoided traveling? Planes were torture for everyone, even for the recently born, who at least had plenty of legroom.

The man in front of him turned around. It was Seth. "Typical," he confided to Sam in a not-very-quiet voice. "There's always a line when my bowels are at their most volatile."

The woman ahead of them pivoted and shot Seth a look of alarm.

"So . . ." Stroking his beard contemplatively, Seth leaned in to Sam. "So you knew the sister. Old girlfriend?"

Sam shrugged. "It was a long time ago. Technically, we were just apartment mates."

"Lived together, no less!" Seth chuckled. "Personally, I think Janie's way hotter, even if she is sort of . . . you know. High-strung. But I sort of go for sophisticated women."

Sam smiled tightly and repeated what he'd told Gina. "Well, when Meredith and I were together—apartment mates—we were a lot younger. Just out of college. We're both probably a lot different now. I didn't even recognize her at first."

The washroom door jerked open, and Meredith burst out, her eyes widening at the number of people waiting, then popping open a little more when she saw Sam at the end of the line. She edged past them all as the person in front of Seth gave him her place.

"Hey," Meredith greeted Sam. "I had no idea you were coming on this trip."

"Me neither," he said. "I mean . . . I didn't know about you. Of course. I didn't even know you were in New York. Or that Gina and your sister knew each other."

She nodded. "That's New York—big city, small world."

"For all I knew, you were still in London."

Was he mistaken, or did she flinch a little? "No, I'm back. Have been for some time. Years, actually."

The smile disappeared, and suddenly he regretted mentioning London. The Meredith of his memory was usually such a good-natured, laughing kind of person that he'd forgotten her way of looking wounded. It was something about those big brown eyes in her pale face, framed by that reddish hair. In the blink of an eye it was so easy for her to appear fragile, under siege. Her war-orphan look.

"Well . . ." She moved to continue to her seat, but was stymied when she saw the drink cart. She was trapped now too. Her brows knit for a moment, but then she laughed. "Eventually, aren't we all going to end up crushed into the flight attendant alcove? It's going to be like the Marx Brothers with all the people crammed into the stateroom."

"'And two hard-boiled eggs,'" he piped up, not quite succeeding at a Groucho impersonation. He and Meredith had seen *A Night at the Opera* together one night at the outdoor summer movies in Bryant Park.

A chortle erupted out of her, and suddenly seven years didn't seem that long ago.

Ten rows away, Janie's head bobbed over the top of her

seat. She peered back at them for just an instant, but an instant was all it took. Sam's smile dissolved.

Meredith's laughter trailed off too, and she eyed him curiously. "How long have you and Gina been together?"

"Not long . . ." He shook his head. "Well, eight months."

She tipped her head to one side. "Longer than . . ."

Longer than he and Meredith had lived together. Not that there was any comparison. He and Gina were more serious—thinking about marriage. Something he and Meredith had never reached the point of discussing. They'd been at a different stage in their lives then, so it wouldn't have made sense. Also, she'd run off to London.

Technically, he and Gina hadn't discussed marriage yet, either, except in a "maybe someday" kind of way, but he hoped this trip would change that. Unconsciously, he patted the ring box in his pocket.

Awkwardness stretched the seconds out to their ragged limits, until Meredith nodded over his shoulder. "Restroom's free."

Sam fled into the tiny compartment, nearly bashing his forehead against some ceiling protuberance in the process. Despite the fact that he couldn't stand straight, the coldness, and the general ick factor, it was a relief to have a little privacy. His heart thumped. He wished he had thought of something better to say to Meredith after all these years. But what? What was there to say?

Not a day went by that I didn't think of getting on a flight to London to find you.

Of course, saying that would have been entirely inappropriate. Gina occasionally dressed him down for being socially tone-deaf, but even he knew that sometimes the best thing was to stay mum. Especially to an old girlfriend. Especially when new girlfriend was waiting for you in 9A.

When he left the washroom, there was no line. The drink cart had vanished. He hurried back to his row, careful not to look at Meredith and Janie as he passed. As he dropped into his seat, Gina twisted her lips at him. "I thought maybe you'd decided to camp out in there," she said. "I had time to draft an entire damage-control message for after the recall."

He stammered about the line and the drink cart, ending with, "Meredith was stuck too," spoken so breathlessly it sounded as if he were confessing some indiscretion.

"You poor thing," Gina said. "So what did you guys talk about?"

"Oh, I don't know. What's there to say?"

"To her? Not much. She's never been chatty the few times she's come to the studio. From what I can glean from Janie, Meredith is one of these goofballs who's never quite gotten it together. She does catch-as-catch-can legal proofreading for a living—and I'm sure without Janie, who's an attorney, she wouldn't even have that. Occasionally she lands an audition. The rest of the time she's involved in some theater in Astoria. Modern stuff—you know, showcasing original works by undiscovered genius playwrights in Queens. Bet they're packing them in."

"Well, being an actress can't be easy."

Gina nodded. "Especially not when you're the size of a caribou. I mean, who wants to look at that?"

He framed a diplomatic answer, but she didn't give him time to use it.

"Anyway, from what I can tell she'd be lost without her sister. Janie goes way beyond the call of duty to keep her from making stupid mistakes. Even packed her off to London once."

Sam froze. "London?" He sensed he should stop Gina, yet was unable to form words that would do the trick.

"Poor Janie. She buttonholed some professional contact there who could give Meredith a BS internship. And believe me, if Janie was willing to shell out for a plane ticket, she must have been desperate—that woman is cheap. But apparently baby Meredith had attached herself to some loser."

"Loser," he repeated.

She snorted. "Mr. McBoring-Boring, to hear Janie tell it. Evidently he wasn't even very well-off. It's hard to see what Meredith saw in this zero. And then, to top it all off"—Gina lowered her voice—"Meredith had a miscarriage, and the guy's basic reaction was *phew*." She shook her head. "A real gem."

It was all he could do to stay in his seat. It hadn't been a miscarriage—it had been a false alarm. And he'd never said *phew!*

He'd said, "Oh, thank God."

His face felt fiery hot, and he looked out the window into an opaque sky of clouds.

McBoring . . .

This was all coming through the Janie filter, he reminded himself. Janie had never thought he was good enough for Meredith. But even so, *some* of it must have come from Meredith . . . and some of it was simply the truth.

Gina beetled her brows at him. "You aren't feeling airsick, are you?"

He shook his head.

"Good." She leaned her head against his shoulder and sighed. "I'm so glad you talked me into going on vacation. I'm not doing another lick of work. Every mile farther I get from the office, and Perfect Pride, and fish food recalls, the happier I feel. How about you?"

He nodded, which she probably couldn't see anyway. Inside his head, questions roared over the 747 jet engines. So Janie had admitted she'd talked Meredith into going to London all those years ago. That would indicate that Meredith hadn't been so eager to leave him as he'd always assumed.

So why had she?

CHAPTER 2

"If you really want to lose weight, wheatgrass juice is the way to go."

Meredith glanced at Seth and then back to the line in Starbucks, where Janie stood with a couple of others from the yoga group. Meredith had been watching her and Janie's carry-ons while Janie talked to the airline person at the gate and then grabbed coffees for them.

Seth didn't drink coffee. To hear him tell it, his diet consisted primarily of wheatgrass juice and macadamia nuts.

"Have you ever tried wheatgrass juice?"

She shook her head, only half paying attention. Her gaze kept sweeping the terminal, searching for signs of Sam and Gina. They had gone off by themselves. Thank heavens. Seeing him had rattled her brain, dislodging memories she'd tried to keep buttoned down for years. The best strategy for this trip would be to avoid him as much as possible.

"I would have been able to give you a taste right now, if they hadn't confiscated my bottles." Seth shrugged. "But I'm not worried. I'll probably be able to buy more in Cuzco. And if not, they make tea from coca leaves that's supposed to have amazing healing properties." He chomped another nut. "They probably have lots of natural diet remedies too."

She turned to him. "I'm not on a diet."

He bobbed back on his heels. "Just sayin', wheatgrass juice is a lot more healthful than brownies."

"I don't eat Slim Delites products." The brownie had tasted like cardboard, for one thing. But the commercial had been a once-in-a-decade windfall that had allowed her to take this trip. "That's a commercial. Just because you see people on the television doing things, it doesn't mean those people do those things in real life."

The man wasn't listening. He nodded toward Claudia, the group leader, who was in line next to Janie. Janie should have been the actress. She'd inherited Liz Taylor looks from their mother, and she was also the sister with stage presence and command. But of course, Janie wouldn't have been able to stand a life based so much on whim, chance, and uncertainty. Though heaven knows, there were enough of all those things in the law. But with a much better payoff.

"Don't you think she's hot?" Seth asked.

"Janie?"

"God no. I know she's foxy."

Meredith blinked. She wasn't sure she'd heard a man call a woman foxy since . . . well, ever.

"Claudia," he clarified.

Hot? Meredith was accustomed to thinking of Claudia as a mentor or goddess figure rather than an actual corporal being who could be gauged for hotness. Her face was fixed in that serene look Meredith imagined came from having done yoga forever and never experiencing a cramped muscle or negative thought. She was The Other.

"I've never heard that she's involved with anyone." Seth's expression was set in contemplation. "Think I have a chance?"

She squinted at the specks of nut lodged in Seth's black beard.

He sighed. "Me neither." His gaze fixed on Meredith. "Are you seeing anyone?"

Oh God. Another person to avoid. She imagined herself a few days from now, cowering in remote corners of Incan ruins while the rest of the group did their sun salutations at Machu Picchu.

Seth chuckled. "I mean, I know you and that Sam guy were an item once, but he's taken now. Anyway, that was forever ago. College, right?"

"Just after." She tilted her head. "Did he tell you that?"

"Well, he mentioned you were *a lot* younger then. In fact, he said you looked so much older now he hardly recognized you."

Meredith bent down to retie her shoe to cover the fact that her cheeks were on fire. Her skin was too pale to be able to camouflage a blush. So Sam had said she looked like an old hag. Well, maybe not in those words, but that's probably what he'd meant.

Meanwhile, Sam looked better than ever. The planes of his face were more angular, less boyish. He wore nicer clothes, more expensive clothes. Even his glasses had become more stylish, instead of the big geeky wire frames that used to perch on his nose. He'd been updated, buffed, while she had just lost her bloom.

She'd thought he'd been avoiding her gaze because of awkwardness. Maybe it had just been complete lack of interest, or discomfort at how different she seemed.

When she straightened up again, Janie was hurrying over. Her sister handed her a café au lait. "What are you two talking about?"

"Wheatgrass juice," Meredith said, fearing Seth would blurt out the truth. The last thing she wanted was for Janie to think she was obsessing about Sam. Even if she was.

Especially if she was.

Janie tugged her away, saying in a low voice, "I wouldn't spend too much time around Seth. He might get ideas."

Meredith chuckled. "He's already got them, but I don't think he's particular. He thinks you're foxy, by the way."

Janie tossed a gaze back at him. "Really?" Then she shuddered a little. "No. I might get past the Anton LaVey look and the John the Baptist eating habits, but that guitar is a threat. Last Valentine's Day he showed up with it at the studio and did an entire afternoon of romantic folk-rock favorites in a unitard."

A few yards from their gate, Janie stopped, pivoted on her heel, and dragged Meredith in the opposite direction, toward a seating section that was a gate away from where they needed to be. "Why don't we go sit over there, next to the window? You brought your sunscreen, right?"

"I checked it."

"Not too close to the window, then."

"I'm not a vampire," Meredith grumbled, looking over her shoulder to the gate to see why Janie had fled. Sure enough, Sam and Gina were sitting together, Gina leaning against him, ferociously focused on some electronic device. Sam's hand rested on her leg, but his gaze darted nervously toward Meredith, almost as if he expected her to swoop down and break up the happy twosome.

She realized now that Janie was trying to keep her away from Sam, to spare her feelings. Of course, she herself had decided to use the same strategy. But now it seemed silly, almost teenager-like. All Sam saw when he looked at her now was someone old. So different he hadn't recognized her.

Which made sense. When they'd split up seven years ago, she'd been twenty-two years old. She was a different person now, as different from herself at twenty-two as her twenty-two-year-old self had differed from herself at fifteen. By that logic, it would be just as ridiculous for her to pine after Sam now as it would have been for her to have lusted after the Backstreet Boys in college.

"What are you thinking about?" Janie examined her face

avidly. Meredith's glance back at Sam and Gina hadn't escaped her notice.

"The Backstreet Boys," Meredith said, intending to put Janie's fears to rest.

But she might as well have answered *Sam, my one and only true love,* because that was evidently what Janie heard. "I am *so sorry.* If I had known Gina was in a relationship with Sam—of all people!—I never would have come on this trip. I certainly wouldn't have encouraged you to come. And I *really* wouldn't have arranged it so that we'd all be seated in the same row during the next flight."

Meredith tensed. They would all be sitting together?

"I tried to convince the stupid airline person at the gate to switch our seats," Janie said, "but the flight is booked except for first class. Which is hideously expensive. But don't worry—I will sit between you and them. I hate window seats anyway."

Janie was terrified of heights.

"It doesn't matter. Honestly."

"If only I'd known," Janie said. "But Gina was so cagey. She and I would go for coffee, and she'd talk about this fantastic guy she was seeing—successful, good-looking, fun. Does that sound like Sam to you?"

Meredith didn't answer. He was obviously different from his twenty-three-year-old self too. But not so different that she didn't recognize him even in that brief description. He had been fun, in a low-key way, and she'd always thought he was good-looking. He hadn't been successful, but who was successful right after college? He'd been hardworking, focused. Studious, even when they weren't in school.

"Even when she griped about him, it didn't sound like him," Janie went on, aggrieved, as though Gina had conned her by inadvertently going out with a mutual acquaintance. "She'd talk about how he was always too eager to do couply, romantic things, and to take a big vacation. Does that sound like your Sam?"

"He's not my Sam."

"Thank God!" Janie sent an eagle-sharp glance back at him and Gina. "Although I will say he's not as bad as I remembered. His taste in clothes has improved from the postgrad, rumpled look. That's a Ralph Lauren leather jacket he's wearing—I saw it at Barneys. Not cheap. Gina said he's an accountant at some big firm. Guess graduate school worked out for him."

"I'm glad. He deserves success." His family hadn't had much money when he was growing up, and he'd had to work several jobs and take an extra year to get through college, which had fueled him with ambition.

They'd moved into an apartment together after going to college in Boston because they were both moving to New York and he'd been the roommate of her friend's boyfriend senior year. For a while, it had seemed as if Sam didn't even realize she was female. He just viewed her as someone who used all the hot water in the mornings and was too fond of dumb TV shows. But somewhere around the end of June, she noticed she was no longer alone on the couch during *So You Think You Can Dance*.

One night while they were making popcorn in the tiny, airless kitchen, he had bumped into her, and she had turned and found herself flush against him. He'd kissed her for the first time then, kissed her until the popcorn burned and the smoke detector screeched at them.

"But of course, it all could have turned out differently," Janie said. "Like I told you at the time, he was practically a baby then. You both were. Which was the problem."

Looking back on the breakup, Meredith could see that she and Sam had been as Janie said. Blundering children, making all sorts of mistakes. They hadn't known how to communicate like adults yet, how to weather life's problems. And Janie had been one hundred percent correct—Meredith hadn't yet seen anything of life and would have missed out on a lot by settling down. But sometimes, in her weaker, lonelier moments, moments usually fueled by margaritas or cup-cakes or whatever comfort fuel was on the menu, she won-dered if taking Janie's advice and money and breaking up with Sam hadn't been her most childish mistake of all.

"But he's still the same person, underneath all the up-dated trappings," Janie went on. "We can't forget that."

"We won't," Meredith deadpanned. *We* wouldn't let our-selves.

Her sister tapped her fingers fretfully against her coffee cup. "It's just so unfortunate he's here—and that you're here."

"Why? Who cares?" The more Janie went on, the more Meredith saw how crazy it was to freak out. "It's not that big a deal. Just one of those fluky things life throws at you some-times."

"But if anything happens . . ."

"What can happen? I don't care about him, and I know he doesn't care about me."

Janie's eyes narrowed. "How do you know?"

"Because he has a girlfriend. He and Gina have been to-gether for eight months. That's a long time."

"Oh. Right." Her sister frowned. "And that says volumes about his taste, if you want my opinion."

"You like Gina."

Janie drew back as if surprised to hear it. "We were sort of friends, I guess. Coffee after class and that sort of thing. Then she got involved with Mr. Wonderful." Janie rolled her eyes. "*Sam.* If I'd known it was him she was dumping me for, I would have been more incensed. Of all people . . ."

Of all people. Meredith agreed with that. Of all the people to show up on her big vacation, why did it have to be Sam? Worse—Sam with Gina.

Fran, a woman from their group who was on her own, spot-ted them and veered over. "Oh! Sister pic!" Before Meredith could register her intention, Fran held up a digital camera and snapped a photo.

She grinned. "It's going on the blog." Fran wrote a blog called *Yogaholic in Manhattan*. The times Meredith had visited the site, the entries had mostly been gossipy items about Fran's job as an HR person for an insurance company. God only knew what she would write about this crew.

"I'm calling my Peru blog entries 'Yogaholic at the Top of the World.' " Fran said. "This is going to be such fun, don't you think?"

"Where are the others?" Janie asked.

Fran peered around the terminal. "I lost Claudia—although I think Claudia might have lost me. I don't think she's liked me much since I called her a yoga Nazi on the blog. Some people are too thin-skinned for their own good. And I saw the moms in the bar, but I didn't want to pay ten bucks for a drink, so I just snapped a pic and left. And there's Sam and Gina over there. . . ." Fran sighed. "I think it's so cool that we've already got these little groups forming. The sisters, the yoga moms, the lovebirds . . ."

Meredith followed her gaze to where Sam and Gina were still sitting, leaning against each other in lovey-dovey mode.

"Don't forget Seth," Janie piped up. "The gasbag."

"He does talk a lot," Meredith said.

Fran laughed. "*Not* the kind of gas she was talking about. Do not put your mat downwind of his."

Good to know.

"Oh! I see boarding action." Fran's elfin frame hopped in excitement. "Next stop, Peru!"

The three of them headed for the gate, where Gina and Sam were approaching the flight attendant at the door, boarding passes and passports extended.

Gina grinned at them. "Sam got us a surprise upgrade for the flight to Lima. Wasn't that sweet of him?"

Janie looked as if she'd swallowed a bug. "Awesome!"

Gina took her scanned boarding pass from the flight attendant, trilled her fingers at them, and practically skipped down the passageway to the plane. Sam hurried after Gina as Fran snapped a picture of their backs.

Once, Meredith had dreamed that he would follow her onto a plane. Not dutifully, but in a cinematic burst of love involving a sprint down a crowded avenue to hail a cab, mad hurdles over turnstiles and security checkpoints, and finally that long dash down the jetway. Oh, her mind had been on rom-com overdrive as she'd settled into her seat on that flight to London. But the panting, remorseful, loving costar of her hopeful fantasies had never materialized.

"The man obviously had air miles to burn," Janie grumbled as they milled about with the others, waiting for their boarding group to be called. "Either that, or he's a bigger spender than he used to be. More money than sense, if you ask me."

Or maybe he'd heard about the connecting seats and had the same impulse Janie had. But he hadn't let cost stop him.

Or maybe he just thinks Gina is worth it, Meredith thought.

CHAPTER 3

"This is not a luxurious hotel room. It does not exude charm or comfort. It's a tomb with twin beds."

"We have a private bath," Meredith pointed out. She was busy double-checking the sights she'd highlighted that they needed to see in Cuzco. The ruins of Qorikancha were a must-see, and there were at least two museums to hit. "I think some of the single rooms have to share one."

The rooms of the hotel were situated around a narrow, ragged courtyard that featured a long, rectangular strip of weedy grass with a neglected birdbath in the center of it. It was in the Spanish Colonial style, but with a stripped-down, budget effect. No graceful awning shaded the tile walkways outside the rooms, whose doorways were painted a sun-faded and peeling sky blue. There were no archways draped with hanging flowers, no bubbling fountains.

Janie plucked at the stiff plastic shower curtain that evidently did double-duty as a bathroom door. "Your idea of privacy must be different than mine." She peeked through the curtain at the rust-stained toilet and sink. An intermittent *splap* came from the dripping shower in the corner. No shower curtain encircled the shower—it was just open, like something you'd find at an outdoor pool.

"This is completely unacceptable," Janie said. "Where is Claudia? She promised us luxury accommodations. She said there would be charm." She glared at the drain in the center of the green square tiles, next to which lay a small bug carcass. "Completely primitive."

"Pretty tile color, though, isn't it?" Meredith asked.

"Penitentiary green," Janie said flatly. "And frankly, I'm not sure whether that's the tile color or mossy mildew."

Meredith chuckled, and immediately felt Janie's irritation that she could find anything in this situation to laugh about.

"We need to change hotels," Janie said.

Meredith balked at the idea. After losing an entire day of her life to airports and airplanes, she just wanted to be settled somewhere. She'd expected to feel dead on arrival, but during the bus ride from the airport, the countryside and exotic city had awakened her senses. It was one thing to read about a place being the heart of the Incan civilization—but here it was. The air was different. There were foresty peaks in the distance. She forgot about Sam, and Sam and Gina. She forgot about being so old and haggard that the man she'd broken her own heart over didn't even recognize her. This was the vacation of her dreams, and there was so much to do, and so little time.

So the Hostal Tres Chivos was a little primitive. Who cared about hotels? "How much time are we going to spend in our room? We should be out exploring, or going to the pre-Columbian art museum, or lounging in cafés and drinking in the scenery. Having a cup of rich coffee—maybe a yummy empanada."

The sidewalk café/pastry idea created instant mental diversion. Janie sank down onto one of the room's twin beds. The brightly woven pink bedspreads gave the damp, cavernlike room its one cheery note. "Empanada," she repeated. "That sounds good."

"Besides," Meredith continued, "I'm sure everyone is in the same boat, disappointment-wise. We don't want to start out the trip with the group acting as if we're too good for the hotel everyone else is staying in. We've got a whole week ahead with these people."

Egalitarian arguments didn't always work with Janie, but the possibility of being shunned by their temporary cohorts evidently did. And now that imaginary empanada was dangling temptingly in her mind. "You really think everyone else's rooms are the same?" Janie asked.

"Of course. It's not as if the hotel, or Claudia, would have singled us out for the crappy room."

At that moment, Fran flitted down the corridor outside their doorway. A few moments later, she backtracked and reappeared, standing on the threshold, slack-jawed. "Omigod. What a dump!"

Over her sister's head, Meredith began waving a warning, as you might to someone about to light up a cigarette in a fuel depot. Fran seemed too overwhelmed by awfulness to notice. Plus she'd found the most receptive audience ever in Janie.

"Yes!" Janie straightened. "Isn't it the pits?"

"Omigod," Fran repeated, with even more relish. She raced over to the shower curtain/door. "What is *this?*" She peeked into the bathroom and then cackled. "What are you guys supposed to do when you're both in the room together? Hold your poo?"

"That's what I was wondering," Janie said.

"It's not even a particularly clean shower curtain." Fran shook her head, and then her eyes lit up. "Can I take pictures? This is too gruesome not to share."

Meredith hung back during the photo shoot, interjecting halfhearted reminders about the pre-Columbian treasures and lively street life awaiting them while Janie and Fran dashed about, exclaiming over various stains and frayed wires. Also, what first had seemed to be a sponge-painted pattern on the wall on closer inspection turned out to be evidence of some kind of water seepage problem.

"The room is oozing," Janie said flatly.

"It is not—the wall is dry." To demonstrate, Meredith put her hand against the plaster—and then recoiled, eyeing the film of damp, ochre dirt on her hand. She shuddered. "Mostly dry."

"Yuck!" Janie said.

Fran snapped ooze stain pictures and photographed Meredith washing off the ooze dust in the rusty sink.

"But I guess everyone's rooms are sort of damp and dingy, right?" Meredith asked, even though it seemed unkind to be wishing dead bugs and ooze on the others. She just dreaded the idea of precious sightseeing hours being consumed in hotel hunting.

"Mine's fine," Fran said. "And Seth's is pretty nice too."

Janie tensed with bird dog alertness. "*Seth* has a better room than we do?"

"Actually, this is the worst room I've seen," Fran said.

Janie looked resolute. "I'm going to talk to Claudia."

"Good luck finding her," Fran said. "She's staying at a really swank place across town. She said this one was overbooked."

"That's just perfect," Janie fumed.

"But you guys should see the honeymoon suite," Fran said. "It's got a king-sized bed, a forty-inch television with satellite reception, and a Jacuzzi tub. That's where Sam and Gina are."

Meredith froze. The combination of *Sam and Gina* and *honeymoon suite* caught her off guard.

"That's it," Janie said. "Grab the *Frommer's*, Mer. We'll find something better."

Meredith didn't argue. The thought of bumping into Sam and Gina coming out of the honeymoon suite made her stomach churn. She snatched up her purse and the book. "Should we call a few places first?"

All three turned to the bare bedside table and then pivoted slowly, searching the few furniture surfaces for a phone.

There was no phone.

"Let's just go," Janie said, winging out the door.

Fran went back to her own room, and Meredith followed her sister. She wasn't going to argue. At least if they found a new hotel room, this leg of the trip would be Sam-and-Gina free. They would be harder to ignore when the group went to Machu Picchu. The village there, Aguas Calientes, was much smaller, and the group would all be doing the same activities, whereas here they were free to see whatever they wanted.

As she and Janie headed down the walkway toward the hotel's lobby—a charming, rustic room with beamed ceilings, clearly meant to sucker people in—Meredith couldn't help eyeing Janie's red pumps. They didn't look like good tourist gear. "Don't you want to change into walking shoes?"

"These are really comfy," Janie said.

Maybe comfy for a cab ride from Gramercy Park to the Upper West Side, Janie's natural habitat. But for exploring a foreign city on foot?

Cuzco was a big city—a swath of Spanish Colonial architecture with touches of even older civilization peeking through, along with splashes of modernity. Most of the city had seemed level, but the hotel was set high on a steep street in a hilly section of town.

Meredith hadn't noticed the incline of the street so much when they had arrived on the bus. The entrance to the hotel was in the center of a steep staircase that rose up from the street. It almost felt like a vertical alley, with walls of buildings within arm's reach on either side. Many had exclaimed how charming it seemed, even as they lugged their bags up the stairs. Now, as she teetered down the uneven, narrow sidewalk, she thought about having to go up that staircase every time they returned to the hotel.

Hostal Tres Chivos. It was beginning to make sense. "Maybe they named the hotel 'Three Goats' because it took goats to make it up the street."

"Or maybe it was where the goats lived," Janie muttered, her arm poised to grab the wall for balance.

As sightseeing strategies for viewing a town went, hunting for a hotel wasn't bad. They encountered bad luck—no free rooms—at the first several places they looked, but Meredith was just excited to be out wandering the streets and stretching her legs after being folded up in airplane seats for so long. The strange city and the mountains in the distance energized her. At moments she felt she could have bounded through the streets like a gazelle.

Janie wasn't so enthusiastic. "It's more crowded than I expected," she complained, clutching her purse tightly to her side. "And so touristy."

"It's the big tourist season," Meredith said.

"That Claudia," her sister muttered. "She would get us stuck here when there are mobs of people."

"The mobs are here for the same reason we are, though. The weather's so nice."

In fact, Hostal Tres Chivos aside, it felt as if they'd touched down in paradise. The weather was insanely gorgeous—sunny and a perfect seventy-five degrees. Hard to believe this was winter here. She'd take it over the already sweltering weather they'd left in NYC. Seeing the mountains made her antsy to put on her hiking boots and start exploring the ancient ruins hidden in those green peaks. Meanwhile, the streets busy with vendors, locals, and tourists of all stripes provided constant distraction. Only Janie's single-minded focus on hotels kept Meredith from wandering down side streets or stopping to snap pictures of every building and vendor.

After less than an hour tracking down five-star hotels, Janie started to look dispirited and complained of fatigue. Fifteen minutes later, her ankle turned on a cobblestone. One second they were trudging side by side, Janie's nose in the guidebook while Meredith gawked at the world around them. The next thing Meredith knew, Janie let out a bleat and then was leaning against the wall.

"What happened?"

Janie was holding her foot. "These crazy sidewalks," she complained, glaring at the offending stones. "Doesn't this country know how to make concrete? I might have broken my ankle."

"Oh no," Meredith said.

Janie closed her eyes and took a deep breath. "I think the universe is trying to tell me something. I need to get back and take it easy."

"To the hotel?" Meredith asked.

"Where else? I can't take a cab to Manhattan from here, can I?"

"But if you're hurt, shouldn't we get you to a doctor? The guidebook probably has the name of an emergency clinic. . . ."

"Nah, that's not necessary." Her sister limped toward the nearest intersection. "It's probably just sprained. I'll rest it for a bit and see how I feel tonight." She stuck out her hand and whistled at a vehicle barreling toward them. How she knew it was a cab was anyone's guess. Janie seemed to have a longtime New Yorker's unfailing instinct for flagging down taxis.

"You'll have to carry on the hotel hunt without me," she said, handing Meredith the guidebook, open to the pages with the best hotels underlined.

Meredith started to protest. She didn't even care about the hotel, and now Janie seemed perfectly happy to go back to their revolting little room. "Maybe we could look again tomorrow."

"It's not rocket science," Janie assured her. "Just find a five-star hotel. Double beds or better—preferably queens, en suite bath with a working door, non-crumbling walls, and room service." Janie got in the vehicle. Then, before the cab could speed away, she rolled down the window and called out, "And we don't want to spend more than eighty dollars per night."

Meredith stared after the retreating cab. A feeling of being ill-used made her breathe in shallow huffs, but she continued on. The first hotel she went to had a room, but there was just one bed in it, and she was not spending her vacation sharing a bed with her sister. At the next hotel—a beautiful Colonial building with long corridors of arched hallways overlooking a courtyard with flowers and a fountain—the clerk laughed at her when she asked for a room for eighty dollars or less. The cheapest room they had available was two hundred dollars.

She returned to the street, stewing. She loved Janie, but for heaven's sake. They only had a few days—she wanted to see something of the city beyond hotel lobbies. She'd been so happy when Janie had encouraged her to take her money from the stupid commercial and accompany her on vacation. She'd looked forward to getting away from all their usual routines and traveling together. Now she saw the downside. They might be seeing new sights, but they were their same old selves.

Why was this hotel hunt up to her? Even if she secured the perfect room, she suspected Janie would find fault with it. And then there would be more friction between them—Janie feeling huffy, Meredith inadequate. A wave of pre-resentment washed over her over this future hypothetical fight. Why did Janie have to be so uncompromising, so particular, so bossy?

It was just like Janie had been about Sam all those years ago. Okay, he hadn't been perfect. Who was perfect right out of college? Meredith certainly hadn't been. And yet Janie had nitpicked over his faults in Meredith's ear until those aspects of his character began to bug Meredith too. He wasn't fun-loving enough; he didn't care about culture; he thought she was hopelessly left-brained and unorganized. And how often did these post-college hookups work out, anyway? He was her roommate, for heaven's sake. Sleeping with your roommate was lazy and showed woeful lack of imagination. And where was the romance? Instead of flowers, he gave her Excel spreadsheets.

And how naïve, impressionable, and just plain stupid had Meredith been? At the first sign of trouble, she'd allowed herself to be talked out of a relationship by someone who wasn't actually in it. She'd let Janie influence her and whisk her away to London, as if she were an heiress in a Victorian novel being sent to Europe so she could forget she was in love with the chauffeur. And how often had the heiress actually forgotten about the chauffeur? Not often, Meredith bet.

It hadn't entirely worked with her, either. Leaving Sam had created a sore that had never quite healed. And, though rarely spoken of, the Sam question had always remained a point of friction between herself and Janie, the burr in the blanket of their sisterhood going on seven years now.

Meredith steamed down the street, furious with herself—again—for having been such a doormat when she was twenty-two. And for still being one today. What on earth had possessed her to come on this vacation? This should have been a grand adventure—the kind of vacation to savor each second exploring and discovering new things. Not to spend angsting over shower curtains. It was the kind of place to come to with someone you were crazy in love with, or even alone.

That last thought caused her to stop in her tracks. She *was* alone. Alone with a guidebook and the whole afternoon stretching out in front of her. So what was to stop her from doing whatever she wanted?

Looking back at the ruins of Qorikancha, Sam caught sight of Meredith shading her eyes to stare up the six-meter walls at the convent perched above it. He stopped, feeling a shock almost as big as the one when he'd first spied her at the airport in New York. After that, he'd known he would probably be seeing her often, with the group. But he hadn't imagined this—spotting her by herself, outside a ruin. He found himself staring, wanting to take a mental snapshot of her. Locals might think she looked like a typical tourist, in her red tank top, shorts, and walking shoes, with a little leather purse secured over her shoulder. They wouldn't notice the way sunlight glinted off her auburn hair, making it seem positively red. They wouldn't recognize the stillness that could overtake her when she was concentrating on something she found fascinating.

Maybe no one who hadn't known her would notice these things. No one who hadn't spent a significant portion of his young adulthood dreaming about her, wondering about her.

A part of his brain protested the injustice of it. Why couldn't they have crossed paths again years ago, when it might have made a difference? Not that they would have rekindled their romance. That would have been highly un-likely. He wasn't Charlie Brown, waiting for Lucy to yank that football away again. But it might have given him some closure. It wouldn't have left him dangling, forever questioning what he could have done differently.

He was getting ready to turn around and head back to the hotel when Meredith pivoted, as if a sixth sense had alerted her to him standing there. She caught his gaze, and red heat crept up his neck. He half expected her to cross the street and chew him out for ogling her.

Instead, a beaming smile overtook her formerly pensive expression, and she bounced excitedly on her toes. Then, im-pulsively, she rushed across the street, almost getting run down by a moped.

The near-collision stopped his heart. Hadn't she heard the motorbike's angry mosquito engine buzzing directly toward her? He was opening his mouth to scold her when she fin-ished her death-defying dart and then hopped up onto the sidewalk with a triumphant smile. Like an aerialist who's performed a triple flip with a twist under the big top and then touches down on the relative safety of the tiny platform to give a bow.

"Isn't that incredible?" she said, beaming.

He shook his head. "I thought you were a goner."

Her eyes clouded in confusion for a moment, and then a laugh burst out of her. "I wasn't talking about crossing the street—I was talking about *that*." She swept her arm toward the hulking architectural evidence of a lost empire, just in case he'd missed it. "Can you imagine what it must have looked like? An entire fortress wall covered in gold. Filled with life-sized solid gold and silver cornstalks, and golden llamas, and the sun itself. How do you build a golden replica of the sun? It must have been incredible!" She turned and caught him staring at her again. He couldn't seem to help himself. But at least he was breathing normally now. She exhaled on a chuckle. "But yeah, me making it across the street without getting run over? Pretty damn impressive."

Her laugh had the same effect on him as sunshine—the sound permeated him with well-being, making him smile in spite of himself. Of course, every exposed pore of his skin was slathered with sunblock. He had no protection from the effect Meredith had on him.

"Seriously, you should go in and poke around that place and the little museum," she said. "It's worth the ten bucks."

"I did go."

"You mean you just came out?" At his nod, she rolled her eyes. "We were probably wandering around in that place, just missing bumping into each other."

Question: What do Qorikancha and New York City have in common? Answer: The ability to swallow people whole and make them lose sight of each other.

Maybe they could have wandered around that ruin for seven years and never met again.

"Where's Gina?" she asked.

"At the hotel—jetlag." Although he had a hunch she'd

wanted to stay at the hotel and sneak in some work. He raised a brow. "Where's Janie?"

"At the hotel—sprained ankle. Or broken."

He felt his forehead crinkle. "Does she need to see a doctor?"

"She said she just wanted to rest. She might have just twisted the ankle a little. In fact, she might just have felt like taking a nap. I'll probably regret not taking one myself this evening. I can't remember the last time I slept. Jetlag is going to catch up with me sooner or later."

"You're not supposed to sleep during the day, according to the book I read. The best thing to do is make it through a normal day and go to sleep at the appropriate hour, local time. That way you'll acclimate yourself quickly."

"Or get killed crossing a street half-asleep," Meredith said, laughing again.

He'd forgotten how much she liked to laugh at things. Goofy little occurrences during the day and awkward verbal exchanges cracked her up. Even big things that terrified her also tickled her. Seconds before a giant asteroid hit the planet, the last sounds on Earth would be millions of terrified screams and Meredith's final hoot of laughter.

"So . . . you've been sightseeing," he said. It sounded lame, but was infinitely better than *I've missed your laughter.*

"Yes, and now I'm bushed. I was thinking of going to a café near here that's mentioned in my guidebook. It has local specialties."

"Guinea pig?" he asked.

She tilted her head. "Are you trying to avoid *cuy?*"

"I hadn't meant to—I never thought about guinea pigs one way or another. But then on the plane Gina was telling me about the pet guinea pig she had when she was a little girl. Buttercup. And how Buttercup used to like to sleep in a shoe box at the foot of her bed. And now when I see them roasted on those sticks, with the head and everything, I can't help thinking of Buttercup."

"I totally get that," Meredith said. "And guinea pigs make that cute little R2-D2 sound—*wheek, wheek, wheek.*" She did a dead-on impression of a guinea pig.

"But it wasn't even my pet," he pointed out. "It's completely irrational."

"Oh no. I could never eat a horse, all because of *My Friend Flicka.* And that was just fiction." She opened her book, squinted at the map, and then waved to the right, in the general direction of half the city. "I think the café is over there. The review doesn't mention *cuy.* It talks about *chicharrones,* which is chunks of deep-fried pork with mint, onions, and other stuff."

"That sounds . . . good. Disgusting, but good."

"That's what I thought." She looked at him eagerly. "Want to try it? While we're there, we could order something to bring back for our weaker halves holed up in the hotel."

He'd been preparing to beg off, but her last addition—that hint that there would be an element of altruism involved in their having lunch together—decided him. "Lead the way."

Of course she led him the wrong way. They wandered, lost in conversation and increasingly just plain lost, then wound up half a mile from where they needed to be.

"You were always terrible with directions," he said.

"No, I'm not. I think I'm pretty good with directions."

"You used to get lost all the time!"

"But that was in New York, right after we moved there."

"That's what I mean," he argued. "New York is a grid. It's navigating for dummies."

She shook her head. "It's just the way the numbers go—I can never remember if they get bigger when you go east of Fifth, or smaller. . . . There's some system there."

"You still don't know?" he asked, incredulous.

Laughing, she handed the book to him. "Okay, Magellan.

Lead the way. Anyway, you were always the one wagging a map around, like a tourist."

"We *are* tourists."

"But back in New York? I used to worry we'd get mugged while you wandered around with your nose in a city map, even when we were just looking for something basic, like the Brooklyn Bridge."

"You have to know what street it's on to find the entrance," he sputtered. "Besides—we never were mugged."

"Still—a map." She laughed, as if the idea were completely crazypants. As if she hadn't just been looking at one—and misreading it. "Where's the adventure in that?"

Hungry now, they gave up the idea of backtracking all the way to the place in the guidebook, and ended up in a little dive that served nothing but cheese-covered corncobs.

"Peruvians evidently don't worry about the cholesterol," he said, after stuffing himself.

"At least not about the cholesterol of tourists."

"I must say, it wasn't what we were looking for, but it was pretty good."

In addition to the disgustingly good food, there was the fun of catching up with Meredith. He asked her about what she did now, and she told him about the Astoria Garage Players, which ate up most of her free time. "We're doing a children's theater camp this summer. That starts when I get back. I can't wait."

"So you must be doing well."

She let out a blast of laughter. "We're lucky when we break even. And we 'directors' work for free. I do freelance proofreading for law firms, so it'll be interesting to see how much sleep I get between now and September."

"Wow. That takes a lot of . . ." Insanity, he thought. ". . . dedication."

"It's fun, when it's not crazy and overwhelming and tiring. And you know me—I love summer."

Yes, he remembered stifling hot days that she breezed

through in sundresses and sandals. He'd come home from his first suit-and-tie job and want to collapse, but Meredith would still be daisy fresh. Even at night all the concrete in the city would hold its heat like a massive oven, yet Meredith would float down the sidewalks oblivious to the fact that everyone else was baking and wilting. All that pep had been annoying at first, and then, later, endearing and even essential. She was his backup power supply.

That could explain why he'd been in such a funk after she'd left him. Or maybe any heartbreak made you feel like something from *The Walking Dead* that needed to be shot.

But he was glad Meredith's work situation wasn't quite as dire as Gina had painted it. In fact, she seemed busy and happy.

"And what about your other life?" he asked.

Her brow pinched, and she looked amused. "I have another life? Why did I not know this until now?"

"I mean guys. Are there . . ." He struggled for a way to put it. ". . . wedding bells in your future?"

She tossed her head back and laughed. "I love it. It's like I'm being interviewed by *People*."

He was tempted to retract the question . . . except he really wanted to know the answer.

"No—no wedding bells," she answered. "I haven't seen anyone seriously in a long time. Seriously, meaning longer than three months. Since London, really."

He couldn't help doing the math. She'd been back from London for a while. And she evidently hadn't been there all that long. So not many men in her life besides him could have met the three-month rule of seriousness.

"In London I went out with a barrister. Liam. He was serious." She laughed. "A serious jerk, in retrospect. He was always broke, drank too much, never remembered plans we'd made, and I'm pretty sure he cheated on me at least once. He said all the right things, though."

"Every woman's dream, then."

She shot him a look. "Okay, I was an idiot. I knew it wasn't going to work."

"Then why was he an over-three-monther?"

"Oh, you know how it is with dating. You're always re-fighting the last war."

So . . . she was talking about the guy she had dated after him. Which meant that she'd considered him, Sam, to be the war. And Liam, the anti-Sam, was the tank she'd been using to crush the bad memories. He could understand, because in a way, every woman he'd dated for the past seven years had been an anti-Meredith. He'd purposefully sought out professional, self-sufficient women who didn't seem subject to whims and whispers. Seven years was an exhausting amount of time to be on the rebound, though. His goal was to be settled and happy at age thirty, and if all went well, it looked as if he was going to squeak in right under the wire.

Meredith leaned back in her chair, smiling. "This was fun. And think how much more of the city we saw than we would have if we'd just found that other restaurant."

When he'd first seen Meredith at the airport, he'd assumed things between them would be awkward and stilted. He'd used up all his frequent-flyer points to avoid contact for as long as possible. But now that they were face-to-face, and the conversation hadn't faltered as he'd expected, he felt foolish for having worried.

"You never minded calling an audible," he said, remembering. "If one movie was sold out, you were always just as happy to see something else."

"Of course. Because I probably would have gone to see it anyway." She arched a brow in mock disapproval. "Whereas you, if I recall correctly, said you only saw four movies a year, or something insane like that."

"I saw more movies that summer than I've seen before or since."

"Really?" She looked disappointed.

"Why? Does it matter?"

She shrugged. "Well, you always hope that something of yourself rubs off on people you"—she reached forward and took a long sip of lemonade—"people you've known. But, hey, we weren't together that long, right? A summer and some change."

He could have broken it down into hours and minutes for her, but he held his tongue. Or tried to. "I probably do see more movies these days, now that you mention it."

She smiled. "Please, you don't have to lie to make me feel better."

"No, no. I made it a point to go to see almost all the Academy Award nominees last year. Gina likes to watch the Oscars."

Meredith blinked, and for a second the conversation teetered, and they both shifted uncomfortably, as if he'd belched or spluttered a half-masticated kernel of cheesy corn across the table.

"Maybe we should be getting back," she said.

He made a show of checking his watch, but was so distracted he didn't even see what time it was. "Of course." He wanted to kick himself for mentioning Gina.

Then he scolded himself for wanting to kick himself. Why *shouldn't* he bring her up? He was on the trip with Gina, not Meredith. He and Gina were practically engaged. Why should he be on tenterhooks about bringing up his almost-fiancée? Why should he care about sparing Meredith's feelings at all? The woman had never, ever apologized for dumping him. If nothing else, you'd think that she'd at least acknowledge that she'd left him holding the bag for the lease of the apartment.

Although, to be fair, Janie had given him a check to cover three months' rent. It was nobody's fault but his own that he'd mashed the check through the shredder at work.

They paid—separate checks, since Meredith insisted—and headed back to the hotel. Halfway there, he stopped, remembering. "We were going to grab food for Gina and Janie."

"Oh, right." She nodded. "We can stop again before we get there."

They continued back. Near the hotel, they found a restaurant that agreed to give them two orders for takeout. "Although it's so close to dinner now, maybe there's no point," Sam said. "I'm planning a special dinner for two with Gina tonight."

Meredith eyed him, and he felt a little silly for bringing it up. As if he was trying to prove something. *I've gone on to have a rich and rewarding relationship with someone else.* Ridiculous.

"At least she'll know you were thinking about her," she said.

"Of course I was." His tone sounded defensive. Because he'd probably gone a full hour at the restaurant barely thinking of Gina at all. What kind of almost-fiancé did that make him?

Meredith's eyes widened at his change in tone. After a moment's hesitation she said, "Anyway, I'm glad I bumped into you—"

It can't happen again, he almost blurted out. *I'm a practically engaged man. I shouldn't have stopped when I saw you. I shouldn't have even noticed the sunlight on your hair. . . .*

"—and not Seth, for instance," she finished, making him feel like a fool for assuming there had been an emotional underpinning to her comment. "Instead of a tasty meal, I might have gotten another lecture on wheatgrass juice. Or a questionnaire on who among the group he's likeliest to get lucky with."

He frowned. "Has Seth been hitting on you?"

"I think he hits on anything that moves." As Sam was trying to come to terms with how revolting he found the idea of Seth and Meredith together, someone interrupted them.

"Hey, you guys!"

They both swiveled and saw a woman from the tour coming up behind them. "Fancy seeing you two here."

Sam wracked his brain to remember her name. He got all the women a little confused, to tell the truth. He'd probably nail down their names just as the vacation was ending. This one was . . . Ann?

"Hi, Fran," Meredith said.

The newcomer darted glances between them. "Sneaking off for a quiet lunch together?"

"No!" they answered in unison.

"We were just out sightseeing—"

"Separately," Sam interjected.

"Totally separately," Meredith added quickly. "And then we bumped into each other—coincidentally—and then decided to—"

"To get some food for Janie and Gina," Sam finished for her.

Meredith nodded. "So we're grabbing some takeout for Janie and Gina."

Fran's thoughtful gaze panned between their two faces. "Wow—altruism." She lifted her camera and snapped photos of the food behind the counter. Instinctively, Sam and Meredith edged away from each other.

Fran took a picture of them in profile, both with their eyes focused on the food preparation and carefully avoiding looking at each other. It was a relief when the guy behind the counter finally handed them their plastic sacks. Paying was another diversion.

As she was leaving, Meredith frowned in thought. "I should probably find a pharmacy and grab some kind of painkillers for Janie too. Just in case her foot isn't better."

"It is," Fran said flatly. "She's been in Gina's room all afternoon, nursing it in the Jacuzzi tub."

Sam and Meredith exchanged anxious glances.

"I guess it makes sense that they'd want to hang out. Two old friends." Fran's sly smile spoke volumes. "And since you two disappeared for so long . . ."

CHAPTER 4

"Of all people," Janie groaned.

"We just bumped into each other," Meredith said with a dismissive shrug, even though a flush overtook her when she remembered sitting across from him. For a moment, it had felt as if . . . But of course that was ridiculous. They'd had lunch. Shared a couple of cheesy corncobs. Hardly a romantic reunion. "Anyway, I thought you were in bed, resting your foot."

"I was, but it got better. And then I couldn't go hotel hunting, because that's what you were doing."

A pinprick of guilt jabbed Meredith's conscience. "Our target price was too low. There didn't seem to be any point."

Janie sighed. "Oh well. There's always tomorrow. At least while you disappeared with Sam, I visited with Gina and got to sample how the other half lives."

"Sam and I didn't disappear. It's not like we assumed a cloak of invisibility. I'm pretty sure that the whole time we were walking around together, anyone could have seen us."

"Yes. That's the problem. Anyone could, and blabber-mouth Fran did." Janie opened the to-go box Meredith had brought her, eyeing it suspiciously. "What is this?"

"Pork, rice . . . and maybe some other stuff? It smelled good when Sam and I were standing in the restaurant."

The mention of Sam made Janie grimace. "I should never have left you alone. . . ."

"For Pete's sake." Meredith tossed herself facedown on her bed. "We just bumped into each other. It was no big deal. Happens to people all the time. We could have met again by chance in New York City. It's amazing that we never have, actually."

"A miracle and a blessing, I'd call it."

Meredith sat up again. "Why?"

Her sister blinked at her, a forkful of food halfway to her mouth. "Why what?"

"Why would you call it a blessing that I never ran into Sam? What difference would it have made to you?"

"To me? None at all. We're talking about you. I would think you'd want to avoid him. He broke your heart, remember?"

"I left him."

"Because you felt it was a hopeless, dead-end relationship. You were unhappy. You were thinking happily-ever-after, and he was applying to graduate school in California and God knows where else. He wasn't including you in his plans, so he was clearly either thinking of dumping you or he was so arrogant that he didn't feel you needed to be consulted."

Because the summer had seemed so blissful, Meredith sometimes forgot all the frustrations of those autumn months that followed. But, looking back on it now, she wondered if her perspective hadn't been a bit skewed. Being unhappy for a few weeks at age twenty-two had felt like the end of the world. Maybe their rough patch would have been one of those blips that all relationships went through . . . if she hadn't ended the relationship.

"And don't forget the pregnancy," Janie said.

"It wasn't really, though. I was just late, and I was so angsty and keyed up. . . ."

"Still, he let you down."

"He was a twenty-three-year-old guy. I don't think he got it."

"Exactly. You're two different sensibilities. Anyway"—Janie's brow darkened—"what are you saying? That you wish you two had met earlier and rekindled your defunct romance?"

"No, of course not." Meredith pulled her shoulders back, determined to be positive. "If anything, Sam's being here is good. I've always wondered if he and I just met at the wrong time—right after college, so much going on in our lives, wanting to pursue different dreams. . . . It's not like I've been pining for him—you know that—but he's just one of those guys I've wondered about. The one that got away."

"The one you got away from," Janie corrected.

The one you got me away from, Meredith almost retorted. But how dumb was that? She'd been an adult, and Janie had just been trying to give her the best counsel she could, based on what Meredith was telling her. Maybe, with the benefit of hindsight, Meredith wouldn't have bitched so much about minor spats to her sister. Seven years later, she might be inclined to keep her own counsel and not obsess over the small things.

But she wasn't going to blame Janie for her own screw-ups. She'd been twenty-two, and she'd made mistakes, and Sam hadn't behaved like her dream guy. So it ended. These things happened. They were adults now. Real adults. Sort of.

Meredith crossed her arms over her chest. "Anyway, you don't have to worry. Sam was full of talk about some romantic dinner he and Gina have scheduled for tonight."

"Oh, I know all about his plans."

Something in her tone made Meredith wary. "You do? How?"

Taking her time, Janie finished a bite, swallowed, and set

the to-go box aside. "This is totally on the QT . . . but when I was up in Gina and Sam's room today—" She stopped, clucking her tongue. "Honestly, you should see that place. It's like the Plaza compared to our leaky tomb. Their tub is bigger than some swimming pools I've seen." She frowned. "Which reminds me, I should have told you to look for a hotel with a pool. But maybe that would make the search even harder."

Impatient with the distraction, Meredith prompted, "You were saying you discovered something when you were in Gina and Sam's room?"

"Oh—right!" Janie scooted to the edge of her mattress. "So I was in Gina's suite because she offered to let me soak my ankle in her Jacuzzi tub. And while we were sitting around, she mentioned *the dinner.* And how transparent Sam has been concerning what this whole trip's about."

Meredith wondered if there were dots she should be connecting. "What's it about?"

Her sister paused for effect. "Sam's going to pop the question."

Too much cheese. That had to be the cause of the sudden gnashing in her stomach. Meredith tried to keep her expression placid, though she doubted she succeeded. "Gina thinks this?"

"Thinks it? She knows it. She even showed me the ring."

Meredith hugged her middle. *Definitely need to avoid dairy the rest of the trip.*

Definitely needed to avoid Sam.

"Guy's been carrying it around in his pocket since they left New York, according to Gina. She noticed the bulge in his jacket first thing yesterday morning. Then he transferred it to his hotel safe. He thinks he's being pretty cagey, I guess. Gina caught him locking something in the safe. Naturally, after he left, she looked in it first thing. The schmuck set the lock combination to the same numbers as his bank card PIN."

"He doesn't know that she knows about the ring."

"Of course not—although I'm a little surprised that he can be on the verge of getting engaged to her and not realize that she has X-ray vision when it comes to detecting bling."

Well. That was that.

Meredith straightened, giving herself a mental kick in the pants. What was wrong with her? *That had been that* for seven years. Even while she was out with Sam today, she'd been under no illusion that they were anything but two people catching up on old times. Maybe she had felt a little nostalgia for the old days, a little wistful about all the time that had gone by. They weren't rekindling anything.

"I bet he's going to ask her tonight at dinner. Probably plans to drop the ring in her champagne flute or something completely unoriginal." Janie tapped her fingers on the bare nightstand. "I wonder if I should call her and explain that you and Sam really did just bump into each other."

"No." That was just too ridiculous. "If she doesn't trust him enough to take his word . . ."

She doesn't deserve him.

"You're right," Janie said. "Let them navigate love's rocky road on their own."

Janie leaned back, munching the takeout contentedly again, while Meredith flipped through the guidebook she had read so often she could practically recite it. She could just imagine the two of them—Gina all decked out in the best, slinkiest dress she'd brought, and Sam in a snappy suit. They would come back from their big romantic dinner, tipsy on champagne and love and hopes for the future, and return to their honeymoon suite with the huge Jacuzzi.

Her stomach gnawed at her anew. Way too much cheese.

"When we're looking for hotels tomorrow," she told Janie, "maybe we'll have better luck if we up our price limit. We need to get out of here."

* * *

"It was nothing," Sam repeated for what felt like the tenth time in as many minutes.

Gina, immersed in a bubble bath, smiled at him. "I know."

She did? For some reason, he had expected her to react a little more tartly to his afternoon with Meredith. "I just ran into her . . . and we went to a restaurant. . . ."

"It's fine," Gina said.

Her nonchalant attitude rattled him. "And I brought you back some food." He held up the sack, his peace offering, even though there apparently was no conflict to smooth over.

"I couldn't eat a bite."

"I was worried about you. But you seem . . ." He looked at her face poking up through a mass of bubbles, ". . . fine."

"Sleeping did me a world of good, and then visiting with Janie. You should take a quick nap yourself."

"I'd better not."

"Isn't it great to be on vacation?" She stretched, flicking bubbles across the tile floor. "We lucked out with this room, let me tell you. Poor Janie's stuck with her sister in some kind of dank broom closet."

He frowned. "Really? Meredith didn't say anything to me."

"Well, if what Janie tells me is true, that one's used to primitive conditions. She lives in Queens." When he shot Gina a look, she arched a brow. "I'm serious. What's being a starving artist good for if not lowering your expectations? She's probably just glad to be here."

The vision of Meredith standing in front of Qorikancha came back to him—that smile of amazement, the way her hair seemed to refract sunlight, like an aura in a Renaissance painting. . . . He'd been leaving the ruin, walking away from it. What had caused him to stop and look back?

He wished he hadn't. Talking to her had been pleasurable for a time, but the whole episode felt like a complication now, even if Gina didn't seem to care.

Why didn't she care?

"Scrub your back?" he offered.

"No thanks. I brought my scrunchy-scrubby." She produced the rope of braided plastic netting out of the bubbles. "I'm good."

Amazing. They were on a weeklong trip to Peru, and she'd remembered to pack her bath scrunchy.

"What's the matter?" she asked.

"Nothing." He paced over to the window and stared out, watching the women Gina called the yoga mommies tripping down the sidewalk toward town. The first big night out in Peru.

The afternoon had been so distracting that he'd almost forgotten about tonight. He glanced back over at Gina, who had sunk down into the tub, her head resting against the back, eyes closed.

"Still tired?" he asked her.

She let out a blissful groan. "No—just thinking how glad *I* am to be here."

He smiled.

"Anything's better than work," she continued. "Janie and I played cards this afternoon, and it got my mind completely off fish flake disasters."

Janie made her feel glad to be here? His smile faded. "We never play cards together. We could sometime. Now, if you want to."

"That's okay," she said. "I'm nice and relaxed. Just read a book or something for a while. I'll get dressed soon."

That meant she would *start* getting dressed. So, by his mental calculations, their hour of departure was still an hour and a half away. He lay down on the bed, deciding to read a little before he needed to change clothes himself. He'd bought a thick book in the Miami airport—a page-turner about a hard-talking guy with a mysterious past who was investigating a murder. The bodies piled up at a rate of about one every ten pages, so he had no fear of nodding off. He could just lie back, crack the book open, and be transported.

But after a moment, he found himself transported to the old railroad flat he had shared with Meredith—the kind of apartment that was several rooms divided by glass doors. In essence, the apartment was one long hallway. To get to her room from the living room, Meredith had to go through his room. He had to go through hers to get to the bathroom. This lack of privacy had annoyed him at first. About a month went by before he realized that he actually enjoyed having Meredith underfoot all the time—that they spent more time seeking each other out than trying to avoid each other.

In a wink, he was back in his old room—the futon on a box spring on the floor, next to his shelves constructed of pine boards and milk crates. Due to a dearth of outlets, the television was plugged into the wall next to his bed, but actually stood in the living room thanks to an extension cord that was a fire inspector's nightmare. He studied the cord now—it seemed to be sparking and smoking, like the fuse leading to a stick of dynamite in the old cartoons. He followed the spark, but when he reached the end of the cord, instead of finding the television, he was in Meredith's room. She sat up in her twin bed—a squeaky camp bed they used to refer to as the orphan-home bed. She held the sheets up to her chin.

"What are you doing here?" she asked.

"What are you doing on my vacation?" he demanded right back.

One of those laughs trilled out of her. "This isn't a vacation. This is our life, and you brought Gina along."

The statement confounded him. "Gina? I haven't even met her yet."

"Sam?"

It was so like Meredith to throw a wrench like that into the conversation.

"Sam!" Someone nudged his shoulder, and he opened his eyes—and gasped. Gina loomed over him, draped in a low-cut sheath of shimmery red silk. "You *are* here," he said to Gina through a fog of sleep.

Her brow pinched. "Where did you expect me to be?"

Sam lay heavily against the mattress as if he had been glued there, the forgotten book on his chest. The burning cords and conversation with Meredith had just been a dream.

Gina stood over him, cleaned and coiffed, Chanel emanating from her in a perfumed plume. She shimmered onto the bed next to him and laid a manicured finger on his shoulder. "Are we going out, or are you going to lie here like a lump all night?" Before he could force himself up, she added, "Because I'm starving."

He struggled to unstick himself from the mattress. "I brought you food."

Her nose wrinkled. "I wanted to hold out for something really good."

"Just give me a minute," he said.

A shower woke him up a smidge, although his brain synapses still felt mired in quicksand. His jetlag prevention strategy had backfired. Applying aftershave, he gave himself some sharp slaps and debated taking the ring out of the safe and carrying it with him. There seemed no good way to handle the ring, which he'd spent months deciding on. He'd given more thought to buying it than he had to asking Gina out after they'd met.

The trouble was, there didn't seem any good way to handle the ring now. When he carried it, he was anxious about pickpockets. When it was in the safe, he worried about the unscrupulous hotel employees. It would be a relief when it was finally on Gina's finger. Maybe tonight he would do some spontaneous marriage proposing and put himself out of his misery. Except he'd planned to give it to her at Machu Picchu, and he hated to switch everything up at the last minute.

Maybe that seemed rigid. People like Meredith might scoff at him, but without clear plans the world would unravel.

Still, her laughing voice echoed in his ears. *"A map? Where's the adventure in that?"*

He hesitated, looking down at the guidebook he had put aside to take with them. This was supposed to be a romantic evening—hauling his guidebook around screamed Boy Scout. Anyway, he had the address of the restaurant memorized. He took one last glance at the map in the guidebook—with all his planned destinations marked with red Xs—and tossed it to the bed.

He had his smartphone, in case of emergency. He patted his jacket to make sure the familiar telecommunication lump was there. He'd checked ahead and purchased a local SIM card that would allow him to use it here, just in case.

To get a taxi, they had to scale down the narrow stairs and then the torturous hilly street until reaching the more crowded avenue at the bottom. And then there was competition. Several others waited to flag something down, and when a car barreled down the street toward them, a jostling war broke out at the curb.

Sam lost the battle, but consoled himself that he was new to the fight.

A young man approached him. *"Taxi? Quiere taxi?"*

Sam nodded more out of reflex than agreement, but that nod was as good as a contract to the young man. He hooked onto Sam's elbow, beckoned Gina with a crook of the head, and hustled them around the corner into a waiting car. Sam dug into his pockets for change and handed the boy several nuevos soles before the door shut.

Dazed, he gave the driver the name of the intersection closest to the restaurant.

Gina took his hand. "You handled that with aplomb."

He had? "I'm not certain whether this really is a taxi," he mumbled, "or part of some kidnapping racket."

"I'm just glad to be off my feet and on my way to food."

The cab sped through streets, which became slightly emptier, more residential-looking, as they traveled out from the city center. The sun hung lower in the sky, and a cooler breeze whipped through the cracked driver window to the backseat. Next to him, Gina hummed along with the rhythmic, fluty Peruvian music bleating out of the dashboard, but he remained alert. How far was this place? It was supposed to be a restored monastery that had been converted to a restaurant, so the guidebook had warned that it was on the outskirts.

At last, the driver rammed the brake as if to avoid a collision, although the street had no other traffic on it. Sam and Gina, splattered against the back of the front seat, righted themselves. He thanked the driver, negotiated for him to come back in two hours, and gave him a fifty percent tip.

Holding hands, Sam and Gina started strolling up the street dominated by stucco houses in white, with red tile roofs.

"This place really is something," Gina said, inhaling and exhaling. "So foreign. I just love it!"

He squinted at the surrounding buildings. It was growing darker, and not all the numbers over the doorways were metal—some were stenciled in faded, peeling paint and hard to read.

"Where is this restaurant?" Gina asked.

"Should be in this block . . . or the next one."

"I hope it's not too far. Did you hear my stomach rumbling?"

He squeezed her hand.

She grinned back at him. "No pressure or anything."

They passed the building where Sam was fairly certain the restaurant should have been, although he tried to avoid giving any indication of this at first. The windows of the large stone edifice were boarded up. His heart sank, but he kept walking, and when they arrived at the next intersection, he surreptitiously checked the street names.

But the street was right. Maybe he'd memorized the wrong number?

He'd just begun to panic when Gina said, "You said we'd only have to walk a block or two. Otherwise, I would have made a different shoe choice."

He glanced down at her sexy backless stilettos and winced. "I thought it would be in this block, but it's . . . not. Or if it is, it's that boarded-up building."

"Which one?"

"The one we just passed."

Gina twisted and gaped. "Are you serious? Because that place is definitely not a working restaurant. How old is your guidebook?"

"I'm not sure."

She held out her hand. "Give it here. We should double-check the address."

"I didn't bring the book," he confessed. "But I had the address memorized. I'm sure that was it." He took a breath. "Almost sure."

Gina blinked in astonishment at their predicament. "How are we going to get back? The taxi's not coming back for two hours."

"There are other taxis."

"Where?" she asked, gesturing at the quiet street around them.

This, he supposed, was the downside of choosing an out-of-the-way spot for dinner. It was . . . well, out of the way. Still, he chuckled. They might not be in Manhattan anymore, but they were still grappling with first-world, easily fixed problems.

He reached for his phone. His smile faded.

"What's the matter?" Gina asked.

"My phone." He patted down all his pockets. "It's gone."

"You left it at the hotel?"

"No—I had it in my pocket when we left. I must have dropped it in the cab." But how did a phone drop out of his breast pocket? Even when the driver had slammed on the brakes, Sam would have noticed a cell phone flying up from his chest through the vehicle's interior. That hadn't happened.

He remembered being jostled on the street as he'd tried to flag down a taxi. It might have been stolen then. And then there was that kid who'd hustled him around the corner—he could have been a pickpocket, which would explain why he would be working in tandem with a driver who obviously wasn't hurting for business.

And if the pickpocket and the driver were working in tandem, what incentive would the driver have to show up for a fare from whom he'd just stolen a phone?

Crap. "I think we'd better start walking."

He said this with every confidence that they would run into another cab, or find a phone to call one. Instead, they ended up walking for blocks and blocks, past houses, parks, and churches, and then through a warehouse area that he hadn't noticed during the ride over. He pulled Gina close, but her body was rigid and spiky with irritation.

"How is it that we haven't hit a major street yet?" she asked.

"This is a major street, I think."

"But it doesn't have any restaurants or stores. Even a little bodega would be welcome. I'm so hungry I'm about to faint. Plus, my feet are killing me."

He had given her his jacket already, but he couldn't do anything about shoes. And the shoes were slowing them down. In a classic bit of displacement, he redirected the irritation he felt toward himself for getting them into this mess at those ridiculous shoes. They were basically expensive, spike-heeled flip-flops. What was the point of them? Why would a person bring them to Peru?

Because this is what he'd planned. *"Let's have one real night on the town by ourselves,"* he'd suggested. And why? Because he'd worried he wasn't romantic enough. Because all those years ago, Meredith had thought that. And he had left his map at the hotel tonight because Meredith had criticized him this afternoon. And then he'd lost his phone. . . .

Okay, maybe that wasn't Meredith's fault.

"I should never have left the choice of restaurants up to you," Gina muttered, startling him. Although he might have guessed that her thoughts would be circling the same who-to-blame territory as his were. "Why did it have to be so far from everything else?"

"I thought it would be romantic," he said. "I thought that you would like that."

"Oh sure—women love being dragged into the middle of nowhere so they can cripple themselves walking home. Great idea."

"Maybe someday we'll laugh about this."

She sent him a withering look. "*Someday* might never arrive if I drop dead from hunger before we reach the hotel. Are you even sure we're walking in the right direction?"

A feverish wave of doubt hit him. Then, in the dying light, he nodded toward the large spire of the cathedral. They were still heading toward it, although it still loomed far away. "Of course we are."

"I'll never make it," she said with a groan. Then, she stopped. "What's that?"

He squinted down the street toward a distant figure in the twilight.

"That's a food cart." Like a marooned desert traveler seeing a mirage, Gina licked her lips. Her feet moved forward briskly, her heels tapping in urgency.

He hurried to keep pace. "We can find another restaurant—somewhere nice."

"I don't care about nice. I'm ravenous."

Hunger must have sharpened her eyesight to raptor clarity, because after speed walking several blocks, they came upon what was indeed a food cart run by a small old woman wearing a shawl over a long-sleeved T-shirt, and a baseball cap. The metal cart with wheels was little more than a traveling grill with a shelf containing a few plastic condiment bottles. Over the hot coals lay several skewers of what Sam first assumed was sausage, but upon closer inspection appeared to be an entire small animal—skinned, gutted (presumably), and roasted. *Cuy.*

Gina held up one finger to the woman, who produced a skewer with a charred guinea pig impaled on it, its little skinned, cooked head attached. Sam's stomach lurched.

"Don't you want something?" Gina asked him.

He shook his head, trying to clear the echoes of the *wheek wheek* sounds Meredith had put there.

Gina took a bite, tearing at the meat with her teeth as if she hadn't eaten in weeks. She rolled her eyes in appreciation. *"Delicioso,"* she told the vendor, loudly, between swallows. *"Gracias."*

The woman broke into a toothy smile. *"Por nada."*

Gina continued walking, scarfing down *cuy* with every step.

"I can't believe you're eating that," he said.

"Why not?"

"Well, because . . ." He shook his head. If she didn't remember her childhood pet, he would not be the one to remind her at this sensitive moment. Still, when he looked at that pathetic grilled, impaled animal—its mouth gaping as if frozen in the agony of its dying moments—he couldn't help thinking of Buttercup.

CHAPTER 5

Sitting at a table in a busy bar with Nina, Pattie, Jennifer, and Amelia—aka the yoga mommies—Meredith had to remind herself that she was in a different hemisphere. Yes, the atmosphere felt a little more rustic, and there was more Spanish being tossed around at other tables than you'd hear in some parts of New York City, but otherwise, this could have been anywhere. Drinkers Without Borders.

She'd arrived with Janie and Fran and had joined Seth and Claudia, but she'd wanted to branch out and talk a little with the rest of the group, so she'd switched tables and joined this group. The women were welcoming, but they were all really good friends. They talked over each other, and random buzzwords would send them into whoops. As they slugged back tequila shots like sorority girls on spring break, their conversation ricocheted from annoying teachers to annoying playdate parents, from husbands who didn't help enough with the house stuff to all the things that could go wrong with kids.

"The worst is when you're in the car and somebody gets sick," Pattie said.

The rest of the table groaned in agreement.

"Oh!" Nina, the woman next to Meredith, held up a hand. "Last week I'm in my car, it's bumper-to-bumper on the Triborough Bridge—we're all strapped in, of course—and then, boom. Conor hurls. I mean, so hard I could feel the vomit tsunami hit the back of my seat. Poor kid's groaning, bless his heart, and his sister starts wailing, because she got splattered. And then—"

"The smell!" the table chorused.

"My gag reflex kicks in," Nina continued, "so I'm rolling down the window, and the diesel exhaust fumes from the eighteen-wheeler in front of us start to mix with the *eau de upchuck* we're already contending with—"

While the story went on, Meredith noticed Janie and the others weren't at their table anymore.

"—And you're stuck," Amelia was saying.

"No darting to the fridge for a 7UP in that situation."

"I always give Madison ginger ale for her tummy. Ginger ale and saltines—my mother swore by that."

One of the others released a guttural bellow of laughter. "My mother swore by tossing us a towel or two and barricading herself behind her double-locked bedroom door."

Someone chuckled. "The old ways were the best ways."

"Do you have kids, Marilyn?"

It took Meredith a moment to process that she'd been addressed. She turned to the speaker—Nina?—and considered correcting her, but then she wasn't one hundred percent certain she was putting the right names to faces either. "No," she answered. "Maybe someday."

"Well, don't hope too long. Get busy," one of them told her.

They all nodded. "The older you get, the worse everything is."

It was a subject they all had strong opinions about—which they hurled at her, rapid-fire.

"Harder to get pregnant."

"Much harder!"

"Then you end up doing IVF."

"Hormones!"

"You become, like, this lab rat."

"And the risks get worse."

"Bed rest! It sounds good at first, but—"

"I nearly went out of my mind."

"Then, when it's all over and they hand you a baby, you're so damn exhausted."

"And you stay exhausted for the next eight years."

"Eighteen."

"I just handed the kid over to my mom."

"I wanted to kill my mom. And don't get me started on my mother-in-law."

Exclamations of sympathy ended in their flagging a waiter over for another round.

Meredith pushed back her chair. "I think I should go back."

The women exchanged glances, grinning. "We drove her away with our pregnancy talk."

"And we didn't even bring up episiotomies."

Amelia snorted. "We didn't need to. It was probably mentioning my mother-in-law that did it. That woman always clears a room."

They laughed.

"No, honestly," Meredith said. "It's been fun, but I need to find my sister."

Amelia blinked at her. "Those guys left about fifteen minutes ago."

Janie had left her without saying anything?

Returning to the hotel, Meredith tried not to feel disgruntled. After all, she was the one who had switched tables. Janie had probably thought she was enjoying herself. And just that afternoon, Meredith had been kicking herself for being trapped as part of a sister act for her vacation. It was good that they did things separately, autonomously. She just hadn't expected to be trudging back to the hotel by herself at night. But she hadn't felt like waiting to go back with the yoga moms. From the looks of things when she'd left, those ladies had another hour or so in them, at least.

On her amble back to the Tres Chivos, one look overhead shook off any sense of being disgruntled with Janie. Above, a million stars hung tantalizingly close. She couldn't remember the last time she'd seen such a dazzling display. Maybe never. It was as if the heavens were a few million miles closer to Peru than New York.

At the hotel, Meredith passed the dozing night clerk and headed straight to the room, which was at the bend of the corridor. The passageway was quiet—no televisions or radios in the rooms, no murmurs of conversations through the doors. Her footsteps on the tiles seemed too loud, so she was practically tiptoeing by the time she reached her and Janie's room.

Being extra quiet with the key, she snicked open the lock and slipped inside, glad to see that Janie had left a light on. She turned, took a step toward the beds, and let out a yelp. At first she wondered if she'd entered the wrong room. But her luggage lay on the empty twin bed, just where she'd left it. And after a few blinks of shock, she confirmed that Janie was on the other bed. Except that she was half dressed, and had Seth attached to one of her nipples.

The two of them noticed her and jerked up to sitting just as Meredith was pivoting away. Too late. That image of Janie and Seth was burned on her eyeballs for all time. She fumbled for the doorknob.

"Meredith," Janie said.

"I'm just going back to the lobby to . . . uh . . ."

She lunged out the door before she could think of a reasonable end to that sentence, besides the obvious. *Escape.*

She sprinted toward the reception area, where she collapsed onto a rustic wooden seat. The heavily carved bench jabbed into her back. What was it? An Incan torture pew? As if her psyche wasn't tortured enough at the moment . . . God, she wished there were some kind of brain cleanser that could erase that image of Janie and Seth.

How much had Janie had to drink? Meredith should have kept closer tabs on her. She just wasn't used to being her sister's keeper. It had always been the other way around.

Meredith half expected her sister to run after her, but several minutes went by before she heard footsteps hurrying toward the lobby. She jumped up, wanting to avoid a confrontation about Seth in front of the desk clerk . . . on the off chance that he ever woke up.

Instead of meeting Janie at the door, however, she nearly slammed into Sam. He jumped back from their near collision, his face pale and anxious. Meredith breathed a yip of surprise and stepped away, but he grabbed her like a drowning man reaching for a lifeline. The frantic look in his eyes wasn't caused by bumping into her again. "I need help. Gina's really sick."

Meredith shifted mental gears, glad for a problem to think about that might get her mind off his strong hands clamped around her arms. "Does she have a fever?"

"No." He stepped back, letting go. "That is . . . I don't think so. But she's been . . . ill. Like, for hours. Ever since we got back from dinner." He lowered his voice. "And there are intestinal issues. . . ."

Meredith raised a say-no-more palm. "Stomach bug."

"Well, yes. Obviously."

"I mean, a bad bacterial stomach bug." She remembered the one beach vacation she'd taken to Cancún a few years before. She'd spent all but one day in her hotel room, worshipping at the porcelain throne. *Bug* was a hilariously benign word to describe the Godzilla that had been stomping around her digestive tract for days on end. "Montezuma's revenge."

One of his brows arched above the rim of his glasses. "In this case, it's Buttercup's revenge."

Meredith didn't know what he was talking about.

"The only thing Gina ate tonight was a guinea pig from a street vendor," he explained.

Bad pet karma was a bitch.

"What should I do?" His voice was strained with worry. "I know the human body is mostly fluid, but there's got to be a limit to how much somebody can lose."

"A pharmacy will be able to give you something."

His eyes widened as if this was an idea that hadn't occurred to him. "You don't think I should call an ambulance?"

"So you can haul her to a crowded hospital emergency waiting room while she's nauseous?" She shook her head. "No."

"Okay, the pharmacy it is." He was already looking toward the hotel entrance.

She grabbed his arm before he could rush off. "Let me go for it."

"I was sort of hoping you could stay with Gina," he said.

"Me?"

At her hesitation, panic showed in his eyes again, and she understood. He needed to be out doing something, taking action. And face it—it wasn't as if she had anywhere to go now that her room had turned into the site of the weirdest booty call since Ernest Borgnine met Ethel Merman. She fished through her purse and found a pen and an old receipt. On the back, she wrote the name of the drugs she'd been prescribed in Mexico. As an afterthought, she added ginger ale and saltines to the list. Her time with the yoga mommies had not been wasted.

She handed him the paper, and he was about to run out the door when she stopped him again. "Sam, wait." She turned to the desk clerk and cleared her throat loudly to wake him. "Can you help us? We need a pharmacy. One that's open late."

"Farmacia?" he asked.

"Sí." She added, "Can you go with him?" And as she called up her remedial Spanish, she made gestures that she hoped

brought to mind a person accompanying someone and not, for instance, mugging someone in an alleyway. *"Vaya con él, por favor?"*

Understanding—or seeming to—the man jumped up and disappeared into a back room. He returned a few minutes later with a rumpled-looking teenager in tow. Meredith recognized the youth from when they'd arrived. He'd helped lug suitcases up the staircase from the street. The desk clerk rattled off something to him that Meredith didn't quite catch, but the boy nodded and sped for the door, beckoning for Sam to follow.

Not that Sam needed encouragement. He moved as if jet-propelled, stopping only to turn and toss Meredith his room key. "If you could just check on her . . . Tell her I'll be back as soon as possible. Tell her . . ." He looked so pained, for a moment she worried he was going to ask her to convey some sort of love message. ". . . tell her I'm sorry."

She nodded. Sorry she could handle. *But sorry for what?* she wondered. Had they had a fight?

Not your concern.

After she watched him go, the brass key weighed heavily in her hand. She smiled at the desk clerk and said *gracias* for his help, then turned and made her way back to Sam and Gina's room. It was at the back of the hotel on the opposite side of the courtyard from her and Janie's. At the door, she rapped lightly, not wanting to disturb Gina if she'd managed to fall asleep.

Receiving no answer to the knock, she put the key in the lock and turned it as quietly as possible. *Just check on her,* he'd said. She'd make sure Gina was still alive and then go. Leaving the door ajar, she stepped inside and peeked into the suite. *Damn.* Janie had been right—it was huge, with freshly painted buff walls (no ooze) that reflected the warm light from the glass-shaded decorative lamps and the cozy brick fireplace in the corner. Double glass doors looked out on what appeared to be a private patio. Though it was dark,

Meredith saw hanging plants laden with blooms just on the other side of the glass.

A bricked archway divided the suite in two. On one side was the bedroom; on the other was a sitting area bigger than Meredith's living room in New York. A couch and two chairs faced off at the end of the room. Nearby, a forty-eight-inch television held court on a low antique table. The wood floors boasted several rugs that seemed to have been woven locally and probably cost more than most Peruvian workers earned in a year.

Wow. This room was either the hotel's loss leader, or she and Janie really had gotten screwed, roomwise.

In the bedroom, Meredith spotted Gina strewn across the bed like something that had been flung there. She lay on her back, her arm draped over the edge, her manicured hand nearly dragging on the floor. Sometime after getting back from the restaurant she'd managed to change into a filmy negligee in silky peach. Meredith was impressed. The woman might be sick, but she was being elegant about it.

Gina squinted one eye open. "Oh, it's you," she said in a gravelly voice. "What are you doing here?"

Meredith crossed toward her. "I ran into Sam in the lobby. He's going to the pharmacy to find something for you."

"The only thing that could help me now is a cyanide pill."

Meredith laughed nervously. The fact of the matter was, Gina didn't look good. Despite her high-end sleepwear and comfy surroundings, her skin had a decidedly greenish hue. And when Meredith took another step toward the bed, it hit her: that unmistakable sour-milk smell of sickness. Meredith gulped in a breath and tried to put on her best Florence Nightingale front. She wondered if it was too cold to open the patio doors.

"Can I get you anything?" she asked.

"God, no," Gina groaned. "Nothing is crossing these lips

till I'm back in the U.S. I don't care if I starve to death before I get there."

"You'll feel better when Sam comes back. I sent him to find drugs to help you."

"Where's Janie?" Gina asked. "Does she know I'm dying?"

"No, I think she's . . . asleep." Meredith shuddered as that awful vision returned.

Gina sighed and handed Meredith the cloth that she'd been holding to her forehead. "Run some cold water over this for me," she said.

Meredith grabbed the cloth, glad to be somewhat useful and to get her mind off Janie. She found the bathroom, flipped on the light, and—

Whoa. The bathroom really was impressive. Fuzzy hotel bathrobes hung against rustic tiles—not green—and a Jacuzzi tub stood next to another, smaller fireplace. Trying to think like a nurse and not so much like an envious hotel patron, she hurried to the double sink and ran fresh cool water over the cloth. At the same time, she caught a glimpse of herself in the massive mirror inside a carved frame. She'd spruced up to go barhopping, but her makeup had faded and the strain in her eyes indicated that her body was fading too. Crawling into bed sounded so good . . . if her room ever freed up. Maybe she could beg to stay on Sam and Gina's couch.

She shook her head. Crashing in Sam and Gina's honeymoon suite—now *that* was a dumb idea. Tempting, but dumb.

She turned to go back to the bedroom, but Gina nearly flattened her as she came streaking in. The woman sprinted toward the toilet, yelling, "Get out and shut the door!"

Meredith didn't have to be told twice. She scooted out and threw herself onto a chair.

What a night.

Several minutes later, Gina came dragging out again. She held her hand out and snapped her fingers to ask for the cloth Meredith had forgotten she was still holding. "I should run it through the tap again," Meredith said.

"Screw it," Gina answered. "It's fine."

She took the cloth and collapsed in a Camille-like faint on the couch opposite. "I should never have come on this stupid trip," she moaned. "I didn't even want to. Even when Janie started blathering about bringing you, the place held no appeal."

"Then why'd you come?"

Gina let out a raspy chuckle. "For Sam. Sam saw the flyer I brought back from the yoga studio and latched onto the idea. It was all his doing."

"But you must have wanted to."

"Oh, sure. He's so sweet. Who could resist a guy who wants to whisk you away, even if it means traveling with this group of nuts?"

Meredith nodded. *She* had not only resisted Sam; she had run away from him. But back then, he hadn't been interested in whisking her away.

"It seems sort of unlike him. . . ." she couldn't help saying.

Gina squinted open one eye and looked at her. "Oh, that's right. You knew him back in his student days, right?"

"And just after."

"I guess he was a little different back then. More rags, few riches. He told me all about how he struggled to pull himself up by his bootstraps."

That was true. They'd been in the ramen noodle phase of post-graduate life. They both had had student loans to pay off.

"I guess he was probably a bore when you knew him," Gina said.

"No. . . ."

"I like to think I've broadened his horizons. I've certainly made a difference in his wardrobe."

Meredith frowned. She tried not to be too judgmental. Yes, Gina sounded superficial. But she herself had noticed how good Sam looked now. She just hadn't known she was admiring Gina's retail handiwork.

"And he's gotten me to do things I wouldn't normally," Gina said. "Unfortunately, this is one of them. And it might kill me. How can I possibly take a three-hour train ride when I feel like this?"

"You have all tomorrow to recuperate."

"By the end of this night I might be dead." Gina shook her head. "We might just have to stay behind."

"Oh no." Meredith hated herself for the thoughts roiling around in her head. As awkward as it was to be here with Sam and Gina, she didn't want them to drop out of the trip. The thought of them staying behind while she went trudging into the mountains alone with her sister, Seth, and the rest made her unreasonably sad. At the same time, she knew she *shouldn't* feel that way.

And what right did she have to think that Gina didn't deserve Sam, when she herself was the person who had abandoned him? After all, Gina was here with him, when she'd just confessed that she hadn't even wanted to come all that much. It sounded as if this were a compromise vacation for both of them. And if that compromise wasn't a show of love . . . or something like it . . . what was?

Last but not least, there was the small matter of that ring Sam was reportedly carrying around with him.

The door pushed open, and she jumped up. "Here's Sam now," Meredith said.

"Thank God."

"You'll feel better tomorrow," Meredith predicted. "You'll see."

Gina grunted, then jumped up and ran to the bathroom again.

Sam took in Gina's bathroom dash and looked almost

distraught that Meredith was leaving so quickly. He opened a bag to show her all the things he'd brought back. "I got just what you said."

"Good." She gathered her purse and headed for the door.

"You're taking off so soon?"

She muttered, flustered, "Well, yeah . . ."

He nodded, as if suddenly realizing how silly his words sounded. "Of course. It's late. You probably want to get back to your own room."

She thought about that and braced for a wave of revulsion. "Well, it is late."

His eyes were warm with gratitude.

"Thank you."

She averted her gaze. "Good night."

"My night will probably be spent on the couch, so Gina won't be disturbed." He looked down at it. "I hope it's comfy."

The evil streak in her felt strangely buoyant at the thought of Gina and Sam sleeping in separate rooms in their honeymoon suite.

That inner smile disappeared as she neared her own room, though. What was she going to say to Janie? *"What were you thinking?"* *"How much did you have to drink?"* Or just, *"Ew"?*

When she let herself in, however, it was clear that she wouldn't have to face this problem tonight. Janie was gone.

CHAPTER 6

Meredith's travel alarm buzzed her awake in time to make the morning yoga session. She slapped the Off button with a groan and opened her eyes to the unslept-in but still rumpled bed next to hers. Janie hadn't come back. Maybe she was already outside with the others.

Meredith crawled out of bed, slipped into yoga pants and a long-sleeved T-shirt, and went outside to face whatever this day had in store.

The morning yoga session was already in progress, but her sister wasn't among those gathered in the weedy courtyard. Aside from Claudia, there were just the yoga moms—looking startlingly sober—and Fran. Meredith hurried over and unrolled her mat next to Fran's. Even though the others were already on the ground in a cobra pose, she did an apologetic Namaste in Claudia's general direction and tried to catch up. Nothing like hectic yoga to start the morning.

"Isn't Janie coming?" Fran whispered to her.

Meredith hesitated, both because she didn't want to receive one of Claudia's disapproving stares for chatting and because she didn't know. Also, what would Janie want her to say? Whether her sister saw last night as a onetime indiscretion or the beginning of something big was impossible for Meredith to guess. She was still in the baffled stage. Janie was usually so persnickety about boyfriends, so cautious.

Meredith opted to avoid the subject of Seth altogether.

"Sleeping in," she said. "She might be a little sick."

Fran nodded knowingly. "Gina's down, I hear. Seth isn't here, either—maybe he has the same bug."

Meredith was glad when Claudia shot them the evil eye. She winced apologetically, gave Fran a shrug, and tried to concentrate on what they were doing. Stretching felt good. So did focusing. After a few minutes, some of the tension fell away, and she turned her face up to the blue sky and sun, and smiled.

I'm on vacation. Who cared about all the things that had happened yesterday—about Sam and Gina, Janie and her drama. Meredith felt good, and the day was gorgeous, and she was in Peru. There were still five glorious days before she even had to think about going back to her old life, to the stresses of her everyday routine. This was heaven.

The clicking open of a door interrupted her bliss. Seth's door opened and Janie came out, dressed in her skirt and blouse from the night before and flip-flops. Her jaw dropped to see them all out there—apparently Janie had forgotten that her walk of shame this morning would have witnesses. She trilled a wave at them and hurried toward the lobby. A minute later, the group in their downward facing dogs craned to watch her as she came back out and flapped back to Seth's room carrying two glasses of juice.

Not a walk of shame, then. Breakfast in bed.

"The one time I left my camera in the room," Fran muttered.

After yoga, Meredith returned to the room and took a quick shower in the icky bathroom. Even under the disappointingly lukewarm spray, her good spirits from the class remained intact. There was so much to do today. Once Janie extricated herself from Seth, they could resolve the hotel problem and hit a museum or two. Or maybe take a bus to one of the nearby ruins. Nothing too strenuous, to give Janie's foot a rest. Meredith frowned. Come to think of it, Janie had been walking pretty well on her way to the breakfast buffet set up in the lobby.

Still, maybe they could take a bus trip to one of the nearby ruins, just to be on the safe side. That would be fun, and it would get them in the mood for tomorrow's trip to Machu Picchu. They would stay overnight at Aguas Calientes, take the train back to Cuzco, then fly on to Lima for two days. And then home. She wanted to conserve her energy for the highlight of the trip—Machu Picchu—but she didn't want to waste her time.

When she came out of the shower, she found Janie perched on the edge of her bed, putting on makeup. "Sorry about last night," she said. "Didn't expect you back so soon."

"Obviously."

"You don't have to sound scandalized," Janie said.

This was too much. "*Seth?* You never even said you liked him."

"I never did until I had a few Pisco Sours in me. Also, I got a peek into his room earlier yesterday afternoon."

Meredith shoved her legs into a pair of jeans. "His room?"

"It's not the honeymoon suite, but it has a queen-sized bed." Janie widened her eyes in the mirror and made her long, applying-mascara face. "And a big tub."

"Wait. You slept with Seth because he has a better hotel room?"

"Well. Not entirely . . ."

"But last night, you two were in here."

"That was the alcohol's doing. Otherwise we would have made it farther down the corridor."

Unbelievable. Meredith felt as if the solid ground beneath her feet had turned overnight into marshmallow fluff. Janie's judgment had always been so important to her. Her whole life had been influenced by Janie's opinions. But now Janie was acting like a . . . a room slut.

"What's the matter with you?" Janie asked.

"You could at least acknowledge that this was a weird thing to do."

Her sister looked at her as if Meredith had lost her mind. "Having a fling on vacation?"

Yes, a fling. That's all it was. If a coworker had told her about this, or if it were just something she'd read about in a magazine, Meredith wouldn't have thought a thing of it. But this was *Janie*. Janie, who leapt on her every stupid mistake and had actually badgered her about the only really promising relationship she'd ever been involved in.

"If it were me sleeping with Seth, you'd say I'd lost my mind," Meredith pointed out.

Janie blinked at her with newly thick and luscious lashes. "Do you want to sleep with Seth?"

"No!"

"Then what's your problem?"

Meredith sputtered and flung herself down on the bed. What *was* her problem? When she tried to put her finger on it, she couldn't come up with exactly what was bothering her about this situation. She wasn't a prude, and Janie was an adult. If she wanted to sleep with a flatulent, unitard-wearing nut muncher, that was her business.

Meredith took a deep breath and decided to change the subject. "Anyway . . . I thought we could take care of the hotel problem first thing." She flipped the book open to the parts she'd highlighted. "I wrote down several places we can call. Fran would let us use her phone, or the lobby might. Then maybe we can hit a museum, or take a tour bus out to some ruins."

"Hotel problem?" Janie asked.

Meredith nodded. "Claudia gave me the name of someone to talk to at her hotel, which sounds really nice. A little pricier than what we'd planned, though."

"I'll bet," Janie drawled. "But why would we want to move now?"

Was she kidding? "You hate this room," Meredith reminded her. And now she was beginning to see how her sister might be right to hate it. "Have you taken a shower in there? It's like trying to get clean in a dense fog."

"But it's just one more night," Janie said. "And Seth's room is nice. Oh, and Seth wanted to go to the Mercado San Pedro. I thought I'd tag along with him today."

"Oh."

The subtext couldn't have been clearer. Frustration was coursing through Meredith, but it made no sense. Yesterday she'd felt tethered to Janie . . . and now Janie was telling her to do her own thing. Why should that make her resentful?

She laughed humorlessly. "I didn't realize you two were inseparable already."

Janie dropped her mirror on her bedspread. "You don't have to take that tone with me."

"What tone?"

"That disdainful tone. What's the matter with you? It's like you're prematurely turning into a judgmental old spinster."

She was judgmental? "You were worried about my even having lunch with Sam yesterday."

Janie's face screwed up in confusion, as if she didn't quite grasp the connection. "Of course I was worried. You two have a history."

"Ancient history. And yet you treat it like it's this unspeakable thing—you and Sam both. As far as I can tell, no one's even told Gina that Sam and I were a couple. I would think you'd want to score some points over your frenemy, if nothing else."

"How would that score points on her? He improved,

makes good money, and now she's got him." Janie shook her head. "That's *not* a win for our team."

"He's more than a snappy wardrobe and a bank balance," Meredith said, growing angry. "He's warm and funny and intelligent—he always was. Okay, he brought me spreadsheets instead of roses. That seemed like a huge deal when I was twenty-two. But you know what? I'd love it if someone did that for me now. I hate doing stuff like that for myself, but any idiot can pick up a ten-dollar bouquet at the deli."

Janie's expression fell slack. "God, you really do still love him."

"No—no, no." Meredith slapped her hand against the mattress. "This isn't about me. If I'd really been carrying a torch for him, then I could have Googled him and looked him up years ago. I'm not selfish. I want him to be happy. But I don't know if Gina really appreciates what she has." Which sounded . . . weird. She felt her face redden, especially when Janie's penetrating gaze bored into her. Meredith shook her head. "But of course, she probably *does* appreciate him. I mean, I was with her last night. And she was talking about him and coming on this trip when she didn't even really want to, just for his sake, so . . ."

The more she babbled, the more her sister's shrewd look took on a pitying cast. "You were talking to Gina about Sam last night?"

"I looked in on her while Sam was at the pharmacy."

"Why?"

Meredith shrugged. "Sam asked me to."

Janie's lip jutted out sadly, and she reached across the gulf between the two twin beds to grab Meredith's hand. "I'm *so sorry* about this. It's just opening all sorts of old wounds."

"No, it's not." Meredith put her sister's hand aside and chuckled. How many times did she have to reassure her? "I'm not some pathetic, heartbroken spinster, or a jealous psycho who is going to try to wrestle Sam away from a relationship that he seems perfectly content to be in. You said it yourself—the ring's bought."

Janie's brows rose. "A generous cushion cut with a diamond band. I'm guessing he loves her to the tune of sixteen grand, at least."

Meredith lurched off the bed, hiding her dismay at her sister's stubborn insistence on putting a numerical value on emotion, and also . . .

Well. Sixteen grand. Maybe dollar signs didn't equal love, but there was no denying they made Sam and Gina's relationship seem more . . . concrete. Irreversible.

Not that she'd ever thought about reversing anything.

Good grief. Her brain kept going in circles. "I should probably get moving. I think I'll go on the tour to Tipón."

"What is that?"

"A ruin outside of town. Sure you don't want to go?"

"No thanks. I'm sure I'll have seen enough ruins by the time this trip is over."

Meredith loaded up the backpack she'd brought with her with essentials she might need during the day—a bottle of water, her guidebook, and her emergency kit. (Tylenol and Band-Aids.) At the storefront where the guidebook sent her to buy tickets for the tour bus, she gave the man her fare and turned to wait the twenty minutes he said it would be before their transportation arrived. A familiar figure was waiting on the concrete bench he pointed her to. Fran looked up at her. "Oh, hi! Are you doing this tour thingy?"

"I planned to."

"Me too, only I don't know if they have free Wi-Fi. Could you ask the guy selling tickets?"

Meredith laughed. "You're overestimating my Spanish. Also, I think you're overestimating the modernity of these buses."

"That's probably true." Fran sighed and slumped against the wall. "I'm getting this weird vibe from the rest of the group, aren't you? It's pissing me off."

"What weird vibe?"

"Well, the yoga moms were running off to go mountain biking and wine drinking, which don't even sound like two things that should go together. They're sort of insular, if you ask me. Claudia is living in her ritzy Zen bubble, and everybody else seems to be paired off. It's a little boring, and frankly, it makes for lackluster blog posts."

"Well, maybe this tour will give you something to blog about when you get back."

Fran didn't look convinced. "Ancient irrigation systems? Meh. I shelled out for this trip thinking it would be a mini version of *Eat, Pray, Love*. Instead, it feels more like *Drink, Walk, Yawn*."

"Tipón looks pretty in my guidebook."

"Yeah, but it's going to take the whole day." Fran said this as if she had a million things to accomplish that day.

Meredith inhaled a calming breath. What was the matter with all these people? Never had so many incurious people come so far to see so little. At least, the ones she was hanging out with. The yoga moms were adventurous. Pickled, but adventurous.

"It's only thirty kilometers, but I'll go ask the ticket guy how long the drive is," she told Fran. "That is, I'll do my best."

She got up and went back in the little shop front to ask. On the way back out, she met Sam on the shop's stoop. He was clearly heading inside. Her heartbeat ramped up before she could give herself a stern command to cool her jets. *Sixteen thousand dollars.* She smiled at him in greeting, even though she felt her heart sinking. What a day-trip this would be. Her and Fran, and Gina and Sam.

"Are you catching the tour bus?" she asked.

"I hope so. I'm not too late, am I?"

"No, but . . ." She looked behind him, wondering where Gina was. She was a little surprised that Gina would be up for a trip like this. Usually when a person was sick to her stomach, the last place she wanted to be was on a tour bus.

He took hold of her elbow. "I'm so relieved I can talk to you. I was worried I wouldn't be able to tell you how wonderful you were last night."

The hair on the back of her neck prickled. She could feel Fran's gaze on her. The woman was standing several feet away, no doubt was watching with interest. "It was nothing—"

"It meant so much to me," he said. "I was a mess, and you really knew exactly what I needed."

Oh God. Before she could say anything, or flash him a warning with her eyes, she heard Fran call out, "Smile, you two."

They both turned a fraction of a second before a camera clicked. Too late, they both froze, aware of their closeness, huddled in the doorway, his hand on her arm.

Fran grinned. "You know, I don't think I will go on this outing, Meredith. But you two have fun."

When she was gone, Meredith groaned. "Great. Where's Gina?"

"Back at the hotel," he explained. "She's still not feeling very well. She said I was just bugging her hanging around the room."

"Poor Gina." And poor her. She was not going day-tripping alone with her ex-boyfriend. Janie would flip.

"We might have to give Machu Picchu a miss," Sam said.

Meredith felt her eyes bug. "Miss it entirely?"

"I don't want to drag Gina out there if she feels bad."

Sam's disappointment was palpable, but he was willing to give up the main event of the trip for Gina.

"It's too bad you might have to miss it, but I understand."

"So this might be my big chance to go look at ruins," he said. "Better make the best of it."

She felt torn now. Should she bow out of the trip to

Tipón? The only reason for doing so was purely superficial: She was worried about what Janie might think. But Janie's moral compass had plummeted in value since she'd basically admitted to sleeping with a guy to gain access to a better bathtub.

Plus, wouldn't running away be proof that she still had uncontrollable lingering feelings for Sam?

Of course, it would have helped if she *didn't* have lingering feelings for Sam. If not uncontrollable, then at least unresolved. And contradictory.

A van rumbled around the corner, its tailpipe letting out a belch of black smoke that in itself seemed ominous. "I'm not sure if I should go, either," she said.

He looked disappointed. "Why not? It'll be fun."

She swallowed. "I know, but . . . Well, I wouldn't want there to be any talk."

"Who's going to talk? Fran?" He laughed. "Anyway, who cares?"

She eyed him sharply. "Gina might."

He shook his head. "I doubt that. When we came back from lunch the other day, she wasn't even fazed. I don't think she sees you as a threat."

He turned and headed in to buy a ticket for the ride to Tipón.

Of course she doesn't see me as a threat. I'm not one.

So why, moments later, did Meredith feel so odd climbing into the van behind Sam? As if she were heading off on an illicit, clandestine adventure? Why did she feel so guilty?

The van was smaller than he'd expected. Smaller and older. The first ones on, he and Meredith gravitated toward the back bench seat, and then found themselves squished together when a group of late arrivals showed up. It was a beautiful day outside, but the sun beat in through the windows of

the van—windows that didn't all open, he discovered—
which caused a trickle of sweat to run down his temple. Also,
Meredith's left thigh was pressed against his. He practically
hugged the inside wall of the vehicle, but that didn't relieve
the space problem.

She smiled. "Tight squeeze."

It was impossible not to smile back and not to feel a
surge of affection for someone who could make him feel so
at ease and uncomfortable all at once. For a moment back in
town, he'd feared she wasn't going to come . . . although
maybe that would have been better after all. He'd intended to
make this a solitary day journey, but once he'd seen her waiting at the little pick-up spot, his heart had lifted at the idea of
spending time with her. When he'd feared she was going to
back out, a kind of panic had overtaken him.

She jumbled up his emotions without even seeming to
try. Under the circumstances, he shouldn't be so glad to be
with her. But he was.

"Is this how you expected it to be?" she asked now.

I never expected we'd be together again, he almost said. *I
never expected to see you again at all.*

She pointed out the window and elaborated. "The countryside. Peru."

"Oh!" Thank God his tongue had remained tied. "I'm not
sure." He hadn't really anticipated what the scenery would
look like, apart from eyeing the spectacular pictures of
Machu Picchu and trying to judge whether it would be worth
the time, money, and inconvenience to get there, and if it
would be a suitably dramatic backdrop for his big romantic
moment with Gina. "How about you?"

The van trundled past a field where some kind of reddish-
topped grain was being cultivated. "I suppose I hadn't expected it to be so agricultural," she said. "When you're looking
in a guidebook and online, you forget that the whole country
doesn't exist just for tourists. Sort of like when you go to

England—that millions of people live there, but a part of your brain expects the place to be one giant history pageant. You know what I mean?"

His heart juddered like an engine stalling out. England. An entire country with millions of people and thousands of years of history, but all it brought to his mind was coming home to an empty apartment. "I've never been to England."

He didn't mean the words to sound so resentful, but Meredith winced a little and looked away. The minute she did, he felt foolish for his reaction. He wanted to reassure her that he wasn't bitter. Of course, he would prefer not to have that conversation when they were stuffed like sardines in a tourist bus.

Meredith turned to the middle-aged couple next to her—British, wouldn't you know—and struck up a conversation. But her chirpy tone belied her real mood, if the tension in her thigh was any barometer.

The couple mentioned a place called Hay, where they were from, and Meredith seemed to know something about the town, or at least about some kind of festival they held there.

Sam tried hard not to eavesdrop, but when the man asked, "Are you two married or just on a romantic adventure?" he couldn't help pivoting.

Meredith hesitated. He could practically hear the hitch in her throat.

To help her out and fill the awkward silence, he blurted, "Neither."

In tandem, the man and the woman turned their gazes to him. A red stain rose in Meredith's cheeks before she laughed and explained, "Sam and I used to live together, actually, but he's here with his fiancée."

Too much information. The expressions on the couple's faces morphed from curiosity to confusion to speculation. Meredith didn't see it, of course. She went on, "But she's sick, and so Sam thought he'd seize the opportunity to get out and about."

Two pairs of eyes zeroed in on him, and he read the couple's thoughts at once. *Left his sick fiancée to sow wild oats with the ex.*

He wanted to refute the misperception, but for the life of him, all he could come up with was, "She's not my fiancée."

Meredith turned to him sharply. "How can you say that?"

Yes, how could he? He'd been thinking of himself and Gina as almost engaged for a while now. But nobody else knew that. Nobody. "Why did you think we were?"

"Because of the—" Her words stopped abruptly, and she reversed course. "Well, aren't you?"

"No."

She folded her arms. "Interesting."

The couple had been following the conversation like spectators at a tennis match. Now their gazes turned back to Sam. Before he could explain the technicalities of the situation—or even decide if he wanted to explain them—Meredith stole his turn.

"Sorry, I must have misunderstood," she explained to them. "Or maybe it's just beginning to dawn on Sam that things are serious, and he's decided to cut himself off emotionally from his partner. He has a history of that."

He sputtered at the unfairness of that. "*I* have a history of cutting myself off? Who was the one who bought an airline ticket and flew off without a word of warning?" He appealed to their audience. "Getting on a plane bound for another continent. Isn't that an example of shutting someone out?"

Their eyes widened. The man shook his head in confusion, while his wife nodded.

"And what made you think Gina and I were engaged?" he asked Meredith.

She lifted her shoulders. "I just assumed."

"You sounded pretty sure."

"Well, Janie told me some things."

Janie. He faced forward and was dismayed to discover the people sitting in front of them were now angling back to listen to their argument. "And of course you believed her. Janie's word is gold. She's your touchstone."

"No, not anymore," Meredith said with a sharpness that surprised him. "But when I was younger? Yes, I valued her opinion. She raised me, Sam."

He looked at her. "That didn't mean that she was right."

"No, it didn't." One of her brows arched. "But is she right about the ring?"

"Yes," he bit out, unaccountably irritated. That was supposed to be his secret. The idea that everyone knew about it—that even Gina knew about it, and had told people—seemed to take something away from him. Even if it was just the element of surprise.

"So you're engaged."

"Practically," he said.

The van braked, and the driver called out, "Tipón."

Thank heavens. He didn't want to continue this conversation.

He'd expected to lose himself in a tour of the place, but the busload of people found themselves dumped on a path at the bottom of a hillside with nothing but a stone marker letting them know they'd reached their destination. The driver—evidently not a tour guide—stayed in the van with a newspaper. The others started up the hill in their own little groupings, leaving only Sam and Meredith.

Awkward. He considered turning and walking away, alone, but that would seem rude. But he was still chaffing from the things she'd said in the van, and from the way she'd characterized him. As if he was emotionally distant—as if he'd been to blame for the breakup.

"What's the matter?" she asked.

"What's the matter with what?"

"You've stopped talking."

"So have you."

"And you were doing that thing where you focus straight-ahead and clench your jaw so that I can see your mandible hop under your cheek. You used to do that in the old days."

Mentioning the old days didn't help, and in fact sent a surge of irritation through him. "That's because I'm the same person as in the old days, which only are the old days because *you* left, which you seem to have forgotten. And now you show up on my vacation—"

A strangled cry interrupted him. "Excuse me. I thought I was on *my* vacation."

"—and then get in a snit every time I mention Gina."

She bristled. "I wasn't in a snit; I just ran out of things to say. You of all people should know about conversation-killing silences. You were always sinking into uncommunicative funks. It drove me insane. Whenever I had something I really wanted to talk about, you clammed up."

"I'm not a chatterer."

She tossed her head back in a challenge. "I didn't want you to chatter. I wanted you to listen."

"I always listened."

"But it didn't *feel* like you did."

"What could I have done about that?" He sighed. "For Pete's sake, Meredith. You're accusing me of being uncommunicative, when you were the one who ran out without a word. What was I supposed to do? You always just expected me to read your mind. That's what drove *me* insane."

She took in a breath, puffing up as if she might escalate the argument, but just as quickly, she deflated with a laughing sigh. "It's a good thing I left when I did, apparently, or we both might have ended up in padded rooms."

He nodded, although he could have mentioned that her leaving had done nothing for his peace of mind. In fact, he'd been depressed for months afterward. Only when he'd gone back to school for his graduate degree had he begun to slough off the malaise he'd felt since she left.

She hitched her backpack over one shoulder. "Anyway . . . I read in the guidebook that there's an interesting village nearby, with a zoo. I think I'll check it out."

He shook his head. "Liar. You hate zoos."

She laughed. "I didn't count on your memory being so good."

"I remember more than you think I do," he said. "Look, it would be silly for us to try to avoid each other while we're here." When she didn't argue, he tilted his head toward the sign. "The whole day would be *ruined*."

She groaned. "The zoo's sounding better and better."

They headed toward the rough paved walkway, climbing the hill together.

He'd felt a pang of guilt after he'd denied being engaged to Gina, as if he'd betrayed her. Now he was wondering if it wasn't Gina who was betraying him. Could telling about a ring be categorized as betraying a confidence? He wasn't sure. Hard even to call it a confidence when he hadn't told her about it. Yet it should have been private, and she should have known that.

He tried to sort out his feelings. It was just a ring, but it seemed much more than that. And yet it would be crazy to make too big a deal of it. Especially now that nothing in life seemed as certain as it had forty-eight hours ago. Before he'd seen Meredith at the airport, he'd been sure of what he wanted.

A strange thing happened to his muddled thoughts as he huffed up the incline. They didn't resolve—they simply dissipated. He concentrated on breathing. The air was thinner, forcing him to breathe in wheezy gulps of it. Still, once he'd acclimated, there was something calming about this spot.

He stopped and looked around, impressed. The hillside in front of them was terraced gracefully, the levels divided by stone walls that had stood for centuries. All through the area, clear water flowed in narrow stone channels, its rushing providing a soothing sound track.

"What is this place?" he asked, awed.

Lacking a guide or even a tourist information booth, Meredith told him what she remembered from her book, giving the essentials of the five hundred–acre, self-contained ruins. "They aren't sure if this was meant to be a sort of resort for the Incan nobility or an agricultural center."

Or maybe, Sam thought, the place had been an ancient mental-health center. Instead of handing their stressed-out citizens a Xanax, the Incas just sent them up the hill to listen to the trickling of calming, life-giving water.

They continued to climb. Occasionally, precarious-looking steps would jut out of a wall to lead them to the next level, and he would take those, giving Meredith a hand up once he reached the top. The gesture was reflexive, but touching hands felt strangely intimate. He remembered the looks the people in the van had given him—as if he were some kind of tour lothario. And the feeling in his gut made him wonder if maybe they were right. Looking into Meredith's bright eyes, it was easy to forget the last seven years. He was twenty-three again, living through his first hot summer in New York, but humming Black Eyed Peas songs while he worked his boring bank job, just happy to come home every night to the apartment. To Meredith.

Was Meredith as blissed out by their surroundings as he was? He couldn't tell. He was afraid to ask, to break this moment of peace.

After a few moments, she cleared her throat and turned to him. "I'm sorry about how I spoke earlier—saying that you were emotionally cut off."

He shifted uncomfortably. "Please, it's—"

"No, what you said was true. I was wrong to run away like I did, without explaining myself. I've felt bad about that for years."

"Well . . ." There it was. The apology his bruised ego had been craving for the better part of a decade. And now he felt no better for it. "Water under the bridge."

"I know, but I wanted to say it. I'm sorry. If I had it to do over again—" Abruptly, her words stopped, and her eyes widened in mortification.

His mind filled with what she might have said. *I wouldn't have gone.*

But for all he knew, she might have just meant to say that she would have written a note, or returned her overdue library books. Why did his brain jump to the idea that she wouldn't have gone at all?

Because that's what he'd wished for . . . still wished for?

He reached out to her, just meaning to brush her arm. Instead, he took her hand and pulled her to him. The tug wasn't even conscious on his part. He angled her body against his and lowered his mouth to her lips, brushing them lightly. The moment his lips touched hers, he felt like a lost man—lost in the vanilla scent of soap or shampoo, in the taste of her, in memories.

How many kisses had he taken for granted when they were young? Had he appreciated the feeling of her pressed against him, his hand on the curve of her waist, and the gentle warmth of her breath? Now he wanted to stop time, savor every moment. . . .

She groaned and with a thump against his chest pulled away.

"Meredith . . ."

She shook her head. "Okay—that was wrong. Very wrong."

But it felt so right. It had to happen. . . . Nothing came to mind that didn't sound like bad Top 40. "I couldn't help it. I've tried to forget about us forever. I wanted to move on—"

"You did," she pointed out. She added quickly, "We both did."

"Then why am I still so drawn to you?" He reached out for her hand again, and she sidestepped a safe distance away.

"Everybody has feelings of nostalgia for old girlfriends

and boyfriends," she said. "Occasionally they act on them, like we just did. It doesn't mean anything."

"It could."

"No, it can't. There's Gina, remember?" She crossed her arms and almost glared at him. "If you've become the kind of man who would cheat on a girlfriend during his vacation—when you're practically engaged—then you're not the Sam I knew."

Just the mention of Gina's name was like a douse of cold water. He took a deep breath. Meredith was right. What had he been thinking?

He hadn't been thinking at all. That was the problem.

"We just got carried away," she said. "It's my fault too. I've been moping about old times since we met up at JFK." She shrugged. "We're on vacation. Out of our element. It's easy to forget there were reasons things didn't work out between us. And in any case, we can't change history and start over as if none of it happened."

Did she want to? He didn't have the nerve to ask. She was right. It was insane even to be having this conversation. When he'd seen her at the bus stop, he should have turned and headed to the hotel, or at least to another tour.

She glanced at her watch. "Maybe we can catch an early bus back."

He nodded. That knife-edge of tension was back between them. He wanted to kick himself.

"Meredith, I—"

"Please don't apologize again," she said. "I'll forget about it if you will."

"All right." He meant the words, but as he said them they felt like wishful thinking. Forgetting evidently wasn't his strong suit. "But just let me say that I wish I'd done things differently too. I know there were moments when I didn't step up to the plate. Like with the pregnancy thing. Maybe you thought I was being callous—"

She looked him straight in the eye. "You said 'thank God.' Like you were so relieved you wouldn't be saddled with me."

"Because I wasn't ready. If you *had* been pregnant, I would have reacted differently. But I don't think either of us were ready for parenthood at that point."

She let out a knowing laugh. "Obviously. We weren't even ready to deal with the hiccup of *worrying* about being pregnant."

"But after that, I didn't have any idea that you were unhappy."

"I wasn't *unhappy*. I was just worried that you didn't actually want a long-term relationship, and that the false alarm was really my wakeup call that you weren't serious about me, that our relationship was just something you'd fallen into out of convenience and didn't take all that seriously."

"How could you think that?"

"You sat around talking about grad schools all that fall. Some in California. You weren't asking if *I'd* want to live in California. I figured you'd get in somewhere, and then that would be the end of us."

"So you dumped me preemptively?"

"I didn't want to get stuck in a happy-for-now thing that went on and on and then fizzled." She laughed. "That kind of logic made more sense to me then. I was younger, and I had crazy ideas. I thought that true love was what I was supposed to be looking for."

"It *is* what you're supposed to look for," he said.

"Then you're lucky you've found it."

The words scalded him. Right now, he didn't feel particularly lucky. He'd come on this trip hoping to get his life settled—just like he'd mapped it out on his Day Runner. In a matter of days, his heart had pretzeled itself into a confused knot.

Thank God Buttercup's revenge was putting the kibosh on their trip to Machu Picchu. Maybe those couple of days alone with Gina, away from Meredith, would give him a cool-down period. And time to decide what he really wanted.

Back at the hotel, he and Meredith parted ways in the lobby, and he continued down the corridor to his and Gina's suite, opening the door quietly to avoid waking her.

He didn't need to worry about that. The room was a blizzard of activity. Gina was up, striding across the room in her bathrobe. She seemed to have upended all their luggage over the furniture. Her eyes flashed at him with impatience. "Good. You're back. Finally."

Something was definitely wrong. "It's a ways out to that place," he explained, frowning at the clothes everywhere. "I'm glad you're up and feeling better."

"I feel like hell," she said.

"What's going on?"

"I'm packing things for tomorrow's trip to Machu Picchu."

They were going after all? He swallowed. "So . . . you must be feeling a little better if you still want to travel."

"I just don't want to stay behind here. And *you're* obviously bored."

The wire-tautness in her tone alerted him that there was something besides restlessness behind all this frantic repacking. Suddenly, the memory of pulling Meredith into his arms flashed in his mind. Guilt swallowed him. But no one else had been there. Gina couldn't know about that kiss.

"This morning, you were telling me to get out," he pointed out cautiously.

She planted her hands on her hips. Another bad sign. Very bad. "And you were more than eager to go off on some group tour this morning. But come to find out, you didn't go with our group . . . or at least not all of it. You went off on your own, with Meredith."

Uh-oh. "Meredith just happened to be there." He cast

back in his mind to this morning—it seemed so long ago now—and came up with one exonerating detail. "I bumped into Fran, too."

Gina's eyes narrowed. "Believe me, I know. The whole world knows you two chased her away with your lovey-doveyness."

How? How did she know? Fran couldn't have witnessed the kiss.

"What?" he asked, feeling confusion now, on top of guilt.

She snatched her iPad off the end table and madly finger-scrolled until she found what she was looking for. Then she thrust the device at him with an outstretched arm. *Yogaholic in Manhattan,* the blog's title read. And there below was his and Meredith's picture with the caption: *More pairing off. The plot thickens. . . .*

He pushed the device back to her. "That was when we met up at that tour place." His heart thumped with both relief and a renewed conviction of his own weaseliness.

"Apparently Fran's been narrating the whole trip to her faithful audience in the blogosphere. All four of them, not that it matters. If you had bothered to read the blog post, she's talking about you *thanking* Meredith for last night. And saying how much you needed her."

He sputtered. That was what Gina was so upset about? "Well, yes. Of course. I was thanking her for sitting with you. And for keeping a cool head when I was so worried about you that I got rattled."

"Oh, I bet she was very cool. And so happy you turned to her." Gina stared him down. "You might have told me that you two had been . . . intimate."

"I told you that we'd been roommates." As he repeated the words, their evasiveness pricked at his conscience. Why hadn't he confessed how much Meredith had meant to him? He wasn't a liar, but he'd been lying by omission the whole trip. He was still doing it.

"Roommates with benefits," Gina said. "When Janie came

in to show me that wonderful blog post, she let me know that you two had been quite an item. In fact, you were the one dating Meredith when she went to London."

"Exactly. She dumped me. And I hadn't seen her since until we ran into her at JFK. Believe me, it was not a delightful surprise."

"You were Meredith's zero. Why didn't you tell me?"

"First, because it's not pleasant to be called that. Also, because defending myself would be like my arguing against Janie's version of events, and I wasn't going to stoop to that. And the whole thing just didn't seem important anymore." A niggling discomfort sliced through him. To claim Meredith wasn't important to him seemed like a travesty now, but he couldn't explain that to Gina. "Anyway, you're way off the mark about Meredith."

"Oh, please. She's probably been dying to get you alone this whole trip."

This seemed incredibly unfair, given that Meredith was the one who had put a stop to the kiss, and was the one who had reminded him of his nearly engaged state when he had been about to throw scruples to the wind.

"You're wrong. This afternoon she assumed that we were already engaged because she knew about the ring."

Gina had the grace to blush a little. "Ring?" she asked with not-quite-convincing innocence.

He crossed to the room safe in the corner, where he'd locked it up the night before. He set the combination, yanked opened the door, and pulled out the turquoise box. Crossing back to her, he snapped it open. "This ring. Which I assume you're already acquainted with."

She gasped, pulling her gaze away from the brilliant stone to look up at him apologetically. "I just happened to run across it once, Sam. While you were in the shower. But it's so beautiful." She plucked it out of its cushion and slipped it on. "I *love* it."

He watched it taking up its new residence with no help

from him and felt oddly put out. "I wanted to give it to you as a surprise. I had this big scenario all built up in my head."

"And I ruined it." She sighed, but he couldn't tell if the sigh was a commiseration for having ruined his surprise or love for the ring. She smiled at him. "So this is our moment now. It just caught you unawares."

She hugged him, and it took him a moment to process what was happening. After all his planning, he'd ended up giving Gina the ring by accident. He'd just intended to confront her with her sneakiness, and by some jujitsu on her part, she'd taken it as a proposal. The jeweled band was on her finger now—his engagement had happened without his even prompting it. At least, he was pretty sure he was engaged.

She hugged him. "Oh, I'm so happy! You are *the most* incredible, wonderful fiancé ever."

Fiancé. Yes—definitely engaged. The thought stunned him. This was supposed to be the happiest moment of his life, but all he felt was a gut-churning sense of doom.

He pushed his glasses up the bridge of his nose, trying to figure out what to do. What to say. This had been the goal of the trip, and yet he felt blindsided. "Does it fit?"

She held her hand out, modeling it. "It's a little loose, but that might just be because I'm dehydrated. I can get it adjusted when I get back to New York."

He leapt at this detail. "Maybe we should put it back and keep it locked up safe until we get back to New York."

"No way. This puppy's mine now, and I'm going to wear it."

She pulled away and practically did a pirouette across the room, tossing a sweater into her small rolling bag. "This is going to be so much fun! Even if I end up puking the entire way up those damn mountains. I'm going to love it!"

"There's no reason for us to go running off if you're still weak. Honestly. I'd be just as happy to stay here."

Spending two days with Meredith had confused him

enough. Meredith and Gina together, on a train and then in a smaller town, struck him as even more problematic.

"I'm not *running off*," Gina said. "And I'm just not going to allow my reaction to a few bites of toxic rodent to give people—especially Janie—the satisfaction of thinking I'm afraid of letting you go to Machu Picchu. Especially when I can show them this." She trilled her ring finger.

He shook his head. "Nobody will read anything into our staying back here. And if they did, it would just be idle speculation and gossip. Who would bother?"

Her gaze turned almost pitying then. Pitying and amused. "You're adorable. You still don't know anything about women, do you?"

CHAPTER 7

The ring was the talk of the tour. After receiving it, Gina had left her room just long enough to let it be seen by a few people, including Fran, who'd immediately updated her blog with a correction and a photo.

"Insanely gorgeous," one of the yoga moms declared it during drinks the last night in Cuzco. Everyone at the table had swiveled toward Meredith in unison, a Greek chorus of pity for the woman shunned. They traded glances with one another, and in the next moment changed the subject to preschool admissions.

Subsequently, Meredith tossed back one more glass of the local corn beer than was good for her. Both the drink and the news about Sam left her numb. Of course, she'd known the kiss they'd shared had just been a moment's madness. She certainly wasn't expecting him to break up with Gina over her.

But she hadn't expected him to go directly to the hotel and get down on his knee to Gina, either.

The next morning, only four people showed up for sunrise yoga, which Meredith dubbed hangover yoga. She tried her hardest to banish her headache and all thoughts of Sam. Every time she remembered their kiss now, she was filled with equal parts desire and horror. For a moment, she'd sunk against his chest and let herself respond to him as if she actually belonged in his arms. As if they existed in a vacuum where the past didn't exist, where Gina didn't exist. All her arguments to him about why they shouldn't take the kiss seriously had been for her own benefit as well as Sam's.

After yoga, Claudia approached her, blocking Meredith's path to the breakfast bar. Meredith's stomach gnawed both from hangover and nerves.

"Do you see what's happening?" Claudia's usual mask of calm showed a fracture of impatience. She obviously wasn't pleased with dwindling attendance.

Meredith glanced around. "People are realizing they don't want to get up at seven thirty during vacation?"

"Is that really what you see?" Claudia's earnest tone beseeched Meredith to grasp the gravity of the situation. "Have you looked inside your house lately?"

Meredith shuffled uncomfortably, pretty sure that question had something to do with matters spiritual and not architectural. "Not this morning . . ."

"I think you should. You're carrying Sha Chi." When Meredith failed to comprehend, Claudia shook her head, more in sadness than recrimination. "Corrosive, attacking energy. It's spilling off of you and rubbing off on the tour. You need to examine that, both for yourself and the others. Negative Chi hurts everyone and causes friction. It's bad for morale."

That was so unfair. *She* was causing negative thoughts? She was just doing her own thing. She wasn't writing *Peyton Place*–type blog posts like Fran, or gossiping like practically everyone else, or holing up in an entirely different hotel as if the rest of them didn't exist, like the Goddess Claudia here.

By the time Meredith could begin to form a comeback that didn't sound like the negative, corrosive spew Claudia was clearly expecting from her, the woman had turned and was floating toward the lobby.

Meredith glared at her until Claudia was gone before scuttling in that direction herself. Normally she didn't believe in things like auras and Chi, but Claudia had spoken with such conviction, Meredith couldn't help feeling like a kind of fifties sci-fi monster. *Attack of the Bad Chi Creature.*

At the beverage table, Fran sidled up to her. "What was Claudia saying?"

"Oh . . . nothing much." Meredith couldn't quite own up to being called the group's morale suck.

"Must be a tough day for you, huh?"

"Just because of the rush to get ready to go." Meredith reached for an orange juice, then thought better of it. This morning called for a taste of the strong stuff. Grapefruit.

Fran eyed her almost apologetically. "Honestly, I never would have written that about you and Sam if I'd known that he was about to give her a rock bigger than a basketball." Her brows knit together in annoyance. "Clearly, I need better sources."

"You shouldn't have written it anyway."

Fran drew back. "Oookay. Someone's *a little touchy* this morning. Why would that be, I wonder? Methinks because the one that got away just got away again."

"Because it just wasn't true."

At least, not as far as Fran knew.

"Whatever you say . . ." Under her breath, Fran added, "Which isn't what other people are saying, by the way."

Meredith splashed coffee into a to-go cup. *I'm not taking that bait.* For once, though, she wished Janie were here to play big sister and give someone a verbal smackdown. But Meredith hadn't seen Janie since last night.

Fran appeared to hesitate, but then asked, "Have you seen the ring yet?"

"No." Meredith reached for a piece of bread.

"It's un-effing-believable. Seriously. The diamond is bigger than your breakfast roll."

Meredith was careful not to react. "It must be beautiful."

"Plus, they barely came out of their room last night."

"Well, Gina's sick."

Fran chuckled. "Right. They were in bed together last night because she was *sick*."

Meredith turned on her, a smile bolted in place. "I'm going to take this back to my room. Got to finish packing."

The bus that was going to take them to the train station was due to pick them up in less than an hour.

As she headed for the door leading to the corridor, she heard Fran belting out the chorus of Adele's "Someone Like You," which Meredith always thought of as a psycho-girl stalker song. Great. After yesterday, probably most people thought she was trying to throw herself in Sam's path to remind him that she was still carrying a torch.

She couldn't wait to be on the train and out of here. Yesterday when Sam had told her he wouldn't be going to Machu Picchu, she'd felt a pang of loss. So far, their meetings had been awkward and bittersweet, but she'd enjoyed talking to him. He might not have been in her life for seven years, but she had the feeling that he knew her.

But now—what a relief it would be to get away from him and Gina. And that damn ring.

When, balancing her breakfast, she pushed through the door of her room, Janie was perched on the unslept-upon bed. "Here you are!" Her sister hopped up and rushed toward her. "I'm so sorry about everything, Mer."

Oh, for Pete's sake. "Not you too. Once and for all, I don't care. We both knew about the stupid ring."

"Yes, but he hadn't given it to her yet. Now it's so permanent. Irreversible—at least for a few years, until they start thinking divorce." She took the grapefruit juice from Meredith and sank onto the bed. "And what an idiot, to choose her over you."

"It was never a contest," Meredith insisted. "I was never in the running."

"But after yesterday . . ." Janie was the one who'd discovered Fran's blog—and from her account, she'd taken not a little glee in pointing it out to Gina while the woman was lying sick in bed. Now that her concern trolling had backfired, Janie looked deflated.

"Why do you care? You don't even like Sam."

"True." Janie drummed her fingertips against the glass. "Although . . . he is better than he used to be."

She didn't say it, but obviously Janie couldn't help thinking that no man was all bad who gave a woman a ring with a retail value that would put a married couple above the poverty line. It was infuriating. "Sam was always great," Meredith said. "*I* was the one who was mixed up. I was stupid."

"Oh dear."

This time, Meredith didn't contradict Janie's fretting. *Oh dear* about summed it up. She'd been fighting it since Tipón, or maybe longer. A lot longer. If Sam had been available, she never would have broken off that kiss. The world was filled with stories of couples getting second chances. Why not them?

Gina, that was why. Gina was an undeniable fact. An undeniable, beautiful, size-four barrier whom Sam was in love with instead of her. Go figure.

"You blame me, don't you?" Janie asked.

"No."

"You do. That's what you've been so upset about—you like him and you're afraid to tell me, because of what happened all those years ago. Maybe I was wrong. And now if you die a spinster, it will be all my fault." A look of genuine anguish crossed her sister's face. "But things seemed so different back then."

"I know."

"You were so young. For that matter, *I* was younger too." Meredith laughed. "We're not ancient now."

"That's true." Janie brightened. "Well, maybe we'll just

have to set up house together someday. We'll be the crazy old spinsters of our building."

Meredith tossed her nightshirt into her little duffel bag. "I'm just glad we're getting away from this town, and getting away from them for a while." Getting away from Sam and Gina.

Janie looked stricken. "Haven't you heard? They're going."

"To Machu Picchu?" Meredith's voice looped up in alarm.

"I thought you knew. I'm so—"

"Please don't say you're sorry again." Meredith struggled to regroup her emotions. "There's no reason to be. I'm on vacation. Everything's great. I'm going to one of the places on my bucket list. What could be better?"

Janie didn't look convinced. She sat down across from Meredith, a contrite expression on her face. "I haven't been much of a sister to you on this trip, have I? But that's all going to change. I'm going to loan you Seth. You can sit next to him on the train."

"And that would make me feel better how?"

Janie gaped at her as if it should be obvious. "You wouldn't be alone. And frankly, it would give me a breather."

"Please don't tell me you're dumping Seth now that you don't need his hotel room."

"Well . . . it's not just that." She tapped her finger against her chin. "Although I probably should wait and see what kind of dive Claudia has us booked into at Aguas Calientes. . . . But the other thing is, Seth broke out the guitar last night and treated me to a Gordon Lightfoot marathon."

Spending three hours on a train next to the Bald Troubadour was not what Meredith needed right now. "I was going to use the train ride to do some planning for the Astoria Garage Players' theater day camp."

But, naturally, the first person she bumped into while carrying her luggage down the steep stairs from the hotel to the street was Sam. Her steps faltered when he turned and saw her, but she forced herself forward. "Hi," she said. "I hear congratulations are in order."

"Thanks."

He didn't seem ecstatic about it. As they continued their descent, she searched for something else to say. "How is Gina?"

"Fine."

When they reached the bus, the driver came around to open the storage space under the vehicle. Meredith handed him her bag, and when she turned back around, Janie was picking her way down next to Gina. The two of them hesitated at the sight of Meredith and Sam huddled with the driver, and then they hurried forward. Gina hooked her arm through Sam's. Her face was still pale, and she looked as if she might have gone down another dress size in the past day, but otherwise, she was perfectly put together in a yellow linen top, white Capri pants, and sandals. Meredith, wearing a polo, Bermuda shorts, and sneakers, felt gym teachery by comparison.

Something sparkled, and her gaze was drawn to the ring on Gina's left hand. It really was a beauty. The silvery band had a line of little diamonds leading up to the large stone in the center. "What a gorgeous ring," she said. "Congrats!"

Gina smiled. "Thank you."

Meredith and Janie headed to the back of the bus, while Gina and Sam sat at the front. It seemed almost as if there were some sort of group agreement to keep Meredith and Sam separated. This continued at the train station, and then on the train itself. They boarded the blue-and-yellow Vista-dome train, and almost immediately Meredith felt herself being tugged to the opposite end of the train from Sam. Their group made up half the people in their car, and once the train pulled out, the excitement of being on the go distracted everyone from their internecine soap opera. When the tracks pulled alongside a river, the passengers moved en masse to the left-hand side of the train, to get the better view.

The soothing rhythm of the wheels against the tracks worked like a balm on Meredith's spirits. For a while, she just stared out the window as they gained altitude. She would have liked to zone out completely, but as Janie had promised/warned, Seth sat next to Meredith while Janie herself joined a few of the moms for a hearts tournament. Right after they were offered beverages, Seth cracked open his guitar case and settled in for a long, ballad-filled ride.

"I thought of some songs that might make you feel better," he said. His first song was "Crying," a song Meredith actually liked. At least, she liked it when Roy Orbison sang it. His next selection was "All Out of Love."

"Is there a reason you think depressing love songs would make me feel better?"

"Just so you'll know that you're not alone."

Marvelous. She and Air Supply, together in misery.

He leaned in toward her. "Is the pain too raw?"

She gulped down her apple juice, trying not to think of Sam's lips against hers. It was amazing how sappy songs actually could get to you when you were vulnerable. "No."

"You shouldn't feel jealous," he said. "I'm sure there are men who prefer your type. You win some; you lose some."

"I'm not jealous."

He shot her a skeptical look and launched into a dirge-like, gender-inappropriate version of Patsy Cline's "She's Got You."

Though she tried not to, Meredith couldn't help stealing glances at Sam, who was sitting on the aisle on the empty side of the train. He didn't even seem all that interested in the scenery going by. He looked tired. Glum. Something wasn't right.

Or maybe she was just projecting her own feelings onto him.

She wished things were normal and she could just go up and talk to him. But the way things stood now, any attempt to approach him on her part would be interpreted as her making a play for him. It was so ridiculous to feel self-conscious about just talking to someone because people assumed she was eaten up with jealousy. Which wasn't the truth at all—or was just a tiny part of it. If anything, she had only just now realized how much she wished all the best for Sam. If he thought he could find his happily-ever-after with Gina, so be it.

He didn't look happy, though. And how could he, facing a life sentence with that awful, superficial harpy?

All right. Maybe she was a little jealous.

After an hour of watching the train's progress out the window as they made their way along the brown, rushing river, she got up to use the restroom at the back of the train. As she approached the door, Gina came out.

They exchanged smiles. Gina's was especially big. Every time Meredith had an interaction with the woman now, she felt as if she were onstage, playing the part of a person trying not to appear heartbroken and jealous.

It will get easier, she told herself as she shut herself in the bathroom. Emotions were ornery things. She'd lived seven years without Sam, and for most of that time hadn't felt this raw emptiness inside. After this trip, she'd get back to her old life and be on an even keel again.

After washing her hands, she snatched a towel from the dispenser. Drying her hands, she heard a light *clink*. Something sparkly winked at her from the stainless-steel sink. She blinked twice to absorb what she was looking at—Gina's engagement ring. It must have been left on the lip of the sink, and Meredith's towel had probably brushed it. Now, right before her eyes, that hugely expensive ring was clattering and spinning around the sink's deep bowl, beating a swirling, elliptical path to the drain.

Dexterity had never been her strong suit. She stank at video games and any activity that required hand-eye coordination. So in the nanosecond that she watched that Tiffany cushion-cut diamond with its flashy parade of little stones on the band rolling toward that opening that would suck it into a pipe and then take it God knows where—the bowels of the train, or perhaps the very track they were rushing over—panic hit her hard. Panic fueled by the memory of having been picked last in PE for every game, and of thousands of missed shots, swings at softballs that hit nothing but air, of being the only girl in third grade who absolutely sucked at jacks.

The ring made its final narrowing rotation around the drain, and she darted her hand out, slapping her entire palm over the ring and drain both. When she felt the stones pressing into her index finger, a wave of relief hit her. Not trusting herself to let go, she dragged the ring up against the steel several inches before picking it up.

What had it been doing here? Was Gina so cavalier with jewels that she could just toss it onto a stainless-steel sink and forget about it? Meredith wasn't taking any chances. She jammed it onto her finger for safekeeping and then raised her hand to inspect it up close. It really was a little dazzler. She could just imagine how much anxiety Sam had undergone, both in picking it out and carrying it with him on this trip. It made her nervous to have it in her possession for just a minute.

She exited the bathroom and walked right into a stampede. Gina was leading the charge down the train aisle toward the bathroom, her eyes wide and frantic, her raised fist poised to pound on the bathroom door. Perhaps to batter it down if necessary. Behind her were Sam, Fran, Janie, and several of the yoga moms who obviously understood the pitfalls of taking off wedding jewelry in a public restroom.

Gina rampaged past Meredith, tossing a searching look at the bare sink. She swung around, grabbing Meredith's shoulders. "Did you see it?"

Meredith had intended to go straight to Gina's seat and return the ring to her. She'd hoped she could save Gina panic and probably embarrassment, as well, when she realized what she'd done. Now all she could do was hold up her hand.

"You mean this?" She smiled, hoping it would puncture the tension around them.

Instead, as the blood returned to Gina's cheeks, the woman's panic flared into indignation. When Meredith looked at her hand, she realized why. She'd mashed the ring onto the third finger of her left hand. It probably looked as if she'd been in the bathroom modeling it and fantasizing it was hers.

Heat leapt to her cheeks. "I was just bringing it back to you," she explained quickly.

From scanning the expressions of those gathered around, she could tell that not everyone was convinced. Even Janie eyed her doubtfully, as if worried that Meredith had finally gone round the bend.

Rolling her eyes toward the windowed dome ceiling of the train, Meredith tugged on the ring, eager to get rid of it. She frowned and tugged again.

Unfortunately, the ring wasn't eager to get off of her finger. "I think we might have a problem," she announced.

Convincing everyone that she wasn't a jealous ring-snatcher proved nearly impossible when the ring in question refused to budge from her hand.

Luckily, the yoga moms proved themselves invaluable—between them, they were a regular *Hints from Heloise* index on the subject of stuck rings. First, they advised her to soak her finger in ice cubes and then elevate her hand. When that failed to do the trick, anything greasy from people's handbags was brought out to aid the cause. Hand lotion. Antibiotic ointment. Chapstick. Even a nut butter sandwich Seth had brought along for the train trip. Each substance was slathered on, and then passengers took turns tugging on her finger. When dislocation threatened, Nina remembered a trick involving dental floss. The floss was wrapped around Meredith's finger—compressing the flesh until it felt like the thread tourniquet was going to cut off her circulation. Painstakingly, the ring was wriggled free.

During this ordeal, she'd barely been able to meet Sam's eye. Did he suspect that she'd done it on purpose too? After their kiss yesterday, he might well wonder. Especially since he'd gone straight home and proposed to Gina—probably relieved that he'd escaped a fatal near-mistake.

She felt like such an idiot. She wanted nothing more than to catch the next train back to Cuzco.

The bus ride from Aguas Calientes to Machu Picchu changed her attitude. As the vehicle lumbered and zigzagged its way up the mountain road, Meredith couldn't think about herself—except perhaps the peril she felt when she glimpsed occasional hair-raising drops into the valley below. The view was spectacular. From a distance, the impossibly vertical mountains covered in cloud forest jutted straight into the heavens. It took her breath away. When she looked out the window at the passing scenery up closer, splashes of color caught her eye. Orchids and wild begonias peeked from behind shrubs and vines.

"I think I'll get up early tomorrow morning and walk up to Machu Picchu," she said to Janie, who was sitting next to her, white-knuckling the armrest with one hand. She had her nose in the guidebook, presumably trying to avoid looking at the dead drop below them. For the first time, it occurred to Meredith how much her acrophobic, comfort-loving sister was enduring on this trip.

"You've got to be kidding," her sister said. "The book says that hike takes an hour and a half. And you'd need to be a goat or a llama."

"But it's so pretty."

"Mm." Her sister darted a quick glance out the window and then stuck her nose back into the book. "Besides, we're supposed to take the first bus up again tomorrow morning. Claudia is going to have us do sunrise yoga at some temple or another."

"My corrosive Chi and I would probably be unwelcome anyway."

Janie patted her leg, but didn't contradict her. "Well, if you do walk it, remember to bring money. You'll be thirsty at the top, and they charge you an arm and a leg just for water, according to this. Even to use the washrooms costs you."

She felt a strange swell of affection for her sister then. Janie was still looking out for her, just like that thirteen-year-old who had led her by the hand on day one of first grade. The conscientious older sibling who had reminded her to bring her milk money—something their stepmother always forgot. The sister who, when she got her first paycheck, had made a date with Meredith to take her shopping that weekend. Who had seen her floundering after college and tried to rescue her. Who hadn't wanted her to settle for the first guy who came along.

The sister who'd had no way of knowing that the first guy might have been the best guy for her. Because Meredith hadn't known it herself.

Not until it was too late.

She put her hand over Janie's, causing her sister to jump in alarm. "What? What's wrong?"

"Thanks," Meredith said.

"For what?"

"For everything." She gestured out the window. On any normal vacation, the fantastic scenery would have been the highlight of the trip. But this was just the buildup to the main event. Maybe it was foolish to feel so crazily sentimental when they were stuck on a tourist bus, but Meredith couldn't help herself. Tears stood in her eyes. "I wouldn't have done this if you hadn't convinced me."

Janie studied her closely and smiled in understanding. She patted Meredith's hand. "Thank me when it's clear that we're not going to plunge to our deaths."

* * *

It was the most beautiful place he'd ever been, maybe the most beautiful place he would ever be. But as he climbed centuries-old steps and gazed at the terraced mountainside down to the distant valley below, the magnificence and marvel of it all barely registered. He'd felt numb since yesterday and distracted by a niggling voice in his mind telling him that he was doing something wrong. But the only way out seemed wrong too. Or at least, not good.

Another voice also distracted him. Gina's.

"I swear I can still smell nut butter on my ring." She lifted her finger to her nose, sniffing in distaste.

"It can't be," he said. "Platinum isn't porous enough to absorb a smell like that. Especially in so short a time."

"Short!" Gina grunted. "I thought we were going to have to slice off Meredith's finger to get my ring back. I'm still not sure why she put it on to begin with."

"She told you why. She'd been terrified it was going down the drain. You might ask yourself why you left it there."

"I just forgot. It's loose, so I took it off before I washed my hands." Her eyes widened, and she did a double take. "Wait. Are you saying it was *my* fault?"

He sighed. "No. I'm just saying you can't read too much into things. She said she did it instinctively, and I believe her."

Gina released a throaty laugh. "Quite a coincidence that she *instinctively* sticks the ring of the guy she's in love with on her finger."

"She's not in love with me."

"Of course she is. Haven't you noticed? She's been moping all day."

"Probably because she's self-conscious after that blog post of Fran's. Believe me, she's not in love with me."

"How can you be so sure?"

"Because she told me."

After he blurted out the words, the world fell silent. Sounds of birds and the conversation of other tourists faded.

Gina held her arms rigidly at her sides. "You two were discussing love? When?"

"Yesterday. At Tipón."

"I suppose she gave you a long speech about how you shouldn't worry about her, because she no longer carried a torch for you."

"Not exactly." He took a deep breath. "The truth is, I kissed her. And she was the one who broke it off. *That's* when she told me that it wouldn't go anywhere."

When he met Gina's gaze, shock swam in her eyes for a moment before anger took over. "You kissed her," she repeated. "Yesterday."

He nodded. Confession was supposed to be good for the soul, but he was suddenly aware that it could be treacherous for physical well-being. One strong shove could send him toppling over a stone wall. His might be the first sacrificial death that the Temple of the Sun had seen for a few centuries.

But Gina stayed perfectly still. "So . . . you kissed Meredith while I was in bed sick. And then she rejected you. And then you came back to the hotel and gave me an engagement ring."

Pointing out that it hadn't been a matter of his giving her the ring so much as her taking it didn't strike him as politically astute at the moment. He made do with a nod.

"Well! That's just thrilling to know," she drawled. "I'm your fiancée by default."

"I swear, I never intended this to happen. You know how excited I was about this trip. I had everything planned. And then Meredith showed up." Seeing the color rise in Gina's cheeks, he decided that wasn't a good route to take, either. For lack of a better alternative, his brain fell back on repeating breakup clichés. "I never meant for this to happen. You deserve better."

She gawped at him. "Wait. You're *dumping* me? You dragged me all the way to South America to let me know that you're running off with Meredith?"

"I'm not running off with her. I'm not even sure she'd want me at this point."

She continued to stare at him incredulously. "I can't believe it. You're serious."

"It's not about Meredith. It's about us. We've been content to be going out together, to have someone. But I don't think we love each other enough to be married for fifty years. At this point, I'd be surprised if we made it five years."

She glared at him. "I would be too, considering you can't even stay faithful during our engagement vacation." She shook her head in disgust. "I was so wrong about you. I thought, 'Okay, he's a little on the unexciting side, but he's not one of those guys you'll have to keep tabs on all the time.' But it turns out, behind that unassuming accountant exterior, you're just another undependable, cheating dog." She yanked the ring off her finger. "Well, all right. If that's the case, and you want your stupid ring back . . ."

To his horror, she hauled back and then hurled the ring over the side of the wall. The pitch would have done Sandy Koufax proud. The precious metal glinted as it arced toward the sun, then dropped out of sight.

"Go fetch!"

CHAPTER 8

There were so many things to look at here. When she'd read about Machu Picchu in the guidebooks, she'd envisioned something compact. Now, she feared two visits wouldn't be enough to explore everything. She kept stopping to film, panning with her camera across the spectacular panoramas in all directions. And then she'd start down a new path and be distracted by a llama. They were all over and stood sentry around the site like the slightly bored security guards at the Metropolitan Museum of Art. She snapped about a hundred pictures of them.

She also couldn't believe how many stairs there were. The Incas must have had glutes of steel. She puffed her way up a particularly long rise that the map she'd picked up at the entrance promised would lead her to another temple. She stopped to gather her breath and frowned down at the map. Maybe this staircase was leading to the ceremonial baths.

Damn. Sam was right. She really sucked at directions.

Do not think about Sam.

Something hit her hair, causing her to jump. At first she thought it might be a particularly hardy bug performing a kamikaze dive onto her scalp. She shook her head, and in the next moment perceived a light tinkling metal hitting stone. What the hell?

She peered in the direction the sound had come from, then bent over, studying the ground. Something silvery winked at her.

She crouched farther to pick it up, and then froze. *Oh no.* It couldn't be.

She frowned at the ring for a moment and gave herself a sharp pinch to make sure she wasn't hallucinating. But no. There it was, her old nemesis, Gina's ring.

She picked it up gingerly, careful *not* to put it on her finger this time. Any finger. She wished she had tongs or tweezers so she wouldn't even have to touch it.

Why had it been flying through the air? She glanced up, but she couldn't see over the wall above her head.

And why her? She just couldn't seem to shake free of this ring. She couldn't help wondering if Dorothy Gale had felt this way when she realized she was stuck wearing the ruby slippers the Wicked Witch would kill her for. Pretty, yes, but she hadn't asked for the damn things. Meredith certainly didn't want the ring.

She peered up again and caught sight of Sam's head. He was looking over the edge of the wall. She waved and started climbing. Might as well get this over with. Maybe Gina could be convinced to Scotch tape the ring to tighten it up until she could get home and get it fitted better.

When Meredith had puffed to the top of the stairs, she found Sam standing alone. Several expressions marched across his face—from a glad smile, to wariness, to a shuttered look she couldn't read at all.

"Where's Gina?" she asked.

He jabbed his thumb in the opposite direction. "She went thataway."

Meredith shifted uneasily. "You're not going to believe this," she said, holding out the ring. "I found it again. Please tell Gina it wasn't on purpose."

He didn't seem inclined to take the ring back at first. Then, almost glowering at it, he plucked it out of her hand and stuffed it into his pocket.

Something was seriously wrong. "I don't know how it got from up here to bouncing off my skull, but—"

"Gina threw it," he said, interrupting. "She was angry because I'd called off the engagement."

Her heart lurched uneasily in her chest. She wanted to be glad for him, but he was clearly still in turmoil. Or shock. "Please tell me this had nothing to do with me and that stupid ring."

"It had nothing to do with you and the ring. But it had everything to do with how I feel about you."

She shook her head. "Oh, Sam." She wasn't sure whether to laugh, cry, or throw herself into his arms. Nothing seemed quite right. "What a mess."

"No kidding," he said. "I've got four more vacation days to go with the girlfriend I just broke up with. Including a fourteen-hour plane trip home."

She couldn't help it. She laughed. "This will give Fran something to blog about."

He hesitated a moment, then stepped toward her. She pivoted slightly, taking in the view of lush greenery and rediscovered hidden city, and trying to process the avalanche of feelings going on inside her.

"What do you think?" he asked.

She sucked in a deep breath. Maybe it was the altitude that made her light-headed, or the air itself, which smelled pure and earthy at the same time. It was a million times cleaner than what her lungs usually got. "The climb was definitely worth it."

"I meant, what do you think about my breaking off with Gina?"

Elation? Maybe that was the altitude too. "I'm not sure. I didn't want to come between you two."

"It wasn't your doing. It was mine. I've been an idiot. I forgot what love was supposed to be."

She glanced up at him, unsure of what to say.

He took her hand. "Maybe I shouldn't bring this up just now," he said. "But just suppose that when you got back to New York an old boyfriend called you up on a Friday night. What would you say?"

Her heart skipped, but she managed to maintain some poise. He looked so worried. "I probably wouldn't answer my phone. I'm usually at the theater on Friday nights."

He shifted in frustration. "Saturday afternoon, then. What if this old boyfriend were to ask you out for coffee, to talk about old times."

She thought about that. "I think I'd rather talk about current times. Or maybe the future."

The anxiety pinching his brow lifted. "Then you'd say yes?"

She looked into his eyes, and resistance melted. "Yes. Definitely."

He squeezed her hand. The happiness inside her seemed to expand to fit the landscape.

"When we get back to New York," she said, for clarification, "this old boyfriend won't wait seven more years to call, will he?"

He smiled. "More like seven minutes after he gets back to his apartment from the airport."

That sounded perfect. Except for one thing. "I like the idea of taking it slow. But maybe we need a little something to tide us over?"

A spark leapt in his eyes. "Good idea." He pulled her into his arms, and when their lips met, she realized that she'd never looked forward to the future more.

She couldn't wait to tell Janie.

SUMMER MEMORIES

HOLLY CHAMBERLIN

As always, for Stephen.
And this time, also for Ruth.

Acknowledgments

Thanks to John Scognamiglio for his
patience, care, and encouragement.
And thanks and gratitude to Stephen
for everything, always.

CHAPTER 1

"Well, Ellen Tudor. Welcome to your new temporary home."

Ellen stood in the middle of the living room of the house she had just rented at a ridiculously expensive price for the three months of summer. She didn't mind the ridiculously high price, because she had come home. She would have paid more than she could have afforded to be back in Ogunquit that summer.

The house stood at the end of the picturesque and private Wisteria Lane. It was a simple, two-story wooden structure set on an acre of land. The owners had kept the grounds well tended. The grass was freshly mowed, the trees trimmed, and there was a very pretty garden of wildflowers out back. Ellen had been offered the choice of tending the land herself (the owners would pay for her time and supplies), or having a professional gardening service come by on a regular basis.

Ellen chose the gardening service. She loved flowers, but she wasn't much good at keeping even the hardiest of green plants alive. She loved to buy good silk imitations of her favorites—blue-tinted hydrangeas, fat pink peonies, cream-colored roses—and when the real things were in season, she bought those lavishly. At the moment, most of the surfaces in the living room were decorated with vases of blooms. A squat, square container showed off the vibrant and colorful energy of three large sunflowers; a tall, narrow glass vase displayed several elegant stalks of bells of Ireland; and a classic, V-shaped vase allowed a dozen Fire and Ice roses to claim pride of place.

Yes, the house on Wisteria Lane would suit Ellen perfectly. A modest-sized kitchen, a generously sized living room, and a room that had once been a parlor or sitting room were to be found on the first floor. On the second floor, reached by a center stairway, there was the master bedroom, a smaller bedroom for guests, and the house's one bathroom. It had been modernized enough to please the finicky bather, but retained a good deal of old charm. The white porcelain tub was a genuine claw-footed one; there was molding halfway up all four walls; and the light fixtures looked to be expensive and very good replicas of those from the early twentieth century.

The house came furnished, so Ellen had brought only the basics with her—clothing, books, computer, and the like. Her rental apartment, back in Boston, was standing empty for the summer. Her mail was being forwarded to Ogunquit. Only her parents and Caroline Charron, her closest friend, knew where she was spending June, July, and August.

In short, she would be left virtually alone. It was how she wanted it to be, after what had happened with Peter.

Ellen decided that she was hungry. As she passed through the living room on her way to the kitchen, she caught sight of her reflection in the mirror over the fireplace. Well, the topmost bit of her reflection. Ellen, who had turned thirty-one the previous February, stood at only five feet two inches tall. Her hair was very blond, and she wore it short in the pixielike style Michelle Williams had made popular again. Her eyes were large and brown; she thought they were probably her best feature. When she was younger people had said

that her eyes made her look like a Disney character, all innocent and lovable. Well, Ellen wasn't entirely sure about the
lovable part! She had her bad and sad moods like everyone
else, although they never lasted very long.

Why Ogunquit, Caroline had asked when Ellen had announced her plans to "escape" for a few months. Why not
some other pretty coastal town? The answer was easy. Ellen's
parents had owned a vacation home in Ogunquit. She had
spent every summer there from the age of eight, after that
one summer at sleepaway camp. (Her memories of Camp
Norridgewock were mostly vague; the only bit that stuck out
vividly was the memory of that fiendish boy named Bobby
who had called her that awful name. It was a name that had
haunted her for months, if not years, afterward.)

Anyway, five years earlier the Tudors had sold the beloved
house in Ogunquit and moved to Arizona for the famously
dry heat. They came to visit Ellen for a week each spring, and
they all kept in touch as most long-distance families did
these days—they Skyped and e-mailed and texted, and they
even used the good, old-fashioned telephone.

So, when Ellen had decided that she needed time to heal
after Peter's betrayal, Ogunquit, the "beautiful place by the
sea," had seemed the logical choice of destination. It was in
Ogunquit that she had built sandcastles and collected shells
on Maine Beach, and it was there she had lost her virginity
at the age of sixteen to a cute and very sweet seventeen-year-
old guy named Etienne, visiting from France. It was there
that she had her first paying job waiting tables at a fish and
chips joint in Perkins Cove, and it was there she had spent
lazy summer evenings on the front porch, swinging and sipping her mother's lemonade.

But why go back there now, her mother had asked. *Why
retreat from the people who love you, like Caroline and your
other friends in Boston? What possible good could come of
being all by yourself, surrounded by virtual strangers?*

Because, Ellen had answered, though silently, *virtual strangers will have no idea of what a fool I made of myself with Peter Hall.*

Caroline had warned her against Peter from the start. She had declared him untrustworthy on no evidence that Ellen could see, and after a while this difference of opinion had caused tension between the two friends. Peter was just so—just so perfect!—and after all, Caroline wasn't exactly known for her success with men. She hadn't had a relationship in three years! Ellen knew that Caroline wasn't jealous of her relationship with Peter; Caroline wasn't the jealous type. Still, Ellen just couldn't understand what was causing Caroline's antipathy.

Eventually, Caroline had begun to keep her opinions about Peter to herself, and the women's friendship had gotten back on track. When Peter had proposed to Ellen with masses of her favorite flowers and a four-carat diamond ring, Caroline had warmly and sincerely congratulated her friend.

Unlike Caroline, Ellen's parents had thought Peter was as perfect as Ellen had thought him to be. When Peter had proposed with such drama and romance, both JoAnne and Louis had been dizzy with joy. It was amazing, Ellen thought now, how much influence a dozen bouquets and a sparkly ring could have over even the most levelheaded and practical of people.

And then Peter had cheated. Well, it turned out that he had been cheating for some time before he got sloppy and left evidence behind for Ellen to find. And she had also found evidence that a good deal of the money she had contributed to their household fund had disappeared without a paper or electronic trail. In short, Peter Hall had proved to be a liar, a cheat, and a swindler.

Caroline had been one hundred percent correct about Peter. And though she didn't gloat or say, "I told you so," Ellen felt embarrassed by her own poor judgment. She was uncomfortable facing the friend who had had the courage and the honesty to warn her of a danger she had not been able to see.

But this was nothing new. Since childhood, it had been Ellen's habit to retreat when she was upset, to seek emotional isolation until her wounds had healed. And then, she would emerge from her seclusion, more cautious than before, but whole. And she always emerged.

In the beginning of their relationship, Peter had found her habit of emotional withdrawal annoying; Ellen guessed that by the end of their relationship he had come to find it very convenient for the pursuit of his own illicit adventures.

Now, this summer, Ellen had chosen not only emotional but physical retreat, as well. The best thing for her to do was to go away for a time.

Eventually, even JoAnne Tudor had accepted her daughter's decision. She had witnessed just how badly Ellen had been hurt by Peter Hall. It was Mrs. Tudor who had urged Ellen to sell the ring Peter had given her; it more than made up for the money he had filched. And it was Mrs. Tudor who had urged Ellen to confront Peter and demand an apology.

That confrontation had taken every ounce of courage Ellen possessed. Not that it had changed anything. Peter had refused to apologize for destroying her life, or for destroying the life they had been building together.

Now, two months after the breakup, Ellen wasn't sure she had anything left in her to fuel another big stand. But if she were very lucky and very, very cautious, she would never be fooled again. . . .

Peace and quiet. That was what she was hoping to find in Ogunquit. Time alone to recoup and to recharge.

"Well, as long as you're going back to Ogunquit," Mrs. Tudor had said, "would you do me a favor and look up my old friend Cora Compton?" And Ellen would. She remembered Cora as more than slightly eccentric. Interestingly, she had been called "Old" Mrs. Compton for as long as the Tudors had known her; now, Ellen thought, she must be approaching eighty and almost deserving of her moniker. As for Mr. Compton, well, no one seemed to know anything about him. It didn't seem to matter now.

What did matter was food. Ellen had brought in groceries earlier that day, and now selected a package of ground turkey from the freezer. A turkey burger and a big salad were just what she wanted. She set about preparing her dinner, aware that after only a few days back in Ogunquit she already felt calmer and more at ease. It boded well for a restful and restorative summer.

one, simply everyone will be there, and they are all dying to meet you. Well, those who haven't met you in the past. Those who have are eager to renew their acquaintance."

Ellen highly doubted that, but she quickly agreed, more to make Cora feel better than because she wanted a night out hobnobbing with the locals.

"Well, then," Cora said with a tone of immense satisfaction, "I'll look for you at the opening. It will be such a marvelous occasion."

Ellen watched as the older woman made her way—sailed, rather, a ship in full mast—down the drive to where she had parked her car, a massive, ancient black Cadillac.

She was really a wonderful old girl, Ellen thought as Cora Compton pulled away. Woman, rather. Why, Ellen wondered, had she thought of Mrs. Compton as a girl? She had meant no disrespect. Maybe she had been watching too many British period mysteries lately, the ones in which even the nicest of men referred to older women as "girls" and suspected them of fanciful thinking, odd behaviors, and a penchant for cats and doilies and sherry.

Ellen turned away from the view of the front drive and headed toward the kitchen. Some people might not think so, but a love of British period mysteries went very well with a financially attuned mind, one that could make calculations and decipher complicated facts. In her professional life as an independent financial advisor, Ellen was in some ways a detective, reading signs, making educated guesses, and rapidly solving riddles the average person could not solve given months or even years.

It was just too bad that she couldn't solve people as easily as she could solve their financial matters.

Her stomach rumbled loudly, and Ellen reached for the door of the fridge. She would solve no mysteries, financial or otherwise, until she got some hot coffee and food inside her.

CHAPTER 3

The Noise Gallery (what a ridiculous name, Ellen thought; it certainly didn't bode well for what lay within) was located on a small, one-way street off a main road through town. It was a cramped space. The ceilings seemed dangerously low, and there was very little natural light. The artificial lighting was poor, especially for a venue dedicated to showcasing art. Well, maybe poor lighting was a good thing, Ellen thought, taking a glance around the rooms. She was no artist, but she prided herself on having some native taste. And that taste was telling her that the work hanging on the walls of the Noise Gallery was—well, it was not very good. Amateurish would be a kind way of putting it. Just plain bad would be a less kind though maybe more accurate way of stating things.

Ellen eyed the refreshments. They didn't look any better than the art. A paper cloth that had seen better days covered a long metal folding table. (Wasn't the point of paper table-cloths to use them once and toss them?) Plastic cups pre-filled with wine of a suspiciously bright yellow color were lined up along the back of the table. The hors d'oeuvres were laid out next to the cups—pale yellow squares of cheese Ellen

supposed was an anemic sort of cheddar piled on store-bought
crackers; rubbery shrimp stuck on plastic toothpicks; and
dry little chunks of some awful nut bread. Nut and bolt
bread was more like it, Ellen thought, as she desperately
swallowed half a cup of wine (it was horribly sweet) to wash
it down her protesting throat.

Still, in spite of the bad art and worse food, the opening
had drawn a large crowd. Virtually everyone was smartly
dressed; no baseball caps or white crew socks here. There
was the usual scattering of eccentrics to be found at every
gallery opening everywhere—women in billowing garments
and oversized jewelry and men in badly faded velvet vests
and sporting ponytails. And then there was the better-heeled
set, or the ones who considered themselves so, the men in
navy blazers, pressed chinos, and pastel ties, the women
wearing tailored skirts or dresses and stack-heeled pumps.
In general, both sets of people were genial and seemed
happy to be there.

Ellen hadn't thought about what to wear until almost the
last minute. She was lucky she was built slightly; most
everything sat nicely on her, like the sleeveless A-line linen
dress she was wearing at the moment. And it was all right
that linen be slightly wrinkled. In fact, it was almost expected that it be wrinkled.

"Ellen!"

Ellen startled. Cora Compton was charging in her direction, sending patrons of the gallery scattering for safety.

"Ellen, my dear, I am so glad you came!"

Ellen smiled. "I wouldn't have missed it for the world."

The older woman was decked out in what she proudly told
Ellen was one of her finest outfits. Finest and, Ellen thought,
most conspicuous. It was a dress of a shocking shade of purple,
with a fitted bodice and a full, floor-sweeping skirt. Adding
to the Edith Wharton effect (though Ellen doubted that Mrs.
Wharton ever wore such a garish shade), Cora's hair was

piled particularly high, causing Ellen to wonder if she had inserted a few pieces of faux hair into the structure. From Cora's earlobes hung magnificent, glittering gems; they might have been real diamonds, they sparkled so cleanly and brilliantly. No less than three diamond and ruby rings adorned her fingers. For the first time Ellen wondered what the mysterious Mr. Compton had done for a living. As far as she knew Mrs. Compton was unemployed and had been for—well, forever. Had her husband been a latter-day robber baron? Had he left her millions when he died? That might explain a few things, like her presumptuous nature, as well as the obviously expensive jewelry.

"You of course remember my dear friend, Miss Emily Camp," Cora said now.

"Of course," Ellen lied, startled to finally notice the woman tucked under Cora Compton's right arm. "How do you do?"

The truth was that Ellen had completely forgotten and now only began to remember Miss Camp, and it wasn't surprising that memories of the woman should slip her mind. Compared with Cora Compton, Miss Camp—well, she didn't compare much at all.

Emily Camp, who Ellen thought might be anywhere in age from seventy to ninety, was as diminutive as her friend was massive, as birdlike as her friend was—well, ursine, as soft-spoken as her friend was thunderous. Side by side they made for a classic pair, the forceful leader and her loyal, subtle sidekick, a contemporary Gertrude Stein and Alice B. Toklas. They routinely finished each other's sentences and straightened each other's clothing when a bit went awry, and Emily slipped her tiny little arm through Cora's sturdy limb when they went walking. Ellen now recalled that there had been rumors once (and there probably still were) of the women being witches—of the good sort, of course. Well, Ellen thought now, if they are witches, I might have to ask them for a charm to ensure against choking. The nut bread was still working its laborious way down into her digestive system.

Emily's outfit befitted her lack of definitive presence. She wore a dun-colored dress that came to mid-calf; held a dun-colored handbag in the crook of her right arm; and her feet were shod in dun-colored, low-heeled pumps. Ellen looked closely without seeming to. Yes, Miss Camp's eyes were dun-colored, too. Her hair, white like her friend's, was the only spot of brightness about her. Unlike her friend's, it was neatly scraped back into a low bun. On her head sat a dun-colored, narrow-brimmed straw hat.

"Hello, dear," Miss Camp said, in a voice oddly strong and clear for such a wee person.

"Hello, Miss Camp," Ellen replied, unsure if she should attempt to shake the woman's birdlike hand. She was sure she would crush it.

Cora came to the rescue. She suddenly hailed a fellow art enthusiast across the room with a cry that made Ellen wince, and sailed off, Emily following in her wake.

With nothing else to occupy her—there was no use spending any time pretending to admire the paintings and collages—Ellen turned back to the table of pathetic refreshments. Standing there, reaching for a piece of the deadly nut and bolt bread, was a very attractive man about her age.

"I'd avoid that stuff," she warned.

He startled, as if he hadn't at all sensed her standing next to him. "Why?" he asked, turning to face her.

"Trust me. Try the cheese instead. It's tasteless, but harmless."

The man thought about her advice for a moment and then chose a cracker with a piece of the tasteless cheese.

"Ellen Tudor," she said.

He finished chewing and then said, "Rob Penn."

"You're an artist."

Rob seemed surprised. "How did you know?"

Ellen pointed. "Paint-stained fingers. It's a dead give-away. Unless of course you're a house painter. Are you?"

Rob managed a smile. "No. I paint canvases. Pictures."

"Do you have any work in the show?" Ellen asked.

Rob's face underwent a remarkable series of expressions, from outright horror to injured ego to dark amusement. "No," he finally said. "My work is—er, it's different."

"Oh." Ellen restrained a smile. Different. What a nice way of saying, "the work in this place is awful."

"What are you . . ." Rob's question wandered off, as did his eyes. It—and they—were back in a moment. "I mean," he said, "are you here for the summer or . . . ?"

So, Ellen thought, he's not good at small talk. That was okay. She didn't think she was so good at it, either. "I'm renting a house for the summer," she said. That was the simple truth. She did not want to share the more complicated truth with anyone who didn't already know.

Rob nodded. "Me too."

"Oh," Ellen replied.

"Yeah."

When nothing more seemed forthcoming, Ellen opened her mouth to ask some sort of polite question, but before she could form words, Rob was wandering off, his eyes scrunched in what Ellen thought might be horror at the "art" surrounding them.

Ellen watched him wander. He's handsome, she thought. Nicely built. Not too buff and not too thin; tall, but not too tall. His hair was a rich shade of brown. And his eyes were particularly nice—large and very dark brown with lashes Ellen would kill to have for her own. But the cuffs of his button-down shirt were seriously frayed, and the shirt was missing a button right in the middle. And his sneakers . . . They were tattered and looked just about to fall to pieces.

Ellen wondered if he cared and decided that he probably did not. He was an artist, after all. Artists weren't supposed to care about frayed cuffs and missing buttons and torn sneakers, were they? Certainly, Rob Penn didn't seem at all self-conscious. In fact, he carried himself with what struck Ellen as a sense of ease and confidence. Not bravado or cockiness, just confidence. That was also attractive, and in Ellen's opinion, pretty rare. Peter certainly had his share of bravado. . . .

Ellen dismissed thoughts of her former fiancé with some difficulty. And along with them, she dismissed any thoughts of Rob Penn. The last thing she needed or wanted was an emotional entanglement, for a very long time. She simply didn't trust herself to see the truth before her eyes. She had made such an enormous mistake with Peter. How could she have loved someone—and she had loved him, very much—who could treat her so cruelly and with such duplicity? It really didn't bear thinking about.

Ellen spent another twenty minutes or so answering polite questions about her parents from longtimers claiming to remember them well. Ellen recognized very few of these people, though she refrained from admitting as much. Finally, seeing her opportunity, Ellen snuck out of the gallery before Cora could corral her into another round of small talk.

She didn't regret having gone to the opening. It hadn't been a painful experience. Then again, nothing had been gained by her being there, and the food had been less than appetizing. Ellen's stomach grumbled with hunger; she was glad the nut bread wasn't causing total disaster on its journey through her digestive system. She slid behind the wheel of her car and mentally scanned the fridge back home. A nice bowl of pasta with shrimp and peas would be delicious and easy to prepare, followed by a quiet, peaceful evening all by herself.

A few moments later she pulled into the driveway of her rental home and turned off the engine. In the half-dark of the summer night, the house at the end of the road seemed suddenly very isolated, not charmingly alone, as Ellen had thought it in the light of day.

She got out of the car, walked up the front steps, and opened the door of the house. For a moment the silence that greeted her was deafening.

Ellen shook off the sense of loneliness that had overcome her, stepped inside, and firmly closed the door.

CHAPTER 4

Two days later Ellen found herself at Cora's house. She might have visited as a child, but for the life of her she couldn't remember if she had. Looking up at the Compton residence now, she felt sure she would never have forgotten such a structure.

The house could be described as a cottage, albeit a mammoth one. In that way, it was on a scale suited to its owner. It appeared to be out of proportion, though Ellen didn't know enough about architecture to say exactly how. There was something about the windows; maybe there were too many of them? And the porch seemed to be something transported from a much larger and older structure, maybe a manor house or a faux castle of the Victorian imagination. It seemed to swallow the house itself, to embrace it in a strangling hug. The entire pile was painted dark green; trim and shutters were painted black. Cora Compton's home, Ellen decided, was something out of a fractured fairy tale.

The interior was decorated in what Ellen decided could be dubbed "hodgepodge meets fussiness." But in spite of what seemed to be thousands of objects on top of the surfaces—books, figurines, framed photos (was Mr. Compton in one of those photos?), and doilies—the surfaces (what could be glimpsed) were dust free; the throw rugs looked almost new; the wooden floors beneath them (what could be seen of them) shone. Even the walls—some painted a soothing ivory, others covered in pretty flowered wallpaper—were conspicuously clean. Even the ornate crystal chandelier over the formal table in the formal dining room shone with brilliance. Old Mrs. Compton might enjoy collecting trinkets and amassing keepsakes, but she was a stellar housekeeper.

Cora had invited Ellen for tea, and, once again, in spite of her determination to suffer in silence, Ellen had not known how to say no to her mother's old friend without causing offense. She had been prepared for a tea bag and a cup of water heated in the microwave. How mistaken she was. Cora's idea of tea included said beverage (piping hot and delicious, made from a mix of green and black loose tea leaves), milk, sugar, lemon wedges, cookies, tartlets, half a pound cake, and a cake that resembled an overgrown sticky bun. Everything was served in or on obviously fine and frighteningly delicate china. With what she thought was admirable restraint and dignity Ellen carefully placed a cherry tartlet and a piece of the giant sticky bun on her plate. That would do for now. Maybe.

They sat eating pastries and drinking tea for a while, Ellen listening to Cora's colorful commentary about the bad behavior of neighbors (some of it was indeed shocking!), and the backstabbing involved in the local politics, and the terrible trouble the farmers had been having due to a particularly dry spring and summer.

Suddenly, something at the corner of Ellen's eyes caught her attention, and she started. An enormous, black, short-haired cat, sleek and powerful-looking and easily standing a full two and a half feet off the ground, slunk into the room. If he was trying to be inconspicuous, he was failing miserably. (He was like his mistress that way, Ellen noted. Neither could possibly slip under anyone's radar should it ever occur to them to try.) He stopped several feet from Ellen's chair and glared up at her.

"Oh, my God, what is that?" Ellen exclaimed, involuntarily sitting back in her chair.

Cora frowned. "It's a cat, my dear."

"Oh, I know that. I mean—it's just that he's enormous."

Cora considered. "Is he? Well, yes, he might have gained an ounce or two recently."

"I don't mean that he's fat," Ellen explained. "He's just—huge. Are you sure he isn't a puma or a mountain lion? Are jaguars black? His paws are like catcher's mitts! He's got to be at least half wild!"

"Oh, dear, not at all," Cora replied with nonchalance. "I was a witness to his birth. Though he did give his poor mother quite a hard time of it, he is one hundred percent domesticated, I assure you."

Ellen was not assured. "He's looking at me."

"So he is."

"Um, what's his name?" Satan, Ellen thought, what with the black glossy fur. Goblin or Lucifer, what with the yellow eyes. Maybe even Snake, what with the way he slunk. He probably even slithered, so maybe . . .

"Clovis," Cora said.

Ellen blinked. "That's an unusual name."

"The famous Frankish king, my dear. Clovis was of the Merovingian dynasty. He ruled his kingdom from 481 until his death in 511."

"Oh," Ellen said. "Right."

Cora squinted at her. "Surely you know your European history?"

"Well, not all of it . . ."

"The Merovingian dynasty was followed by the Carolingian dynasty. That was in the eighth century."

Ellen laughed a bit. "Of course. The Carolingians. Who could forget them?"

Cora gave her a look that managed to combine pity with disappointment. Clovis stalked off, his tail touching the floor.

Ellen had never been made to feel stupid in front of a cat before. But she guessed there was a first for everything.

"I saw you speaking with that nice young painter we have with us this summer," Cora was saying. "At the gallery opening, I mean. Rob Penn. He's renting a house down by the water off Sand's End Street."

"Yes," Ellen said. "We spoke for a minute."

"He's such a handsome man, don't you think? One might even say distinguished. And from what I understand, he's quite a good painter. I am told he specializes in landscapes. Well, that makes sense then, for him to come to Ogunquit, doesn't it? We have all sorts of wonderful landscapes, and seascapes for that matter. Maybe he'll have his own show soon at one of our local galleries!"

Ellen had more than a slight suspicion of Cora's motives in introducing the subject of Mr. Penn.

"You know," she said, "I should tell you that I'm not at all interested in dating. Not that I don't appreciate your concern or your good intentions. I do."

Cora released and recaptured a small, brief smile. "But I'm not at all interested in matchmaking, dear!" she declared. "Really, I have much more important things to do with my time than orchestrate the romantic lives of my friends."

Ellen blushed. "Oh," she said. "I'm so sorry. Forget I said anything. . . ."

"Forgotten. Now, you never did tell me exactly what it is you do for a living. Something marvelous, I'm sure."

Ellen explained as simply as she could the nature of her work as an independent financial consultant.

"I'm actually very lucky," she told Mrs. Compton. "I find

the work interesting and challenging, but at the same time not very difficult. Well, most times. And it pays really well, and I can work from pretty much anywhere."

For a moment, Cora's expression wavered between outright distaste and supreme pity. "Well," she said finally, "I must say that sounds like rather dry work. For a woman, I mean."

With difficulty, Ellen restrained a smile. Well, it was confirmed. Cora Compton was firmly implanted in the Old School of thinking about "the fairer sex."

"Are you quite all right, dear?" Cora was saying. "Your face has grown alarmingly pink."

"No, no," Ellen lied. "I'm fine. I'm just—just overheated. It must be the hot tea."

Cora picked up the plate of cookies and offered it to Ellen. "Of course. Do you know who also likes tea?" she asked. "Rob Penn!"

With even more difficulty, Ellen stifled a laugh.

CHAPTER 5

The next morning dawned clear and bright yet again. Imagine, Ellen thought, contemplating the garden of wildflowers through the kitchen window as she drank her coffee, becoming suspicious about endless perfect weather. If only there were a cloud on the horizon or an unexpected chill in the air, something to mar the seeming perfection. In Ellen's experience, seeming perfection was not to be trusted.

Take Peter Hall, for example. Handsome, jovial, successful, attentive. Also, a liar and a cheat.

Ellen spent most of the morning with her laptop. Around eleven, feeling she had been particularly productive so far that day, she drove into town. After stopping in Bread and Roses for a bag of fresh whole-wheat rolls, she popped into the local deli cum specialty foods shop for a pound of butter and some raspberry preserves to go with them.

And there he was, Rob Penn, Cora Compton's distinguished and talented painter, standing before the dairy case, staring at the large selection of milk.

For a moment, Ellen wondered if Cora Compton had orchestrated this sighting. She immediately dismissed the idea as nonsense and almost laughed out loud at her wild imagination. Everybody needed milk on occasion. Even starving artists. Though Rob didn't look particularly hungry. As a matter of fact, in the light of day, he looked downright robust, the proverbial picture of good health. Maybe he really was a talented painter. Maybe he made a great deal of money from the sale of his work. Maybe his tattered clothing was a style statement, not a sign of financial distress or unconscious, habitual carelessness.

Ellen took a closer look at Rob and noticed that his fingers were free of paint stains. Interesting. He cleaned up to go to the market, but not to attend a gallery opening. (What did that say about his priorities?) He was wearing a pair of jeans and a T-shirt, nothing special, but they fit him perfectly.

There was no doubt about it. He was an attractive man.

"Hi," she said.

He turned and frowned at her for a moment, clearly puzzled, and then his expression cleared and his eyes widened. "Oh," he said, "right. The opening."

Ellen felt a twinge of disappointment. Was she that forgettable? Still, what did it matter? She wasn't in Ogunquit to make friends. She was in Ogunquit to hide and to heal all on her own.

"Yes," she said. "How are you?"

"Fine."

"That's good," she said. "I'm fine, too."

Rob blushed. "Oh, right," he said. "I should have . . . Sorry. I guess I'm a bit out of it lately. Distracted. I'm trying to solve a problem with the painting I'm working on right now and . . . Well, the answer isn't coming. It's kind of driving me crazy."

Ellen smiled. "I don't know how you do what you do," she said. " 'You' meaning artists. It's as foreign to me as . . . well, as financial analysis might be to you. But I'm making an assumption."

Rob laughed. "Believe me, there are times when what I do is as foreign to me as financial analysis. Like, right now. What made you say that, about finance?"

"Because that's what I do. I'm an independent financial consultant."

"Oh. Wow."

"There's really nothing wow about it. It's a job like any other." But unlike any other, Ellen thought, it can make people think you're some sort of machine. Some sort of machine intent upon evil. (Did machines have intentions?)

"I'd better be off," Rob said suddenly, snatching a carton of milk without looking to see if he had chosen low-fat or soy or chocolate-flavored. "I've just had an idea. . . ."

He dashed off toward the checkout counter before Ellen could say good-bye. She smiled at his back. In spite of his flighty behavior, there was something honestly charming about Ogunquit's newest resident artist.

Not that it mattered. Ellen finished her shopping and drove home, her mind on what she would make that evening for dinner. By the time she walked through the front door she had decided on steak and green beans. And maybe the rest of the double fudge ice cream.

But dinner was hours away. Ellen brought her laptop to the kitchen table and checked her e-mail. There was a mildly amusing joke forwarded by her mother, something about a cranky husband. There was an obviously dubious offer of a loan from an obviously dubious lending institution, and there were the ubiquitous Facebook and Twitter and LinkedIn updates. Finally, there was an e-mail from Peter. It was headed, *Please don't delete until you've read this.*

Ellen's heart began to race with an all too familiar combination of fear and anger. Was there really nowhere safe to hide these days? With the click of a mouse or the tap of a key, anyone could follow you anywhere. She felt exposed, sitting there at the kitchen table, unprotected.

Well, Peter might reach out to her, but there was nothing

to force her to take his hand. With a firm touch, Ellen hit the Delete button.

It was not that she hadn't forgiven Peter his sins. She had forgiven him. And it wasn't that she held a grudge against him. She was working hard to let go of the past, and holding a grudge or refusing to forgive was hugging the rotting, decaying past to one's chest. It was a form of self-torture. You didn't retreat to hold a grudge. You retreated to forget as much and as completely as you could manage.

With a sigh, Ellen put her laptop aside and proceeded to make a cup of tea. When the tea was brewed, she took the cup over to the window and peered out at the back lawn. Ellen noticed that it was a little dry in spots. That was to be expected. Cora—and the local papers—had informed her that the area had been short on rain since spring. For Ellen, this was a minor inconvenience, if an inconvenience at all. But for the farmers it could very well spell disaster. That, in turn, would have a ripple effect on the broader local economy and, possibly, at some point, on Ellen's own business. People had to have money in the first place—at least, some money—in order to hire someone to manage it.

But Ellen wasn't particularly worried. She knew she would always find a way to survive. She was nothing if not resourceful. And she didn't need much in the way of "stuff," unlike Peter, who seemed compelled to accumulate every new electronic and mechanical gadget the moment it hit the market. His house was cluttered with things Peter had just had to have, iPads and super-duper phones and state-of-the-art cameras that were ignored almost as soon as they were acquired.

Stop thinking about Peter, Ellen scolded herself. Well, it would be easier to stop thinking about him if he stopped trying to contact her!

Ellen turned away from the window. I wonder, she thought, what the inside of Rob Penn's house looks like. . . .

CHAPTER 6

"Ellen, my dear! So good of you to come!"

"Thank you for having me," Ellen said, submitting to Cora's hearty hug.

"Come in, come in. You're almost the last to arrive."

Cora took Ellen's arm and whisked her into the cottage, already loud with laughter and good cheer.

So much for my vow to enjoy a party-free summer, Ellen thought. Cora Compton had a way of getting what she wanted, at least as far as Ellen was concerned. *Oh, well,* Ellen thought. *Maybe she'll tire of me by midsummer. After all, I'm not the most exciting person around these days!*

This evening Cora was wearing an ensemble in fuchsia. Fuchsia dress. Fuchsia shawl. And, most surprising, fuchsia shoes. They must be dyed, Ellen thought, eyeing her hostess's boatlike feet with suspicion. Would anyone really mass-produce shoes in that eye-shattering hue? *Maybe I'm just a boring dresser,* she thought, giving the older woman her due as she contemplated her own rather sedate outfit of white blouse, navy cotton pullover, and dark, skinny jeans. In the latter months of their relationship, Peter had often commented on her style or lack thereof. . . .

In stark contrast, per usual, Cora's sidekick, Miss Camp, was in taupe from head to toe. Ellen greeted her with trepidation. If she tripped and knocked into the lady she was sure Miss Camp would break into a million little taupe pieces.

Clovis was nowhere to be seen. "He doesn't care for crowds," Cora explained. For a moment Ellen had a strange desire to seek out Clovis in his hiding place; she really didn't care much for crowds, either.

Cora sailed off to see to her other guests, and Ellen got herself a glass of wine from the drinks table in the living room. As she sipped the wine (it was very good, another indication that Cora Compton was not in financial difficulty), she surveyed the room. She recognized a few of the faces from the Noise Gallery opening; others were new to her, though she might have known them in passing as a child. There seemed to be far more women than men. Among the men that were present, Ellen was not surprised to find Rob Penn. After all, he was a favorite with Cora and already a bit of a local celebrity; in the past week Ellen had heard his name mentioned on three separate occasions—once at the post office, once at the Hannaford a town away, and once in Reny's. Still, Ellen felt a wee bit suspicious. Had Cora invited Rob Penn so that he and Ellen could chat, fall in love, and wed? Don't be silly, she chided herself. *I'm sure Cora Compton has far more important things on her mind than me!* After all, Cora had said as much the afternoon Ellen had been at her house for tea.

Hmm, Ellen thought now. There was Cora, leading Rob by the arm toward a tall, willowy woman.

Ellen watched as almost immediately Rob fell into animated conversation with this willowy woman. She must be very interesting, Ellen thought. Or maybe Rob liked women with long, dark, glossy hair.

Ellen turned away and came face-to-face with another guest.

"Greetings," said the man.

Ellen returned the greeting; she had seen this man at the gallery opening, but had not spoken with him. He was of medium height and weight and maybe about sixty years of age. His long, gray hair was pulled back into a neat ponytail. His clothes were black, as were the beret perched on his head and the frames of his glasses. His shoes, Ellen noticed, were bright green.

He introduced himself as Richard Green. (Hence the shoes? Ellen wondered.) He said he was an old friend of Cora's and asked how Ellen knew their host. Ellen explained.

They chatted amiably for a few minutes until Ellen noticed that Rob, across the room, had put on a jacket and was headed for the front door. Cora was with him, and she beckoned to Ellen to join them.

"Excuse me for a moment, won't you?" Ellen said to Mr. Green, interrupting a tale of his fourth marriage. (He claimed that none of his wives had understood him. Maybe, Ellen thought, they hadn't approved of his taste in footwear.) She headed toward her hostess.

"Rob has something to ask you, Ellen," Cora announced when Ellen had joined them.

Ellen looked up at Rob's expression of discomfort and braced herself.

"Um," he said, "I was thinking that maybe we could have lunch someday."

"The day after tomorrow," Cora said brightly. "Why not the day after tomorrow?"

Rob attempted a smile. "Um, sure. Why don't you come to my place? If the light is good I can paint while we have lunch. I hate to miss good light."

Ellen attempted a smile back. "Sure," she said. And because it was painfully obvious that Cora had put Rob up to offering this invitation, Ellen suggested that she bring the food. It was, she thought, the least she could do.

Rob nodded. "Thanks. Sometimes I forget to go to the grocery store. . . ."

Ellen assured him that it was no trouble at all.

"Good then," Rob said. "See you around noon. Oh, do you know where I live?" He told her, and Ellen made a mental note.

Task accomplished, Cora sailed off, and with a little wave Rob left the party.

Ellen's thoughts were a jumble. So Cora had lied. She was interested in the romantic lives of her friends! Ellen hadn't been imagining Cora's nascent matchmaking. Well, it wasn't the end of the world, she decided promptly. Clearly, Cora meant well, and also clearly, Rob Penn wasn't in the least bit romantically interested in Ellen Tudor! She would be safe enough eating a sandwich with him.

If she kept up her guard.

Ellen found Cora standing by the drinks table, saying farewell to an elderly couple in matching yellow sweaters. She waited until the elderly couple had gone off and then thanked Cora for inviting her. She did not mention the lunch date with Rob Penn.

"Of course, my dear," Cora said graciously, squeezing both of Ellen's hands in hers. "I hope you enjoyed yourself?"

"Yes," Ellen said. "Thank you. I had a very nice time."

Was Cora giving her a searching look? "Thanks again," Ellen said, and hurried out the door and down the drive to her car, flexing her squished fingers as she went.

She just knew that Cora Compton was watching her from the front window. And what, Ellen wondered, was the crafty older woman planning now?

CHAPTER 7

Before she had finished her coffee and breakfast the next morning, Ellen was considering the wisdom of canceling her lunch date with Rob. He probably wouldn't care—if he even remembered that they had made a date. He might even be relieved; he might possibly be delighted. After all, Cora had put him up to offering the invitation.

But Ellen realized that canceling without a very good reason like a verifiable illness the town folk could witness (a freshly broken leg might suffice) might only serve to bring more attention to her nonexistent relationship with Rob Penn. Even if he had told no one of the lunch date, and she doubted that he had, someone, a third party (other than Cora), was bound to know about it.

Nothing, absolutely nothing, was private in a place as small as Ogunquit. Her mother had reminded her of that terrifying little fact often enough. *Then why,* Ellen thought, *did I come back here?*

Better to bite the bullet as the saying went and eat a sandwich with Rob Penn. Or rather, eat a sandwich while he painted.

As a matter of course, Ellen checked her e-mail before

reading the news online and settling down to work. The only message of interest was one from Caroline.

> *Hey, you! Whassup? No, really, I haven't heard from you in days, and although I know, I know, you're doing your hiding away thang right now, trying to erase all traces of the dreadful Mr. Hall from your system, your old friend Caro misses you and wants to hear something, anything from sleepy little Ogunquit. So—write! Call! Sheesh, send a text! Mucho love, Me. Xxxx*

Ellen smiled and quickly typed out a note in return. She did not mention Rob Penn and his forced invitation to lunch. There was really nothing to tell.

It was another beautiful day, warm and sunny and dry. (Too dry. Even Ellen was beginning to worry about the near-drought conditions and had checked to be sure the house came with a fire extinguisher.) She thought of taking her laptop out to the garden—there was a small wrought-iron table and chairs where she could work—but she suspected she would soon lose focus. The colorful flowers, the songs of the birds, the warmth of the sun on her skin would distract her. And you didn't want to be distracted when you were handling other people's financial futures. Ellen was nothing if not responsible.

She had been working in the living room for close to an hour when she heard an odd sound at the front door. It was a heavy sort of scraping. . . . Peering through the front window, she saw Clovis, all one thousand pounds of him, standing on his hind legs and scratching at the door.

Ordinarily, Ellen liked cats, but she wasn't entirely sure this was just a cat. In short, Clovis disturbed her. She wasn't afraid of him exactly, just—wary. Still, she opened the door. Clovis tumbled to all four feet.

"What are you doing here?" she asked. And how, she

wondered, had he known where to find her? Cora's house was at least a ten-minute drive away. Was he used to wandering miles away from home? Was his being there merely a coincidence?

Clovis did not deign to answer her question.

Ellen tried again. "What are you doing here, Your Merovingian Majesty?"

Clovis replied with a face-shattering, jaw-splitting yawn.

"I see," Ellen said. "Uh, do you want some water or something?"

In response to this question, Clovis walked past her and into the house, as if he had lived there all his life. He made his way to the kitchen without erring, where he plopped his massive hindquarters down in front of the fridge and turned his enormous yellow eyes up at her. They were not amused or friendly eyes. One might be tempted to call them malevolent.

"I can't open the door unless you move back," Ellen, who had followed him into the kitchen, pointed out reasonably.

Clovis rose and stepped back just far enough for Ellen to ease open the door of the fridge.

"Thanks," she murmured.

She reached for the bottle of milk. Clovis groaned. Ellen was certain that he was eyeing the carton of eggs, but there were only three left, and Ellen had no intention of sacrificing the omelet she planned to have for dinner to this beast. "You can have some milk," she said firmly. "And there's a bit of cheese. . . ."

Clovis lapped up the milk Ellen poured for him and stared her down until she poured another bowl. Then she crumbled the bit of cheese for him. He ate that, too.

"I hope you're not lactose intolerant," Ellen told him with a frown. "If you are, I don't want to be around to witness the results of this feast."

When he had finished licking his chops, Clovis set about what looked to Ellen like a particularly elaborate session of facial grooming. She left him to his ablutions and went back to the living room and her computer.

All was quiet for close to another hour. Ellen was just contemplating a brief break in her work when Clovis stalked from the kitchen, through the living room, and dropped his rump on the floor just in front of the door.

"I'll get it," Ellen said unnecessarily, putting her laptop aside.

She opened the door, and Clovis stalked out.

"You're welcome," Ellen said pointedly.

Clovis continued on his way, his tail twitching wildly.

Watching him walk off with all of his native feline power and grace, Ellen found herself grinning. It had been nice to spend a bit of time with someone. Correction. A cat, not an actual someone. Flowers were all well and good for contemplative and aesthetic purposes, but you couldn't really communicate with them the way you could communicate with a person. What she meant was, a cat. An animal with whiskers and four furry legs.

She thought again of Caroline. She missed her friend. Ellen would be lying if she said otherwise. But she had come here to Ogunquit for a reason. There was a real purpose to her having retreated. A real purpose.

Suddenly, Ellen realized that she was hungry. Hunger, she knew, could make you feel sad and grumpy and maybe even lonely.

She was glad she hadn't given the last three eggs to Clovis.

CHAPTER 8

Ellen pulled up in front of Rob's rental home and got out of the car, carrying the plastic bag with their lunch. She was determined to have a pleasant time. They would have a quick meal—after all, Rob didn't want to waste the light—and then she would be on her way. And maybe, when she got back home, Clovis would deign to show up for more snacks. Funny how the beast had so quickly stomped his way into her affections.

Ellen paused and looked up at the house. The one-story structure could be described as a big square box, with two walls made almost entirely of glass. It wasn't a particularly attractive house, at least in Ellen's opinion, but she supposed it suited Rob's professional purposes.

She had to knock twice and ring the bell three times before Rob came to the door.

"Sorry," he said, a bit breathlessly. "I was just finishing a difficult area and couldn't put my brush down. Come in."

Once inside Ellen saw that the house was really no more than one large room that had been sectioned off into functional areas—a tiny kitchen, a large all-purpose room, and a bedroom (that, simply a bed behind a large screen). The bathroom was minuscule and off the kitchen. Ellen wondered how someone Rob's size could fit into the tubular shower. There was, of course, no bathtub.

Most of the all-purpose room was devoted to Rob's work. There were no fewer than four easels. On each easel there was propped a work in progress. Finished works (at least, to Ellen they looked complete) were propped along the walls and windows; a few works hung above them. A long worktable was heaped with paint-smeared rags, brushes in old coffee cans, open sketchbooks, various kinds of pencils, palettes, and, of course, tubes of paint.

"It's been used as an artist's residence for years," Rob explained. "It's not meant as a home as much as a studio where you can also crash. Hence, the massive windows. Luckily, there aren't any neighbors close enough to invade my privacy. It's just me and the Atlantic."

"The view is spectacular," Ellen said. And the light really was amazing; you didn't have to be an artist or particularly artistic to tell that. And Rob's paintings . . . Ellen felt her breath almost literally taken away. They were beautiful. The evening landscapes were luminous and atmospheric. The seascapes were powerful. The landscapes painted in the light of a summer day seemed to vibrate with life.

"I'm a realist, as you can see," Rob said. "And a romantic. They are not incompatible."

"Yes, I know. Rob, your work is—it's incredible."

"Some of it is pretty good; I'm not unnecessarily modest. Some, not so much. Like that one by the—"

"Don't ruin it for me," Ellen cried. "I love them all."

Rob shrugged.

"Did you solve that problem you mentioned? When we were at the deli in town?"

"You remembered." Rob sounded genuinely surprised.

"Yes. Of course."

"Yes, I did solve it, as a matter of fact. The full solution came to me late last night. Which is probably why I'm a bit more coherent today than I have been lately. At least, I think that I am. Am I?"

"Yes," Ellen said promptly. She pointed to the plastic bag she had brought and put on the small round wooden table by the kitchen that seemed to serve as a dumping ground for mail, hats, sunglasses, and whatever else Rob didn't want in his hands when he came into the room. "I don't know what you like to eat so don't complain if I didn't bring your favorites."

"I never complain when someone chooses to feed me. And my favorites are pretty much whatever it is I'm eating at the moment."

"So, you're not a fussy gourmet type?"

"Nope."

"Good. There's a tomato, basil, and mozzarella sandwich on a baguette and a ham and cheese on rye."

"Let's do halves," Rob suggested.

Ellen shrugged. "Sure."

"I have beer. And for some reason, I have a bottle of ginger ale. I really can't remember why or when I bought it. I hate ginger ale."

"Me too," Ellen said, with a laugh. "It reminds me of being sick as a child. My mother always gave me flat ginger ale. I'll take a beer, thanks."

Rob retrieved two bottles from the fridge and joined her at the table.

"I thought you were going to work while I ate," she said.

"In a minute. I'm starved. I was so excited about solving my problem I forgot to eat breakfast."

With a sweep of his forearm Rob moved the junk to one half of the table. They sat, and Ellen distributed the food.

"So why did you choose to come to Ogunquit?" she

asked after a moment. "New England is stuffed with pretty, scenic places."

"Yeah, but Ogunquit is special. It's been a destination for artists since the nineteenth century. But I guess you know that. Cora said something about your family having summered here for years."

Ellen nodded. "My parents bought a place in town when I was a little girl. They sold it five years ago."

"I often wondered why my parents never bought a summer place," Rob said. "It's not as if they were into traveling, dashing off to a new destination every year. Mostly they stayed home and sent me packing. One summer to a relative, one summer to a sort of learning camp abroad, the next summer to an old friend of the family. But never the same place twice. Odd."

"Maybe you were a naughty little boy and people didn't want you back?" Ellen suggested with a smile.

"Hardly. I never got in trouble, and not because I never got caught. I just wasn't a bad kid. I didn't act out or disobey. I wasn't generally obnoxious. Maybe I should have been."

Ellen wondered if Rob's assessment of his younger self was true, or if his memory had worked wonders on reality. She would probably never know. There were vast tracts of her own childhood she could hardly recall and others she had probably edited over time.

"My parents sent me to a camp one summer," she said, "here in Maine. But only the once." And that had been more than enough, Ellen noted, thinking of that awful boy Bobby. "My father was sick at the time, and my mother didn't think having a seven-year-old underfoot while he was going through chemo was a great idea."

"I hope your father recovered?" Rob said.

"Oh, yes," Ellen said, "completely. He's the healthiest person I know."

"Good. I went to sleepaway camp one summer, too. I

mean, a good old-fashioned camp, one without a pretense of being a learning experience. For the life of me I can't recall what it was called. But I'm positive it was in Vermont. Well, I think."

"Where?" Ellen asked. "I mean, near what town?"

"I don't remember that, either."

"Okay. Near what mountains? The Green Mountains?"

Rob shrugged. "I don't know. I guess there were mountains. . . . We didn't go hiking, though. There was definitely a lake. I remember swimming in a lake. I hated the mushy bottom. Ugh."

"Vermont isn't the only state with lakes," Ellen pointed out. She kind of liked the mushy bottom of a lake, but decided there was no point in mentioning that. It wasn't as if they would ever be going swimming together.

"I know that. But, see, one of the counselors used to sneak in maple sugar candy for us. Well, for me. I paid him by giving him the cardboard health cookies my mother sent me. I had a ridiculous sweet tooth, and I guess he was a masochist."

"You can get maple sugar candy all over New England," Ellen said. "Not just in Vermont."

"Oh. I guess that's true."

"Why don't you ask your parents where you went to camp?" Ellen suggested. "They should remember if anyone should."

Rob smiled. It looked a bit pained. "You would think. But I'm not so sure my mother remembers what shoes she put on this morning. And as for my father, I'm not sure he remembers he's married to my mother."

"Oh, I'm so sorry." Ellen hesitated before asking, "Are they suffering from dementia?"

"No," Rob replied promptly. "Sorry to give a false impression. My mom's been addicted to prescription pain pills for as far back as I can remember. And my father's been checked out from his wife and son for well over twenty years. I understand from one of his gossipy colleagues that he has a very nice girlfriend. Mistress. Whatever she's called. I've never met her, and I doubt an invitation will be forthcoming."

"Oh, I'm so sorry," Ellen said again. "That all must be so hard for you."

Rob seemed to consider before speaking. "Maybe it was, once. Honestly, I don't remember. It's funny what you can get used to. What weirdness. And it's not like my mother ever abused me. She's actually quite sweet and very smart. She's just—sick. And I can hardly blame my father for giving up on her, can I?" Rob went on. "Who's to say I wouldn't do the same thing in his situation? Though I hope I'd be better able to help someone I loved before she got in too deep."

"Why did your mother start taking medication?" Ellen asked. "Do you know?"

Rob shrugged. "No. Once, way back when I was in college, my father attempted an explanation. But he chickened out in the middle. Or maybe it was too hard to admit the truth to his son. Whatever that truth might be."

Ellen thought of her own family, how relatively normal her parents were, how steady and reliable. They drank in moderation. They didn't smoke. They weren't even divorced. Maybe they were an aberration. Normal is the new abnormal, she thought. She felt very lucky in that moment.

"You know," Rob said suddenly. "It's really strange that I'm telling you all this. I hardly know you. It's not like me to spill my deep dark family secrets."

Ellen smiled. "Well," she said, "your secrets are safe with me. I won't tell a soul."

That, Ellen could promise. She could keep a secret, even from Caroline and her mother if necessary.

"I really should get back to work," Rob said suddenly. "I didn't plan on taking so much time off."

Ellen jumped to her feet. "Oh," she said. "I'm sorry."

"Don't be," Rob said. "I'm glad you came. Thanks for the food. And thanks again for listening. Maybe I can return the favor at some point."

Ellen smiled and took her leave. Just before she ducked into her car she looked back at the house. Through the enormous bank of windows she caught sight of Rob standing before one of his easels, paintbrush poised. The sight made her smile.

CHAPTER 9

Ellen was preparing a cup of tea. She had worked steadily from eight until eleven that morning and felt that she needed a bit of a break before tackling a few tasks she had scheduled for the afternoon.

As the tea bag seeped in a large white ceramic cup, she found herself wondering what Rob Penn was doing at that very moment. Was he also enjoying a break from a productive and tiring morning? Was he just rolling out of bed? Or was he deeply involved in a painting, unaware that lunchtime was approaching?

She was surprised by how much she had enjoyed the time she had spent with Rob the day before. He was smart and funny and boy, was he talented with a brush. And it didn't hurt that he looked the way he did. Not that looks mattered one whit in the end, not to Ellen, anyway.

Still, she found herself wondering about the willowy, dark-haired woman Rob had been talking to at Cora's party. Had Cora forced Rob to invite her to lunch, too? Had they exchanged numbers all on their own? Did she live locally? Was she also an artist; had they bonded over the agonies of a life devoted to the aesthetic principles?

Ellen took a sip of the now fully brewed tea (it was not half as tasty as Cora's) and wondered how she could find out if Rob was dating that woman or anyone else without coming right out and asking and thereby causing the entire town of Ogunquit to assume she was romantically interested in him. Within hours if not minutes every shopkeeper and farm stand employee and waiter or waitress in town and as far away as Kennebunk would be convinced that Ellen Tudor had a crush (what an odd expression!) on that handsome painter Rob Penn.

That could not be allowed to happen.

Ellen caught sight of something large and dark against the green of the grass out back. She took her cup of tea to the kitchen window. Yes, it was Clovis, stalking some poor unsuspecting animal across the lawn. She considered opening the window and calling to Clovis, distracting him and thereby giving the victim a sporting chance to run for his or her life. After all, it wasn't as if Clovis was homeless and hungry. He was probably just bored.

She knocked loudly on the window, but Clovis either didn't hear or he ignored her. Ellen sighed. She supposed it was the way of the world. So many people, just like cats, took what they needed to survive—or, what they wanted badly enough—without a thought for someone else who needed—or wanted—it more.

Maybe, Ellen thought, flinching as Clovis pounced with deadly accuracy on the chipmunk (she could see now that his prey had not been a mouse or a bird), maybe she should learn to be more like those people who acted boldly in their own self-interest.

She respected people with a sense of reasonable entitlement and a toughness of spirit, even if in some cases, she also feared them.

Ellen took another sip of the cooling tea. Ever since that long ago summer, when her father had been sick and she had been banished to camp, she had felt vulnerable in a way she assumed that most people did not, not quite as resilient as the rest of the world. It was not self-pity. It was not that at all. In fact, she didn't like feeling less able than others to deal with life's blows.

Once she had reached adulthood she had worked hard to overcome her hesitations and fears. After college she had traveled through Europe for a month all on her own. And upon her return she had gotten her own tiny little apartment rather than join up with a roommate in a bigger, nicer place. And she had opted to establish her own business rather than join an already established firm, though the obstacles were many and large. She had tested her toughness and her resilience and mostly, she had earned a good grade.

Those three years with Peter, that's what had set her back so badly. His spectacular betrayal had made her feel once again like that scared and questioning child, kept in the dark, subject to name-calling (memories of that despicable boy at camp!), vulnerable to her own inability to correctly read other people.

Clovis was rolling on his back now, the poor chipmunk between his gigantic front paws. Ellen flinched again. Life could be so cruel.

For a bitter moment she remembered what she had felt when Peter asked her to marry him. Safe, and secure, and grateful that she had found someone with whom she could share the burdens as well as the joys of this dangerous journey through life.

So much for safety and security.

Ellen frowned as she watched Clovis enjoying his game of intimidation with the chipmunk. She doubted that cats ever got their hearts broken. Though they most definitely had egos, and they did not like to be embarrassed or shown to be wrong . . . or, Ellen surmised with a sort of dark grin, left almost at the altar.

Ellen took a final sip of tea. She wondered if Clovis would like to come inside when he finished torturing the poor little chipmunk. She wished she had a way to ask him.

Wait, she thought. Maybe she could entice him with a can of tuna fish. . . . There was some in the pantry.

As if he had read her thoughts, Clovis suddenly released the chipmunk (who, much to Ellen's relief, darted off at great speed) and came trotting toward the house.

CHAPTER 10

The doorbell rang—three times in rapid succession—at eight o'clock the next morning.

Ellen knew it had to be Cora Compton. Patience didn't seem to be one of her strong suits. This morning she was bearing a plate of scones. They were lightly browned and still warm and fragrant from the oven.

"You'll make me fat," she said to Cora, accepting the plate. "Not that I won't enjoy the journey."

Cora made a clucking sound with her tongue. "Young women today are too concerned with their weight. Why, I could knock over most of them with one big breath!"

Ellen smiled at the image that came to mind. "Let's go to the kitchen," she suggested. "By the way, Clovis has been hanging around. How does he know this house?"

Cora's eyebrows arched in surprise. "I wasn't aware that he did know the house. I suppose he followed your scent here. It would seem he likes you."

"Huh." Pretty impressive, Ellen thought, to follow my scent all the way from his home to this somewhat remote house on Wisteria Lane.

She put the plate on the counter. She wondered if Clovis

liked scones. She suspected he ate everything that came his way. He certainly had devoured that can of tuna fish she had offered him the day before.

But enough about Clovis. Ellen was sorely tempted to ask about Rob, in spite of the dangers involved. After all, she was an honorary local, wasn't she? She should be entitled to know all the gossip.

Oh, what the heck, Ellen thought, experiencing an unexpected moment of bravery. Or maybe it was carelessness.

"So," she said, "who was that woman Rob was talking to at your party?"

Cora's eyes widened. "What woman would that be, dear?" she asked. Ellen thought Cora knew very well what woman she meant.

"A tall, thin woman. With dark hair."

Cora now scrunched up her eyes. "Tall and thin, you say? Dark hair? Hmm . . ."

"Yes. Long, dark hair."

"Oh, that woman! That's Annabelle Morris. She owns a charming little restaurant in Portsmouth. She does quite well, from what I'm told. I hear that she's opening a second restaurant in the fall. Not that I go down to Portsmouth all that often. Usually, I prefer to give my money to our more local business owners."

"Oh," Ellen said. Not an artist, then. A businesswoman. Interesting.

Cora reached out and put her hand on Ellen's arm. "My dear, are you asking about Mr. Penn's romantic status? Because I can assure you that he's unattached. He told me so himself."

"Oh," Ellen said quickly. "I mean, no, I don't care one way or the other if he's seeing someone."

"You really should give him a sign of your own growing romantic interest," Cora suggested, ignoring Ellen's protestation. "How else will he know? He seems a sensitive sort, but I'm quite sure he doesn't read minds. Not many people do."

Was Cora insinuating that she could read Ellen's mind? Maybe she was a witch after all!

"No, no," Ellen said hurriedly. "Really, I have no romantic interest in Rob Penn. No interest at all, actually. I mean, other than as a neighbor."

Cora raised her dark eyebrows again until they came very close to the lower portion of her magnificently upswept hair. "Cora knows all," she intoned.

Ellen was compelled to grin. "Like Hercule Poirot? He says, 'Poirot knows all.' "

"If you like, dear."

"Well, in this case you're wrong. I'm sorry." Ellen wondered why she was apologizing.

Cora nodded. "If you say so."

"I was just curious. That's why I asked if he was—I mean, that's why I asked about that woman. I'm just a curious person."

"Of course."

"You might not think that a person who works in the financial industry would be a particularly curious or creative person, but in my case you would be wrong."

Cora put her hand over her heart. "In your case, I would never make such a wrong assumption."

"Because I am a creative person," Ellen went on, all too aware that she was protesting too much. "Even if I can't draw a straight line or write a novel or—"

"Now, Rob Penn certainly can draw a straight line, and a crooked one and a wavy one at that. His ability with the brush is astounding. Don't you agree?"

It's a lost cause, Ellen thought wearily. She'll throw us together until we finally stick, even if she has to move mountains and use a vat of Krazy Glue to do it. And then she'll swear she had nothing to do with it. "Yes," Ellen said, momentarily defeated, "his work is astounding."

Cora seemed to have gotten what she came for. "Well," she said briskly, "I must be off. Dear Miss Camp and I have an appointment for an early lunch with her solicitor, and we mustn't be late."

"Her solicitor?" Ellen said, following Cora back to the front door. "I hope she's not in legal trouble."

Cora looked puzzled. "Why would you think that? Emily's solicitor is a dear old friend. We three get together once every month to catch up on the gossip and share recipes. Mr. Frechette is a whiz in the kitchen. His beef bourguignon is beyond compare. His courgettes are divine. And his crème brûlée is the best I have ever tasted."

Ellen smiled. What could she reply? (Well, she might have asked the definition of a courgette. Obviously, it was something edible and French and probably delicious.) She watched Old Mrs. Compton sail down the drive and, with surprising grace for such a large person, settle into her Cadillac. Then, Ellen headed to the kitchen to have a scone while it was still warm.

And if the rumor mill was in full operation by lunchtime, then Ellen only had herself to blame.

CHAPTER 11

The next morning, around nine o'clock, Rob Penn called to ask Ellen if she wanted to drive with him up to Portland later that morning. He said that he needed to visit an art supply store and would appreciate the company.

"Did Cora suggest that you ask me along?" Ellen blurted. She wondered if Cora had gone straight from her house to Rob's the day before, full of misinformation about Ellen's romantic intentions.

"What? No." Rob laughed. "Why would you think that?"

Ellen cringed. "No reason. Sorry."

"Okay. So, would you like to come along?"

Ellen considered. "Sure, yes," she said after a moment. "Thanks. I could pop in to some of the shops on Exchange Street while you buy paint or whatever it is you need."

Rob came by a half an hour later. He was driving a beat-up old Mazda. It was missing all four hubcaps, and several low-lying areas were fragile with rust. Ellen got in with caution, only to find that the car was surprisingly clean inside, particularly given the run-down condition of the exterior. The engine seemed to be in good shape, too. At least, it didn't make any unsettling noises as Rob pulled back onto the road.

Ellen fervently hoped that no one saw them together before they were able to get on the highway and away from nosy neighbors and enthusiastic matchmakers.

"I don't know Portland well," Ellen admitted, once they had reached the relative anonymity of the highway. "Except for the Old Port, of course, the touristy part of town. Irish pubs. High-priced stores and way too many spas and salons. I can't imagine how they all stay in business! Not that it isn't a charming area."

Rob nodded. "It's an interesting city, especially once you get beyond the Old Port. It's got a little of everything. Quiet neighborhoods like the West End, great food sources and restaurants, a unique urban vibe, and of course, the museum and galleries."

"I guess you're a member of the PMA?"

"Card-carrying. I shouldn't brag, but I will. I had a painting in a show there a few years back. The show featured Maine artists under thirty. It was the highlight of my career."

"So far," Ellen pointed out.

Rob smiled. "So far."

Once in Portland, Rob dropped Ellen off at the top of Exchange Street and headed off to the art supply shop. After about forty-five minutes they met at the Portland Lobster Company for lunch. The place was packed, the band was good, the food was substantial, and the sun was shining. Ellen felt pretty good; she was glad she had come along for the ride, even if (in spite of Rob's denial) Cora Compton had arranged it.

Rob raised his hand in greeting to a scruffy group of young guys and girls who were settling at a high, round table near theirs.

"You know them?" Ellen asked.

"A bunch of my students," Rob explained. "For the past

five years I've been teaching a few courses each semester at the Maine College of Art."

"Really? What's that like? Teaching, I mean."

Rob shrugged. "It's okay. I like teaching, but I don't love it. I'm always worried my students are going to find that out about me and suffer for it. A lousy teacher, even a lackadaisical one, can be death to a young talent, let alone a tender spirit. So I try to work extra hard to make up for my lack of enthusiasm. So far, so good. I think. At least, no one has complained to my boss."

Ellen laughed. "I'd be an awful teacher. I can't seem to understand why someone doesn't know what I expect him to know. If something—like math—comes easily to me, I just can't grasp why it doesn't come easily to everyone. I'd be fired on the very first day for shaking a student in frustration. Fired and sent to prison."

"Well, at least you're aware of your—your weakness."

Ellen laughed. "How very tactful! So, where do you live when you're not in Ogunquit?"

"Here, in Portland," Rob said. "I have a small apartment in the East End. I'm subletting it for the summer. It's how I can afford to rent in Ogunquit. Barely. And, well, I sold three paintings so far this year. It might not sound like much, three measly paintings, but trust me, it's huge. Especially since I don't have an agent and get to keep all the money!"

Ellen was dying to know what one of his paintings commanded on the current art market, but thought it might be rude to ask. "That's great," she said instead. "I don't own any art myself. Well, just some prints. But nothing original."

"Maybe I'll convince you to invest in me," Rob said. "Just kidding."

Ellen smiled enigmatically. Honestly, she would love to own one of Rob's paintings. His work spoke to her. But first she would have to know what a painting cost! She doubted he sold on an installment plan.

"I've actually been considering moving full-time to Ogunquit," she said now, surprising herself by admitting what had been only a passing thought. "I can work from practically anywhere. And it's high time I bought a place and stopped wasting my money on rent."

"It's an awfully quiet town for—"

"For what?"

Rob shrugged. "At the risk of sounding like an old busybody, I'll say it. It's an awfully quiet town for a single person. Unless, of course, meeting someone isn't on your agenda."

"No," Ellen said quietly. "It's not on my agenda."

As if sensing this was not a topic Ellen wanted to further discuss, Rob turned the conversation to a more neutral subject—movies. They both had seen and liked the new biopic about Katharine Hepburn. They both had seen and abhorred the latest installment in an otherwise fine series about a popular comic book hero.

"Should we head back?" Ellen suggested after some time.

Rob checked his watch and agreed. "If we leave now I can get down to the beach by four and do some sketching."

And I, Ellen thought, can . . . Can what? Work, of course, but . . . Why had she suggested they leave Portland to head back home? It had been years since she had enjoyed an afternoon with someone as much as she was enjoying this afternoon with Rob. Maybe, she thought, I'm just not used to having fun, not since the early days with Peter. And look where that got me.

Fun was risky. It could lure you into a false sense of security and happiness. Peter had been such a jovial guy, the proverbial life of the party, a magnet around which everyone gathered and stayed put. He had so thoroughly disarmed her with his good humor that . . .

"You're frowning," Rob said as they turned onto Commercial Street. "Crab roll not sitting well?"

Ellen smiled. "Sorry. I mean, I don't know why I was

frowning. Habit, I guess. It's not the crab roll or the company."

"Good. Because I thought I was being pretty darn charming."

He was, Ellen thought. But she only smiled.

CHAPTER 12

"Oh, I'm so sorry!"

Ellen reached out to steady the person she had accidentally bumped into as she stepped back from one of the library stacks.

"No problem! I am off-balance with this load!"

It was a young woman, no older than nineteen or twenty. She was very thin and was dressed in a black T-shirt and black jeans. She had an arresting face with large, luminous dark eyes and a wide, mobile mouth. In her arms she held a mammoth stack of magazines.

"I read as many of the magazines as I have time for," she explained, noticing Ellen's look of astonishment. "It is a good way to keep up-to-date on the current slang. And, some of the articles are pretty good. At least, in some of the magazines. By the way, I'm Nadia."

"Ellen." She laughed. "I doubt *Tween Fashions* prints stimulating stuff!"

Nadia grimaced. "What are you here for?"

"I came in to see if the library had a collection of Sherlock Holmes stories. I forgot to pack my copy."

"You are not a local? You're visiting?"

Ellen explained her family's history in Ogunquit. "So, no, I'm just here for the summer. Then, it's back to Boston." Maybe, she added silently.

"Boston is home?"

"Yes. You're here for the summer, too?"

"Yes, working as a waitress and saving as much money as I can."

"And then, it's home?"

Nadia shrugged. "Where is my home now? I was born in a country in Eastern Europe I can no longer name. It's too painful for me. But for the last few years I have been most of the time not there. Anywhere but there."

"Oh." Ellen didn't know quite what to say to this bit of information.

"You see, my parents were killed in a conflict when I was thirteen," Nadia said then, taking Ellen entirely by surprise.

"My God!" she cried. "How awful."

"My brother and I went to live with our grandmother after the death of my parents. Then, she died, and soon after, Stefan went to Australia. I have not heard from him since. So, I have been alone in this big wild world since I was fifteen."

Ellen shook her head. "I . . . I don't know what to say. I'm so sorry."

Nadia shrugged. "I thank you for your sympathy, but really, I do not need it. I am simply impossible to hold down for long! My spirit is—what is the word?—irrepressible. Is that correct?"

Ellen nodded. "I think it's exactly the word you want. Your vocabulary is wonderful."

"It is just my way. I do not know why I am so—like a rubber ball. I hit the floor, and I bounce back!"

"I would consider myself very lucky to have such a positive outlook on life," Ellen admitted.

"Positive?" Nadia frowned. "Maybe not positive. Life is often very nasty and always very hard. But what is the point of moaning about it? What is the point of hiding away, yes? Face life! It sometimes will back down. I am proof of this!"

Ellen laughed. "You certainly seem to be!"

Nadia checked her watch, with some difficulty given the stack of magazines in her arms. The watch looked to Ellen like an antique, and she wondered if it had belonged to Nadia's mother or perhaps her grandmother. "Look, I must go to work," Nadia said. "If you will let me have your number I will give you mine and perhaps we might meet some time for coffee. I would like to ask you what you do for a career. I need the ideas for my future!"

Ellen found herself happy to exchange numbers with the young woman, though she doubted that Nadia was really in need of anyone else's help.

Nadia dashed off, and Ellen resumed her search. She found a copy of Sir Arthur Conan Doyle's stories and headed back to the house. As she drove, she reflected on her meeting with Nadia. It had heartened Ellen to hear that brave young woman tell her story with such a lack of self-pity. It had shamed her a bit, too.

Imagine being so alone, she thought, as she pulled into her driveway, so truly alone, and yet so free of self-pity. Imagine being so alone and so fearless.

Nadia was not only irrepressible; she was inspirational.

Well, Ellen thought as she opened the front door. This summer is proving to be restorative after all—and in an unexpectedly social way!

CHAPTER 13

Two days later, Ellen sat at a table for two in the garden of one of the more popular restaurants in Perkins Cove. She was waiting for Rob to join her for dinner. He had called her that morning with the suggestion, and she had said yes, sure, without hesitation, Nadia's encouraging—and irrepressible—voice in her head. "Face life," Nadia had said. And so Ellen had accepted Rob's invitation.

After all, it was just a meal.

It was an undeniably idyllic setting. The Cove itself was chock-full of charming old wooden structures that now mostly housed expensive shops and galleries. The restaurant's garden was lush; the owner seemed to have gotten around the water restrictions, or else he employed a magician of sorts. There was no sign of drought here, not if the masses of red and yellow and purple tulips and the profusion of pink and white roses were any evidence. In the water bobbed beautifully kept pleasure boats, as well as working lobster and fishing vessels and touring boats. Crowds of ambling tourists made driving into the Cove a long, slow nightmare, but they were a well-behaved bunch on the whole.

Ellen's phone alerted her to a text. It was from Rob, apologizing for running a little late; he had been waiting for an important package that had finally arrived, and he would soon be on his way. Ellen shrugged (when you worked from home, package deliveries could be the bane of your existence; there was no mail room clerk to be there when you couldn't be) and decided to turn her attention to those ambling tourists. People watching could be fun. And, she supposed that for a novelist people watching was also profitable. Weren't novelists always making mental notes on people's behaviors and appearance? She was glad she didn't know a novelist personally. She would constantly be worried about finding herself described in a book.

Ellen watched as a family of four passed by. The mother and father wore matching baseball caps that proclaimed they were Lovin' Lobstah; the son, about ten, wore a voluminous lime-green T-shirt and baggy shorts; the daughter, about thirteen, was wearing a hot pink sundress and big, white-framed plastic sunglasses.

With a melancholic sigh, Ellen wondered if she would ever have a family of her own. Peter had talked about having children, three or four he had said. She had often thought about what kind of a father he would make. A good one certainly; she had been sure of that. Until she had learned his true nature.

And what kind of mother would I make, she wondered now. Would she be overprotective? Probably. Would she be strict? Possibly. One thing was for certain. She would never send her seven-year-old away to protect her from a family crisis. She would hold her tightly, and together, they would weather the storm.

Ellen recalled what Rob had told her about his parents. None of it was very encouraging. She wondered if in spite of his somewhat miserable home life he wanted a family of his own. She didn't feel it was something she could ask, not yet. Maybe never.

"Hey."

"People watching is really an extraordinary pastime," Ellen announced to Rob as he joined her.

"I'm glad you weren't bored waiting for me. I'm sorry I was late. But the package came, and it wasn't smashed, so that's something."

The waiter came by then and took their orders. Ellen ordered a glass of wine and a lobster salad, and Rob ordered a beer and the mussels special. Ellen didn't object when he also asked for an order of fries to share.

The meals were brought to the table promptly, and for a while they ate in contented silence. When they had finished off the fries, Rob sat back.

"You know," he said with a grin, "I think Cora has been trying to hook us up."

"Matchmaking?" Ellen felt a tingling in her stomach. She had not expected this as a subject of conversation.

"If suggesting I ask you to lunch the other day is matchmaking, then yeah."

Ellen smiled. "I figured as much. Well, she does like to sing your praises."

"And the other day she happened to mention that you made a very good living."

"What!" Ellen cried, appalled and yet amused. "How does she know that?"

Rob shrugged. "As if it would matter to me. And then she pointed out that you were really very adorable."

Ellen felt her cheeks flush and hoped that in the darkening evening light, Rob couldn't tell. "She said 'adorable'? Oh." She wondered if Rob agreed.

"And then," Rob went on, "when you asked me if she had suggested I invite you to Portland, I kind of figured she'd been dangling me in front of you in the same way she'd been dangling you in front of me."

"Like bait before a hungry fish."

"I don't think Cora would see it quite that way. Anyway, do you mind?" Rob asked. "I mean, if she is trying to set us up."

"Do you?" Ellen asked, aware that she was stalling.

"No. And you didn't answer my question."

"I guess not," she said after a moment. "I mean, it's not as if you're a gargoyle or a medieval dungeon master."

"And it's not as if you're a homicidal maniac. You're not, are you?"

"Only on my bad days," Ellen assured him with mock seriousness.

"Well, on my bad days I lapse into spacey behavior. Some might even say rude. But that's only when I'm really focused on a project and it's causing me trouble. I think you've witnessed that already! And then I bounce back to being a nice normal guy."

"Artistic temperament?" Ellen asked with a smile.

"That or immaturity. I have to warn you, though," Rob said, his tone suddenly serious. "I'm not too long out of a relationship. Cora doesn't know about that, by the way. Frankly, I'm not sure how she hasn't ferreted out the information by now."

Ellen hesitated, but then she thought of the irrepressible Nadia. "I am, too," she admitted boldly. "It's been two months since the final, final end."

"Are you able to tell me about it?"

Ellen sighed. "Why not? His name was Peter. We were together for almost three years. We got engaged after about eighteen months and moved in together soon after that. And then, about three or four months ago—some of it is a blur already—I started having suspicions. And then I found proof that he was cheating on me and had been for a long time. Cheating and stealing."

Rob let out a long whistle. "Wow," he said. "I'm so sorry. It must have felt as if your entire world was crumbling around you."

"Pretty much, though my friends and family were there for me." When I let them be, she added silently. "Can you tell me what happened to you?"

"Sure," he said. "I had been seeing this woman, Christine is her name, for about seven or eight months. And I was in love. And she wasn't, I guess. She hurt me. Not on purpose. I mean, she didn't cheat on me or steal from me, like your former fiancé did to you. She just decided to move to California and pursue her life out there. She had every right to make that decision. Anyway, it's been about nine months now since she ended it, and I like to think I've moved on." Rob frowned, then nodded. "I have moved on. I can say that definitely."

"So," Ellen asked, "if she called you tomorrow and said, I'm moving back East, let's get back together, what would you say?"

Rob smiled. "I'm a romantic, not a masochist. I don't like to be thought of as a convenience."

A convenience. Was that what Peter had considered her? Ellen wondered. Until she had become an inconvenience, of course. Had she been just a warm body with whom to pass the time? It wasn't the first time Ellen had considered this possibility, but it still gave her a chill. That someone could have so little respect for another human being was really appalling.

"I'm over Peter completely, too," she said then. "Not the damage, but the person."

Rob smiled. "Good. I'm glad."

They sat there quietly as the sky darkened and twinkling lights came on in the houses across the Cove and families with small children headed back to their motels for the night. Ellen felt more peaceful than she had in a very long time.

"So, let me see if I've got this right," Rob said at last. "We're not dating."

Ellen was startled, but she hid the fact behind a smile. "Right," she said.

"But we might be interested in each other someday."

Ellen hesitated. "I guess you could say that," she finally admitted.

"But neither of us is immature enough to rush into anything."

"Right," Ellen said firmly.

"At the same time," Rob went on, "neither of us is silly enough to walk away from something that seems like it could be a really good idea."

Ellen didn't quite know about that, but she said, "Also right."

"Good." Rob smiled. "We're in complete agreement then."

They paid the check soon after. As they were leaving the restaurant, Rob took her hand. Ellen smiled up at him.

Oh, my gosh, she thought as they headed for the parking lot. What, oh what am I doing?

CHAPTER 14

"What a perfect evening," Rob said. "I know, what a cliché, but at this moment I feel it's true."

Ellen nodded. "So do I."

They were sitting at the little wrought-iron table in Ellen's backyard. The air was warm and soft and scented with flowers. The candles Ellen had lit gave off a warm glow. In the distance a night bird was singing its melancholy song.

It was not the first time Ellen and Rob had seen each other since the dinner in Perkins Cove. One afternoon they had visited the Ogunquit Museum of American Art, and afterward they had gone for steamers and corn on the cob at Chauncey Creek in Kittery Point. Another afternoon they had gone to a really awful action film, just for the fun of it. It turned out they both liked popcorn with an extra squirt of life-threatening artificial butter.

This evening, Ellen had invited Rob to her house for dinner in the garden. She had served wine and a Caesar salad, a crisp French-style baguette from Bread and Roses, and a plate of cold shrimp with a curry dipping sauce. For dessert she offered chocolate chip cookies, also from Bread and Roses. Conversation had been nonstop and easy. Ellen told

Rob about her idyllic childhood summers in Ogunquit. Rob told Ellen about his wild days in art school. Ellen told him about how she had met her good friend Caroline at a charity event; they had been seated at the same table and had bonded over rubber chicken and dull speeches. Rob admitted that though he had a few buddies, in his free time he often chose to take long, solitary rides on his bike. Ellen revealed that she was content being an only child. Rob said that for years he had wanted a kid brother to boss around. "But it's probably a good thing my mom didn't have more kids," he said.

Only a few shrimp and one cookie remained when suddenly, Rob grabbed the arms of his chair.

"Holy . . . !"

"What's wrong?" Ellen cried. Rob's face had gone deadly pale, and his eyes were abnormally wide.

"Don't turn around," he whispered hoarsely. "Maybe it will go away."

Of course, Ellen turned around. And then, she laughed.

"What are you laughing about?" Rob hissed. "It's a panther. A young panther. Its mother could be just behind those trees! It probably wants to kill us!"

Ellen turned back and with difficulty tried to quell her laughter. "Oh, Rob, that's only Clovis, Cora's cat."

"Her what?"

Ellen called over her shoulder, "Clovis, would you like a shrimp?"

With his characteristic groan, Clovis walked over to join them at the little table. Ellen held out a shrimp, and with one engulfing bite it was gone. She fed him the other remaining shrimp, and then with a long, penetrating stare at Rob, Clovis stalked off.

Rob put his hand to his chest. "I think I'm having a heart attack," he said. "I've never seen such an enormous house cat in my life."

"Cora swears he's not a half-breed, but I have my doubts,"

Ellen admitted. "Your color is coming back. Have some wine. Maybe it will help restore you."

"Thanks," Rob murmured. "I guess I acted like a Victorian lady just now, on the verge of fainting dead away."

"I would have fetched the smelling salts," Ellen assured him.

"And loosened my stays?"

Ellen laughed. "If I knew what a stay was, yes, I would have loosened it."

"Though I doubt you'd have the strength to carry me inside, out of the elements."

"Yes. I'd have to call the fire department for help."

"And my reputation as a man would be forever ruined!"

Ellen laughed. "And what would Cora and the other ladies in your fan club think about that!"

"You know, I never expected this sort of thing to happen," Rob said after a moment.

"What sort of thing?" Ellen asked lightly. "The sudden appearance of a massive four-footed beast?"

"No, silly. This. This friendship we seem to be developing. I mean, I came to Ogunquit this summer with the full intention of sticking to myself and my painting. I didn't at all expect—or, to be honest, even want—a, well, a relationship with someone."

"A relationship," Ellen repeated, wondering if her voice had shaken.

"Yes. Like what we have now, whatever exactly it is. We're having fun together, aren't we? Not raucous fun, but real fun."

"Yes," Ellen agreed. "We are. And as long as we're being honest, I have to admit my intentions for the summer were pretty close to yours. I came here to be alone and to forget all that had happened with Peter. At least, to put it all behind me. I even had to force myself to spend time with Cora. But

I didn't want to insult her; she had been friends with my parents."

Rob smiled. "And I suspect that Cora Compton does not take 'no' for an answer from anyone!"

"I wonder if even Emily can resist her," Ellen said.

"Emily is probably the only one who can!" Rob got up from his chair then. "Look," he said, "I hate to come across as such a workaholic, but I do want to finish some preliminary sketches tonight. If I'm to get anything done in the morning, when the light is back, I'd better get cracking."

Ellen got up as well. "Of course," she said. "And you don't have to excuse a devotion to work to me! My friend Caroline is always telling me to lighten up and leave work at the office."

"But home is your office," Rob pointed out.

"You see my dilemma!"

They parted with a warm hug. Ellen was both relieved and disappointed there had been no kiss. Mostly relieved? Or mostly disappointed? She didn't know.

She watched as Rob drove off. At the end of the road he tooted the horn. She waved and went to the garden to clear the remains of their meal.

JoAnne Tudor called later that night, just as Ellen was putting away the last of the cleaned and dried dishes.

"Hey, Mom."

"You sound good," JoAnne replied promptly.

"What do you mean?"

"Your voice. There's something light in it. Maybe all that time alone is proving of some benefit after all."

Ellen laughed a bit guiltily. "Maybe," she said. "So, what's going on in sunny Arizona?"

They chatted for some time, and though it felt somehow dishonest not to share with her mother the news of Rob Penn's presence in her life, Ellen did not. She wasn't entirely sure why, but she suspected that embarrassment had something to do with it. Against her mother's—and Caroline's—advice she had made a commitment to spend the summer alone and in relative isolation, and here she seemed to be developing a—yes, a relationship, of whatever sort it was, with someone.

But if something . . . definitive . . . were to happen with Rob, whatever that might be, then, of course, she would share the news. She might even shout it from the rooftop.

"Good night, Mom," Ellen said finally. "Give my love to Dad."

"I will. And keep at whatever it is you're doing," JoAnne urged. "You're sounding a lot more like the Ellen we know and love."

Thanks to Rob? Ellen wondered.

CHAPTER 15

Ellen was on her way to Rob's house for dinner. They had seen each other only that afternoon, but already she missed the sound of his voice and the way she found herself smiling so freely when they were together.

Rob answered the door on her first knock. His shirt was open to mid-chest. Ellen felt a tingle of nervous excitement course through her.

"Come in," he said, stepping aside. "I'm almost finished getting dinner together."

While Rob was busy in the kitchen, Ellen occupied her time looking at the paintings in progress. If things between them went well, she thought, she would buy a painting. And even if things didn't go well, whatever that might mean, she would buy a painting anyway, purely for the aesthetic pleasure it would bring her for years to come.

Suddenly, an enticing aroma from the tiny open kitchen caught her attention. Rob must have taken something from the oven.

"You can cook," Ellen exclaimed, turning away from the easels. That was no frozen meal she smelled. That was savory heaven.

Rob looked up from whatever it was he was now chopping. "Don't sound so surprised."

"You said you weren't a fussy gourmet."

"And I'm not. I made us mac 'n' cheese and a salad, and for dessert, we're having Ben and Jerry's. Simple."

"What flavor?"

"Is this a deal breaker?" Rob asked.

"No. I just want to know so I can have something to look forward to if dinner is awful," she teased.

"Thanks for the vote of confidence. I got vanilla in case you like your ice cream clean and classic, and I also got some concoction with coconut and cherries and chocolate fudge in case you like your ice cream complicated."

The meal was not awful at all.

"Where did you get this recipe?" Ellen asked. "This is not like any old plastic mac 'n' cheese I've ever had!"

"From Ina Garten, you know, the Barefoot Contessa. She's my celebrity chef crush."

Ellen approved of his choice. Ina Garten—now there was a woman who would chow down with you. And how adorable was she with her husband? That was still what Ellen wanted, wasn't it, in spite of the damage Peter had done to her heart and soul? A long and happy marriage with someone who was, first and foremost, her best friend.

After dinner Rob and Ellen moved to the battered and sagging couch in the main area of the house. Ellen curled her legs up under her. Rob extended his out before him.

"You know," he said then, "since that conversation we had the first time you were here at my place, I've been thinking about that summer I went to sleepaway camp. All these memories came back to me, things I haven't thought about in years."

"Really? Like what?" Ellen asked.

"Well, there was a woodworking course. I remembered how much I loved it. I remembered the smell of the freshly cut wood and how satisfying it felt to carve a recognizable shape out of a boring old log. It gave me a great sense of purpose. And I remembered that, when I got home at the end of the summer, I asked my father for a saw. It didn't go over so well."

Ellen laughed. "I should say not! You were a child!"

"Oh, it wasn't that my father had any objection to giving a saw to an eight-year-old. It was just that he didn't want his eight-year-old to have anything to do with craft work or manual labor."

"Then why did he send you to camp in the first place?" Ellen asked. "Everyone knows that camp involves getting down and dirty and building stuff."

Rob shrugged. "It was a cheap and easy way to get rid of me for a few months?"

Ellen thought that was sad, and from what Rob had told her about his family, she also thought that it was likely. She wondered what the senior Mr. Penn thought of his son's being a working artist. Was he ashamed? Was he disappointed? And what did poor Mrs. Penn think of her son? Had she ever seen one of his paintings in a show?

"What else do you remember?" she asked, pushing aside those unspoken, unhappy questions.

"Tuna melts," Rob said promptly. "We learned how to make tuna melts over an open fire. That was fun. And delicious. And s'mores. Boy, did I love them. The food at camp was way more kid friendly than it was at my house. Oddly enough, given her troubles, my mother has always been a health food freak."

Ellen smiled. "It sounds like you had a great time that summer." Far better, Ellen thought, than the time she had when she went to camp. That summer would always be associated in her mind with fear—fear of her father's dying, fear of her parents' abandoning her, fear that the awful boy who had teased her with that awful nickname would somehow follow her back to her real life. In spite of the warmth of the summer night, Ellen shivered.

"Hey, are you okay?" Rob asked. "Do you want a sweater?"

Ellen smiled. "No, I'm fine. Thanks."

"All in all that summer was a lot of fun." Rob laughed. "Except for one thing. There was this girl, oh boy, she was a terror!"

Ellen grinned. "Why? I mean, what did she do that was so bad?"

"If it was something that would annoy me, she did it." Rob paused for a moment, as if more closely remembering. "Steal my soda when my back was turned. Stick out her tongue every time she passed me. Poke me in the arm and then run away. Stuff like that. She was really pretty, too. She had this long blond braid, and she wore these cute pink glasses, but she was a horror. I think that's what freaked me out the most, that she was so adorable and yet so—so . . . obnoxious!"

A blurry image came to Ellen then, a vague memory of having worn a braid at one point in her childhood. . . . But then again, most little girls with long hair wore a braid at some time. And there was that brief period of her childhood when her eyes had been weak, and she had had to wear glasses. . . . Had they been pink? And when was that, exactly? She couldn't really remember.

"She drove me crazy!" Rob was saying. "I don't know why she got to me so much. One time, I even spoke to a counselor about her. I demanded she be thrown out of camp. Can you imagine? I guess I thought pretty highly of myself back then if I, a puny eight-year-old kid, could demand a fellow camper be tossed—and a girl, at that!"

Ellen's stomach clenched. Maybe, she thought, she shouldn't have had a second helping of the mac 'n' cheese. Maybe she shouldn't have had all that ice cream, either. "What was the worst thing this girl did?" she asked.

"The absolute worst? Well, hmm, I guess that was when she put big globs of red Jell-O in my sneakers."

"Jell-O?" Ellen smiled a weak smile. "That doesn't seem too bad. . . ."

"It was, for me. I was a squeamish kid when it came to blood. Anyway, I'd just come out of the lake. I'd left my sneakers on the shore. The shore was all rocky and pebbly. . . . So, I got to my sneakers and jammed my feet into them—I don't think I ever tied the laces—and suddenly all this red goo came squirting out. I screamed. I thought I'd cut my feet on the rocks. I remember feeling suddenly light-headed, and I woke up in the infirmary." Rob chuckled. "I tell you, this girl was a brilliant criminal mind in the making."

Ellen put her hand to her forehead. It was hot. Red Jell-O . . . No. It was impossible . . . "Um," she said, "how do you know this girl was responsible?"

"Because she admitted it! She must really have wanted to be sent home. Or maybe she was just in serious need of attention and didn't know how else to go about getting it." Rob pretended to shudder. "I wouldn't be surprised if she grew up to be a psychopath. One thing's for sure. I wouldn't want to run into her now."

There was a very loud buzzing in Ellen's ears. She felt as if she were going to pass out. The past . . . That summer had always been such a fog. . . . But now . . .

This could not be happening. And yet, it most certainly was.

"Um, what was her name?" she asked.

Rob shook his head. "I'll never forget it. Nellie. Cute name, really. It fit her. I mean, it fit the cute part of her."

"Nellie," Ellen repeated numbly. "What was her last name?"

"I never knew. I probably shouldn't admit this, but after a while she made me so mad I started to call her Smelly Nellie. I didn't expect the nickname would catch on with the other kids, but it did. I felt bad about that, until I got home at the end of the summer and didn't ever have to set eyes on her again. Then, I guess I just didn't care any longer. Not very nice of me, I know, but . . ."

Ellen jumped to her feet. Her hands were shaking. She felt sweat prickling at the back of her neck.

"What's wrong?" Rob asked. "You look sick. I should have gotten you that sweater. . . ."

"What's wrong?" Ellen said, her voice wobbling. "What's wrong is that I'm Smelly Nellie!"

"What?" Rob shook his head. "What are you talking about?"

"And you were Bobby. Bob. Rob. I never put it together. I never thought . . ."

Rob's face became a remarkable shade of pale. "But— You're kidding me. Right?"

"I wish I were," Ellen said, her voice trembling with disbelief. "I can't believe I've been falling for the person who tortured me that awful summer!"

"I know, I was horrible," Rob said promptly. He reached a hand out to Ellen, but she jumped away. "It's not right to call someone a bad name, even when you're a stupid little kid. Ellen, I'm so sorry. I—"

"You ruined my life for months!"

Rob flinched at the volume of her words. "Please, Ellen, I—"

"I hate you!"

Rob gave a choking little laugh. "Well, that's pretty inconvenient because you see, I've fallen in love with you. I wasn't planning on telling you just yet, but—"

"No, you haven't. You're just saying that to trick me."

"Right now, I almost wish that I were. But it's true, Ellen. I am in love with you."

"Well," Ellen said, with a wild little laugh. "That's just too bad."

Rob was silent for a moment, his head bowed, his hands on his knees. "You were mean to me, too," he said finally. "But you know how despicable kids can be, boys and girls. I'm sure neither of us really meant any of it. I'm sure if either of us had known what damage we—"

"Just—don't."

Ellen grabbed her bag from the chair onto which she had tossed it earlier, and ran out of the cottage, making sure to slam the door behind her. The window next to the door rattled in its frame. Ellen hoped that it fell out and shattered into a million pieces and that Rob had to pay to replace it and . . .

Behind her she heard Rob calling out: "Ellen, wait! Don't leave like this!"

She ran down the little drive, got into her car, and drove off until out of sight of the house. Then, she pulled over to wait until her hands stopped trembling.

She waited a long time. And during that time, through the clamor of anger and indignation and surprise, she realized that what she felt most of all was very, very sad.

Once again she had badly misjudged someone, let down her guard when she shouldn't have. Once again she had made a bad, bad mistake. She had liked Rob. She had really, really liked him.

When would she ever learn!

CHAPTER 16

At eight fifteen the following morning Ellen was behind the wheel of her car, on her way to Cora Compton's house.

She had spent a sleepless night, her mind a dreadful blank. She had expected to be haunted by memories of the time she and Rob had spent together these past few weeks, to be tortured by every laugh and smile and kind word. But this blankness, this deadness was somehow far worse.

Still, one thought had taken firm hold in her mind. She had been able to make one decision. She should have stuck to her guns in the beginning, politely and firmly refused Cora's invitations to socialize. Maybe it wasn't too late to salvage a summer of solitary healing. God knew she now had more misery from which to recover.

Cora was at home. At least, her old black Cadillac was in the drive. Ellen pulled up behind it and walked to the front door. It opened after one knock. Cora must have seen her coming.

"Ellen, what a nice surprise." Cora's eyes narrowed. "But no. I see from your expression that you are rather upset. Come in, come in."

Ellen had to clear her throat before she could speak. Even

then, her voice was a dreadful rasp. "No, thanks," she said. "I won't take long."

"My dear—"

Ellen lowered her eyes. "Please, Cora. I won't—I can't—go into details. Something has happened, and I'm very upset. Please . . . Please understand that I can't see you for some time. I can't see anyone. I never should have . . . It's my fault. We can leave it at that."

"But you must let me help you, dear." Cora reached out to put a hand on Ellen's arm.

Ellen, raising her eyes, stepped back. Cora's face was gray with concern.

"No," Ellen said, as steadily as she could manage, which was not very steadily. "You can't help me. No one can, not right now. I'm sorry, Cora. Please believe me. Please don't come to my house."

There was a long and horribly awkward moment of silence. Ellen lowered her eyes again, unable to face the older woman. She felt like an enormous coward in that moment.

"I acknowledge your need to be alone," Cora said finally. Her voice was chilled with hurt and rejection. "And I wish you well. Now, if you will excuse me, I have gardening to do."

Cora, gathering her voluminous skirts, walked past Ellen, and headed around to the back of her house. Clovis appeared from behind her and followed his mistress.

"Hi, Clovis," Ellen whispered.

He brusquely twitched his tail at her and stalked on.

With a heavy heart, Ellen walked back to her car. She wasn't entirely conscious of the ride home. It seemed as if a moment after leaving Cora Compton's driveway she was pacing the living room of her rented house, struggling to understand what awful and destructive thing had happened to her life in the last twenty-four hours.

Could it be, she thought in one wild moment, that Rob had planned their reunion all along with the intention of humiliating her? No, it could not be. She felt stupid to have even considered such a crazy notion. Calm down, Ellen, she scolded. Be sensible.

But it was hard to be sensible when there were so many questions with no solid answers.

Was Rob lying about how badly she had behaved that summer at camp? But why would he lie? And why couldn't she remember more?! So much of that summer was a blank. Bits and pieces of memory had only begun to come back to her when, the night before, Rob had told his tale.

A fairy tale in which she had been cast as the wicked witch.

She was glad now that she had said nothing to either her mother or to Caroline about Rob. What a travesty!

For the remainder of that dreadful day, time alternately scurried past and crawled by. At seven thirty that evening, Ellen went to bed. She didn't expect sleep to come, but it did, almost immediately and with a heavy hand.

"No!"

Ellen shot up in bed, tossing the lightweight blanket aside as she did. The illuminated clock on her bedside table told her that it was a quarter to three, the middle of the night.

Her heart was beating madly, and she felt worn-out and sweaty, as if she had been running for a long time over difficult terrain.

She had been dreaming of that long-ago summer at camp. The dream images had been so terribly vivid and so terribly . . . terrible.

Had she really been such a little beast? Had she really dumped a bottle of black paint over Rob/Bobby's art project? Or was that an exaggeration of her unconscious (and guilty?) mind? Had she really stolen Rob/Bobby's favorite T-shirt from the laundry room and cut it to shreds with blunt-end scissors filched from the art teacher? Had she really put a garden snake in Rob/Bobby's bed? No, that didn't sound possible. Ellen was afraid of snakes. She always had been. Hadn't she?

And then . . . This was the most disturbing part of the dream. At one point she had seen her seven-year-old self, long braid and pink glasses, sitting on a fallen tree, deep in the woods. Pine trees loomed all around her. Night was coming on and the temperature was rapidly falling as the sun went down. But she did not feel afraid. She felt—annoyed.

Why annoyed? Why was she alone in the woods feeling annoyed? What normal seven-year-old girl wasn't scared out of her mind in such a situation?

My God, she thought, falling back against the pillows and rubbing her temples, if even one of those episodes was real, I have an awful lot of bad behavior to answer for!

Ellen realized that she was desperately thirsty. Why did bad dreams make a person thirsty? She got out of bed and went down to the kitchen for a glass of water. She drank it down and leaned back against the sink.

No, she decided. Those dream images weren't memories at all. They were unimportant fictions; they were inventions; they had to be. They were fictions brought on by Rob's wild accusations. Because if they were memories—long buried in her unconsciousness—well, what else about her life was a mystery to her? It was a terrifying question.

With dragging steps, Ellen went back upstairs to her bed-room, wondering—dreading—what the rest of the night would bring.

CHAPTER 17

"What has happened to you? You look awful. Like you have seen the ghost."

Ellen grimaced. "Thanks."

It was two days after the explosive revelation at Rob's house. Ellen was leaving a hardware store in Wells; she had needed lightbulbs and had guessed that it was unlikely she would run into Rob in Wells when he could fulfill his hardware needs much closer to home. So far, so good. There had been no sign of Rob Penn or of Cora Compton.

Nadia, it seemed, had been shopping at the secondhand store next door. "Well, you do," she said. "Come, I don't have to be at the restaurant for an hour. Let us get a drink, and you can tell me all about what has put you in such a state."

"No, thanks," Ellen said quickly. "I really don't want to talk about it."

Nadia peered closely at her. "There are the dark circles around your eyes."

"I haven't been sleeping well."

"And your hair. It has no luster."

Ellen laughed a bit wildly. "All right, I'll come with you."

There was a tiny little pub close by, a place Nadia knew,

and at this time of the day, two thirty in the afternoon, she said it would be fairly quiet. Except for an elderly couple sitting at the bar watching a sporting event on television, Ellen and Nadia were the only customers.

They sat at a little table out of earshot of the older couple and ordered two beers.

"So," Nadia said. "What has happened?"

Ellen sighed. "What happened is that yet again I made a mistake in judgment."

Nadia frowned. "You speak in enigmas."

"Sorry. I just can't bear to talk about the details at the moment."

"I understand. But then, I am afraid there is not much I can do for you. Of course, your trouble involves a man."

Ellen managed a smile. "How did you know?"

"Trouble always involves a man. That is, when it does not involve a woman. And in your case, I think it is a man."

"Yes." Ellen hesitated. "You know," she said, after a moment, "it's funny you should have said I looked as if I'd seen a ghost. I have, actually. A specter from the past. Someone I used to know—in an odd way—a very long time ago. Someone I had hoped never to see again. Someone I—someone I failed to recognize."

"Someone—a man—you realized that you like. Maybe even more than like."

"Yes."

"So, what is the problem? He does not like you?"

Ellen looked down at the glass of beer. She simply could not answer that first question for Nadia. As for the second question . . .

A long moment passed before Nadia spoke again. "This thing people call closure," she said. "I am not so sure there is such a thing, but if there is, it must be something very different for everybody who seeks it. Don't you agree? Maybe it would be good to decide what this closure would look like for you with this man. And then, maybe it would be good to seek that closure."

Ellen looked up. "Maybe," she said. "I just don't know."

"Better to do something, no, than to wait and—what is the word? To wallow?"

"That's the word."

Nadia looked at her watch. It was the same one she had been wearing the first time Ellen had met her.

"Is that an heirloom?" Ellen asked.

"The watch? Yes. It belonged to my mother. It is all I have left of her. But I must go to work," she announced. "Come in to the restaurant some time. The chef is very good."

Ellen smiled. "Thank you for listening. And for caring."

Nadia shrugged. "Maybe one day you will do the same for me."

"I would be honored," Ellen said. "Really."

CHAPTER 18

It was yet another one of those perfect midsummer days. The sun was out in full force, the sky was cloudless and blue, and the water sparkled. It was mid-tide, so there was plenty of sand for everyone to enjoy. The humidity was low; it hadn't rained now for a month.

Ellen had gone down to the beach in an attempt to shift her spirits to a happier place. Shimmering water, a bright blue sky, and clean, white sand. Who couldn't be—who wouldn't be!—positively affected by such pristine beauty? Ellen Tudor, that's who. Her spirits were as dark and troubled as they had been in the middle of that night when she had woken from those disturbing dreams. . . . Or, from those disturbing memories disguised as dreams.

"Oh, no," she murmured. Up ahead . . . Yes, it was Rob Penn. He was sitting cross-legged on a yellow blanket, a sketchbook on his lap. He was not wearing a shirt. Ellen tried to ignore that fact. And the fact that his thighs were admirably muscled. And the fact that his magnificent hair was tousled and glinting in the sun.

Turn around and walk the other way, she told herself. He

hasn't seen you yet. You can easily avoid an unpleasant encounter.

But no. Ellen took a deep breath. She remembered what Nadia had said about figuring out what closure between she and Rob might look like, and pursuing it. Well, she hadn't been able to determine that yet, but maybe, once she spoke to Rob, a sense of closure might be achieved. Maybe.

Ellen continued on until she stood within a few feet of Rob.

"Oh," he said, taking off his sunglasses and squinting up at her. "Hello."

"You're so tall." Now, Ellen thought with dismay, why did I say that?

Rob put his sunglasses back on. "Well, that wasn't exactly a greeting."

"It's just that you were so short that summer back in camp."

"I was eight. People do change over the course of time, you know. Like the fact that when I got to college I started calling myself Rob. It seemed more mature."

"How was I supposed to recognize you?" Ellen asked, vaguely aware of the absurdity of the question. This conversation was not going well at all.

"You weren't supposed to recognize me."

Ellen shook her head. "What do you mean?"

"What I mean is, I didn't know you were—Nellie." Rob laughed. "It's not like I came to Ogunquit knowing you were here and planning to trick you into falling in love with me just to get back at you for some childish pranks."

Ellen recalled her own thoughts along that line and blushed. "I didn't fall in love with you."

"You made that abundantly clear. But I fell in love with you. Look, do you want to sit down and—"

"No," Ellen said. "The other night you called me a psychopath."

"I'm sorry about that."

"You said I had a criminal mind."

"I believe I said it was a brilliant criminal mind."

"That doesn't make it any better."

Rob sighed. "I know. I'm sorry. It was a poor choice of words. Okay, you don't want to sit. Then do you want to go and get a coffee or—"

And suddenly, Ellen was helpless to stop the tears that coursed down her cheeks. "Do you know how afraid I was that that awful nickname would follow me back to school that September? I lived in fear of my classmates finding out. I swear I could hardly sleep at night for worrying. I was miserable for months."

Rob looked appropriately stricken. "I'm sorry," he said. "Really, I can't say how sorry I am. Do you wear glasses anymore?"

Ellen wiped her cheeks with the back of her hand. "No. It was a childhood weakness. I outgrew it."

"That's good."

Ellen waited, for what else she wasn't quite sure. Certainly not for closure! Maybe Nadia had been right when she said there might not even be such a thing.

After a moment, Rob said, "Since the other night it's occurred to me that maybe you got on my nerves so badly back at camp because unconsciously I was attracted to you. You know, you like a girl, so you dunk her braid in the inkwell."

This was not at all what Ellen had expected to hear. "We were prepubescent," she said. "We were too young for romance."

"Boys and girls—and boys and boys and girls and girls—can like each other at a very young age."

Ellen shook her head. "I thought all boys were disgusting."

"We probably were."

"I would never have—have done those things to you—because I liked you."

"Okay."

"I must have done those things because I didn't like you."

"All right."

"In fact," Ellen said, "I must have hated you." But even as she said the words, she knew they weren't true. Could a seven-year-old really experience the ferocity of hate?

"Okay," Rob said wearily. "But why didn't you like me? Why did you single me out as the kid to torture? What had I ever done to you?"

Ellen opened her mouth, but not a word came out, no witty reply or stinging retort, no accusation real or false. Nothing. Had Rob/Bobby ever done anything to her to make her torment him? Maybe she just hadn't liked anyone that summer, not even herself. It was the first time she had been away from her parents, and her father had been sick and she had been afraid she would never see him or her mother again. And she had been so young!

"Well, I guess you're right," Rob said after the silence had grown even more uncomfortable than the conversation had been. "I guess I didn't like you. If I had liked you I wouldn't have called you a nasty name. I would have ignored you."

"I've kept you long enough from your work," Ellen finally managed to say.

Rob looked back to his sketchpad. "Good-bye, Ellen."

Ellen turned and started back in the direction of the Wells town line. Her eyes were still blurred with tears. And with every step forward she had an increasingly strong urge to turn back, to sit down in the sand next to Rob, to take his hand, to . . .

"Ow!" Ellen stumbled and clutched her shoulder.

"Sorry!" It was a girl about twenty, one of a group of people playing volleyball. "But you kind of walked right into the middle of the game. Didn't you see us?"

Ellen bit back another flood of tears. She shook her head, unable to trust her voice. And she did not turn back to Rob.

CHAPTER 19

A week had passed since that awful night at Rob's house. And it had been a fairly miserable and lonely week. Clovis had not come to visit Ellen since her last and very awkward conversation with Cora. The mail had consisted only of bills and coupons. The new printer cartridge she had been expecting had been delayed; she had not even had the opportunity to exchange greetings with a UPS driver. Nadia had been working double shifts at the restaurant and had barely had time to send her a text. Caroline had not reached out via e-mail or text or phone call. Even her mother had been silent except for a brief e-mail to say that she was suffering a bad cold.

So, Ellen had concentrated on work, which was always at least a partial antidote to misery. She had watched a slew of British period mysteries on Roku. She had caught up on laundry and ironing and had swept and vacuumed a ridiculous amount.

And she had thought. And thought. And thought some more. But still, the answers hadn't come.

By the week's end, the cupboard had grown quite bare, and if she wasn't going to starve, she would have to go into town for groceries. She would just have to pray she wouldn't run into Cora Compton or Rob Penn.

Ellen finished the grocery shopping in record time, avoiding people she knew even vaguely. Hoping her luck would hold, Ellen next stopped at the post office. The clerk behind the counter was a round-faced, gray-haired woman about forty-five years of age. Her name tag proclaimed her to be Marion. Ellen was relieved to find that she didn't at all recognize the woman. Maybe the woman wouldn't recognize her.

"You're Ellen Tudor," the woman said cheerily, before Ellen had quite reached the counter.

"Um, yes," she answered glumly. "I am."

"I heard you were in town. I remember your parents. They were lovely people."

Ellen managed a smile. "Yes. Thanks. I—"

"I remember they were friends with Old Mrs. Compton."

"Yes. I just need—"

"You must have seen her since you've been back in town. Mrs. Compton, I mean."

"As a matter of fact I—"

Marion leaned forward over the counter, as if she were about to impart important or confidential information. "I'll tell you who's been seeing a lot of Cora," she said. "That nice young painter, Rob Penn. He's renting the old Harper house, well, studio, really, out on Sand's End Street."

"Yes. I heard that he—"

"He and Cora have become great friends. And Miss Camp, too. Mr. Penn took Miss Camp to the podiatrist just the other day. You know she has terrible trouble with her bunions, poor old thing."

"Really?" Ellen said. "I mean, I'm sorry. About the bunions."

Marion shook her head. "Terrible things, bunions. And the other day Mr. Benson from the gas station across the street saw Mr. Penn escorting Cora and Emily into the Cape Neddick Lobster Pound for luncheon. You know, don't you, that it's Cora's favorite restaurant? She just loves their French fries. Personally, I think their steamers are the best around, but I know people who differ."

Ellen managed a sickly smile. "I didn't know about the restaurant being Mrs. Compton's favorite. Or about the fries. And the steamers."

"Oh, yes," Marion went on. "And yesterday afternoon Mr. Penn took both old dears to the Hannaford for their groceries. What they would do without Mr. Penn I don't want to think about!"

Ellen swallowed hard. Could it really be that she had misjudged Rob Penn the adult so badly? Yes, she thought, it most certainly could be.

But in her mind Rob would always be the obnoxious little boy from camp. The connection to that dreadful summer could never be severed.

Right?

Or, wrong?

"Well, what is it I can help you with today?" Marion asked brightly.

Ellen hesitated. She had almost forgotten what she had come in to purchase. "A roll of stamps, please."

"Will that be all then?" Marion asked, handing them over and taking Ellen's money.

Ellen could barely meet the woman's eye. "Yes," she said quickly, "thanks," and hurried back out to the street.

Darn a small town, she thought. Did everybody know everything about everybody? Had Cora or even Emily told her neighbors (who would in turn have told their neighbors) that Ellen Tudor had had a falling-out with Rob Penn and had announced she was not going to be a friend to Cora Compton as a result? It seemed entirely possible.

Ellen walked through the parking lot to her car. She thought she caught a sidelong, accusatory glance from a grizzled old farmer getting out of a pickup truck, and an admonishing frown from a skinny, well-dressed matron exiting a Mercedes.

Ellen slid behind the wheel of her own car. It was clear that she had made a huge mistake in coming "home" this summer. This was not her home, not any longer anyway. She should have retreated to someplace far more isolated and sparsely populated.

When she reached the house she went inside and locked the door firmly behind her. She was considering pulling down the shades when the ringing of her cell phone startled her.

The call was from her mother.

JoAnne Tudor was recovered from her cold. "Cora called me," she said by way of greeting. "Ellen, what in God's name is going on? She said you told her you couldn't see her anymore, or some such nonsense, and that you gave her absolutely no explanation."

There was no point in beating around the proverbial bush.

"Do you remember my ever mentioning a boy named Bobby when I was a kid?" Ellen began. "Specifically, that summer Dad was sick and I went to camp?"

"Let me think." Her mother hummed. "Bobby. No. Not that I can recall. In fact, I don't think you mentioned anyone from that summer when you came home, boys or girls."

"Well," Ellen said, "here's the thing."

She told her mother about meeting Rob Penn, and about Cora's matchmaking efforts, and about what had happened between her and Rob over the course of a few weeks, culminating in the awful revelation that he was her childhood nemesis.

Her mother was silent for a long moment. A long moment, Ellen thought, during which her mother was no doubt regretting the fact that she had produced such an idiotic child.

Finally, JoAnne Tudor spoke. "First," she said, "talk to Cora. She befriended you when you were new to town. Apologize for hurting her feelings and be humble about it. She's not the sort to understand someone 'needing her space.' You should know that."

"I know. I will apologize," Ellen mumbled. But would Cora Compton accept her apology? She certainly was under no obligation to do so.

"Then," her mother went on, "consider the fact that it's only been a few months since the breakup with Peter. Your emotions are still riding high. So what if this Rob person was mean to you that long-ago summer? What does it matter now? Ellen, you're thirty-one years old. Let it go. Let bygones be bygones."

"Mmm," Ellen said.

"After all," JoAnne continued, "I remember getting several calls from the camp supervisors that summer about your troublesome behavior. I'm not making an excuse for what this Bobby/Rob person did to you, but you weren't exactly an angel yourself."

"So I've heard. The camp people really called you?"

"They most certainly did. But I set everything right. I explained that your misbehavior was probably due to the fact that you were away from home for the first time and were worried about your father."

"I was really that bad?" Ellen felt slightly sick. So, Rob was telling the truth. And maybe some of what had happened in those dreams the other night was real, too. "Tell me, Mom," Ellen asked. "Did I ever run away from camp?"

JoAnne sighed. "Oh, yes. Do you mean you don't remember?"

"No. I don't remember. But I had a dream the other night. . . ."

"I was frantic, of course, until the counselors and the police found you after about ten hours. And then, I was—puzzled."

"What do you mean you were puzzled?" Ellen asked. "I could have been hurt. I could have been mauled by a bear! I could have died from eating poisonous berries! I was probably cold and terrified and . . ."

"Not according to your rescuers, dear. From what they told me you were angry that you had been found—'an ungrateful child,' I was told."

"This is awful, Mom," Ellen cried. "Then why didn't you and Dad bring me home, if I was so miserable at camp?"

"You swore you weren't miserable. You begged us to let you stay on at camp. You said you liked it." JoAnne sighed. "Frankly, the camp supervisors were pretty eager to ship you back to Massachusetts, but you put up quite a fuss. They concluded that you had run away just to get some attention. But then in the end it wasn't quite the sort of attention you wanted. Whatever that was. I doubt you knew yourself."

"I don't understand any of this," Ellen admitted.

"Children are irrational and emotional. You were going through a hard time."

Ellen thought it sounded as if her mother were quoting from a manual.

"Ellen," JoAnne went on, "I might as well tell you now that it wasn't the first time that year you'd run away. You did it once just after school got out. I thought you were afraid to go away to camp. But you said that no, you were excited about going to camp. You just wanted to see what it was like to run away."

"How far did I get?"

"The neighbor's house."

"I see," Ellen said. *But I don't see at all,* she added silently.

"I've often thought that we should never have sent you away that summer. But at the time your father and I really thought it was the right thing to do. Still, so many times afterward I've wondered. . . ."

"What happened when I got home from camp?" Ellen asked, afraid to know. "How did I act?"

"You were a model child once more, even more well-behaved than before you had gone off to camp. There was no more running away and certainly no acting out. It was almost as if that summer had never happened."

That's not how it feels to me, Ellen thought.

JoAnne Tudor sighed. "Ellen, you should know by now that running away—whether it's into the woods or back to your childhood haunts—rarely solves anything. You take yourself everywhere you go, Ellen. At least when you're home you can turn to your friends or your family."

"Yes," Ellen murmured. "I know."

"Well," her mother said briskly, "I have to run. Your father is giving me that I'm-going-to-die-if-I-don't-get-lunch-immediately look."

"Is he feeling okay?" Ellen asked. "Did he catch your cold?"

"He's fine. And of course he can make his own lunch, but I like to make it for him. Plus, I'm a lot neater in the kitchen."

"Mom, what do I do about Rob?" Though of course, Ellen knew the answer to her question.

"Apologize?" JoAnne suggested. And then she hung up.

Ellen collapsed onto the couch. She had an awful lot to think about.

CHAPTER 20

The following morning found Ellen parked outside of the house her family had once owned. There was no car in the driveway and no garage in which a car might be stowed, so Ellen assumed the current residents were away at the moment. The last thing her tarnished local reputation (if indeed she had one and wasn't imagining it) needed was an irate homeowner chasing her away from the property. An incident like that would make the local news and papers and follow her forever.

Ellen sighed. The house looked so small now, even though she had last seen it only five years earlier, just before her parents had sold it. So small and so foreign. That was the sad thing, that the house she had lived in for months on end over so many years now seemed as unfamiliar as a roadside motel chain. She knew the upper right-hand window was the window in her old bedroom, but she couldn't remember sitting at that window, looking out onto the front lawn on cool late summer evenings. And yet, she must have done so!

She knew there was a big old pine out back (she could see its top even now), but she couldn't remember gathering its fallen cones for crafts. She knew she had made crafts with the cones and other random bits of found nature. Her mother still had some of the pieces Ellen had made as a child. The problem was that she simply couldn't remember the making.

Did everyone experience this weird disconnect between the past self and the present self? It was odd, too, the things that did stick with her after all these years, like how hurt she had felt when Rob—Bobby—had made her an object of ridicule. Memories of the motivation behind his childish cruelty—her own bad behavior—were still largely buried somewhere, but she could feel the hurt and the sense of vulnerability his nickname had caused her as if it all had happened yesterday.

Looking up at her former home, Ellen wondered if her seven-year-old self had had any sense of the consequences of her mischief. Had she been at all aware of the trouble she was causing? Or had she acted with conscious intention, relishing the mayhem that ensued? Why couldn't she remember!

Maybe, Ellen thought gloomily, *I should go to the bookstore and pick up a book on psychological development in children.* Maybe her father's being sick that summer she was seven had warped her in some irrevocable way.

Ellen rubbed her hand over her eyes. She must, she thought, have been so very angry with her parents for sending her away to camp; she must have been furious with them for banishing her from their lives. She must have seen being sent away to camp as a supreme abandonment. She thought about what her mother had said on the phone the day before, that she and Ellen's father had since wondered if they had done the right thing by sending her off.

Well, second-guessing would help no one now.

Ellen looked up again at what had been her bedroom window and made the decision almost without thinking.

"Carpe diem," she murmured to the interior of the car, as she pulled away from her former home and headed toward Cora's house. "If not now, when?"

She was nervous. What would she do if Cora refused to

talk to her? Ellen really didn't know. Burst into tears? Have a long-overdue nervous breakdown?

Cora opened the door on Ellen's first knock. She was wearing a splendidly embroidered caftanlike garment in a riot of pink and red. It almost made Ellen smile. Almost.

"I'm glad you're home," Ellen said, aware that her voice was a bit unsteady. "I'd like to talk to you. Please."

"Of course, dear." Cora's expression was understandably guarded.

"Cora, please accept my apology. I'm so sorry. I behaved badly. There's no excuse for turning my back on you when you've been such a good friend to me."

Cora's expression softened as rapidly as butter melting in a hot pan. "There's always an excuse for our behavior, dear," she said gently.

"No good excuse then."

"I accept your apology. Now, why don't you tell me why you felt the need to run away from your friends back home, too."

Ellen sighed. "You've been talking to my mother, haven't you? All right. But can we go inside?"

Cora led the way to the kitchen where the two women took a seat at the table. Ellen glanced around, hoping for a glimpse of Clovis, but he was absent.

"Why don't you begin at the beginning, dear," Cora said, reaching across the table to pat Ellen's hand.

Ellen did, starting with that summer at Camp Norridgewock, up through the disaster that was her relationship with Peter, and then her decision to hide away for a while in Ogunquit. "And so," she finished, "just when I was on the verge of—of something good happening with Rob, I learned that he was the boy who had saddled me with that horrible nickname. It . . . It made me a bit crazy, I suppose. And I have a bad habit of running away from everyone I love when difficult things happen. . . ."

Cora was silent for a few moments. "I met your parents

the summer after you had been at camp," she said then. "I never knew about your father's struggle with cancer. Your mother never said a word. And he looked so robust."

Ellen shrugged. "I guess she felt there was no point in bringing up the past once it was over. My father was well. That's all that mattered to her."

"Yes, I can certainly understand her wanting to move on. And to keep what had worried or troubled her to herself."

"I suppose I can understand, too. I didn't tell anyone that my father had been sick until I was in college. I was superstitious about it. I felt that if I didn't mention what had happened aloud, the past would somehow be changed. Well, it makes no sense." *And*, Ellen thought, *look at how I erased all memory of my bad behavior at camp that awful summer.* The mind was a very strange beast, often out of its own control and sometimes acting against its own self-interest.

The two women sat quietly for some minutes. Cora broke the silence.

"Your mother isn't the only one to keep a painful past a secret," she said, her eyes on the table before her. "I myself have kept silent about something that for a time I truly believed would kill me. But it didn't. I lost my husband, you see, as a very young woman."

Ellen felt numb with surprise. She could only shake her head in sympathy.

"He passed away only a few months after our wedding," Cora went on, now looking directly at Ellen. "It was quite sudden. A heart attack. He must have harbored some weakness since childhood. He certainly didn't see it coming. And of course, neither did I, though for a long time I wondered if I should have. I wondered if somehow I could have saved his life."

"I'm so sorry." Ellen had found her voice, but not sufficient words to express her sorrow and sympathy. "Oh, Cora, what can I say but that I'm so very sorry?"

Cora's smile was almost beatific then. "Do you know that

even if I had known he wasn't going to live for very long, I would have married him anyway? John was the love of my life."

"And all these years," Ellen asked gently, "has there been anybody else?"

"Who else would there be?" Cora replied simply. "No, there was never any question of my falling in love again."

How noble and strong she is, Ellen thought. But how terribly sad it all was, too. Unless Cora's memories, the good ones, had been enough to keep her company.

"I never knew," Ellen said, more to herself than to Cora.

"No one does. At least, no one alive now other than you and my dear Miss Camp."

"I'm honored that you told me. Thank you."

"Well, I'm not so sure I should have told you my story," Cora replied, almost brusquely. "I know all too well I sound like a woman imprisoned by the past. But what I want you to remember, dear Ellen, is that whatever happens between you and Mr. Penn, it's the present and the future that count most. Not some silly childish mishap that is better forgotten. And," Cora added, her expression growing fierce, "not some blackguard who broke your heart!"

Ellen knew there was wisdom in Cora's counsel. She just wasn't sure she was capable of acting on the older woman's advice.

Clovis crashed his bulk against her leg. Ellen jumped. She hadn't seen him come into the room. Hot tears of gratitude sprang to her eyes. "Thank you, Clovis," she murmured. "And Cora? I really like your dress."

CHAPTER 21

This time, Ellen had to ring the bell five times and pound on the door for close to a full minute before Rob appeared. His hair was disheveled, and his clothes were covered in daubs and streaks of paint. In his right hand he held a brush and a palette knife.

He was frowning.

"I'm sorry I didn't call ahead," Ellen said in a rush. "I . . . I was afraid that maybe you would tell me to get lost."

"I might have," Rob admitted. "But you're here now so . . ."

He stepped back, and Ellen followed him inside.

"So . . ." he said. "I'm not sure what else there is to say."

"There's an apology to offer," Ellen said. "I'm sorry I stormed off that night when I found out who you were. I mean, that you were Bobby. And I'm sorry I was so—well, so difficult that day on the beach, when you were sketching."

"You're forgiven."

Ellen felt her eyes widen. "Just like that?" she asked suspiciously.

"Yeah."

"Why?"

"Because I can tell that you mean it," Rob said. "You're

sincerely sorry. It would be rude and childish of me not to accept your apology."

"Thank you. Um, do you remember if I put a snake in your bed that summer at camp?"

"A snake?" Rob smiled. "Not that I remember." He reached for her hand, but Ellen took a step away from him.

"No, Rob, please," she said. "That can't . . . That can't happen now."

Rob looked genuinely puzzled. "Why?"

"Because—"

Because, she thought, she was a mess and Rob was a nice, normal guy, someone with energy and talent and a good nature. He didn't deserve to be saddled with a person who might once again try to destroy his art projects or cut up his clothing for reasons she couldn't even name.

"Just because," she said lamely.

"That's all the explanation I get?"

Ellen looked at her feet. "Yes," she said. "It's all that I can give. I'm sorry."

Rob sighed. "I guess I'll have to accept it, but I don't have to like it."

"You should know that I apologized to Cora, too."

"Why?"

"She didn't tell you?"

Rob shook his head. "Tell me what? Okay, to be honest I assumed that something might have happened between you since she hadn't mentioned your name in a few days."

"And you didn't tell her what had happened between you and me?"

Rob shook his head again. "It's our business."

"Well, you see, I kind of . . ." Ellen took a deep breath. "I told Cora that something had happened—I didn't say what—and that I needed my space so I wouldn't be seeing her for some time. And I asked her not to come to my house."

"Ouch. That's not something Cora would understand."

"Yes. My mother pointed that out to me. Anyway, I turned away from her like I turned away from my friends back home. It's a habit I have when things go wrong. I know it sounds ridiculous."

"Not ridiculous. Maybe not the best plan of action, but not ridiculous."

Ellen smiled. "Thanks. Anyway, I think I went a bit crazy. I was just so completely surprised by the things you said about me. I mean, about the seven-year-old me. And I couldn't remember having done any of it. At least, I'm beginning to remember, but who knows how much of that summer will come back to me now."

"Maybe," Rob suggested, "it's better not to remember that summer too clearly."

Ellen didn't know about that. "After all this time," she said, "you'd think my unconscious would be tired of carrying around all that mess and just let it out."

"It must have been an incredibly difficult time for you," Rob said gently. "When you were back home, it probably made sense to erase the past two months. And then, the erasure just became a habit. I believe it's called a coping mechanism."

"I guess. But what else have I forgotten? At least I know for sure that I was the scourge of Camp Norridgewock!"

"I'm sure there were worse kids than you in the camp's history. After all, how much harm can one seven-year-old girl do?"

"According to you," Ellen said darkly, "an awful lot."

"Well, maybe I'm misremembering, you know, exaggerating how bad you were."

"Somehow, I don't think so." Ellen forced a small smile. "I should be going."

"Why? I mean, do you have somewhere else to be?"

Did she? No.

"You're working," she replied. "I interrupted you."

"I need a break. Stay for a while, please."

Ellen fought back tears. Why did Bobby—she meant Rob—have to be so nice? She had not misjudged him this summer. She had recognized him as a person of quality. "I can't," she said. "But thanks."

And before she could relent and fall into his arms, she turned and hurried out to her car. She did not look back at the house before driving away.

CHAPTER 22

Ellen neatened the stack of art books on the coffee table in the living room. The stack hadn't needed to be straightened, but she had needed to do something, to keep occupied. Next, she dusted the mantel over the fireplace. Then, she reorganized the kitchen pantry and changed the sheets on the bed for the second time in as many days.

But busy work only went so far in keeping the darker thoughts away. The fact was that Ellen had decided to move back to Boston within the month. Yes, she would lose a huge amount of money; the rent on the Ogunquit house was nonrefundable. But she felt that she had no choice. Until then, she could manage to hide from prying eyes, go into town only when absolutely necessary, shop at the Hannaford farther away in Wells, rather than the one in York. Until then, she could manage to virtually disappear.

Of course, Cora would invite her to parties and events, but Ellen would politely and firmly decline. It could be done. It had to be done, and now Cora would understand, if not entirely approve. There was simply no way Ellen could stand being in the same room with Rob, pretending to make small talk with the likes of Mr. Green and Marion from the post office, while across the room Rob chatted with tall, willowy women who no doubt had never pulled a nasty prank in their lives.

Yes, settling down in Ogunquit year-round was now out of the question. Rob Penn had gotten to her the way no one, certainly not Peter, had gotten to her ever before. She could never handle seeing him arrive at the start of every summer, a tall, willowy, dark-haired woman, or even a short, plump, blond-haired woman, on his arm. And what if he got married and had kids and rescued a big fluffy dog from a local shelter and she had to pass the happy Penn family in the street and run into them on the beach and bump into them at the grocery store?

The very idea was unendurable.

An intense scraping at the front door interrupted Ellen's depressing thoughts. It was a sound she knew well by now. She would have to pay her landlords for the damage Clovis was inflicting on their home.

This time, instead of heading straight for the kitchen, Clovis stalked into the living room, jumped up onto the couch, and glared at her until she took a seat next to him. Ellen was surprised and pleased. His purr was deafening, but she was glad for the comfort of his proximity. She reached for her laptop and began to type out an e-mail message.

> *Caroline—*
>
> *I should know by now that a friend is someone who doesn't judge you when you make a mistake, even if it was a big one, like I made with Peter. I should know by now that a friend is not someone who says, "I told you so" when the man she warned you against hurts you.*
>
> *The fact is that my embarrassment is beginning to feel a lot like pride, and that can't be good, can it? The wrong kind of pride, I mean. And it also feels a bit like cowardice. That's not good, either. I think I*

*have to learn not to run away from the ones who
love me when bad things happen, but to let them
help me in all of my weakness and despair. Then,
when it's my turn to help them, I'll be ready, able,
and willing!*

*By the way, I've decided to come home at the end
of the month rather than stay on through August. It
would be wonderful if you could find some time to
visit me here before then. The house is beautiful,
there's plenty of room, and I have so much to tell
you—face-to-face. And you just have to meet Old
Mrs. Compton and her sidekick!*

*Many thanks, Caroline, and much love from your
friend, Ellen.*

And then, she pressed Send.

Clovis shifted his bulk so that he rested heavily against
Ellen's thigh. Carefully, she placed her hand on his back.
"I'll miss you," Ellen whispered. Clovis sighed, stuck a claw
in her leg, and went back to sleep.

CHAPTER 23

Ellen woke the next morning to a sky that was burdened with clouds, heavy, low clouds the deadly color of lead and dirty puddle water. The local news stations were predicting a storm of almost freakish intensity. Freakish was Ellen's adjective. Gale force winds, accompanied by hail (hail!), rain, thunder, and lightning. If that wasn't freakish—and frightening!—what was?

Of course, it was a good thing that the rain was finally coming. The farmers would be happy, and maybe the water restrictions would be lifted. That would please the serious gardeners, too. But a storm of the power the meteorologists were predicting could also be a very bad thing. Mother Nature had a tendency to make up for months of her absence and neglect, but she could do it in a perversely nasty fashion.

Ellen drank her coffee and waited. And watched.

By midmorning, the rain had begun in earnest, and it continued loud and unceasing all day.

At noon, the temperature had risen to eighty-eight, and Ellen could feel the humidity seeping past the house's powerful air-conditioning system. Nadia called and told Ellen that she and a few of her friends from the restaurant were driving inland to the house of the restaurant's owner. "Come with us, Ellen," she urged. "It will be safer there, and we will have a good time. There is plenty of room, and we will have a feast."

Ellen thanked Nadia, but refused her kind offer. She couldn't say why, but something, some instinct compelled her to stay put, some sense that she might be needed—but by whom? And how? She was hardly a match for Mother Nature.

"I'll be fine here," she assured Nadia. "But thank you."

"Okay," Nadia said, her tone concerned. "But we will not be leaving for another half an hour, so if you change your mind let me know."

By midafternoon the electricity was flickering on and off, and there were several puddles decorating the recently parched backyard.

By late afternoon it was as dark as night, but without any of a nighttime's clarity and deep color. The electricity had finally died completely. Ellen's T-shirt and jeans stuck uncomfortably to her skin. The candles she had lit against the darkness did little to dispel the sense of doom and gloom she felt pushing against her, bowing her shoulders.

She had been calling Cora since just after lunch and getting no answer. At three o'clock, the line had gone dead. Cora didn't have a cell phone, and Ellen's cell phone battery was running dangerously low.

Ellen had a very bad feeling, and it was about her friend Cora Compton.

She thought of calling the police and asking if someone could check on the older woman, but she knew the police and the fire department would be responding to actual emergencies, not ones that existed in a young woman's fertile imagination.

By four thirty, her phone was completely useless, and Ellen was frantic with worry. She couldn't just sit around and wait for disaster to strike. She had no plan other than to reach Cora's house and be certain that Cora was okay. If the older woman were not okay, well, then she would take charge of the situation and get Cora the help she needed. Somehow.

Ellen blew out the candles, grabbed two flashlights from a drawer in the kitchen, and tossed her rain slicker over her shoulders. Throwing caution to the howling wind, she dashed out to her car.

Driving was a nightmare. The roads were slick and littered with debris—fallen branches, trash cans tossed from front lawns, fractured bicycles and kids' plastic toys. She could barely see the road ahead through the sheets of lashing rain and pelting hailstones. Her hands gripped the wheel until they hurt. She saw only one other vehicle on the road. Correction. In a ditch on the side of the road. The driver was alive and seemed unhurt (he was examining the front tires), and though Ellen considered stopping to pick him up, she drove on. Every moment might count. Cora's very life might be on the line.

After what seemed to be a lifetime, Ellen reached Cora's house. She recognized Miss Camp's tiny car next to Cora's in the drive. And then, she saw that the two women were huddled in the backseat of the black Cadillac.

Looking toward the cottage now, Ellen was dismayed to see that a massive oak tree had fallen across the roof. Beyond the house, in the field that backed it, a fire was moving inexorably toward them.

Ellen leapt from her car and ran over to the Cadillac. Cora and Emily let her inside, and Ellen scooted in as far as she could without sitting on Cora's lap.

"That tree . . . The roof looks like it's going to cave in at any moment!"

"We got out as soon as we could," Cora explained. "But—"

"The fire, it's spreading! Why didn't you drive out of here? Did anyone call the fire department?"

"The Cadillac won't start," Cora explained. "And Emily's car is worthless in conditions like this."

"But the fire department," Ellen insisted.

"Yes," Emily said, her voice rising. "Rob called from his cell phone. It was still working, but barely."

"Rob? Was he here? Where is he now?"

"Inside the house," Cora told her. Her lips were trembling.

"What? Why?"

"We couldn't stop him," Emily assured her. "We tried."

"My God, it's too dangerous. . . . What was he thinking! What's so precious it needs to be rescued at the risk of his own life?" And then, Ellen knew. "Oh, my God, Clovis is inside! That's why he went in . . . Rob! Rob!"

If anything happened to that good, foolish man she would . . . She slammed the car door shut behind her and dashed toward Cora's cottage. There was an ominous creaking and moaning coming from the structure, and Ellen, under ordinary circumstances not one for prayer, sent out a loud and heartfelt plea for Rob's safety.

She was within yards of the front steps when a hailstone smacked into her arm. She continued on. Better a bruise from a hailstone than a roof collapsing on you. How would she rescue Rob if he were trapped under heavy debris by the time she reached him? What if he had been knocked unconscious or was bleeding profusely? What if the fire reached the cottage before help came? What could she do then but—

A terrible sob of fear mingled with relief escaped Ellen's throat when through the cascading curtains of rain she caught sight of a hunched and bedraggled form running awkwardly toward her.

"Oh, Clovis, Clovis, you're all right!" she heard Cora cry, just feet behind her. And then she saw that the form was that of Rob clutching in his arms an enormous black beast.

"Rob!"

Ellen flung herself at Rob and Clovis, forcing the three of them to stumble a few paces together.

"Oh, Rob!" Ellen sobbed. "Clovis . . . He's okay!"

"Yeah." He grinned. "My God, how much does this cat weigh?"

"You're a hero!" Ellen laughed while tears mingled with rain streamed down her face. "Oh, Rob, I do love you! I really do!"

Clovis roared in protest; clearly, he did not relish being squished between two soggy humans. And then Cora was with them, gently removing Clovis claw by claw from Rob's soaked shirt and enfolding him in her massive arms.

Which left Rob and Ellen free to draw even closer into each other's arms.

CHAPTER 24

"I see the Cadillac is running again," Ellen noted, offering a plate of cookies to Cora.

"Oh, yes," Cora said. "Nothing keeps it down for long. I've had it for close to thirty years now, and I expect to have it for another thirty."

A vision of a one hundred (or more)-year-old Cora Compton behind the wheel of the black behemoth flashed through Ellen's imagination. She shuddered.

Cora and Emily were at Ellen's house, as was Rob. It was a few days after the storm had torn through the area, drenching the land and wreaking havoc with buildings and mailboxes and anything not bolted down. The fire that had been spreading across the field behind Cora's house had been contained before it reached the Compton cottage or any of the other homes that backed the field. And the damage done by the tree that had fallen onto Cora's roof had not been as bad as Ellen had feared it might be. Cora and Clovis had spent three nights at Emily's house while repairs were made and then had been able to move back home.

"A raging fire in the rain," Ellen said, shaking her head. "It was the most spectacular and unusual thing I've ever seen—

and I hope never to see it again. It was—otherworldly. The act of an angry entity. I know I'll never forget it."

Rob nodded. "What's amazing is that the damage around town from the storm wasn't too bad. It could have been so much worse. Thank God no one was killed. A woman out on Bainbridge Road lost control of her car and smashed into a tree. A broken leg, a few broken ribs, but otherwise she's okay."

"By the way," Ellen said then to Rob, "I can't believe it hasn't occurred to me to ask this before now. Where did you find Clovis when you went into Cora's house to rescue him?"

Rob grinned. "The big coward was under Cora's bed, backed against the wall. I had a hell of a time extracting him. Witness the scars on my arms and hands! And to think when I first saw the creature I was deathly afraid of him!"

Cora sniffed. "Clovis is most certainly not a coward! It's just that he's never been fond of rainstorms."

Rob looked properly chastened. "Of course. I'm sorry. Well, on another note, we have some big news for you ladies."

Emily chirped, "I just love big news. If it's big good news, of course."

"It's good news," Rob affirmed. "Ellen and I are engaged."

It had happened in Ellen's car on the way back to her house the night of the storm. (Rob's car, parked at the side of Cora's house where Ellen hadn't seen it, wouldn't start, so they had first driven Cora and Emily to Emily's house and then gone on to Rob's.)

"Ellen," Rob had said, wiping rain from his face with the hem of his soaked T-shirt, "I love you. Will you take a chance on me and consent to be my wife?"

"Will you take a chance on me?" Ellen had replied. For an odd reason his proposal had not surprised her. Maybe that was what had kept her from driving to safety with Nadia. . . .

"Yes. But I asked you first."

"Yes," Ellen said, blinking fiercely to clear her eyes of tears and praying she wouldn't drive off the slick road. "Yes, I will."

And that had been that. The kiss that sealed the deal had come once they had safely reached Ellen's house.

Cora now seemed to have been struck speechless. Her mouth hung open, and her eyes were wide. Emily's eyes flooded with tears, and she daintily dabbed at them with a lace handkerchief.

Ellen handed around glasses of champagne. "To good friends," she said, raising her glass.

"To the happy couple," Cora added, having regained her senses. "You see? I was right about you two all along!"

Ellen had the good grace to blush. "Thanks, Cora. For seeing what I couldn't see."

Cora downed her glass of champagne with admirable speed. "And I have just the thing for such a wonderful young couple," she went on. "My neighbor's cat is expecting a litter momentarily, and it has come to my attention that Clovis is in all likelihood the father. I have promised to relieve my neighbor of two of the kittens as soon as they are weaned. One will come to live with me, and the other will go to live with you, dear Ellen and Rob. It is my wedding gift to you both."

"Thank you, Cora," Ellen cried. A son or daughter of King Clovis. She would have to research other names from the Merovingian dynasty. . . .

"Where will you two live?" Cora asked, her expression eager. "We would hate to lose you as neighbors."

Ellen looked to Rob. "Well," she said, "we've been talking about that. Rob owns a place in Portland, which is convenient for his day job. So we're thinking that I should buy a place here in Ogunquit. We can commute together between the two."

Cora beamed. "Excellent."

Emily, her eyes now dry, clapped her little hands; it made a surprisingly sharp sound. "I must get started on your trousseau!" she exclaimed.

Ellen choked a bit on her champagne.

Cora fixed a stern gaze on Ellen. "Have you even begun to think about what you'll wear on your wedding day?"

"A dress?"

Rob sniggered behind his hand.

Cora and her companion shared a look; it said, "Young women these days are simply hopeless." At least, that's what Ellen thought it said.

The women took their leave soon after, Emily murmuring about lacy night clothing and Cora planning the wedding menu. It included her famous cherry tartlets.

"They're incorrigible!" Ellen said, when the big old Cadillac had pulled away.

"They're adorable," Rob said.

"That, too. Let's finish this bottle of champagne. It doesn't get any better if it sits around."

Rob agreed. They took their glasses to the living room and settled together on the couch.

"You know," Ellen said, "just the other day my mother admitted she's always wondered if she and my father made a mistake by sending me away to camp that summer he was sick. But I've been thinking that if they hadn't sent me away, I would never have met you. . . ."

"And suffered for it," Rob pointed out.

"Well, for a while, though I know now that you weren't the real source of my anxiety! But, I don't know, somehow it seems like Fate had a hand in bringing us together back then and now, this summer."

Rob shrugged. "I've never been a big believer in Fate but sure, why not? We'll certainly have a story to tell at parties."

"I'll say!"

"Do you think your parents will accept me?" Rob asked then. "I mean, given how awful I was to you as a kid. Parents can be pretty protective—or so I hear."

"They'll accept you," Ellen assured him. "As long as you don't call me Smelly Nellie."

"No chance of that! I don't know why I came up with that name in the first place. You didn't smell at all. Well, maybe of sunshine and flowers . . ."

Ellen smiled. "What about your parents? Will they accept me, do you think?"

"Will they even notice you is more like it."

"Now, Rob, are you sure you're not being just a little bit unfair?"

"Well, maybe a little. We'll go to see them soon, okay? Maybe we'll be pleasantly surprised."

"I hope so, too."

"You know," Rob said. "I was thinking. It might make you feel better about that infamous summer of long ago if you make up a nasty nickname for me."

"Oh, I already have."

Rob's expression stiffened, but just a bit. "Oh," he said warily. "What is it?"

Ellen laughed. "I'm not going to tell you. It's my own little secret."

"But nasty nicknames aren't worth anything unless the person being persecuted knows he's being persecuted. Not that I condone any of this." Rob leaned over and kissed his fiancée. "But come on," he said. "I deserve the punishment. Consider it payback."

"Well," Ellen said then. "Okay. Ready?"

"As I'll ever be."

"Slobby Bobby."

Rob tried to hide a smile. "Okay."

Ellen frowned. "You don't seem very upset."

"Well, it could be a lot worse," Rob pointed out. "I am kind of a slob at times."

"I'm sure if I try again I could come up with something much more hurtful and—"

"No, no, that's okay. I'll just be Slobby Bobby."

"You'll just be my Slobby Bobby."

"It's a deal. Yup, we'll have a fantastic story to tell not only at parties but to our children someday," Rob noted. "How you and I met as kids and hated each other, and then how we met again as adults and—"

Ellen put up a hand. "Children? That's kind of leaping ahead, no? I mean, we just got engaged. We haven't even picked a wedding date."

"Yeah," Rob said. "It is leaping ahead. But we're not getting any younger and—"

"And, carpe diem."

Rob grinned. "What say we get started on that family right now?"

RETURN TO
HAMPTON BEACH

MARY CARTER

This book is dedicated to April Rain Carter.
Like memories of perfect summer days,
you will be cherished and loved.
May your beautiful spirit soar.

Acknowledgments

Thank you to the usual suspects: my editor, John Scognamiglio; my agent, Evan Marshall; and the staff at Kensington who work tirelessly on covers, and publicity, and editing. Thank you to my parents, Carl Carter and Pat Carter, who took my sister and me on that calamity-filled vacation that finally had a happy ending in Hampton Beach.

CHAPTER 1

Most people think of genies as living in green glass bottles. Shapely, colorful things that beg to be rubbed. They imagine magical men and women in silky pantaloons emerging from the top in a puff of smoke, ready to grant one lucky so-and-so three whole wishes with a bob of his or her head. What would you wish for? It's a fantasy people play, just like spending imaginary lottery winnings.

But sometimes, magic is a little softer, a little subtler. Sometimes, genies emerge from tin coffee cans. And sometimes wishes can be granted that one didn't even dare to wish. Longings a person buried long ago, like a dog with a bone. Why torture yourself with things you think can never be? Celia Jensen had stopped wishing a long time ago. Why wish for anything when there was a long list of people ahead of her who deserved to be taken care of first? Not that she didn't know what she would wish for if it were her turn. *Jacob Have I Loved.* . . .

But at the very top of that list was her father, Pete Jensen. And from the look of things, her fervent wish for him was going unheard.

She pulled up to the assisted living complex, parked in

her usual spot far away from the door, and turned off the engine. On the passenger seat was the gym bag filled with things she had promised to bring her dad. She shouldered it and began the long walk to the gardens. Parking far away always helped her prepare for the visit. Despite the fact it was the best assisted living facility money could buy, Pete Jensen just wasn't cut out for an assisted life. Like it or not, he was a fixer, a Marlboro Man, a wanderer. Idle hands always made him brood. They both knew that Celia was the only reason he was hanging on. He could care less about bingo, or karaoke, or movie nights in the lobby. A familiar lump formed in her throat. It wasn't fair. He was only sixty-seven. In regular years. But in cigarette years he was way into his hundreds. He didn't complain. *I did the crime; I'll do the time*. At least the sun was out and they could sit on the grounds, facing away from the facilities, and make believe they were somewhere else for an hour. Relief flooded her as she spotted his wheelchair, his baseball cap, his tanned arms. Then her eyes moved to the oxygen tank, and she bit her lip as hard as she could. The one thing that was guaranteed to ruin a visit was tears.

Celia wheeled her father down the path, looking for a cool patch near the goldfish pond.

"Only May," her father mused. "You're going to have a hot summer."

"So are you," Celia said lightly, punching him on the shoulder. She found the perfect spot, a little grassy square of shade just a few feet from the pond. She set the brake on his wheelchair, then laid out a blanket for herself.

"How's work?" he asked in between breaths.

It would be just downright selfish of her to tell her father that she hated her job. That lately, every time she stepped into the office building, she was hit with the strangest feeling. It was as if she were being slowly strangled. Spending all day at a desk, in front of a computer, underneath a bank of fluorescent lights. She made a lot of money investing other people's money, but what was that worth when she spent most of her time at the office? She felt a little bit trapped, okay a lot trapped, in almost every aspect of her life. It was a far cry from the life she used to dream of having.

All through her teens she had been convinced she would be a beach girl forever. Boardwalks, bare feet, BBQs, and Jacob Vernon. Nothing made her happier, and she never imagined she would have to give any of them up. Especially Jacob. She knew for sure she would love him forever. And so far she had. She just didn't get to keep him forever.

Wow. If anyone knew she was still secretly hung up on her very first love, she'd be assigned a small team of head-shrinkers. She'd been thinking about Jacob and Hampton Beach a lot lately. Death's approach had a way of making her take a close look at her life. And Celia hated what she saw. Who she'd become. In a way, she'd been so passive. As if she'd been waiting, just waiting for someone to come up to her, pull her out of her work chair, and say—"What the heck are you doing? This isn't you. Get out of that suit, put on your swimsuit, and stop all this nonsense." Of course, no-body did. She was the one who needed to take charge. But there were too many people depending on her income. Her father had taken care of her when it counted, and she was more than happy to return the favor. Nothing was more important, absolutely nothing. And she certainly wasn't going to burden him with any of it. "It's fine. Busy as usual."

"Busy, huh? I suppose it would be. All those rich twats expect you to be at their beck and call."

"Dad." Celia looked around, relieved to see that the only other resident in earshot was Todd Buckley, and he was fast asleep in a lawn chair, head thrown back, mouth open, snore rumbling across the lawn. Pete lifted his arm, and Celia realized what he was doing too late. The acorn her father tried to toss into Todd's mouth plunked Todd on the nose and then fell to the grass.

"Missed."

"Dad. He could've choked."

"That's why I missed. Twat!" Pete yelled at the snoring man. Celia looked around again. Assistants were planted at various locations on the grounds, and Pete Jensen had been repeatedly warned about using the word *twat*. It had only started after the doctor upped his medication, although the side effect was hardly listed on the bottle.

"I'm not even remotely thinking of the female anatomy— I just like the word."

"Other people find it very offensive."

"I can't walk. I can hardly breathe. I'm dying. No twat around here is going to stop me from using the word *twat!*"

"They can kick you out."

"Good." Pete started to cough. They both knew there was nowhere else for him to go. To Celia's relief, he didn't want to live with her. For him, it was a matter of pride. He'd taken care of his little girl his whole life. He didn't want her to bathe him, feed him, remember him this way, and frankly, she didn't either. But she was willing to spend top dollar so he could make the best of the worst situation. And, because of investment banking, like it or not, she was technically one of the rich that her father liked to ridicule. "How's your mother?"

Drinking again. After ten years of abstinence. But by now her mother's troubles were nobody's problem but her own. Sometimes Celia got the feeling her father had never stopped loving her mother. It was a mystery to her. "I guess she's fine."

"You guess?"

"You know how she is. She's the same."

"Is she going to her meetings?"

"I don't ask." That was true, too.

"How's Ben?"

"You hate Ben."

"But you don't. Right?"

Ben. Attractive. Dependable. A fellow investment banker. He wanted a family. He wanted her. What was there to hate? It wasn't his fault he didn't send a zap of electricity running through her when their eyes met. It was childish to expect it. "Of course I don't."

"So if you like him, then I'm going to ask about him."

"He's—"

"Fine," her father finished for her. "You think you're fooling me?"

"What do you mean?"

"You're not happy."

"Happiness is overrated."

"You used to be happy."

"So did you." Hampton Beach. She'd give anything to have one of those good old days back. Before everything hit the fan, of course. Celia reached up and grasped the handrail of her father's chair. "I'm sorry. But some days I don't want to talk about work, or Mom, or Ben. I just want to be with you." Her father reached his hand over the side of the chair, and Celia grasped it. "How are you feeling?"

"Peachy. You bring what I asked?"

"I did." Celia unzipped the bag and removed a large pair of red flippers. "Why in the world did you want these?"

Pete grinned. "Stick 'em on my feet, would you?"

Celia knelt before him. "Socks on or off?"

"Off. I want to feel them on my toes." Her father had been a scuba diver in his day. He and these flippers had plunged a lot of depths. Celia slipped the socks off, ignoring the sight of her father's toenails—she'd have to ask the staff to clip them—and slid the flippers on his feet. He smiled. It was the first time he'd ever asked her for such a thing, and it was worrisome. He looked at the bag and nodded. Celia removed the coffee can. He took it, saw the brand, then threw his head back and roared with laughter. Celia tried to remain composed, but ended up laughing with him. He opened the lid.

"It's empty," Celia said. "Like you asked."

"I know." He stuck his face in it and inhaled. "I can still smell it though. Isn't that something? To smell something that strongly long after it's gone."

"Never really thought about it."

"You'll probably still smell me long after I'm gone."

"Dad."

He put the lid back on and placed the can on his lap. Celia took the last two items out of the duffel bag. A red crayon and a paper bag. Despite her best efforts, tears began to well in her eyes as she handed them to him.

"Sassafras."

"I know what you want with these. I remember."

"Noggin like a steel trap," her dad said, treating her to a proud wink. *When I die, I'm going to write my Last Will and Testament on a paper bag, and I want my ashes to go in a coffee can.*

Maxwell House or Folgers? Celia used to say without missing a beat.

Surprise me. As long as it's caffeinated.

As if having the same memory, he held up the coffee can again, and the chuckling started all over. "It's perfect," he rasped.

Chock Full O'Nuts

The cough shook him for a long time. When he settled down, tears were in his eyes too, although more than likely from the coughing fit. "I only have one regret," he said, taking her hand.

"Smoking?"

"Two regrets."

"I don't want you to have any."

Her father sat straighter. "Exactly," he said, slamming both hands onto his thighs. "And I don't want *you* to have any either. But only one of us can do something about it now."

"Dad." He was dropping too many hints that he thought the end was near. It was getting harder and harder to hold back tears.

"We should've stayed, Sassafras. But I didn't want any of it to hurt you."

"You mean you didn't want *her* to hurt me," Celia said. Just the thought of that woman, and Celia's blood pressure began to rise. Elizabeth Tanner. The Wicked Witch of the Boardwalk.

"Now, now. I'm not carrying grudges. I'm just telling you that I'm sorry if you thought your old man was a coward for turning tail."

Celia grabbed her father's hands. "You're the bravest man I know." It was true too. Nobody would have ever thought Pete Jensen was cut out to be a father, let alone a single one. He had literally kept her together all those years when her mother fell into a bottle. If it weren't for having a little girl, Pete Jensen would've taken off to scuba dive around the world. Celia knew this beyond a doubt. She used to find magazine articles tucked away in the RV. Gorgeous, underwater photographs of coral, and brightly colored fish, and fascinating sea creatures. Far-off tropical islands. Places he could've gone. Places he would've gone if he didn't have children. Instead, he moved to New Hampshire and gave her the beach, and the boardwalk, and sand between her toes. Those summers with him were the only thing that got her through the winters with her mother. "My only regret is that you didn't kick Mrs. Tanner to the curb on our way out."

"I bet she'll outlive us all," Pete said with a chuckle.

"I don't know how you can laugh about it. She's evil personified."

"Karma, darling. I believe in karma."

"I don't. She's probably still harassing all the men of Hampton Beach."

"She was a cougar, all right." Pete chuckled again. He was probably imagining the thirtysomething divorcée in her bikini. Tanned to the hilt. Blond hair piled on top of her head. Hitting on every male with a pulse. Pete Jensen's true crime? Rejecting her.

"Sometimes you think you're doing the right thing," Pete said. "But you don't know. You don't know, Sassafras."

"You did everything right, Dad. Everything."

"Did I?"

"Those people didn't give you a choice."

"Oh, I don't know about that. I think that's exactly what they gave me."

"I don't want you to be upset about anything. Do you hear me? You are a good man. You gave me a great life."

"Thank you. That's all I ever tried to do. Even though I made a lot of mistakes, that's all I was trying to do."

"I know that. And I'm so grateful."

"I want you to do something for me."

"Anything."

"I can't go back now," Pete said. "But you can."

Celia put her hand on his shoulder. "Without you?" she said. "Not a chance."

"We should've stayed. I should've turned the RV around."

"They made it impossible for us to stay."

"But maybe if we had—you would be happier right now. Not always doing the safe thing."

"You mean my job? Ben?"

"Yes. I mean your job. Ben. All of it. You know the last time I saw you happy? Really happy?"

"Dad—"

"With that Jacob boy."

It was the first time her dad had ever brought him up. Celia's heartstrings danced at the mention of him. Why, after all this time did she still react this way? *You never forget your first love.* How true. She wished she could. His body materialized before her. Tall, and muscular, and tan. Wavy dark hair and green eyes. Beautiful, beautiful man. His intense, quiet nature. Jacob had such a sensitive side. One he had to hide from his twin or risk being mercilessly ridiculed. Still, he stood up to his brother. Despite Chris's out-and-out campaign to tear them apart, Jacob had continued to love her. Twenty years later and there were still some memories she dusted off and let shine. Snapshots in time. The simple things.

Jacob squinting at her in the sunlight. Wrapping his arms around her. Crushing his mouth over hers after years of shyness. God, he was such a good kisser. The best she'd ever had. How sad was that? Holding her hand at the top of the Ferris wheel. *Jacob Have I Loved.* "That was a long time ago. I was just a kid."

"You were a young woman. And that boy was so in love with you he couldn't see straight. I thought for sure you'd put up a fight when I said we were leaving. And there was something else I should have—"

"Dad. Stop. We didn't have a choice." She could tell he was getting way too worked up. She put her hand over her father's.

He nodded, paused for a while to catch his breath, then spoke again. "I half expected him to chase the RV down on our way out of town."

So did she. She was truly stunned when Jacob didn't come after her. Chris must have told him they were leaving. "Well, he didn't now. Did he?"

"That's my true regret. What if because of me—you missed out on the love of your life?"

"He was my first love." That was the truth. No matter what really happened on the beach that night, Jacob was the one she loved. "Doesn't mean he was the love of my life."

"You look me in the eye and say that." Celia looked at her

father, then looked away. "That's what I thought," Pete said. "That's what I thought."

She had loved him, fiercely. But it wasn't her father's fault it didn't work out. If he knew what had really happened, he'd pop out of his wheelchair and hike to Hampton Beach just to kick a couple of twin asses. Celia let herself indulge in the fantasy for a moment, then tried to calm herself in the ripples of the pond. "It's not like you ever ended up with a great love, either," she said quietly.

"You were my great love, Sassafras." This time Celia didn't even try and stop the tears. When she was a teenager and would cry, her father had been totally out of his depths. He usually just bought her ice cream. This time, Pete Jensen placed his hand on her knee. "I just want you to be happy."

"Life promises the pursuit, Dad. Not the result."

They watched the goldfish dart back and forth in the pond, gazed out at the gardens, chatted about the weather. Thirty minutes later Celia wheeled him back like she'd been doing every day for the past year. She kissed him, and hugged him, just like normal. But as she started to leave, his hand darted out and grabbed hers. She stood, once again, fighting back the tears with every ounce of her being.

"I'm so proud of you. You know that, kiddo, right?"

"I know." This time it was her voice that was a mere rasp.

"I'm sorry you basically grew up without a mother."

This was the first time he'd ever admitted this, and Celia felt the lump in her throat grow. "I didn't need one. I had you."

"No. I loved you like daylight, but you turned out so good because you're special. So special even your mother and I couldn't mess you up."

"I was always proud to have you as my dad."

"I didn't take that ring, Sassy."

Celia knelt before her father and stared at him until he looked at her. For a split second she saw a little boy looking out of the eyes of a man. She'd never realized how deeply the accusation had hurt him. He always seemed so tough. At that moment, she hated Elizabeth Tanner with an all-consuming rage. "I never thought for a single second that you took that ring. Not. One. Single. Second."

An image of the ring rose to mind. A two-carat princess-cut diamond. It belonged to Chris and Jacob. Left to them by the mother they couldn't remember. The twins were only one and a half years old when Angela Vernon walked out of their beach cottage with a yellow gym bag over her shoulder and never came back. She told her husband she was going out to get the boys mac and cheese. Harry Vernon spent years kicking himself for not realizing the twins were too young to eat mac and cheese, not to mention who goes to the grocery store with a yellow gym bag? As if knowing those things, he could have stopped her. Supposedly she'd left the ring on the kitchen table with a note: *Give to the boys when they're older.* That was it. Not, *I'm sorry.* Or—*Tell them it's not their fault,* or *I will always love them.*

As if all two little boys needed was a princess-cut diamond ring in place of their mother. How could she have been so cruel and selfish?

Celia had felt a fierce bond with Chris and Jacob over their mother troubles. After all, she had a few of her own. Celia was the one person who truly understood how much that ring meant to them. A little piece of their mother. And she knew their secret thoughts. Who would leave something so valuable unless she were planning on coming back?

The day the ring went missing, Pete Jensen had stopped by the Vernon cottage to pick up some tools. Elizabeth Tanner had swooped in like a predatory hawk and accused Pete of stealing the ring. She had formed an impromptu Neighborhood Watch group, and by the time she was done, Pete Jensen was history. Nobody wanted to hire a handyman suspected of stealing diamonds from motherless twins.

Jacob Have I Loved. . . .

After five years of trying to fit in, Pete Jensen and his

daughter Celia had left town in the dead of night, the same way they'd come in. Sometimes, when she closed her eyes at night, Celia could still hear the crunch of the gravel under the wheels as they pulled out of the mobile home park, and she could feel the cool glass on her palms, which were planted squarely on the rear window, as she stared at Jacob's cottage, silently pleading with him to come running after them.

Then again, soon after they left and landed in Boston, Pete Jensen had gotten a job with a signing bonus that paid for the first year of Celia's college. Maybe, on some level, some things were just meant to be. No matter what or who you had to leave behind.

Her father was overtaken by another coughing fit. They were getting worse.

"Do you want me to stay? I can call in sick." A clawing panic hit Celia. She had an overwhelming desire to turn back time, even for a day, just so she could have her strong, invincible father back. She used to hide his cigarettes, smash them, flush them. If only it had made a difference.

Her father let go of her hand. "Don't be silly. There's a new nurse on the dinner shift. She's hot." Celia laughed, shook her head, and bent down to plant a final kiss on his cheek.

"Hot to twat," she whispered. The last thing she heard, as she headed back to the car, was her father's laughter echoing through the sunbeams.

CHAPTER 2

Celia and Ben sat behind an enormous oak desk, across from Landon Biggs, her father's estate planner. Celia wished there was a nice way to tell Ben to go away. He wouldn't stop fidgeting. Landon was struggling to decipher her father's last wishes scrawled on the paper bag in red crayon.

"Being of sound mind but not body, this is my Last Will and Testament," Landon said slowly. Celia suppressed a little smile, even though there was nothing sadder than her father's athletic body giving out on him. He had a sense of humor about it nonetheless. She wondered why he had bothered writing a will. Besides his red scuba flippers, which were on top of Landon's desk, her father owned very little. *What are you up to, Dad?* Ben couldn't stop staring at the coffee can, absolutely horrified that it was filled with her father's ashes. Unlike Celia, Ben had grown up with money. And apparently, people with money were appalled by such things.

"I hereby leave my daughter one final piece of advice and one request." Landon Biggs cleared his throat, then peered at Celia overtop reading glasses. "Maybe you'd like to be alone for this?"

And how.

"Of course not," Ben said. He grabbed Celia's hand and squeezed. His grip was painful.

"First, the advice. Dump Ben." Landon stopped again, stared at Ben. "Sorry, Ben."

Ben let go of her hand, crossed his arms over his chest. "It's not your fault Mr. Biggs," he said. "No need to apologize."

"I'm not," Landon said. He turned the paper bag around and pointed. Celia and Ben leaned in. Landon's finger was just under the words **SORRY, BEN.**

Celia burst out laughing. Ben stared at her, hurt stamped on his face. "I'm sorry, I'm sorry," Celia said. "It's just so Dad."

Ben shook his head, glanced at Celia. "I told you he never liked me."

"Please continue," Celia said.

Landon leaned close to the bag, then sat up and put his hand on his heart. He looked up at Celia as if she were a camera and he was an actor in a film. "It's never too late to reconnect with your true love."

"Reconnect?" Ben said. "What does that mean? Reconnect with who?"

"I believe it's 'with whom,' " Landon Biggs said.

"Gentlemen," Celia said. "Focus."

"Open the coffee can," Landon said. He glanced at Ben.

"What?" Ben said. "No."

Landon turned the paper bag around. Celia and Ben leaned forward. **OPEN THE COFFEE CAN** was written in red capital letters. Celia reached for the can. "Here?" Ben said. "Now?" He scooted his chair back, as if he were afraid that the ashes were going to explode the minute she opened them. Then again, knowing Pete Jensen, they might.

Celia lifted the lid. Sticking out of the ashes was a white card, like the kind that accompanied bouquets of flowers.

She took it out and held it up. Instead of red crayon, this card had its message typed on it in old-fashioned typewriter script.

RETURN TO HAMPTON BEACH

Celia stuffed the card back in and slammed the lid back on. "What?" Ben said. "What's in there?"

"Amityville Horror in a can," Celia said. Ben's mouth dropped open. His eyes widened. Oh, she knew it wasn't nice to tease him like that, but sometimes he made it just too darn easy. Or she had more of her father in her than she liked to admit. "Just kidding." She opened the can again, and once more took out the card.

RETURN TO HAMPTON BEACH

Something was written under it in small letters.

Take me with you.

Tears sprang to her eyes. Conflicting emotions crashed over her. Would she actually do it? Could she? *Jacob Have I Loved.* . . .

"Celia. You're scaring me." And Ben did look scared. He looked like a scared, uptight investment banker. And he was still waiting for an explanation.

"He wants me to take his ashes to Hampton Beach."

"Nice," Landon Biggs said. He was wearing a gray suit, a sky-blue shirt, and a pink tie. Topped off with his shiny bald head, he looked like a giant Easter egg. "Never been, but I'm just figuring it must be nice," he added. He drummed his fingers on the desk. "Where is Hampton Beach?"

"New Hampshire," Celia and Ben said at the same time. Landon held his index finger up as if making a proclamation. "That makes a lot of sense," he said. "Listen. I hate to rush you, but that's really all there is to his estate. Nice flippers though. Do you dive?" He put his hands in the flippers and walked them up his desk. Celia just stared at him. She found this an effective way to deal with most people. If she stared long enough without saying anything, they usually took the hint and stopped talking. In this case, it didn't work. Landon kept talking. "I don't dive. I'm phobic. Seen *Jaws* way too many times, you know?"

Celia continued to stare, but Ben nodded. Celia wondered if he was being polite or if he too had seen *Jaws* too many times. She had watched it several times with Jacob. They had loved it. Sometimes he'd grab her ankle in the ocean, scaring her to death. Then he'd pop up laughing, singing the warning tune. This was how it always went. Everything always reminded her of Jacob. It was torture. Landon was still talking.

"My wife likes the water. Mostly she just tans. But she pretends to like the water. No public pools though. On account of all the pee. Or hot tubs. Saw a TV special once where this gal got her hair caught in the drain. Luscious, curly blond hair." Landon held his hands near his head and mimed his vision of luscious, curly blond hair. "She must have been leaning back." He leaned his head back. "Just a tip is all it took; the drain grabbed hold." He gyrated his hands and made a horrific sucking sound.

"Jesus," Ben said.

Landon nodded. Righted himself. Straightened his jacket. "Not a pretty sight. Ever since she won't so much as dip a big toe in a hot tub. More room for me. Am I right?"

Celia was actually grateful for his verbal diarrhea; it made Ben seem a little less annoying.

"I thought you guys hated Hampton Beach," Ben said, turning to her.

"Hated Hampton Beach?" Celia said. "They were the best years of my life." And the worst.

"I thought your father was accused of stealing or something."

"He was." Humiliated. Accused. Harassed. She could hear Elizabeth Tanner, so clear it was as if she and her shrill, bleached-blond voice were standing right behind Celia. *Pete Jensen was in the house. He's the only one who had keys. . . . He's desperate to send his daughter to college. Jimmy Cluger saw him coming out of the pawnshop. Of course he wouldn't be stupid enough to sell it in town, but it shows what state of mind he was in—getting an idea of what things are worth. Those poor motherless twins. Can you imagine his hands inside your jewelry box?*

It was exactly because Pete wouldn't put his hands in her "jewelry box" that Elizabeth had so maligned him. If there were any reason to return to Hampton Beach, it was to give her the ass kicking she should have gotten a long time ago.

"So why would he want his ashes spread there?" Ben said.

For me. He wants me to find Jacob. "I don't know."

Ben spread his hands and put them in front of the coffee can like a director framing a shot. "We can get him a plot, Celia. With a proper headstone. You can visit." Ben looked to Landon for approval. Landon bobbed his head up and down. Celia wasn't sure if he was giving in or dancing to Bob Marley in his head. "What will people think?" Ben said in a loud whisper, pointing to the can.

"I don't care what people think. I care what *he* thinks." Celia hugged the coffee can to her chest.

He thinks you should go back.

"But he wasn't in his right mind, was he? Deprived of oxygen, the brain can—"

"Could you please be quiet? Just for a minute?" Ben wanted to be helpful; he really did. But it just wasn't the kind of help Celia needed. Because he didn't know her like her father did. It hit her, as she sat clutching the coffee can, listening to Ben plead with her to be practical. Normal. She had chosen Ben because deep down she felt he would never hurt her. Never rip her heart out like Jacob did. What a fool she'd been. Ben wasn't the guy for her. Her father had known it. He had also known she wanted to go back. *Needed to go back.* But wasn't it too late? What were the chances the twins were still there?

Pretty good actually. Their father owned property on the boardwalk. They would have inherited it. There was a pretty good chance they were still there. And sometimes a chance was enough. A chance was more than some people would ever get.

"Are we done here?" Landon said. "Or would you like something? Tea? Coffee?" Horrified, he glanced at the can. Celia laughed.

"Jesus," Ben said.

"Ben." Celia faced him. She tried to smile. "Please go back to work."

"Sweetheart."

Celia stood, clutching the can. "I need to be alone. I need to think."

"We drove here together."

"I'll walk." Celia stood and headed for the door.

"Don't forget these." Landon Biggs waved her father's flippers in the air. Celia went back, retrieved them, and walked past Ben once more.

"I'll drop you somewhere," Ben said.

"Please. Just give me some air. I can't breathe."

"Come on. Cel. Isn't there anything I can do?"

Celia stopped, then planted the flippers in the middle of Ben's chest. "Can you look after these?"

Ben held them out by the tips of his fingers, as if dangling a dead rat. "Sure." He made it sound like the word had twelve syllables.

"Thank you."

"Are you sure I can't—"

"Thank you."

* * *

She went to her father's favorite dive bar. At least his favorite when he could still walk, and breathe, and drink. She set the coffee can on the bar and ordered two Miller Genuine Drafts. His favorite, next to a good scotch. The bartender was young, which meant he was new. She wished Jack were here. He had been one of her dad's buddies—if you could count bartenders as buddies.

"Jack still here?" she asked when the new bartender plunked the two bottles down.

"Nah. Retired last year."

"Oh."

"Would you like glasses?"

"So I can see you better?"

"Huh?"

"Never mind. No glasses."

"Oh. I get it."

She slid one of the beers next to the coffee can. The bartender just stood and watched her. She clinked the first bottle with the second bottle and drank.

"You expecting someone?" the bartender asked.

"He's in the can," Celia said. The bartender looked toward the bathroom and nodded. Celia couldn't help but giggle. Her dad would've liked that.

Hampton Beach. Elizabeth Tanner. Chris. Jacob. Whoever said time healed all wounds was an idiot. She touched the coffee can. "Okay," she whispered. "I'll go. I don't know what good you think it will do. But I'll go."

"Pardon?" the bartender said.

"I'll have another," Celia said.

"Do you think your friend is okay?" the bartender said.

"I think he's in a better place," Celia said.

The bartender glanced at the bathrooms. "Then I'm guessing you've yet to make the sojourn."

* * *

Celia threw her suitcase on the bed, opened it, and just stared into it. What to bring. If she were a teenager again, the answer would have been simple. Bikini and one of her dad's extra-long shirts for a cover-up. Never did wear much more than that. Maybe some jean shorts and tank tops. Of course the winters would have been a different story. But she spent those back in North Dakota with her aunt Carla, who had happened to be living with them before her mom disappeared into the bottle. So all her memories of Hampton Beach were summer ones.

Her swim bottoms were shorts now, and her tops more modest. She'd always had curves. "Hello, Marilyn," Ben had said the first time he saw her naked. How could she not stick with a guy who compared her to Marilyn Monroe? He was attractive in his own way. Not gorgeous like Chris and Jacob—but very few men were that sexy. In their prime the Vernon twins had been sex on a stick. The minute they had hit puberty and started doing odd jobs, every female's sink within a fifteen-mile radius mysteriously clogged. Ben never had that kind of animal magnetism and never would. But he had other qualities. He was loyal. Dependable. Practical. Sweet most times. There just wasn't any chemistry. No sweaty palms, or heart tripping in her chest, no adrenaline rush at the thought of seeing him. Celia had only had that once.

It wasn't fair. Like being given the most delicious dessert you would ever taste in your entire life, but unbeknownst to you, you would never get to taste it again. Why couldn't someone have said: "Savor this as much as humanly possible because everything else is going to pale in comparison." Not that it would stop her from craving it.

"Do you need some help?" She hadn't known Ben was home, let alone in the room. So when he spoke, she shrieked. Ben laughed. Celia whirled around.

"It's not funny."

"Sorry. I thought you knew I was here."

"How? How would I know?"

"My car is parked out front, for one."

"I haven't been paying attention."

"I can see that." Ben sat on the edge of the bed. "I want to come with you."

"I appreciate that. But—"

"There's no *but,* Celia. Look. The last thing I want to do is start an argument."

"Then don't."

"I'm the man in your life. You're supposed to want me at times like this." The thought of Ben's coming back with her to Hampton Beach was unimaginable. "Celia?"

"I have to do this alone."

"No. You don't. That's what I'm trying to tell you. Are you saying you want to do this alone?"

"Yes. That's what I'm saying."

"Why?"

"I can't explain."

"Try."

"I have people to confront. From the past. And I have to do it alone."

"You think those people will still be there? How long has it been?"

"Twenty years."

"Who are you going to confront? Some eighty-year-old woman?"

"If you're talking about Mrs. Tanner—she was in her thirties then. Only in her fifties now."

"Is she the lady who accused your dad of stealing her diamond ring?"

"It wasn't hers, but yes."

"It wasn't hers?"

"Nope."

"But she's the one who riled everyone up?"

"Exactly."

"So you think—what? He wants you to fight his battles now that he's dead?"

"Of course not. He wants me to go back to the last place he saw me really happy."

"He was sick. He was on so much medication. He was—"

"He was right."

"Excuse me?"

"I haven't been happy. Not in a long, long, time."

Ben sat on the bed. "Wow. And I suppose that's my fault?"

"Not at all. It's mine. All mine."

"And going back to Hampton Beach is going to make you happy?"

"It's a start."

"How much do you want to bet she's not there?" Ben asked.

"You've no idea how much property her family owned. I bet he's still there."

"You mean *she*."

"What?"

"You said 'I bet *he's* still there.' "

"Oh. Of course. I meant 'she.' "

"Are you sure that wasn't some kind of Freudian slip? Does this have something to do with your father's cryptic message about 'reconnecting with true love'?"

Celia threw her arms out. "You got me. I was really referring to my teenage summer love. I mean most people get over it by the start of school in the fall. But not me. I'm still pining for Jacob Vernon and his hot body twenty years later!" She buried her head in her top dresser drawer like it was a paper bag and she was hyperventilating.

"I'm coming and that's that." Ben marched over to the closet and pulled out his suitcase. Unlike her, he immediately began throwing clothes into it. Celia crossed her arms and just watched him.

"Work isn't going to let us both go," she said. Ben folded a starched shirt into the suitcase. Did he even own T-shirts? Shorts? Flip-flops?

"Hell, Celia." He abandoned the suitcase. "We've been talking about going to Europe. Getting married."

"I know." Her father had saved her. Saved both of them. No matter what happened in Hampton Beach, she'd finally opened her eyes.

"Do you love me?" But that didn't mean that she wanted to hurt Ben. She hesitated, and it was enough. Ben ran his hands through his hair. "Oh my God." He started to pace their small bedroom. "We bought a condo together. Do you know what a commitment that is? In this market?"

"Ben. Ben. I'm very fond of you." She knew the minute she said it, it was a horrible thing to say, but she also knew it was the truth.

"Fond of me? Fond of me? Jesus Christ."

"I can't deal with this right now," Celia said. She went back to packing. A couple pairs of jeans, underwear and bras, T-shirts, and two nice dresses. How long would she be gone? She had no idea. She picked up speed, throwing whatever looked good into her case.

Ben was still pacing the room. He stopped. Tried to communicate in gestures and half-phrases. "Are you. Did you. Did we. Was that a breakup?"

"I'm sorry, Ben. I can't give you any answers." He came up, took a silk blouse out of her hands, and whirled her around to face him.

"You're very fond of me. You don't think that was an answer?"

"I didn't mean to. I wanted to love you."

"Gee, thanks."

"I mean it. I figured that 'in love' feeling was for kids. That with adults, you had to be more rational about it."

"I wasn't rational about you. I was crazy about you."

"I'm sorry, Ben."

"You don't look sorry. You looked flushed."

Flushed? Because she was thinking about Jacob. All these years and he still turned her insides into gurgling lava.

"Oh my God. This *is* about some boy, isn't it? Some childhood crush?" Celia just stared at Ben. He lifted his finger and actually shook it at her. She wanted to bite it off. "You are really, really losing it."

"First of all—it wasn't just a childhood crush—" She stopped short of telling the story of how she lost her virginity on Hampton Beach. To one of the Vernon twins. If only she knew for sure which one. Yes, best keep that story under lock and key. "What do you want from me?"

"I want you to be crazy in love with me."

"I wanted that too."

"But you're not."

"Do you want me to lie?"

"Like you've obviously been doing for the past seven years? No, thanks." Ben headed for the door. He stopped at the threshold, but kept his back to her. "I'm sorry about your father. But think long and hard about this, Celia. I don't give second chances. And ninety-nine percent of the time? Neither does life."

CHAPTER 3

Celia stood on the boardwalk, breathing in the salt air mixed with coconut suntan lotion, feeling the sun kiss her shoulders, and listening to the waves crash on the shore. It was music to the senses. An orchestra of memory. It was all still here. The arcade hall. The ice-cream shop. The giant greasy burgers with fries, the shops selling beach towels and shells and surfboards. Although as kids they had never needed a board; body surfing was the sport. It was how the twins first saw her breasts. Chris got a glimpse of the left one when a wave took her bikini top down, and Jacob saw the right one the day after when Celia pulled her top down and pretended a wave took it down.

It was comforting to see that with the exception of a few new shops, and eateries, the boardwalk remained the same. Celia purposefully avoided walking right past the arcade, given what she'd found out about the new owners. A quick Internet search was all it had taken to learn that Chris and Jacob did indeed live in Hampton Beach still. She could see the sign above the arcade from here. **TWIN-CADES**.

Chris and Jacob owned the joint now.

Chris was married with three kids. Jacob, from what she

could tell, was not. Unfortunately, no pictures of them; she was dying to know if they were still the type of men who turned heads. She'd find out, but it wasn't going to be just after arriving, squinting in the sun. It was strange to be back. As Celia checked into the motel, she wondered whatever became of the mobile home park where she had lived with her father. Elizabeth Tanner had owned the mobile park back then. But Celia wasn't going to think about Elizabeth right now. First, she was just going to relax and relive the good memories. Which is why she had splurged on the best motel on the boardwalk. Her room had a view of the ocean. She threw her suitcase on the bed and stepped onto the balcony with the Chock Full O'Nuts can.

Hold your head up high. Her father used to say that all the time. Usually after she cried and he bought her ice cream. She set the coffee can on a little table situated between two chairs. She would eventually have to spread his ashes in the ocean as he'd always requested, but for now just carrying the coffee can around made her feel like her father was with her. She had even bought a little beach tote, and she was going to stick him in there for all of her "meetings." Celia took a shower and changed into a peach sundress and wedge sandals. She was proud of herself as she applied her makeup. She'd held up well over the years. Her figure was still lovely, and other than a few more lines, she was still the same green-eyed, chestnut-haired girl. The agenda tonight was simply to walk the boardwalk with Dad, get a bite to eat, and enjoy. She'd figure out her game plan tomorrow.

The sand was soft and welcoming. Celia carried her sandals and walked right along the tide line so the waves could kiss the tops of her feet. The tote with her dad's ashes was slung over her shoulder. She stopped to take it all in. She could feel her dad's presence as she stared out at the mighty Atlantic. Although she hadn't been raised in religious households, Celia was always confident there was something out there. An energy, if nothing else, that survived and continued. She'd always felt it the strongest when she was right here at the edge of the ocean. How had she lived without it all these years?

Next Celia bought a hot dog on the boardwalk and loaded it up with everything she used to love. Sauerkraut, mustard, and ketchup. She devoured it and wanted another, but she was going for a fancy dinner this evening, so pacing herself was only wise. She set off to walk off the hot dog, knowing with every step exactly where she was headed.

Located just a half a block from the boardwalk, with sweeping ocean views, at the time, Elizabeth Tanner's corner house had been the best in the area. In Celia's opinion, it still was. Ocean House, as the locals referred to it, was a three-story Victorian Colonial with two sets of wraparound balconies, five bedrooms, and three bathrooms. Or so she'd been told. Celia had never been allowed inside. She stood across the street, staring at it, as the old humiliation washed over her. She had come for the first time with Jacob and Chris; the three of them had ridden the waves and walked the boardwalk before heading to Ocean House. Chris and Jacob had to pick up a check from Mrs. Tanner. Celia remembered the walk like it was yesterday. Celia was beyond excited; she'd been dying to see the inside of Ocean House since she and her father had arrived. And she'd never known a woman like Elizabeth, so powerful and beautiful. Celia had actually practiced what she might say to her. *You have such a lovely home*. Or, *Your taste is exquisite*. Judging from the way Elizabeth dressed and did her hair and nails, the home had to be remarkable. The word *exquisite* was sure to impress Mrs. Tanner. Celia was a voracious reader and loved any opportunity to try out new vocabulary. Regardless, compared to her RV, Ocean House was like an enchanted castle.

So there they were, headed for it. Celia in her hot pink flip-flops, and towel wrapped around her, the boys shoeless and shirtless, a few paces ahead of her. Mrs. Tanner stood on her third-story balcony with a drink in one hand, Kool cigarette in the other, literally (and figuratively) looking down on them. Celia hoped she would offer them lemonade. Elizabeth Tanner was known for her lemonade.

Elizabeth disappeared into the house and reappeared at the front door just as Chris laid on the buzzer. Now Celia was hoping she could use the restroom. How horrible that at just the thought of lemonade, she desperately had to go. Should she say how exquisite it was before or after she used the bathroom? Elizabeth swung the door open and smiled at Chris and Jacob. She waved them in, and kept a lingering hand on Jacob's shoulder. Then, just as Celia was about to step in after them, Elizabeth blocked the door with her body. Celia felt a flush of embarrassment. Celia had never stood so close to a grown woman wearing a bikini. Elizabeth was so tan too. Celia looked pale in comparison. She half wondered why Elizabeth even wore a bikini; Celia was at the beach every single day and she'd never actually seen Elizabeth there. Instead, Elizabeth preferred to sit out on her balcony with her binoculars.

"Did you speak with your father?" The previous week Elizabeth Tanner had made it obvious that she wanted a date with Pete Jensen. And she had fully expected Celia to cooperate.

"Yes. He's mighty busy right now, but he appreciates your interest," Celia had said as politely as she could. Actually, what her father had said was—"That shrill, peroxided barracuda? In her dreams." Celia thought it was mighty nice of her not to repeat it verbatim. Elizabeth was petite, but the minute the words left Celia's mouth, the woman seemed to grow to ten feet tall. Her nostrils actually flared.

"You can't come in. You have sandy feet." Celia looked

down at her feet. They were clean. She always rinsed them in the spigot on the boardwalk. And housed them in flip-flops. Chris and Jacob, on the other hand, who Elizabeth had already waved into the house, were barefoot. "Say hello to your father," Elizabeth Tanner called out just before she slammed the door in Celia's face. Celia walked away, humiliated. She'd only gone a block when she heard someone shout her name. She stopped to see Jacob running toward her.

"She wouldn't let me in," Celia said.

"I just found out," Jacob said. She tingled every time Jacob was near. He had come out for her. Did this mean he liked her too?

"Where's Chris?"

"She has ice cream," Jacob said.

Even better than lemonade. "You didn't want any?"

"Nah," Jacob said. "Brain freeze." She'd seen Jacob eating ice cream plenty of times. It gave her an unexpected thrill. She had never known she could make a boy give up ice cream for her. The headiness of it was almost like brain freeze. "Come on," he said. "Race you back."

Twenty years later here she stood, across the street. At first glance nothing much had changed about the house. It was still painted yellow with white shutters. Its view was still unfettered. There was, however, at least one very remarkable difference, and it had to do with the small front yard. Celia couldn't believe what she was seeing. There, staked front and center, was a definite sign. **FOR SALE.**

Ten minutes later Celia was sitting in the Realtor's office, only two blocks away. The minute she stepped into the small but cozy space she was greeted by a reed-thin woman who shook her hand and introduced herself as Anna Beth. She escorted Celia to a chair, sat behind a desk across from it, and hit her with a high-beamed sales smile. "Are you in the market for a vacation rental or a permanent home?"

"I'm here about the yellow house on the corner with the ocean view."

"It's fabulous, isn't it? You're in luck. I have the keys, and it's available to show—"

"That won't be necessary. I'll take it."

"Pardon?" The woman's smile faded just a touch. She cocked her head at Celia as if she were prepared to press an emergency button under the desk if Celia said or did anything else strange.

"I'll take it."

"You've seen it before then?"

"Just from the outside."

"Okay. And you don't want to see the inside?"

"No."

"Are you a developer?"

"I guess you could say that."

"I have to tell you, the property isn't zoned for business."

"That's fine."

"Do you even know the listing price?"

"I'm sure you'll tell me."

"Why don't you have your Realtor make an offer and fax it to me."

"Aren't you a Realtor?"

"Of course. But I represent the buyer—"

"Elizabeth Tanner?"

"You know the owner. Are you family?"

"Old-timer."

"What is your name, doll?"

"Celia Jensen."

"Doesn't ring a bell."

Of course it doesn't. Because I was just the daughter of a good-looking handyman accused of stealing. If she said "handyman and diamond ring," the woman would know her, all right. Celia didn't know whether to be relieved or insulted that the woman didn't realize who she was. Not that Celia knew Anna Beth either. Celia hadn't been much into real estate back then. "When I was a kid I lived here for five summers."

"Well. Here's the list price." Anna Beth slid a brochure across the desk. The price was in bold letters at the top. It was quite an asking. Celia felt Anna Beth staring at her with pity. What? Because she was in a sundress and flip-flops she wasn't a serious buyer? Celia didn't look like an investment banker because she didn't want to look like one. She had the money. But just. It would wipe out her savings, and her stock, and she'd have nothing to live on until she and Ben sold the condo. "The price is firm," Anna Beth said as if she could see Celia wrestling with dollar signs.

"I'm sure it is," Celia mused. Elizabeth didn't back down. Even when she was dead wrong.

"Elizabeth turned down the sweetest couple for coming in five thousand less than the asking price. She was so insulted she wouldn't even counteroffer." Anna Beth threw her arms up as if in defeat.

"That sounds like her." Celia would have to watch it before her bias spilled all over the place.

"If you want me to represent you as well, I can certainly do that. You'll save on commission, but it will have to be a full-price offer."

"Great."

"But I insist that you see the house."

"No, thank you." Celia didn't want to step a single foot into the house until she owned it. She would walk in with ice cream and lemonade. She would go to the restroom. Then, ice cream in one hand, lemonade in the other, she would walk from room to room murmuring, "Exquisite."

Anna Beth leaned back and crossed her arms. "This is highly unusual."

"Can you tell me why she's selling?"

"I'm afraid it's the economy." So Elizabeth hadn't bagged another rich man. Did it make Celia an awful person that she was happy to hear it?

"Does she still live on the property?"

"Yes. She needs a sixty-day closing."

"She has ten days." Let the witch go live in an RV.

"Excuse me?"

"I'll pay the full asking price, in cash. But only if she vacates in ten days."

"I see. Would you hold on a moment?"

"Certainly."

Anna Beth took out a cell phone and immediately disappeared outside. From the window, Celia watched her pace and talk. Celia lifted the coffee can out of her bag. "You aren't going to believe this." She patted the can, then quickly replaced it as the Realtor came back inside. "Elizabeth can't possibly vacate in ten days."

"Where there's a will, there's a way," Celia said.

"What about thirty days?"

"I'm afraid my offer is ten days or nothing."

"Why don't you fill out an application and let me take a look at your financials. If it all checks out, we'll get back to you in twenty-four hours." Celia hesitated. Elizabeth Tanner would remember her name. Would she sell the house if she knew Celia was the buyer?

"I prefer she doesn't know my name until it's all said and done."

Anna Beth fixed Celia with a laserlike gaze. "Did she sleep with your boyfriend?"

"What?"

Anna Beth moved closer and closer to Celia. "You're too young for it to be a husband. Your brother? Your father?"

"Let's just focus on the sale, okay?"

"Every summer, you say?" Anna Beth said. She tapped her upper lip with her index finger, then sat on the edge of her desk and leaned in. "Was your father a hunk?"

"Not my usual way of describing him, but—"

"Pete Jensen!"

Celia took a deep breath. Would this Realtor be on her side

if she told her, or would she immediately rat her out to Elizabeth? "Yes."

"Oh my God. Of course he was a hunk. How is he? Is he here?" Anna Beth sat up straighter and fluffed her hair. Celia could almost feel the coffee can vibrating with laughter.

"He passed away recently."

Anna Beth looked truly shocked. "Oh my God. I am so, so sorry."

Celia was touched by her genuine reaction. "Thank you. It was his final request that I come back to Hampton Beach."

"Oh my God. Did he want you to buy the house?"

"I'm pretty sure he would. He believed in karma."

"I do too. I totally believe in karma."

"So can you make a cash sale without revealing my name?"

But Anna Beth wasn't ready to move on. "So young. What happened?"

Celia hesitated. Her father had been larger than life. It wasn't fitting to be taken out by cigarettes. "He was scuba diving. In the Fiji Islands."

"Oh, my."

"He died doing what he loved."

"So wonderful." Anna Beth looked around guiltily, then lowered her voice. "How exactly did he die?" she whispered.

"Shark," Celia shouted. Anna Beth's hand flew over her mouth.

"Shark?" Anna Beth repeated.

"I told him to use the cage. He wouldn't do it."

"He was a man," Anna Beth said, her voice low and slightly hoarse.

It was totally awkward, the sexual way in which Anna Beth said "man." Although, truth be told, it was the way Celia would have said it when referring to Jacob. Maybe there was something about the salt air that made all the women of Hampton Beach absolutely man crazy. Celia didn't want to blow this, so she kept her dry heaves to herself.

"My God," Anna Beth said. Apparently, she was still imagining Pete Jensen in the jaws of a shark.

There. That should distract Anna Beth from bringing up the diamond ring fiasco. "So. Will you help me?" Celia asked.

"I'm not sure Elizabeth Tanner would want to sell to you."

"I know she wouldn't. Which is why she doesn't need to know. I'm a cash buyer. You can represent me."

"I'll see what I can do," Anna Beth said.

"My father would be so thrilled."

She heard back by the end of the day. Ocean House would be hers. Elizabeth wanted two weeks to vacate. Celia conceded. In two weeks she would be living in the same place as Jacob Vernon. In the house she had been banned from. She really could feel her father smiling down on her. Karma. Sometimes life not only gave second chances, it delivered them on a silver platter.

CHAPTER 4

Celia turned the key at exactly midnight on the day she was allowed to take possession of Ocean House. She purposefully walked in the sand before entering. *You can't come in. Your feet are all sandy.* With the coffee can tucked under her arm, a new floppy hat on her head, and plenty of sand on her feet, Celia Jensen stepped into the foyer of her new home. A piercing shriek rang out, startling Celia, jarring every nerve in her body. A security alarm. It reached an excruciating decibel level and then continued to pulse. Celia slapped her hands over her ears, and the coffee can dropped out of her hands and clattered to the floor. *Sorry, Dad.* What was going on? The Realtor didn't tell her about an alarm. It was so loud. Were they hoping to make the burglar deaf? Celia couldn't see a thing in the dark. She groped along the wall to find a switch. She flipped it, but instead of illuminating the interior, the porch glowed with a soft, yellow light. People on the sidewalk stopped to gawk. If she were a burglar, she was in no danger of being tackled by a passerby, but they were staring long and hard enough to pick her out of a lineup. She slammed the door shut and headed down the hall. Just a few feet from the entrance a control panel was built into the wall.

Celia stared helplessly at the numbers. A childhood chant echoed through her mind. *One potato, two potato, three potato, four. Very helpful. Thank you.* Next, her mother came to mind, lying on the couch with a cold compress, after a night of drinking. *That noise!* she would say if Celia even tried to walk across the floor. *I can't take that noise!*

Her grand opening was ruined. The coffee can was on its side on the floor, but the lid was still on tight. Celia slid down the wall and sat on the floor. She scooped the can off the floor, ran out to the front porch for some relief, and waited with the moths fluttering by the light.

It took twenty-five minutes for a security guard to show up at the door. Some security company—the place would have been wiped clean by now. Not to mention he was way too skinny to intimidate any burglar, and he wasn't armed.

"Make it stop," Celia said. The young man nodded, headed inside for the security panel, then turned to her once he reached it.

"Do you know the code?" He was completely serious. Celia stared at him. He stared back.

"Why wouldn't I have shut it off if I knew the code?" Celia yelled over the beeps.

"Do you live here?"

"No. I'm breaking in. Hope you don't mind assisting in my life of crime."

"You're breaking in?"

Seriously. The beach could be too relaxing for some folk. This kid should be selling self-serve ice cream on the boardwalk. That wasn't an insult; the job came with free ice cream. "It was a joke. I own this house. I just bought it."

"Oh. Cool."

"Make it stop."

The kid ambled up to the panel. "I don't know the code." He pushed a few buttons. The piercing scream continued.

"If you don't know the code, why are you pushing buttons?"

"Sometimes I get lucky."

Wish I could say the same.

"I'll have to call it in," he said.

Wasn't he the one who had been called in? She wasn't in a big city anymore. She'd have to be patient. On second thought, maybe she'd get lucky for a change. She marched over to the panel and began pounding on it.

"Hey, hey. Don't break it."

"Oh, I'm going to break it all right. I'm going to rip it out of the wall."

"I wouldn't do that if I were you." For a split second she wondered how the kid's voice suddenly got so rich and deep. She whirled around. A tall, muscular man with dark, wavy hair stood in the doorway. Heart-stoppingly good-looking. It was him. Or his brother. It wasn't fair to have that kind of magnetism. Chris or Jacob? Her heartbeat increased. It was Jacob. Chris never fired up every nerve cell in her body. Never made her heart flutter. Her brain couldn't always tell them apart, but her body could. No. It was too soon. She wanted to control every aspect of the meeting. God, the very nearness of him. Those green eyes, that strong jawline. She could gaze at him all day. And she had always loved his height. Made her feel petite. And predatory.

"Jacob?" Celia said.

He frowned. "You have an advantage." He didn't recognize her. Definitely Jacob. Chris would've been miffed that she had mistaken him for his brother. Chris had always thought he was the better-looking one, even though sometimes their own father couldn't tell them apart. What an egomaniac. And capable of being plain cruel. This was definitely Jacob. "And you are?" Jacob said when Celia didn't introduce herself.

She was crushed. She had thought, somehow, he would just know her. She would've known him anywhere. Maybe she was the only one who had been madly in love. It wasn't right. The universe was upside down. *Life doesn't give sec-*

ond chances. "I'm the new owner," Celia said. She turned away, so he wouldn't see how emotional she was getting. What was he doing here?

"Would you like me to shut it off?"

"I'd love you forever," Celia said. Oh God, did she just say that? So much for sweeping in and playing it cool.

"That won't be necessary," Jacob said without even cracking a smile. He went straight for the security panel. Oh God. He wasn't even attracted to her anymore. Not that she cared. He finished punching in numbers, and the obnoxious blare finally ceased.

"Oh, thank heavens," Celia said. She took off her hat. Silly of her to wear it this late. When she looked up, Jacob was staring at her.

"Celia?" he said. "Celia Jensen?"

Celia's heart soared. It had just been the hat. He did know her. Once upon a time they did exist. Once upon a time they had been in love. "Hello, Jacob." Celia grinned.

"My God. Celia Jensen." Jacob began walking toward her. Celia kept still and held her breath. She wanted to touch him so badly. He stopped about a foot from her. Just a little closer and they could be kissing. "*You're* the new owner?"

Celia lifted her foot. "With sand on my feet."

Jacob threw his head back and laughed. "I don't believe it."

"Believe it," she said.

"Call me if you need anything else," the security kid said. Celia had forgotten he was even there. Jacob and Celia fell silent until the kid was out the door. Once he was, Jacob's eyes landed on her, and they locked eyes for a very long time. *Jacob Have I Loved*. . . .

Jacob looked at the floor. Was he gathering his strength or trying to hold something back? He looked upset. Hurt. Was that possible? Had he remained as attached to her as she had to him? Since it wasn't appropriate to throw herself into his arms and nuzzle his neck, Celia tried to lighten the mood instead.

"New Hampshire's finest, eh?" Celia said.

"What?"

"The security guard. The security kid, I should say."

"He's Elizabeth Tanner's grandson."

"Emily's son?" Celia's heart stopped in her chest. Elizabeth had a daughter, Emily. Just a few years younger than Celia, Emily used to follow her around like a shadow. Mostly because she was in love with Chris, and the twins were always hanging around Celia. Was Emily old enough to have a son that age?

"No, no. A grandson by marriage."

"Ah." So Elizabeth was remarried. Was that why she was selling the house? Celia had really hoped it was financial troubles as Anna Beth had said. Normally Celia would feel guilty for such a thought, but not when it came to Elizabeth Tanner.

Jacob bent down and handed Celia the coffee can. She took it with a slight smile. "Thanks." She headed down the hall, then stopped. "I have no idea where the kitchen is," she said.

Jacob laughed. "I heard you bought it without seeing the inside. I thought Anna Beth was pulling a fast one."

"Would you be so kind as to give me a tour?" She linked arms with Jacob. Forget being angry. This was Jacob. He was here.

Jacob glanced at the coffee tin in her arms. "Only if you make some of that coffee," Jacob said.

"I don't think my father would approve," Celia said.

"I don't think my father would approve," Celia said. Identical twins stood just outside the door of the RV. *Hello, Hampton Beach.* They were gorgeous. Sooooooooooo gorgeous. They were even better-looking than the boys she'd cut out of *Teen Beat* and taped to her wall. And they had just asked her to go to the beach.

"Is he here?" one said with a smile that could set a whole town on fire.

"No," Celia said as a blush spread up her neck.

"Then there's nothing to approve, is there?" Celia allowed the boy to pin her with his gaze, then glanced at the other one. He was looking elsewhere. The shy brother.

"I'm Chris," the exuberant one said. "This is Jacob."

"Jacob Have I Loved," Celia said.

"What?" Chris shouted. "She loves you, dude." He hit his brother on the back. Jacob turned a hundred shades of red. So did Celia, for that matter.

"No," she said. She reached around the corner, which was the great thing about living in an RV, and put her hands on the book propped on the counter. She held it up. *Jacob Have I Loved,* by Katherine Paterson. She had bought it at a yard sale on their way here. Ironically, it was about twins too, but twin girls. Celia tried to tell them about the book, but they didn't seem interested.

"Got any books with my name on them?" Chris asked.

"No," Celia said. She wanted to say something a little more clever, but she couldn't think of anything but the fact that her friend Amy was going to die when she heard about this. Did she have film left in her Polaroid? She would have to mail Amy a picture. *Thanks, Dad. I love New Hampshire! And they're talking to me! They're talking to me! At least one of them was talking. So why was it the quiet one who was making everything inside her go ZING!? She couldn't believe she was reading a book with the name Jacob in the title, and here was a Jacob at her front door. Was this fate? She never knew it could be so kind.*

"Grab a suit," Chris said. "Preferably a bikini." At this, Jacob lifted his head and made eye contact. Celia felt it again. A jolt, like an electric current as their eyes locked. No, her dad would definitely not approve. Should she wear the black bikini or the red?

* * *

The house was just as she'd always imagined. The first floor consisted of a large main living room. Its focal points were a marble fireplace and bay windows that looked out onto the wraparound porch and ocean beyond. The hardwood floors could use a little sanding and the light blue paint on the walls wasn't to her taste, but they would be easy to fix. Then again, Celia thought beach houses looked best if they were a tad rustic. This wasn't the Hamptons, nor did Celia want it to be. It looked the type of room that was just begging for a piano, and lots and lots of people standing around and singing.

"It hasn't changed." Startled, Celia glanced at Jacob. He looked into her eyes. There was that old, familiar jolt. It was still electric between them. And emotional. He remembered, obviously, how she'd been shunned. All these years later and she could see affection in his eyes. He still cared about her. He'd never know how much that meant to her. She couldn't look at him too long, because it only took seconds before a current of desire began humming through her body. She'd never had such a passionate night as that first time, under the boardwalk. And here he was, close enough to touch, and she just wanted to do it again, right now. It wasn't possible that she had slept with Chris. It just wasn't.

"What kind of furniture did she have?" Celia said. Not that she cared. She was trying to prevent herself from going over to Jacob and pulling off his shirt. Ripping it down the middle. Running her hands over his arms and chest. Seriously, that body. He still looked as if he had stepped right out of a poster. And he still looked at her as if she were the only girl in the world. Maybe it was nostalgia. There was something so special about the fact that he had known her as a young girl. Coming of age—the first to de—

"Flowery," Jacob said suddenly.

"What?" Celia was completely startled. Could Jacob read minds now?

"Elizabeth had fake flower stuff all over the place. Even the sofa. It was big, and stuffy, and flowery."

"Oh. The sofa."

"Everything else was kind of clunky too."

"You're kidding." Celia had pictured expensive and sleek. Plastic on the couch and such.

"Nope. I should know. Just helped haul it all out."

"You did?" Celia couldn't hide her surprise. He was doing Elizabeth favors?

"She needed all the help she could get. Apparently you said it was fourteen days or no deal."

Actually, I said ten. I agreed to fourteen. "Right," Celia said. She wandered from the main room to a small dining room behind it. Not wanting to linger with Jacob on her heels, she continued through to the kitchen. It was a nice rectangular space. Way too simple, but again, it could all be fixed. White tiled floors and old appliances, but it was large enough to fit an island in the middle. Celia would redo the floors, put in new appliances, throw paint on the walls, and get a table big enough for ten to sit around. Above the sink two windows faced the back. Beach space was tight, so there was no backyard, just a strip of grass and then an alley. From here she could see the backs of the houses on the next street. That was all right. The floors were still dirty, and so was the inside of the refrigerator. Jacob leaned against the wall and watched her.

"Emily wants to come back to clean. She didn't have time."

It was such a shock, hearing all these old names coming out of Jacob's mouth so easily. Elizabeth. Emily. He was still in touch with them. "I don't mind," Celia said. "I like cleaning." It was true. It was nice to see an immediate result of her hard work. Simple and honest. Not like some of the investment deals that made her feel sour. A job she wasn't proud of. A man she didn't love. Was all of it a result of running from the past? Had Celia learned to numb herself to how she really felt? Or was that just life? Did most people find themselves nearly all the way down a path that they never meant to take?

Celia turned back into the hall and headed for the stairs. Adjacent to the stairs were the two downstairs guest rooms. They were on the small side, but the front one had a view of the beach. She went to the foot of the stairs and looked up. She'd always pictured a winding staircase. She headed up, wondered if Jacob was watching her walk as he seemed to take his time behind her.

"Why was there such a tight turnaround time?" he asked.

"Pardon?" She stopped at the top of the stairs, just as he joined her. Was it on purpose? To keep him close in the tight little landing? For a moment, they just stared at each other. They were so close to the bedrooms too. Celia suddenly wished she had an actual bed.

"Why only fourteen days?" Jacob's voice said the words, but his eyes were on her body. He was trying to be subtle, but there was no mistaking the shifts in his gaze.

"Oh. You know how it is." Celia had completely forgotten what they were talking about.

"I'm not sure I do," Jacob said.

"Not sure you do what?" Celia realized, too late, that she was whispering, and bringing her lips closer to Jacob's. For a second, time stood still. Then Jacob took a step back and gestured ahead of him.

"Shall we continue the tour?" he said in a loud voice.

"Of course." Oh God. He didn't want to kiss her. What was wrong with her? Celia forced her attention elsewhere.

Facing her was a small bathroom. Next to it, a bedroom, and yet another bedroom at the end of the hall. They were a little on the small side, and the bathroom was outdated too. A yellow rubber duck sat on a shelf above the toilet. There were curtains with ungodly flowers plastered all over them.

Celia didn't know why she was so disappointed. She'd imagined the house larger than life. Just like Elizabeth. Did it make it better or worse that Elizabeth Tanner hadn't been some rich socialite? The third floor was an attic, although it was a room in and of itself. It was large enough for a master bedroom and office or even a sitting room. It had a circular window that looked out on the ocean. Celia would make this her bedroom. Just off to the back was another bathroom.

"How's your dad?" Jacob said.

Celia's throat tightened at the thought of the last time she had seen her father. Then she thought of his red flippers on the desk, his ashes in the Chock Full O'Nuts can, and she felt a little comforted. "He passed away two weeks ago."

"Oh no. I am so sorry, Celia." Jacob hung his head for a moment before looking up at her. Instantly she saw him as a seventeen-year-old boy, standing in front of her RV, eyes staring at his shoes. Then, before she could even process what was happening, he was in front of her, taking her into his arms. She let him fold her into his chest, wrap his arms around her waist. He was strong, with such a solid feel, as he held her. She was not going to let go first. She was disappointed when he did.

"Thank you," she said.

"For what?" Jacob sounded genuinely surprised.

For touching me. For being here. You're single, right? Why are we waiting? "For the tour," Celia said.

"It was nothing. May I ask—"

"Anything."

"Your dad was still young, wasn't he? What happened?"

"Smoking caught up with him."

"I'm sorry to hear that. I remember how you were always hiding or crushing his cigarettes."

Celia nodded. She'd even gotten the twins into the act a couple of times. She'd never forget her father's grilling Jacob about a pack that he'd just bought—Celia had shoved them in Jacob's back pocket. Poor Jacob! Her father could be intimidating when he wanted to be. But Jacob had stood his ground, insisting they were *his* cigarettes. To both their horror, Pete called his bluff.

"Then smoke one," he said. "Right now."

Jacob looked like a deer in headlights. "I'm saving them," he said. "For after dinner."

"They're not a piece of pie, son," Pete said. "Have one now."

"Celia hates it when I smoke," Jacob said.

"Well then, you might as well hand that pack over to me. Wouldn't want to upset your girl, would you?"

Celia shut off the memory and looked at Jacob, who was patiently watching her. "I was thinking about that cigarette he tried to make you smoke," Celia said.

"I would have done it," Jacob said. "For you."

Celia knew that was true. She was the one who had grabbed the pack out of Jacob's pocket and handed them to her dad. Celia was pretty sure he had known all along, but he still couldn't pass up an opportunity to give Jacob a bit of a hard time. In her dad's eyes, no boy was good enough for his daughter. "I told Anna Beth he was eaten by a shark while diving in the Fiji Islands."

"You what?" Jacob looked startled for a moment, then threw his head back and roared with laughter.

"He's in the coffee can downstairs," she heard herself say.

"What?"

Jacob sounded so startled. His eyes were huge. Then, he started to laugh again. "Chock Full O'Nuts."

Celia began to laugh along with him. She could almost hear her father's voice mixed in with theirs. "It was totally his idea."

"Oh, I'm sure."

She felt so close to Jacob. He understood her. He understood her father. Unlike Ben. Then, talking about her dad, while standing in Elizabeth's old house, brought back a rush of anger. Why was Jacob helping Elizabeth move? Why was he mentioning Emily? "Are you friends with them?"

"Who?"

"Elizabeth Tanner and Emily."

Jacob looked at her before speaking. He had this way of gazing at her that made her feel as if he were more in tune with her than anyone else in her entire life. Did he feel it too? It wasn't a guarantee. After all, Ben had told her he was crazy about her, and she'd never felt that way about him. Not even close. "You sound upset."

"You don't remember what they did to my dad?"

"Of course I remember. But you've been gone a long time, Seal. People change. They mellow."

"You're telling me that Elizabeth Tanner has mellowed?"

"That might be stretching it a little. But I don't take her as seriously as I used to. That's for sure."

"She ruined my father's reputation. She had the whole town thinking he was a thief."

"Not the whole town. You know Chris and I never thought he stole the ring."

"He didn't."

"We even showed up to one of Mrs. Tanner's Neighborhood Watch meetings. We told them we trusted Pete. We tried to calm them down."

"I take it you've never found the ring."

Jacob broke her gaze, stared down at his shoes. "Honestly, Celia. I try not to even think about it anymore."

"You're right. The damage is done. Elizabeth and Emily saw to that."

Jacob looked at her again. His voice was soft, but reprimanding. "Come on, now. Emily was just a kid. Like us."

He was right. And the last thing she wanted to do was sound bitter. "How's Chris?" She had to change the subject before she went over the deep end.

"Oh, busy. He's married. Finally has three little squirts."

"I know." It was out of her mouth before she could stop.

"You know?"

Yes. I've been cyber stalking you. You're delicious dessert, and I came back to have another bite. "I, uh—Anna Beth." Truthfully, the Realtor hadn't said a thing about anyone, but at her commission, Celia didn't feel too guilty about throwing her under the bus.

"Ah," Jacob said.

"Did he marry Emily?"

"What? No. No, he didn't marry Emily."

"Oh. Just as well."

"What do you mean?"

"He'd be stuck in that family. I can't imagine anything worse."

"I see." Jacob sounded upset again.

She was jumping into the past too fast. She should talk about good times before she got around to the bad. "Would you like to grab a drink?" What was she doing? Acting like they were old friends. Instead of lovers. She didn't even know if they had been lovers. Her face grew hot at the memory.

Sometimes, we switch places. Chris. Standing in the sun, a suggestive leer on his face.

"Now? You remember where you are, don't you?"

"What?"

"All the bars are closed."

"Oh. Right. I forget I'm not in Boston."

"Is that where you live?"

"Lived."

"Right." They stared at each other again. "I always wondered," Jacob said.

"Me too. About you." Jacob nodded, then turned away. He was the one who had some explaining to do. Did he know what Chris had done? Why didn't Jacob come back to the boardwalk? Had Chris lied to him about something? She couldn't ask without warming up to it. The only alcohol she

had in the house was a bottle of scotch she had bought for
her dad. She figured she'd toast with it after she released his
ashes into the ocean. She could always buy another bottle.
"What about a drink here? I have some really good scotch."

Jacob really looked uncomfortable now. There was something he wasn't saying. "I'd love to, but I have to get home.
The girlfriend's waiting." And he said it.

It felt like a slap to the face. Of course. A home. A girlfriend. Waiting. His life hadn't stayed frozen in time.

"Of course." She headed back down the stairs, taking them
as quickly as possible. "Thanks for coming—" She stopped in
the hall, turned. "Why did you come?"

"What?"

"What were you doing here tonight?"

"Oh. Right." He dug in his pocket, pulled out a key. "I
was retrieving this from the porch." He handed it to Celia.

"Extra key?"

"Emily said it was under the mat. She didn't want anyone
finding it and breaking in on the new owner."

"Ah. Thanks." Soon they were standing at the front door
like strangers at the end of a first date. Only this time it wasn't
going to end in a kiss.

"Of course, she didn't know you were the new owner or
that you would be here at midnight or she'd probably have
come herself," Jacob said.

"Right. So instead she sent you." Jacob looked away.
"Because you're her boyfriend." One look, and Celia knew
she was right. And just like that, she didn't feel like a thirty-
eight-year-old woman; rather she was instantly a seventeen-
year-old girl. Emily Tanner and Jacob Vernon. Jacob Vernon
and Emily Tanner. She was going to cry. She was actually
going to cry in front of Jacob, and for once her father wasn't
here to buy her ice cream. And she didn't have any furniture.
She had thought it would be an "adventure" to furnish as she
went. Only she couldn't afford to buy anything. So now it

was just an empty house with no soft bed. She bet Jacob had a bed. And he shared it with Emily. She had to turn her back on him because the embarrassing tears were really coming now.

"Whoa," Jacob said. "Hey." Oh God, she was acting so immature. She didn't want him to see her this way. "Seal."

Celia melted at the sound of her old nickname. Jacob took her in his arms. She could feel his heart beating against hers. They stood in the embrace for a few seconds until time seemed to come to a halt and the air was thick with sexual tension. Celia pulled away, and Jacob took a step back, as if he had been caught doing something he shouldn't have.

Why? Why did she leave him here to be swooped up by Emily? As a girl, Emily had always loved Chris. Celia wondered what Chris thought of his brother dating his old girlfriend. They'd probably all put the past behind them. It was easier to do if you weren't humiliated and made out to be a criminal, and tormented by the thought that you might have been tricked into sleeping with the wrong guy. She should just come out and ask Jacob. *Why did you leave me all alone on the beach? Did you know Chris came instead? Tried to make me believe I slept with him?*

"You'd better go. I'm sure she wouldn't want to be kept waiting."

Jacob looked at her for a long time. Celia stared back, willing herself not to cry more or even blink.

"Please go." *Please don't. Did we make love, Jacob? Or did Chris trick me? I know it was you. How could I not know? I just can't help it. Chris planted a seed of doubt in my head and it took over all my thoughts, strangling out all reality, choking me like a weed.*

Jacob stood watching her for another moment, then nodded, turned, and walked out the door. It was only then that Celia slid to the floor. Here she was in this empty house. No Dad. No Jacob. She was barefoot in Elizabeth Tanner's house. Owned Elizabeth's house. Jacob was here. And he was with Emily. No matter how much time had gone by, or how hard she tried, the Tanner women were always one step ahead. *I don't give second chances,* she heard Ben say. *And most of the time, neither does life.*

CHAPTER 5

In the week following her run-in with Jacob, Celia threw herself into small home-improvement projects that wouldn't break the bank. She painted the downstairs walls. Red in the dining room. Yellow in the kitchen, and a more vibrant blue in the living room. What an instant and wonderful difference. She purchased a chandelier in town, an ornate one with hundreds of shimmering crystals. She hired a handyman the Realtor recommended, and he hung an antique mirror that she'd bought on eBay above the fireplace. Jacob could have done the work, of course, but she certainly wasn't going to call him. She'd yet to buy furniture, only a blow-up mattress for her attic room. She was no longer feeling as vulnerable as she had that first night, and she still wanted to take her time, consider each piece of furniture carefully. Besides, there was something soothing about an empty house. It felt roomy, and each room still held the anticipation of what it could become.

The one exception was the wicker rocking chair she bought for the front porch. Rocking while listening to the ocean was incredibly soothing. As an investment banker, she had never napped, had to constantly drink Red Bull to keep on her toes.

Here she found herself falling asleep in the rocking chair during the afternoons, little catnaps on her porch.

She spent loads of time looking at furniture in catalogs or online. But buying the house had really wiped her out. To make matters even more challenging, she had officially quit her job via a postcard. *Don't wish you were here—I quit.* She felt both giddy and embarrassed by it, but her father would have loved it. Unfortunately, she only had a few more pay-checks coming to her, so things were going to get really tight really quick. She would have to convince Ben to sell their condo and split the profit. Not an easy feat since he was treating the condo like a pawn in their breakup. It was a really good thing they had never had kids. So far he was pretending she was temporarily out of her mind with grief and was going to come to her senses and return. Celia was tired of being the bad guy, so she was going to let him stew for a while, and then she'd be forced to call an attorney. Legally, he had to either buy her out or sell. She was just praying she wouldn't have to resort to threats.

"Toodle-oo!" a female voice cried out. Celia was knee-deep in grime. Hair pinned on top of her head with a pencil. Kneeling on the living room floor. Scrubbing. She heard the call, then heard the front screen door opening and slamming. Heels clacked across the wood floor, and it wasn't until Emily Tanner came into view that Celia warned her not to step onto the wet floor. "Oh," Emily said. "Just look at Cinderella."

"Does that make you the evil stepsister?" Celia asked.

Emily, hands on hips, looked like a replica of her mother from twenty years ago. The mousey child had transformed into a blond bombshell. Tan and model thin except for a decent-sized chest, nails manicured and painted, hair straightened, eye-lashes carefully applied along with the rest of her makeup. She stood in the doorway holding a basket.

Celia stood, awkwardly shoved a stray bang out of her

eyes, and put on her best smile. She was going to have to be the bigger person and play nice. "Emily. It's great to see you."

"Is it?" Emily held her smile. She had always been such an insecure little girl. Celia used to feel sorry for her. She had even known Emily was just using her to be close to the twins, but Celia hadn't minded. She knew the twins had no interest in plain little Emily. Now, here she was with the looks, but unfortunately, the sweet little girl was gone. The pendulum had swung in the opposite direction.

"Of course. I would shake your hand, but—"

"Not necessary. I brought muffins. To congratulate you. On buying my mother's house."

"How nice of you." As Emily approached her with the basket, Celia found herself involuntarily stepping back, and after an awkward few moments, it dawned on Celia that they were actually circling each other. Celia made a point to stop.

Emily looked her over very slowly. It was remarkable; she used to be so timid. Apparently, that was a quality you could grow out of. "When Jacob told me you were the mysterious buyer, well, you could have knocked me over with a feather."

"I'm sure." It certainly didn't look hard to do. Emily should be the one eating muffins.

"I hope muffins are okay. I'm sure you're watching your weight."

Celia peeled off the rubber gloves, wiped her hands on the sides of her cargo pants, and marched up to the basket. She grabbed a muffin. "Not at all. I really enjoy food. My boyfriend loves my Marilyn Monroe curves." Celia bit into the muffin. It tasted like cardboard sprinkled with a few moldy cranberries. She chewed for a bit and then put the rest of the muffin back in the basket.

"Something wrong?" Emily asked. From the glint in her eye, Emily knew exactly how horrible the muffins tasted.

"Sometimes a bite is all you need." *I'd like to bite you.*

Emily headed for the kitchen without even asking. Celia trailed behind, like she was the uninvited guest.

"Is he here?" Emily said.

For a split second Celia thought she meant Jacob. Maybe he'd stopped going home. "Who?"

"Your boyfriend."

"No," Celia said. She wasn't getting into it with Emily.

Emily set the basket on the counter and inspected the kitchen. Celia got the feeling it didn't pass muster. She half-expected Emily to pull a white glove out of her purse and give it a go. "Mother is thrilled you took this albatross off her hands," Emily said.

"Really? I thought she was forced to sell. Hard times and all."

"Oh, no. Not at all. This place is falling apart. All that salt air. The upkeep is a nightmare. She'd rather travel and live in a newer condominium. She and her husband already have another vacation home in Georgia. It's a Southern dream. This place is a dump compared to it."

"Jacob said she was remarried." At the mention of Jacob, Emily furled her arched eyebrows, but didn't quite swallow the bait.

"Oh, yes. He's rich and handsome."

Celia didn't comment. She'd deal with Elizabeth in her own good time.

"Jacob I Have Loved," Emily said out of the blue.

"Jacob Have I Loved," Celia corrected.

"You still do, don't you?" Emily said.

Way to cut right to the chase! Celia could feel herself heating up. Emily was the one person Celia had confided in that horrible next morning. *I know I slept with Jacob, but he left to get something. A surprise. But he didn't come back. Chris did. He acted like he was the one I had slept with. What do I do, Emily? What do I do?*

Oh God. They're horrible! Both of them. They ruined you.

What do you mean, ruined me? I love Jacob. We're both eighteen—

But you say it was Chris—

No. Chris said it was Chris. You know how he is—

I don't know how he is. Because it's you he wants! It's always you, you, you!

And somehow, Emily had turned Celia's cry for help into her own personal drama. That's when Celia had really understood the price of being used. Celia brought herself back to the present. She was an adult now. She would act like one.

"How is Chris?" Celia said. "Do you still follow him everywhere he goes?" Celia knew the minute it was out of her mouth, it was too obvious, too heavy-handed for the light slapping they'd done so far, but it was too late to take it back. But Emily didn't blink.

"You haven't seen him?" Emily said. There it was again, the same glint in her eye that had accompanied the muffins.

"No."

"He hangs out at the arcade most of the time. You should definitely go say hi."

"He's the last person I want to see. You should know that."

"I didn't realize you were still holding a grudge. Boys will be boys."

Don't ask her. Don't ask her. Do NOT ask her. "Did you ever ask Jacob about it?"

Emily smiled. Celia knew instantly that this was the moment Emily had been waiting for. A chess match. "Of course. I was dying to know." Check.

She's pure hate, Celia realized. Like mother, like daughter. Celia wasn't going to play. It was Jacob she needed to discuss this with, no one else.

"It was Chris," Emily announced. And mate. Except she was lying. She had to be.

"No," Celia said. "It was Jacob. I know it was Jacob."

"Oh. You didn't know it then, but you suddenly know now?"

Mean girl, mean girl, mean girl. Weren't women supposed to outgrow this behavior? "Why are you treating me this way?"

"Pardon?"

"Let's cut the crap. I don't deserve this. You used to be my friend." *Or at least pretended to be.*

"Do you forget all the nasty things you said about my mother?"

Celia didn't know what Emily was talking about. She had *thought* a lot of nasty things about Elizabeth Tanner, but she certainly had never said any of them.

"You called her a liar," Emily said.

"When did I do that?"

"When you shouted to everyone who would listen that your father was innocent."

"My father was innocent."

"Then that implies that my mother was lying!"

"My father did not take that ring."

"See? There you go again. Look who hasn't changed a bit."

"Was your mother in the cottage when the ring went missing? Did she see my father take it?"

"Maybe she did."

Celia was floored. "Excuse me?"

"If not him—then who else?"

"Are you kidding me? That's your criteria for ruining a man's life? Who else?"

"Motive, means, and opportunity."

"And just what was the motive?"

Emily just looked at Celia. "That's what I thought," Celia said. "And we both know the only reason your mother accused my father was because he was smart enough to stay the hell away when she wanted to jump his bones!"

Emily stormed out the door. Once again, Celia followed.

Emily stopped on the porch and turned back. "When you realize you made a huge mistake in coming back, I will buy the house back from you. At a discount, of course. Oh. And you should go say hello to Chris. I'm sure you lovers will have a lot to catch up on."

Celia took a cold shower, threw on another sundress, and headed for the boardwalk. Emily was lying. It couldn't have been Chris. It just couldn't! Oh, why hadn't she asked Jacob when he was in her house? She got the feeling he would have let her kiss him too. And boy, how she had wanted to. He used to be such a good kisser. Such a good boyfriend. Why did it all slip away so quickly?

Celia found herself walking to the spot under the boardwalk where it happened. She stood and stared underneath the boardwalk, as if she could see herself and Jacob. Lying under it, Jacob's beautiful body on top of hers. Making love to the boy she loved. It was the morning of her eighteenth birthday. She had wanted to do it the day before, and Jacob was the one who had said, "You'll be eighteen tomorrow, like me. What's one more day?"

And so they had waited, and Jacob had planned. He had brought a picnic basket with a blanket, and champagne, and condoms. She had been so relieved that he had taken care of it. He had taken care of her. It had been the best first experience a girl could ask for. Jacob was tender, and romantic, and oh, how her body had responded to him. He was so beautiful, and she was so beautiful, and together they couldn't have stopped even if they had wanted to. Afterward, they lay entwined on the blanket. Celia could barely hear the ocean above the beating of their hearts. She had been wondering what he would think of her if she asked if they could do it again, when Jacob spoke first.

"I have a surprise for you," Jacob had said, caressing her face. "Can you wait here one second?"

"You're going to leave me?"

"I was so drunk with anticipation that I left it at home. I'll run the whole way. I'll be back in two seconds."

"I'll come with you."

"You can't. Thus the word—surprise." Celia had grabbed him and kissed him, then shoved him off. She could hear his footsteps pounding on the boardwalk as she lay underneath, officially a woman. She must have dozed off. When she woke, someone had been standing over her. It was Chris. She had known by the smirk. She had known because her heart was still.

"Surprise," Chris said.

Celia had shot up and covered herself with the blanket Jacob had brought. "Where's Jacob?"

The sneer had grown. Chris had looked her up and down. "You know we switch places all the time, don't you, doll?"

"Go away. Jacob is coming back."

"No, he's not. Jacob was never here."

"What are you talking about?"

"You enjoyed it though, didn't you?" Chris had reached out to touch her hair. Celia had swatted him away.

"I know the difference between you and Jacob."

"Do you?"

"And you're wearing different clothes."

"You mean the torn jeans and the blue T-shirt? Just took 'em off."

"I'm waiting here for Jacob."

"Then you're going to wait all day. He doesn't even know you're here."

"He does too. He just left."

"I just left."

"You're lying."

"I was so drunk with anticipation that I left it at home," Chris had said in perfect imitation of Jacob.

"You spied on us," Celia had said. "You perv."

"Do you want to do it again, let me prove it to you?" Chris had advanced on her. Celia had pummeled him with both fists until he backed off. Laughing. Celia had turned away and Chris had walked off, whistling. Celia had waited underneath the boardwalk for three hours, with her knees pulled up to her chest, hugging herself. At eighteen, when she'd just lost her virginity and was supposed to be cuddling with the man she loved, three hours had felt like three days. Jacob had never come back. It wasn't possible, was it? The twins were difficult to tell apart, especially in the dark and after alcohol. But Celia could tell them apart. Chris never gave her a jolt. Only Jacob. And Jacob would never willingly switch places. Never. When Celia couldn't take waiting anymore, she had run to Emily. The very next day word got out that the ring had been stolen. From there, things had blown up so fast and furious that Celia didn't have a chance to be alone with Jacob. And by the time she and her father had rolled out of town, she had been in such a state she had thought she never wanted to see either one of the Vernon twins ever again for as long as she lived. Except, of course, that was a big, fat lie. She had never stopped longing to see Jacob. Unfinished business had a way of keeping you prisoner, torturing you slowly.

CHAPTER 6

Celia comforted herself with a giant, greasy cheeseburger and fries. Then, she sat on the beach and watched the waves roll in. She cupped sand into her hand and funneled it back to the beach. If Jacob Vernon wanted Emily Tanner, then he couldn't possibly be the man Celia thought he was. So forget him. Concentrate on confronting Elizabeth Tanner. Or, she could go see Chris. See what he had to say about the whole matter. He knew better than Emily whether or not Celia had slept with Jacob. Resolved, Celia headed for the arcade.

She entered the open game hall under the familiar neon archway. Immediately, she was assaulted with dings, and grunts, and tire squeals, and crashes. It was a mixed bag. Celia loved the open-air arcade, and the fact that it still had Skee-Ball and Ms. Pac-Man. But it was also ironic to see all these kids inside playing video games when the ocean was right there. Then again, she had managed to split her time pretty well back in the day. She used to love coming to the arcade with Chris and Jacob. Back when both twins had been wooing her, they would give her their tickets, and even though all the prizes were pretty cheap-o, she still loved the attention. Celia walked around, feeling invisible to all the kids. She hadn't spotted Chris and was about to head out when she noticed a large man behind the prize counter staring at her. She smiled at him, then turned to go.

"Celia Jensen." Startled to hear her name come out of his mouth, Celia turned back around. The man got out of his chair and then slapped and rubbed his hands together with a giant grin. "I heard you were back in town."

"Hey there," Celia said, keeping a smile on as she walked toward him. There had been so many boys here during the summer, it wouldn't be easy to narrow down who he was. Hopefully, he would volunteer his name. When Celia was finally about a foot from him, his features began to gel in her mind. Oh my God. It was Chris Vernon. It didn't seem possible. What had happened to him?

"I know," he said. "I'm huge." He held out his hands in a what-are-you-going-to-do shrug. "The wife is a good cook," he added with a wink.

"It's good to see you, Chris," Celia said.

"You are looking hot," Chris said.

Celia had to laugh. He seemed harmless now that he wasn't a stud. Was that an awful thing to think? "Thank you." She had fully intended to be cold to him, but the transformation was so stunning and he was so friendly, she found it difficult not to smile back at him. "I'm glad you're here," he said. "Do you want to go for a beer?"

"Now?"

"It's five o'clock somewhere."

"Sure."

"Great." Chris tilted his head back and bellowed someone's name. Celia couldn't quite make it out. A few seconds later, a teenage boy ambled over. He wasn't as good-looking as the twins had been back then, but he was handsome and he knew it.

"Egotistical cockroach," Chris said with a wink as he put

his arm around Celia and they headed out. "Tell me I was
nothing like that."

"You weren't," Celia said truthfully. "You were worse."

They went to a little beach bar that had a few tables out
on the boardwalk, and sat outside. Chris ordered a beer, and
although Celia would have normally just gone for an iced tea
or lemonade, she thought the situation might call for a little
help, so she ordered a margarita.

"Cheers," Chris said. They clinked glasses and each took
a sip. "So. How's your dad?"

"Didn't Jacob tell you?"

"Didn't Jacob tell *you?*"

"Tell me what?"

"The twins don't speak anymore."

"What?"

"That was obnoxious, wasn't it? Talking about myself in
the third person. Or half of myself." Chris laughed and then
gave her a little wink.

"Why aren't you speaking?"

Chris held his hands up. "Oh, I might have said something like, 'Emily Tanner is the biggest douche on the boardwalk, and you're an idiot if you can't see that.' " He had a
loud voice and dramatic delivery. Almost every word was
punctuated with a hand movement.

Celia had just taken a big sip of her margarita, and she
swallowed as fast as she could so she wouldn't spit it out, but
then it ended up going down the wrong pipe, and before she
knew it, she was convulsing in a massive coughing fit, and
Chris was trying to pound her on the back, which wasn't
helping whatsoever, but Celia could see by the panicked
look in his eyes that he was truly trying to help her. When
she finally worked it all out, she began to laugh, and then
Chris began to laugh. Before she knew it, they were cackling

like a couple of hyenas on bar stools. Both of them had to wipe away tears.

"Nice move, by the way. Buying Ocean House." He jabbed a fork in her direction and grinned. "I like your style."

"She never let me in."

"You have *sand* on your feet." He mimicked Elizabeth Tanner's voice perfectly. He slapped his hands over both cheeks and opened his mouth in mock surprise. Once again, Celia was in stitches.

"Oh my God. You're *funny*. And *nice*." More laughter from the pair.

"I was kind of a dick back then, wasn't I?"

"Yeah. You were."

"Sorry."

Celia stared at the straw in her drink. It was now or never. "Speaking of which."

"Uh-oh."

Celia laughed. "Men hate to be confronted, don't they?"

"We'd rather be mauled by a pack of Bambis."

"A pack of Bambis?"

"Or bunnies. Or anything equally humiliating. Bring it on. Anything other than—'We need to talk.' "

"Good to know."

"Go ahead. I can take it." Chris pummeled his chest. "But if you make my mascara run, I'll never forgive you."

"About that morning on the beach." The words stuck in her throat. Chris immediately dropped the jokes. "I just. At the time I. Chris." She was going to cry. Chris reached over and took her hand. He put his other hand on his heart.

"I'm so sorry. I was such a dick. Such a dick!"

"It's okay. I just—"

"It's not okay. Not okay." He folded his hands on top of the table, and stared at them as he lowered his voice and spoke. "You might not believe this, but I've spent all these years beating myself up about that. I had no idea you guys would skip town and I would never get a chance to set things right."

We didn't skip town; we were forced out, Celia thought. But that wasn't the discussion she needed to have with Chris. Celia looked him in the eye and spoke as fast as she could. "I slept with Jacob, didn't I?"

"Oh my God. Yes. Yes. Yes. I thought you knew I was just being a dick—"

"Oh thank God."

"Now, you don't have to sound that relieved. I wasn't too bad-looking in those days."

"So why did he leave me there? Why didn't Jacob come back?"

"Because he couldn't find the ring, and then he ran into Emily, who told him you were crying and hated him. She told him you were at her house. I had just come back from seeing you under the boardwalk, but when I tried to tell Jacob—well, Emily said you were with her now. I figured you'd run over to her after what I did."

"No. I waited there for three hours."

"I'm so sorry. He still has no idea what I did. Hell, he hasn't spoken to me over calling Emily a douche; imagine if he knew what I did to the love of his life."

Love of his life. The words pierced. It must have showed on her face. "Don't look so surprised," Chris said. "You two were soul mates."

Celia didn't want to think about that right now. Wouldn't soul mates have found a way to make it work? Something Chris had said caught up with her. *Because he couldn't find the ring.* "What ring?" she said.

"What?"

"You said—'Because he couldn't find the ring.' "

"That's right. That's when he discovered it was missing."

"The diamond?"

"Of course."

"Why was he looking—" Celia stopped. *I have a surprise for you. . . .* "Oh my God."

"You didn't know." Chris said it like a statement. "I actually told him he was crazy. You guys were way too young to get engaged. But a locomotive wouldn't have stopped him."

"He was going to propose." Celia just had to say it out loud.

"That and only that was the reason I thought that maybe—just maybe your dad did take the ring."

"What?"

"A few days before Jacob had asked your father for your hand in marriage."

"He did not."

Chris chuckled at the memory. "Your dad threw a paint can at him and told him to grow up and get a real job first."

"Oh God."

"But Jacob stood his ground. After he ducked, of course. Told your dad he was deeply sorry that he didn't have his permission, but he was going to do it anyway."

"Wow."

"Your dad says—'What are you going to give her? A ring out of a crackerjack box? You think that's what my Sassafras is worth?' "

Celia gave a strangled laugh. She could hear him saying that. This from the man who wanted his ashes in a coffee can. It was so strange hearing new stories about her father; in a way it made her feel like she was being given back a little bit of time with him.

"That's when Jacob told him he was going to give you our mother's ring. Jacob showed it to your dad and everything."

"Oh. God." It didn't change anything. Did it? Her father wouldn't have stolen a ring. But would he have temporarily misplaced it so that Jacob couldn't propose? Could he have hidden it somewhere? No. He had told her before he died. *I didn't take that ring.* "I thought the ring belonged to both of you."

"It did."

"And you were just going to let him give it to me?"

"Jacob bought me out."

"Seriously?"

"Every penny he'd ever saved. Jacob was a saver. Plus his baseball card collection, skateboard, and every *Playboy* he owned. And an IOU for the rest. Never did see a penny of that though." Chris chuckled again. It was criminal the two weren't speaking anymore. Especially since Chris seemed like he had grown into a genuinely nice man.

Celia downed the rest of her margarita in one go.

"You still love him," Chris said. He glanced at her empty margarita glass. "Either that or I'd better cart your ass to rehab."

"Don't be silly."

"I know he still loves you."

"He's with Emily. He told me so himself."

"Emily is the safe bet. Not the girl who ripped his heart out and ran away."

Just like Ben was her safe bet. But Celia hadn't run away. And Jacob could have come looking for her. But he didn't. He just let her go. "Emily just lied to me. She said it was you I slept with that night."

Chris shook his head, then pointed at Celia. "Proves my theory right there."

"What?"

"Even Emily knows he never got over you. She's lying, Celia. I wish I would've been so lucky. But it was Jacob. It was always Jacob, wasn't it?"

"It was," Celia said.

"That's why I was such a dick."

"What?"

"I was always crushing on you. But you knew that."

"No. I honestly didn't."

"Come on. How could you not? Jake and I went so many rounds over you." He mimed boxing.

"You did not."

"Well. You and the million other things we fought about."

"It shouldn't be that way. You're brothers. Twins. Take it from me, every second you get with the ones you love is precious."

"You know what? You're right. So what are we going to do to get him away from that skinny douche?"

"I'm not really the type to fight over a guy." Wasn't she? Why else had she come? It wasn't like he was married with kids. And Emily Tanner definitely didn't deserve the likes of Jacob. If Emily was willing to so blatantly lie to Celia to keep her away from him, just how many lies was she feeding Jacob?

"Just keep hanging around. I know my brother. He'll come to you."

"In the meantime." Celia leaned forward and whispered, just in case a summer breeze were to catch her words and carry them down the boardwalk. "Catch me up on everything you've got on Elizabeth Tanner."

"Ah. A mother-daughter takedown." Chris finished his beer, then raised his hand to the waitress. Celia had to laugh; he looked like a little kid in school waiting to get called on, but sure enough a waitress scooped his empty glass up and headed off to get him another. He grinned at Celia. She had to smile back. "Just when I thought this day couldn't get any better," Chris said.

CHAPTER 7

When Elizabeth Tanner had humiliated Pete Jensen, she did it in a very public way. Celia fumed as she remembered the gathering on the beach. Neighborhood Watch, her ass. It was a modern-day witch hunt. At least fifty residents had gathered for Elizabeth's witch hunt. "We're going to take back our community!"

Celia had stood on the boardwalk watching. At first she had simply been looking for Jacob in the mob. She'd been desperate to see him, but also furious and hurt beyond belief. To have him leave so happy—*I have a surprise for you*—and then never speak to him again. How did things like that happen?

The ring. She never would have guessed it in a million years. That's why Jacob had been so upset it was missing. Not because they had wanted to pawn it and use the cash, but because he had been going to propose.

Celia kept seeing her father throwing a paint can at Jacob. It probably shouldn't make her laugh, but it did. She also couldn't help imagining how the proposal would have gone. Jacob would have returned, and held her, and kissed her. He would have gotten down on one knee in the sand. She knew this beyond a doubt. Celia would have said yes. This too was indisputable. They would have been married twenty years by now. With kids, and a house of their own, and most likely a couple of pets. But that's not what had happened. All because of interference from Chris, and Emily.

So who had taken the ring and why? Did he or she know what Jacob had planned on doing with it? Could it have been Chris himself? He had admitted to having a crush on Celia, he had known Jacob was going to propose, and he had come to stop it with a very devious "Chris-like" plan of attack.

But he was different now, and he seemed genuinely remorseful. Surely he would have confessed if he'd taken the ring.

Celia turned back to the beach and, in her memory, saw Elizabeth handing out fliers.

HAMPTON BEACH BURGLAR!

Half the women in the crowd, including Elizabeth, were probably totally turned on by the thought. There was even a picture of her father on the flyer, going into someone's home. Legally, of course. He did work for all the locals. Soon the crowd was stirred up, murmuring about items of theirs that had gone missing. Celia hadn't been able to contain herself. She ran onto the beach, shouting.

"It's not him! He didn't take the ring. My father isn't a thief!" She screamed it over and over, pushing her way through the crowd, looking people in the eye. She could tell by the way they stared back that he'd already been tried and convicted. Celia made her way up to Elizabeth and squared off, looking the woman in the eye. "Tell them. Tell them why you're really doing this."

Elizabeth smiled. "I admire your loyalty to your dad. It must be so hard to grow up with a thief for a dad and a drunk for a mother."

Elizabeth's words struck Celia right between the eyes.

Celia heard the sound of gasping. It came from her. She didn't realize anyone on Hampton Beach knew about her mother. How did they? What horrible gossips they all were. And how in the world could Elizabeth Tanner stand in front of her and say those things to a young girl? With all those people watching? Celia could feel herself shaking with humiliation and rage. She was also stunned, almost paralyzed. She'd never had someone treat her with such blatant cruelty. She should have stomped on Elizabeth's foot or punched her in the face.

But all Celia could manage was to snatch fliers out of people's hands as she pushed her way out of the crowd and back to the boardwalk. When she reached it, she looked up to find her father waiting for her. He glanced at the fliers, then swiftly took them out of her hands and tossed them into the nearest trash can.

"Ice cream, Sassafras?" he said. That was their last night on Hampton Beach.

It's over, Celia told herself. *It was a long time ago. It doesn't matter.* It didn't work. Celia would throw her father a party; that's what she would do. She would furnish Ocean House and invite all the locals to one big party. Elizabeth and Emily included. It was time Jacob knew what Chris and Emily had done; it was time for Celia to look Elizabeth in the eye and tell her she had no right treating people like they were beneath her. It was time to sleep in a real bed instead of on a blow-up mattress. And maybe nobody else would give two hoots. But Celia might feel better. Then, she would spread her father's ashes in the ocean, and turn Ocean House into the welcoming, all-inclusive place it was meant to be. Ever since moving to the ocean as a little girl, Celia had had a reoccurring fantasy of owning a large beach house and inviting city kids whose families couldn't afford a vacation, a free place to stay for up to a week. It was unfathomable to

Celia that some kids had never even seen the ocean. And Ocean House was the perfect place to follow her dream. It looked like she wasn't going to get the guy, but she sure as hell had the house. Maybe everything had led her back here so that she could finally follow her lifelong dream. At the end of the day, you had to feel good about giving others a well-deserved place to just get away.

There was a man waiting for her on the porch. From a distance she could make out the receding hairline and a tan suit. Oh God. Ben? Her only advantage was that he hadn't noticed her. He was staring at the rocking chair. She almost giggled. He was still in the investment banking, Red Bull world. He was like an alien who couldn't fathom what a rocking chair was for. She ducked down by the side of the porch so she could think as she crouched. The next thing she knew, a pair of sneakers appeared next to her. She looked up muscular, tanned legs to find Jacob staring down at her. They locked eyes, and he smiled. Her insides turned to jelly as she smiled back. Jacob lifted his head.

"Can I help you?" he called to Ben.

"Oh. Hello. I'm looking for Celia Jensen." Celia heard Ben walk across the porch toward Jacob. He was going to see her if he came any closer. Jacob hopped onto the porch and led him a safe distance away.

"I just saw her way down the boardwalk," Jacob said. "If you hurry, you can probably catch her."

Celia could just imagine Ben in his suit running down the boardwalk. "I think I'll just wait," Ben said.

"Can't stop you from waiting, but you'll have to move off this porch."

"Pardon?"

"I don't know you. And this isn't your porch."

"Celia is my fiancée."

Fiancée? Why that little . . . twat. How dare he?

"Well. I'm not going to get into any of that, but I am going to ask you to wait until you're properly invited to come up on this porch."

"And just who the hell do you think you are?"

Uh-oh. She didn't want Jacob getting in this deep. Although she loved that he was protecting her. Celia popped up.

"Hello, Ben."

"Celia?" Ben was taken completely aback. Celia felt kind of bad.

"Fiancée?" Celia said. Ben glared at her.

"Can we talk?" he said. "In private."

"We broke up, Ben. You can't go around calling me your fiancée."

Ben looked at Jacob. Then back at Celia. "Is this the guy?" he said. Jacob looked at her and raised an eyebrow.

Oh, he's the guy, all right. Look at him. Is there any question at all that this would be the guy? "All right," Celia said. "Let's go inside." She pulled her key out and marched toward the door.

"What guy?" Jacob said.

"Oh, don't be so smug," Ben said. "Looks like you two didn't waste any time making up for lost years."

"That's enough, Ben," Celia said. "Jacob has a very . . ." She stopped. What was she going to say about Emily? "Well-known girlfriend."

There went that eyebrow again. Did Jacob have any idea how sexy he looked? "I can stay," Jacob said. "If you want."

"No. You can go," Ben said.

"It's okay," Celia said. Jacob nodded, then started down the porch. "Wait," Celia called. He stopped. Looked fully prepared to come back if she asked him to. "What are you doing here?"

"Oh." Jacob faltered. "I just—was going to look at that sink you said was leaking."

"Oh," Celia said. "Right." Her insides lit up. She had never asked him to look at a sink. He was here for something private. God, she wanted to just kiss him and get it over with. If Ben hadn't shown up, they might be kissing right now.

"Where are your tools?" Ben said.

"I have tools," Celia said. "I guess you'll have to fix it later," she said to Jacob.

"By all means, fix it now," Ben said. "I'm not going to let her blame me for prolonging a leak!" Celia opened the door, and Ben headed in. She glanced at Jacob again. He smiled. She smiled.

"Now you have to pretend to fix my sink," she whispered as Jacob brushed past her. He stopped when they were both in the doorway. Once again, so, so close.

"It really does leak," he whispered back.

"Oh," she said. "Can you fix it?"

"Probably not." With that, he walked the rest of the way inside, leaving her longing for him once again.

Celia purposely stayed in the living room with Ben. She didn't want to see Jacob lying under the sink. She would probably toss all decency and decorum away and climb on top of him. Ben paced the living room.

"Okay," he finally said, throwing his arms up. "I like it. We'll keep it as our vacation house."

"What?"

"Come home, Celia. I miss you like crazy."

"Oh, Ben. I thought I made myself very clear." Was she imagining things, or did the clanking in the kitchen suddenly stop?

"It was grief talking."

"Ben. It wasn't. It was *me* talking."

"Is he the one?"

"What?"

"The true love your father wanted you to 'reconnect' with?"

A loud clanging sound rang out from the kitchen. Celia

didn't dare look in that direction. "Please. Let's not focus on that."

"Never play poker, Celia. *Ever*."

"I'll keep that in mind."

"I'm not going to sell the condo. It's a buyer's market."

"Then you'll have to buy me out."

"What? So you can stay here? Chase lover boy?"

Now the kitchen was so quiet you could hear a pin drop. "No. So I can live my life, Ben. I've spent too many years covering up the girl I used to be. Living the exact opposite of the life I really wanted to live. But that's over now. I like you, Ben, and I thought what I wanted was a safe, dependable relationship. But—"

"Not this again. So you don't feel fireworks. They don't last forever, you know. They blow up, and then they're over within seconds. Haven't you ever seen fireworks?"

Yes. Every year. Right here on this beach with Jacob. And not just on the Fourth of July. "I don't want to be with you. My life is changing now."

"You're pathetic."

"Excuse me?"

"You heard me. I put up with you and your crazy dad for seven years, and this is the thanks I get?"

"Get out."

"I'm not selling, and I'm not—"

"The lady said 'Get out.'" Jacob stood in the doorway, shirtless, holding a wrench in one hand and the Chock Full O'Nuts can in the other.

Ben pointed to the coffee can. "What's he doing with that? Better yet. What are you still doing with that?"

"I'm standing in," Jacob said. "If Pete were here he'd want me to throw it at your head."

"Are you listening to this?" Ben said.

"Yes. I think they're asking you to leave."

"Why do you still have that can?"

"Because I'm not delivering his ashes to the ocean until I've done what I came here to do," Celia said.

"And what's that?" Jacob asked. He sounded genuinely curious. Darn it. Why hadn't she kept her mouth shut?

"You didn't tell him?" Ben said. "About your dad's dying wish?"

"Don't be so sarcastic."

"You're the one carrying him around in a coffee can."

"It's what he wanted."

"Just like he wanted you to run and find lover boy."

"Wait," Jacob said. "Me?"

"I don't believe this," Celia said.

"Neither do I," Jacob said. "I thought your father hated me."

"Join the club," Ben said.

"I still have a dent from where he nailed me with a paint can," Jacob said. Celia's head jerked toward him. The paint can her father had thrown when Jacob asked for her hand in marriage. They locked eyes. A current buzzed through them. Celia tore her eyes away from him.

"He never threw anything at me," Ben said. "Is that bad? Does he only throw things at people he likes?"

"Ben. I'm sorry you're hurt. But it's over. I don't know how else to say it. I'll have a lawyer contact you about settling the house."

"Good luck with that. And good luck with getting all your things back."

"You know what? Have at them. I have everything I need right here." Celia threw her arms open.

Ben looked around at the empty room. "You have nothing."

Of course Ben would see it that way. He thought in terms of numbers, and charts, and things. "And I've never felt so blessed." Celia marched to the door. "Good-bye, Ben." Ben threw a disgusted look at Jacob, and then he was gone. Celia had never loved any sound more than the door slamming after him.

Jacob was on her in seconds. "Are you okay?"

She wanted to touch his abs. With hers. "I did what I had to do. What a person should do in these situations." She looked at him pointedly. She wasn't going to kiss him. Or touch. She shouldn't even let him in her house, fixing her sink without a shirt. If he wanted to be with her, he would have to break up with Emily.

"You've always been brave," he said.

"No," she whispered. "There was a time when I was a coward." This time there was something deeper about the connection when their eyes met. "That morning at the beach. After we . . ."

"Made love?" The relief from hearing him say it was immense. She had believed Chris, of course, but Emily had planted such a seed of doubt that it meant everything to her to finally get confirmation.

"I waited three hours for you."

"What? I ran into Emily on my way back and she said—"

"She lied. Just like Chris lied to me."

"Chris? What do you mean?"

"I want to talk about all of this. Maybe we can go somewhere—"

"Absolutely. Now?" She stepped forward. Her hand reached for his face. She just wanted to caress it. "Your father wanted you to come find me?" Jacob said.

Celia nodded. "He said the only time he saw me really happy was when I was with you."

"I knew it." The shrill voice rang through the room, jolting Celia and Jacob apart. Emily stood just a few feet away, hands on her hips, glaring. Neither of them had heard her come in.

"I told you she was after you," Emily said. "Let's go."

"Emily," Jacob said. "What are you doing here?"

"What are *you* doing here?" Emily said. "That's the real question."

"I asked him to fix my sink," Celia said.

"Oh, I'll just bet you did," Emily said.

"It's not true," Jacob said. "I came on my own." He glanced over at Celia. "And I think I might have made the sink worse."

I don't care. I love you.

"We'll talk about this at home," Emily said. "Let's go, Jacob."

"Give me a minute," Jacob said to Celia in a low voice. She started to tell him it was all right, that he should just go, but it would have been a lie. She nodded. Jacob walked out to the porch and waited for Emily to follow. Emily started after him, then stopped and stared at Celia.

"This isn't over," Emily said.

I know, Celia thought. *I think it's just begun.*

Celia wasn't able to hear what they were saying. But she could see Emily's arms flailing on the porch. Emily was doing her best to get Jacob to leave with her. *All these years and she doesn't know him like I do*, Celia thought. Jacob might be quiet at times, more of an observer, but he had never been a pushover. The more Emily begged him to leave or harped on him, the more of a sure bet it was that he was going to stay. And then what? It didn't matter. They were going to talk. And then? Whatever it was, Celia was going to be ready. This time she wasn't going to let him slip away.

CHAPTER 8

Jacob and Emily stood on the porch. "Why are we standing out here?" Emily said. "I want to go home."

"I won't keep you long," Jacob said.

"What do you mean? You're coming with me."

"Emily. This conversation is a long time coming."

"The one with her or the one with me?"

"Both, I'm afraid."

"You are not breaking up with me on the porch of my mother's house."

"We can step onto the sidewalk, if you'd like."

"Jacob. Jacob, please. Please. You can't do this to me."

"I like you, Emily. I do. But I never felt exactly right about this relationship."

"Didn't stop you for a solid year, now did it?"

"You know I've tried to talk to you about this. And you'd get upset." That was an understatement. The first time he had tried to break up with her, she had hinted at suicide. *I'd die, Jacob. I'd just want to die.* He knew she had a flair for the dramatic, but at the time he couldn't handle the thought that she might do something to herself and it would be his fault. Besides, he wasn't interested in anyone else in town, so why not try and make a go of it? But when he had heard Celia's speech to Ben, echoing exactly how he felt, he knew he had to be just as brave.

Hell. He had known it the moment he'd first laid eyes on Celia again, right after she took off that ridiculously floppy hat. *Bang.* There she was. In the flesh. In front of him. The girl he'd always loved. The only girl he had ever thought about proposing to. He wasn't going to go into all of that with Emily, and he'd be doing this regardless of whether Celia wanted to be with him. This time he was just going to have to take the punches, whatever they might be.

"I'm going to kill her," Emily said.

Whoa. That wasn't going to fly. "This isn't because of her," Jacob said. "You know it's been coming."

"Like hell. We would not be standing here having this conversation if she hadn't swooped back into town. She's a liar. And her father was a thief. Why have you always been so blond when it comes to her?"

Did she mean "blind"? Jacob could never tell with her. "I don't think you want to start a conversation with me about lying right now," Jacob said.

"What's that supposed to mean? What did she tell you?" Emily's voice started to shake. She was hiding something, all right.

"Why don't you tell me?"

"Tell you what? I really have no clue."

"There's nothing you want to tell me about that morning on the beach?"

"What morning on the beach?"

"Emily. This isn't cute. I know you know what I'm talking about."

"What did she say?"

"You see? I'm not having a conversation with her right now. I'm having it with you. And I'm asking for a straight answer."

"She wasn't right for you, Jacob. I was doing you a favor."

"She wasn't at your house crying. She was waiting for me. On the beach."

"Chris had me do it."

"Why?"

"Because he went off to find her so he could pretend that he was the one who slept with her."

"What? You're kidding me, right? I didn't even tell him I slept with her."

"You didn't have to tell him. He was so in love with Celia he followed you two wherever you went."

"He did?"

"See? You don't know what goes on under your own nose. No wonder you can't see her for who she really is."

"You're the one who helped set up a girl who had never done anything to you."

"She called my mother a liar."

"First of all, you know that's not true. Second of all, that was after all of this had occurred. This was before the ring 'went missing.' The ring I was looking for so I could propose to her!"

"Which would have been the worst mistake of your life. And don't think I didn't pick up on your little air quotes. I hope you aren't thinking of spilling the beans to your precious little seal."

"Don't call her that."

"Seals bark and they *stink*."

"Hate is not a good color on you."

"You know what? I take it back. I think you should tell her the truth. All of it. You'll see her true colors then."

"You know what? I'm starting to see what the worst mistakes of my life were. And none of them have anything to do with her." Jacob gave Emily a nod, and then headed back into the house without another word.

"This isn't over!" Emily screamed from the porch. Jacob turned to find Celia in the living room, sitting on the floor.

"This isn't over," Celia said. "Those were Ben's words exactly."

"I'm really sorry. Did you hear the whole thing?"

"Oh no—I wasn't eavesdropping. I just heard that last bit because—well, I think the whole neighborhood heard that last bit."

"I think I need a walk."

"Sure. I understand. I'll leave you—"

"With you," Jacob said, holding out his hand. "I want to take a walk with you."

They strolled along the ocean's edge. Celia slipped her hand into Jacob's, and he took it without hesitation. He brought it up to his mouth and kissed the back of her hand, then squeezed it.

"Are we crazy?" Celia asked.

"If we are, I don't want to be sane."

"Me neither."

Jacob stopped, turned her around. "Tell me what Chris did."

"Emily must have told you. I wanted to do it myself."

"Chris should have told me."

"I can't believe how much your brother has changed."

"You saw him?"

"We had a drink on the boardwalk. I was sorry to hear you're not speaking."

"He's going to wish we weren't speaking when I see him again. What exactly did he do?"

"Jacob. I don't want to cause any more trouble between the two of you. Besides, I like the new Chris."

"He needs to lose weight. I hate to see him like that."

"He has to do it for himself. But otherwise he seems very

happy. Except of course when it came to you. I think this cold war is killing him."

"Partly my fault. He tried to tell me what Emily was like. I didn't want to hear it. Not that it excuses any of his behavior."

"It was a long time ago."

"I don't want any secrets between us. They've done enough damage, don't you think?"

"Yes. I do."

"I want to know everything. And there are a few things I need to tell you. But I just don't want to do it today. I've waited twenty years to see you again, and there's somewhere very special I want to take you. Okay?"

"Okay."

"But I promise. We'll talk about everything. Everything."

"Talking can wait, Jacob. I agree. Let's just *be* today." Celia started to walk. Jacob twirled her around, like a dancer being turned. Her chest came into his, and before she could even anticipate it, Jacob kissed her. That's when Celia learned that no matter how much time passes, some things never change. His kiss was just as electric and magical as she'd always remembered it. She should know. They stayed in one spot, kissing, for a very long time.

They headed down the boardwalk. Still hand in hand, neither of them able to wipe the smiles off their faces. "Where are we going?" Celia asked.

"Do you remember what happens this time of year?" Jacob said.

"The fair!" Celia said. Once a year, a street fair came to town. They set up tents and rides, including a Ferris wheel right on the ocean. It was on that Ferris wheel, when they were stuck at the top, that Jacob had told her he loved her for the very first time. And there, swaying above the ocean, Celia Jensen had said it back for the very first time.

* * *

The fair was in full swing. Cotton candy, and rides, and carnival games, including a dunk tank, and of course, the Ferris wheel. Celia felt a bit of her youth recaptured as she stood in line holding hands with Jacob. He wanted to know about her life, her work, her dad. She was honest about everything without sounding like a complete downer.

Jacob filled her in on a few highlights of his life. After Celia and her father had left, it had been quite a while before Jacob or Chris spoke with Emily or her mother again. There had been no more thefts, and soon everyone had simmered down. Emily had gone away to college, and Mrs. Tanner had met an older gentleman and stopped hitting on all the young boys in town. Chris had met a girl, fallen in love, and finally after many years of trying they had three kids. Jacob confirmed the wife was a good cook. When Emily had come back from college, she had morphed into a new woman. She was very attractive, but didn't behave like her mother. At least not at first. As Celia listened to the story of Emily's transformation, then the slow descent into the shrill replica of her mother she was now, Celia figured it had all been orchestrated to get Jacob.

"I think I was a replacement for Chris. Once he got married, she set her sights on me." The arcade was a good investment, and they also had money in a few of the souvenir shops on the boardwalk. Jacob still did odd jobs around town, but only because he liked to, not because he had to. He was in the market to buy a place, but he had known he wasn't going to buy one with Emily.

"I'm surprised you didn't want Ocean House," Celia said.

"I didn't want any place where you hadn't been welcomed," Jacob said. It was their turn to board the ride. Jacob opened the door for her, and then slid in after her. Excitement grew in her as the car swayed, and soon they were moving, rising to the top. Everything looked so small from up here. The boardwalk, the beach, even the ocean. They were on top of the world. Jacob looked at her.

"I'm sweating as much now as I was then," Jacob said.

Celia laughed. "I couldn't tell then, and I can't now."

"I never thought I'd get the words out of my mouth."

"It was the most romantic moment of my life," Celia said.

"Me too."

"What should we do after this?"

"Well. We could get a bite to eat. Some lobster."

"I love lobster."

"Liar. You just love the butter."

"That's partially true."

"And maybe a drink."

"Twist my arm."

"A little more of this." Jacob leaned over and kissed her.

"A lot more of that," Celia said.

Jacob smiled. He traced her upper lip with his index finger. "And then," he said in a voice that was almost a growl.

"Then?" Celia said. *Say it. Say it. I want you too. I want you right here, right now.*

"And then, from the looks of your place, we should buy furniture."

They dined oceanside on lobster and crab. Jacob ordered a bottle of champagne. After it was poured, they held their glasses aloft.

"To second chances," Jacob said. Celia's mouth dropped open. She hadn't mentioned anything to Jacob about all of her ruminations on "second chances." They were just in tune, like they always had been. Celia couldn't have asked for a more perfect afternoon. She wished she could put the day on ice, thaw it out, and relive it whenever she wanted.

"Did you buy Ocean House just so you could walk in with sandy feet?" Jacob asked. The glint in his eye gave away that he was teasing.

"Partly. But this area is home. It's where I wanted to be. I knew no matter what shape it was in, I could make the house work. But it's also because I've always had this idea, and once I get the place up and running, I want to try it out."

"What idea?"

"Do you know there are city kids who have never even seen the ocean?"

"I couldn't imagine."

"Me neither. But it's not hard to imagine all the families who can't afford to take a vacation."

"True."

"Well, I want to open up Ocean House as a free place for families in need to stay. Anywhere from a long weekend to a week. I want to reach out to the right community groups in big cities, and offer up two rooms each summer for families to come spend a few days to a week at a time at no charge. I'm also going to see if I can figure out how to raise funds for their transportation."

"That's amazing. Are you sure you'd want strangers in your home?"

"Lots of them. And they can go barefoot. But seriously, I don't mind. If I partner with a nonprofit agency, they can vet the family first so that I'm not leaving myself too vulnerable, but I'm not going to let fear of a few bad apples stop me from helping a lot of good kids see the ocean and get away from it all, even if it's just for a few days."

"You were a remarkable girl, and you've grown into a remarkable woman. I think it's a fabulous idea."

"You do?"

"Of course. It makes me love you—" He stopped short as he heard what he was saying. Celia wanted to make him feel less embarrassed, but she couldn't stop smiling. Jacob shook his head and smiled too, as a bit of that shy boy came creeping back into his face. "Anyway," he said. "I'll help you however I can."

"I'm just glad you didn't tell me I was crazy. Ben would have hated the idea."

"No offense, but Ben is a . . ." Jacob let the sentence trail.

Twat, Celia heard her father say in her head.

"What do you say to ice cream?" Jacob said, dropping the subject of Ben.

"Yes," Celia said. "As long as I don't have to cry."

After their late lunch, Jacob once again started heading in a certain direction. "Where now?" Celia asked. She loved the adventure, but her curiosity got the better of her.

"You'll see," Jacob said. "If you're willing to climb into my truck, I know a guy."

Ten miles down the road was a warehouse filled with used, but beautiful, furniture. Celia loved the pieces, but it was still out of her budget. She was forced to admit this to Jacob. The owner, a large man wearing suspenders with Bermuda shorts, ambled over. "Pick out whatever you like, darling. I owe this man and his family going back twenty years now."

"We used to do deliveries and such when he first started," Jacob said.

"Once the women in town learned the strapping twins were my delivery boys, sales skyrocketed." The man laughed. "I told them if they ever wanted anything, it was on me. And now that Jacob has told me what you plan on doing with Ocean House—well, it's tax deductible too."

Celia felt a swell of joy and love rise within her. People really were good. They just needed the opportunity to prove it.

"Where do we start?" Celia said.

Celia picked out mostly sturdy, oak furniture. It would complement the floors and the rustic look of the beach house. The sofa was the one exception; she chose a soft fabric in a beautiful sea-green color. She placed a vase of gorgeous sea glass next to it, added a couple of oversized throw pillows and a black-and-white photo of a beach above the sofa, and suddenly the living room looked as if it had come straight out of a designer magazine. Celia couldn't believe all this furniture had been donated. She was going to make sure and promote the store when she set about drumming up publicity for the project.

When everything was in place, Celia stood back and took it all in. What a difference furniture made! There were now several rocking chairs and little tables on the front porch. The living room had a sofa and a coffee table, two end tables, and two oversized chairs near the fireplace. A sturdy, long dining table took up the dining room. A few candles and a vase of flowers would really set it off, along with a large mirror in an old-fashioned gold frame above the fireplace. Each bedroom had a bed and an end table. Finally, a smaller, stone table and a butcher-block island completed the kitchen. Celia would have jars with wildflowers about the place as much as she could. A tall bookshelf greeted visitors in the foyer. Her guests could start a paperback exchange. Nothing went with a beach getaway like a good book.

They announced the neighborhood open house in the local newspaper, along with an article about her plans for Ocean House's future, and in it they asked everyone to bring donations such as lamps, towels, bedding, kitchen appliances—everything the house would need. A local catering company agreed to host the open house at a discount. Celia couldn't believe how smoothly it was all coming together. She was so motivated and excited about her plans that she'd even stopped fantasizing about confronting Elizabeth. In fact, Celia was going to bury the hatchet. After all, if Elizabeth hadn't treated her so horribly, barred her from the house, she might not have ever come up with this idea. In a strange way, every single step was meant to be. If she and Jacob had stayed together, she might have been too wrapped up in their lives to follow through with the dream, and together it was unlikely they would have bought Ocean House.

People spent too much time regretting their choices. Celia realized she could just as easily spend that energy seeing how life sometimes turned out better than you could ever imagine if you just let go and stopped trying to control every little thing. She could feel her bitterness leaving her day by day. She and Jacob were getting so close, although they had yet to make love. Instead they were building back up to it, kissing and petting like teenagers, drawing out the delicious anticipation. In the midst of their renewed puppy-love, she and Jacob never did pick back up on their serious conversation. She had already said her part. Whatever he wanted to tell her could wait until he was good and ready.

Ben was still refusing to sell their condo in Boston, and she was going to have to get a lawyer. Just because she was more relaxed than ever didn't mean she was going to ignore what was only right and fair. And she and Jacob were so over the moon about rekindling their relationship, Celia barely noticed that Emily had been leaving them alone. *It's too good to be true,* Celia thought, momentarily returning to her habit of worrying. *What if it's all too good to be true?*

CHAPTER 9

The morning of the open house, Celia rose early, left a slumbering Jacob in bed, and walked along the beach. She'd forgotten the miracle of seeing the sun rise over the ocean. How crazy was it to forget something like that? What she hadn't forgotten was what it felt like to make love with Jacob. Last night they had been unable to hold back any longer, and had ripped the clothes off of each other like they'd been stranded on separate beaches for decades. It had been like the first time all over again, except they weren't getting sand in places that sand shouldn't go, and Jacob didn't run off afterward, never to return again. But their bodies had melded into each other with the same passion as that first night on the beach, maybe even more, if that was possible. They'd made love five times last night. Every time they tried to stop and get some sleep, one or the other would end up trailing a hand along his or her bare skin, and the passion would ignite again. Every touch, every kiss, every probe sent Celia into space. It was amazing how sex could feel with the right person. Comfortable, yet incredibly sexy and primal. Moaning one minute and laughing the next. Soft kisses and hard thrusts, and—let's face it—orgasms that didn't have to be faked. Celia couldn't believe it. She was so lucky to experience this again, to be able to express decades of pent-up longing. Just thinking about it made her want to run back to the bed and have her way with him. She couldn't stop smiling. She took a deep breath and glanced at the sunrise again.

Red and orange light spilled over the horizon, dazzling the sky with intense, glowing rays. Good morning, sunshine! This was going to be a good day. Celia had no idea how many people would come through the house today, but she would welcome them all. The food was ready. The balloons were waiting to be tied to the mailbox. She'd even hired a small, local band to play on the front porch. She was probably the only person on the face of the earth to throw herself a Welcome to the Neighborhood party, but she didn't care. She and her father had left with their heads down; she was coming back with her head held high.

After spending an hour or so walking along the ocean's edge, Celia made her way back to Ocean House. Just as she reached her corner, she saw Chris standing across the street, looking at the house. It was as if he were afraid to cross over.

"Hey there," Celia said. Chris turned. Instead of showing her the smiling face he had greeted her with a few weeks ago, Chris looked horrid. His eyes were bloodshot. He was frowning. Was he drunk?

"Are you okay?" Celia stopped in her tracks, almost afraid to take another step.

Chris looked over his shoulder as if expecting the boogeyman. "No. Not okay."

"What's wrong?"

"You told Jacob what I did? After all these years?"

Emily had obviously gotten to him. Spread more lies. "No, Chris. Emily told Jacob. Not me."

Chris pointed at her. "She said you would say that."

So Emily was still attacking. Just from the periphery. "I didn't tell Jacob. Emily is furious that we're together. I thought you knew better than that."

Chris looked as if he were about to cry. "She wants me to do something terrible, Celia."

He was a man on the edge. What now? "What?"

"A year ago, we slept together."

"You and Emily?" Celia didn't mean to sound so surprised, but hadn't Emily been with Jacob?

"Just after she and my brother hooked up. I guess I was feeling insecure. I know what you're thinking." He gestured over his body. "How could she still want this?"

"I wasn't thinking that," Celia said. "I was thinking how sorry I was for your wife."

"I know. I know. Don't you think I know? And now Emily's threatening to tell my wife if I don't do this thing for her."

"What does she want you to do, Chris?"

"I can't lose my wife and kids, Celia. I'm sorry. I'd do almost anything to make it up to you and Jacob. You have to know that. But I can't lose my wife and kids."

"What does she want you to do, Chris?"

"I've got to go."

Chris headed off at a fast clip. "Tell us. We'll help you." But Chris didn't answer. Celia turned back to the house. When she reached the porch, she saw large footprints. Chris had apparently been on the porch. Why? What had he done? What was Emily planning?

Celia was going to have to tell Jacob that something was afloat. After all this time, she didn't want another misunderstanding to pull them apart. If Jacob knew Emily was planning something diabolical, and that it involved blackmailing his brother, then at least when whatever it was hit the fan, they wouldn't be totally blindsided.

Jacob was still fast asleep. She stood in the room and watched his chest rise and fall. *I want to wake up to him for the next fifty years. More if we're lucky.* She didn't want to wake him up just to give him bad news. The minute he felt her hand on his shoulder, he pulled her into bed, rolled on top of her, and kissed her before she even got a word out. He kissed her neck, then pulled back to smile at her. Celia could only imagine what he saw on her face: half desire, half dread.

"What's wrong?" he asked.

"Just kiss my neck once more and I'll tell you." He was happy to oblige. Then he rolled off her and lay next to her with his head propped up by his fist. He looked so sexy and concerned. She told him about the encounter with Chris. Carefully. Even though Jacob was no longer with Emily, it was never fun to learn your partner had slept with someone else. Jacob's reaction surprised her.

"That part is actually a relief."

"What?"

"I knew she still loved Chris. It wasn't just me. We were using each other."

"But what now? Emily has asked him to do something she thinks is going to hurt us. And if he doesn't, she's going to tell his wife. I didn't come here to break up a marriage."

Jacob took her hand, and they sat on the edge of the bed. "As much as I've resented Chris over the years—more so since I learned what really happened with you—I still don't wish that on him either. His kids don't deserve that."

"What are we going to do?"

"First, I'm going to find Chris. I'll get him to tell me what she's up to."

"Should I cancel the open house?"

"Absolutely not. Whatever it is, we're not running. She's pulling the same stuff she tried as a teenager. We fell for it then, Celia, because we were young too. But let me tell you something loud and clear. This is your last chance, gorgeous. If you don't want to be with me, say so, and I'll walk out of here forever. But if you do, we're not letting anything—not one thing—ever come between us again. Do you hear?"

It was a relief to hear Jacob echo her earlier thoughts. "I'm not going anywhere either."

Jacob leaned in for a kiss. "Thank God," he said after he got it. "I wasn't really prepared for you to walk away."

Celia kissed him again. "Not on your life."

Jacob worried nonstop as he made his way to Chris's house. Emily and all her schemes. Like it was one big boardwalk soap opera. It did his head in. After he saw Chris, he was going directly to the source. No matter what, she was not going to ruin Celia's open house. Of course, it was a delicate balance because Jacob agreed with Celia. None of this was worth destroying a family. Chris shouldn't have slept with Emily and kept it from his wife, but Jacob wasn't going to be the one to get in the middle of that hornet's nest.

Jacob stopped into the arcade first. They didn't open until noon, and the place was shut tight. Chris's house was only another fifteen-minute walk. Jacob had a car, but walking or biking was one of his favorite things about living on Hampton Beach. Besides, the fresh air and walk were helping to calm him down. He would need to be calm to face the destructive duo. Chris was lucky Jacob hadn't punched him in the face for what he did to Celia all those years ago. Now Chris was pulling this?

The minute he arrived at Chris's house, he saw the driveway. Normally they had two cars parked in it. Today there were none. The windows were shut too, and so was the front door. Normally his niece and nephews could be heard a block away. Screaming, squealing, playing, fighting. They were definitely gone. Maybe Chris had gotten out of town instead of bowing down to whatever Emily demanded. It was ironic. Chris had been the one who tried to get Jacob to see what she was like. Now he was the one who had to deal with her instability.

Jacob knocked on the door, just in case. Silence confirmed his suspicion. Should he go over to Emily's? Dealing with Chris was one thing. Emily was a woman, and Jacob wasn't always very good at figuring out the best way to approach women. He wasn't trying to insult a single woman on earth, but from his limited experience, they could be unpredictable. What if confronting Emily just made things worse? Then again, Chris could be at Emily's house. He'd at least amble by and see. He was just passing the gas station near Emily's house when he heard shouts.

"Uncle Jake, Uncle Jake!" Jacob stopped as the kids piled out of Chris's truck and came barreling into his arms. Chris, who was pumping gas, looked stunned. Jacob hugged and chatted with the kids as he made his way up to Chris. His sister-in-law wasn't in the truck. Chris must have noticed Jacob looking for her.

"She's inside getting snacks," Chris said.

"Road trip?"

"Yes. But I'm also going to tell my wife the truth. All of it."

Jacob nodded. Diana was a good woman. Would she forgive Chris? Was it better not to tell? Jacob didn't have a clue.

"What about you?" Chris asked Jacob.

"What about me?"

"Are you going to do the same with Celia? The whole truth and nothing but the truth?"

"I've been meaning to. Haven't found a way to ease into it."

"Well, you'd better hurry. Or Emily's going to do it for you."

Jacob felt a prickle of fear run through him as Chris looked at him. If Emily revealed the truth before Jacob had a chance to explain . . . Celia would never forgive him.

"Emily sent me to tell Celia the truth," Chris said.

"You were going to do that? You were going to tell her something that wasn't yours to tell?"

"Of course not," Chris said. "I'm not Emily's puppet."

"Celia said you were at the house, she said you told her that Emily wanted you to do something that was terrible."

"She wanted me to drop the bomb."

"She was willing to throw her own mother under the bus?"

"How many times do I have to tell you? She's just like her mother."

"And you were going to do it? You were going to tell Celia everything?"

"No. I came to warn you, dude. I'm still on your side."

"Okay," Jacob said. He put his hand on Chris's shoulder. "I'm sorry I didn't listen to you about Emily."

"I can't tell you how glad I am that Celia's back. Don't let her go this time."

"Does Elizabeth know that Emily plans on—how did you put it—'dropping the bomb'?"

"Apparently, yes. Looks like they'd both risk anything to get rid of Celia," Chris answered.

"Just like old times," Jacob said. It was a head-wrecker. Celia had never done anything to either of them. Celia had never done anything other than be her beautiful, happy self. Imagine how much easier all of their lives would have been without the Tanner women.

Jacob ran his fingers through his hair. There was no other choice. He was going to have to tell Celia first. Shit. Shit, shit, shit. He should've done so already. He'd hoped Celia's father would have just confessed the whole sordid mess. It might have saved Jacob all these years of heartache. But at the time he supposed everyone involved had done what they thought they had to. You gotta do what you gotta do, isn't that how the saying goes? Every one of them had made mistakes. Surely Celia would be able to see it through adult eyes?

There was no guarantee. After all, Celia was fiercely protective of her dad. Ironically, this would have gone down much easier if the old man were still around.

"Hey, handsome." Jacob looked up to see his sister-in-law coming out of the gas station with bags in her arms. Chris hurried over and took them from her. He prayed Chris would be able to make things right. The older Jacob got, the clearer it became. He even understood why Pete Jensen had done what he did. All might be fair in love and war, but there was nothing a man wouldn't do for his family.

Celia was in such a good mood when Jacob returned. She was arranging flowers and jars of sea glass. She was blowing up balloons and tying them to the porch rail. She was making homemade lemonade. Was it really worth ruining her good mood to tell her the truth? Or should he let the good times roll as long as he possibly could? Life was full of such decisions, and Jacob didn't love his track record. It seemed he always made the wrong choice no matter how much time he spent weighing his options. Just had a knack for picking the wrong one. So when his instincts shouted at him and told him to tell her the truth right this very minute, he purposely did the opposite. Instead of confessing he squeezed lemons and blew up balloons and made another pot of coffee and did everything he could, all the while praying that he was for once making the right choice.

Celia couldn't help but wonder what had happened between Jacob and Chris. She wanted to tie him down and ply the information out of him (she also wanted to tie him down just to have her way with him), but she had too much to do to get ready for this day. Jacob was helpful but quiet when he returned. Celia didn't press him; she was just happy to have him by her side. By the time she finished, there was only an hour left before people would arrive. She had to shower and dress. Jacob was actually wiping down all the windows when she slid up behind him and put her arms around his waist. She had never been this comfortable with Ben, couldn't remember a single time she'd slipped up behind him to cuddle. Jacob turned around, and before they knew it they were kissing again. Jacob's hunger for her seemed to grow by the second.

"Want to shower with me?" Celia said.

Jacob groaned. "You know the answer to that. But you also know that you'll never get out in time for your party."

"You're probably right. Although I hate to admit it," Celia said. She broke away and ran up to the shower before she could change her mind. When it came to Jacob, she definitely had that soft spot that she had to watch or she was going to ignore the entire world and spend her days just loving him. *This is our time,* she thought while in the shower. *This is our coming out party. Bring it on,* she wanted to shout at Emily. *Whatever you've got, our love is stronger.*

CHAPTER 10

People began strolling in at one o'clock sharp. Celia had a banner hung near the front door. **SANDY, BARE FEET WELCOME.**

The band arrived and was soon playing beach tunes on the porch. The food was a huge hit: finger sandwiches, and strawberries with cream, prosciutto with melon, and plates of cheese and crackers. Laughter rang out as guests dropped off their donations before meandering through the house. From the looks of it, Ocean House was going to be well-stocked. One older woman spent her entire time in a corner, drinking tea and staring at Celia. Just as Celia joked with Jacob that it looked like she had a stalker, the woman approached.

"You're Celia Jensen," the woman stated.

"Yes," Celia said. She knew there was more, so she waited.

"Your father was a good man," the woman said.

"Yes, he was," Celia said. She tried to catch Jacob's eye, but he was looking away. Maybe he was worried Celia would start crying.

"My husband had just passed away when you came to

town. Your father was a lifesaver. He came any time I called about anything. Mostly, I was just grieving, and I just wasn't used to taking care of a house by myself. I was so terribly sorry when he was unjustly accused of all that nonsense."

Celia impulsively reached out and took the woman's hands. "You have no idea how glad I am to hear you say that. That's what hurt the most. Nobody around here stood up for him."

"Well, I tried, for what it was worth. But instead of getting anyone to listen, I was kicked out of the quilting club."

"I'm so sorry."

"Don't be. I took up yoga instead, and now look at me." The woman winked. Celia felt a load lift off her as the woman walked away. She turned to get Jacob's reaction. He had moved on, was talking to someone else. For a moment she was stung. Didn't he know how much it meant to her, meeting people who believed in her father's innocence? But she shouldn't expect him to read her mind. She should tell him the truth. When it came to her father, she wanted Jacob right next to her, defending his name.

Two hours later, Celia finally started to relax. She'd been carrying so much tension, expecting some kind of Tanner ambush. It looked as if Emily and Elizabeth were going to stay away after all. Endless worrying for nothing. There was a nice crowd still in the home, mostly gathered on the porch to listen to music, and in the living room, where food and drink were readily available. And just as she thought her worrying had been over nothing, she saw them, mother and daughter, marching up the street. She didn't even realize she had swayed, until Jacob put his hands on her waist.

"Easy there, tiger," he said. Celia didn't want to give the impression she was running away, but neither did she want to appear like she was waiting for a fight.

"Pretend we're having a lovely conversation," she said, grabbing Jacob.

"Why don't we just have a lovely conversation?" Jacob said.

"Who's the man with them?" Celia said. Jacob looked out the window. "Don't look. Is that Elizabeth's man?"

"Can I look?" Jacob tried to turn his head to the window. Celia grabbed it and pulled it toward her.

"No!"

Jacob grinned as Celia squeezed his face. "Then I have no idea."

Celia kissed him and let go of him, then straightened her hair. "How do I look?"

"You look amazing."

Celia melted. From the way he was gazing at her, he meant it. "We can do this. We can handle them."

"Celia. I think I made a mistake. I should have told you—" The door opened. Celia didn't pay any mind to Jacob—he was worried they were going to get her goat. But he was wrong. Now that Ocean House had a purpose, so did she. She had Jacob. And a reason for being here. But she still didn't know how to handle the Tanners. Look at them or don't look at them? She was just trying to figure out which way looked more cool when they shoved their way in and bullied their way up to her. Celia didn't have time to process much. Elizabeth looked much older, but also good for her age. She'd definitely had Botox, maybe even a face-lift. Her perfume reached Celia first. Her makeup looked as if it had taken days to apply. Her hair was still blond, or still fake blond, and straightened. She hadn't gained an ounce. Maybe they all just ate Emily's muffins. Nobody would want more than a bite a day. Elizabeth Tanner was the ultimate picture of someone who was "put together." Emily, on the other hand, looked a little wild. She was a woman on a warpath. Next to them stood the mystery man. It was Ben. He was wearing sunglasses, Bermuda shorts, and a parrot shirt. Celia couldn't believe it.

"Ben. What in the world?" Celia said.

"Do you like my new look?"

"Are you a Jimmy Buffet fan?"

Ben furled his eyebrows. "I'm relaxed," he said. "I'm mellow."

"What are you doing here?"

"It will all become clear," Ben said. "I've learned quite a bit about your past in the last few weeks."

"You've been here this whole time?"

"We have plenty of room," Elizabeth Tanner said with a smile. "He was more than welcome into our home." Celia stared at Elizabeth. It was a definite dig from the past. Suddenly, more than anything she wished she had barricaded the front door and turned Elizabeth away. Well, screw being polite. This was her house now. Celia ushered them all into the dining room, where she could give them a piece of her mind away from the other guests. Once they were out of hearing range of the living room, she turned to Elizabeth.

"Didn't take long for the claws to come out, did it, Mrs. Tanner?"

"Excuse me?" Elizabeth fluttered her eyelashes. It was eerie, seeing mother and daughter side by side. They were a couple of Stepford Wives. Celia would certainly be thinking less of Jacob's taste right now if it weren't for parrot-head next to them reminding her that she hadn't made the best choices either.

"You're not welcome here." Celia pointed to the back door through the kitchen. She'd rather they sneak out the back with their tail between their legs. "This is my house now. Free and clear. And *you're* not welcome. That goes for all three of you."

"Have you looked under the kitchen sink yet?" Emily said.

"Don't do this, Emily," Jacob said.

"Why would I look under the kitchen sink?" Celia asked.

"Everything but the kitchen sink," Emily said. "Ever heard of that one?"

What in the world was she getting at? About half the time Emily said things that were so off the wall Celia didn't have a clue how to respond. Did this have something to do with Jacob's fixing it? She couldn't imagine why any of them would care.

"I think you should do it," Ben said.

"Are you sure you want to go down this road, Elizabeth?" Jacob said.

Elizabeth put her hand on her heart. Here comes the Scarlett O'Hara routine, Celia thought. Sure enough, when Elizabeth spoke next, her voice was about an octave higher. "Why, Jacob. I have no idea what 'road' you're referring to."

"You do, Elizabeth," Jacob said. "You sure do."

What are they talking about? Celia hated being in the dark.

"I'm just here supporting my daughter," Elizabeth said. "But if you think there will be no consequences for you if you start spreading lies, well then, that would make you very foolish indeed."

"Except they wouldn't be lies, now would they, Elizabeth? Why don't we all just finally tell the truth?"

"Go ahead," Elizabeth laughed. "Tell the truth, Jacob. See how fast your little love flies away."

Celia was frightened now. Elizabeth seemed so sure of herself. And Jacob looked absolutely terrified. "Jacob," Celia said. "What are you guys talking about? What truth?"

"We'll show you," Ben said. He forged into the kitchen. Seconds later he was rummaging under Celia's sink.

"Ben!" Celia said. "What are you doing under there?" She followed him in, along with the rest of the group, and soon they formed a semicircle behind him.

"You always were out of the loop," Elizabeth said to Celia. "It's not surprising given your father—"

With lightning speed, Celia reached for the sink. She grabbed the water-sprayer, turned the faucet on full blast, then unleashed it on Elizabeth. Elizabeth screamed bloody murder, but Celia was in a frenzy, unable to stop. Until Emily started shouting and Celia turned the water on her next. From the way the two were carrying on, she was definitely going to get in big trouble for this. Was it illegal to turn a hose on someone? She would just tell the police she had thought they were on fire. Before she could turn it off, Jacob took the sprayer from her and turned off the water just as Ben popped up from under the sink. He too was soaking wet, presumably from the leak.

He was holding a pipe from the sink. Water pooled underneath it and snaked onto the floor.

"What are you doing?" Celia said. "Why are you breaking my sink?"

"Did you get it already?" Ben asked Jacob.

"Celia," Jacob said. "We need to talk."

"You think?" Celia said. "Let's start with Elizabeth. She seems like she has something to say."

"You're still nothing but a little wench," Elizabeth said. "A low-class little—"

Celia raised her hand to Mrs. Tanner. She was going to slap her silly, which would definitely get her in trouble, but oh, it was going to be worth it. Jacob intervened again and gently took both of Celia's hands in his.

"You deserve everything you're going to get," Emily said.

"And just what would that be?" Celia said.

"I found it," Ben shouted. He held something up. It caught the sun and glittered. Celia stepped forward. It was the diamond ring. The boys had shown it to her once, when they were whispering about their mother, how she was coming back for them one day. The princess-cut diamond was the largest and prettiest Celia had ever seen. It was definitely the ring. "It was in the toolbox. Jacob must have already found it in the pipe."

"The ring was in this sink?" She turned to Elizabeth and Emily. "Which one of you stole it?" she said.

"Elizabeth did," Jacob said. "When I first refused to give in to her demands, apparently she dropped it down the sink."

"What demands?"

"You still haven't told her," Elizabeth said. "My, my, my."

"Somebody had better start talking," Celia said. "And by somebody, I mean you, Jacob."

"The night after the incident on the beach, I went to talk to Emily," Jacob said. "I was still trying to piece together why you ran to her crying after we—"

"I didn't," Celia said. "I didn't."

"I know that now, Seal. But I didn't then. I ran back to our place that night to get the ring. I tossed our mobile home to pieces looking for it. Chris came in—and that's when he told me that you were at Emily's crying your eyes out. I was a teenage boy. I thought maybe I'd done something wrong. That you regretted it—and you hated me."

Celia glared at Emily. Still dripping wet, Emily just glared back. "Go on," Celia said to Jacob.

"The next night, when I went back to see if I could get more details out of Emily, Elizabeth was waiting for me. She said she had the ring. She said she took it to keep me from making the biggest mistake of my life, and she told me that she hid it. She said she'd only give it back if I stopped seeing you."

"Why didn't you just report the theft to the police?"

"I didn't have proof. I didn't know where she was keeping the ring."

Celia was having a hard time listening to the details. Shock was preventing her from absorbing it all at once.

"When? When did you say you found out she'd stolen the ring?"

Jacob looked at the floor. Then he forced his gaze up and looked her in the eye. "The next evening. After the beach."

"Before she accused my father?"

"Yes. Although I didn't know she'd dropped it down her sink. She didn't admit to that part until after someone else—you—had bought her house."

An image of Jacob at her door that first night rose to mind. "And so she sent you that night. To get it back," Celia said slowly. That's what he had been doing there. Not fetching a key under the mat like he had said.

"I didn't know you were the new owner," Jacob said. "Elizabeth had been in such a hurry to move that she didn't remember the ring until the last minute. That's when I found out what she'd done with it."

"But you still knew she was the one who stole it?"

"Yes."

"The whole time? You sat back while she called my father a thief? Ran us out of town? How? How could you do that? Why would you do that?" Celia could feel herself getting hysterical, but her feelings of grief and rage were so raw, she couldn't tamp it down.

Jacob hung his head. "It's a little more complicated than—"

"Doesn't sound complicated at all," Celia said. "You let my father take the blame for something you knew he didn't do. True or false?"

"Celia," Jacob pleaded.

"True or false?" Celia demanded.

"True," Jacob said. "Very, very true."

"Oh my God." Celia turned on Elizabeth. "You organized a witch hunt against my father when *you* were the one who stole the ring?"

Even dripping wet, streaks of mascara running down her cheeks, Elizabeth Tanner looked triumphant.

"I didn't know what she was planning," Jacob said. "I swear."

"I don't understand. What does it matter what she was planning? Why did you let her spread vicious lies about my father?" Celia pointed at Elizabeth. "She ruined his name all over town!"

"There's more to it than that," Jacob said.

"I don't see it that way," Celia said. "I want you out. I want everybody out."

"It's about time," Ben said. "I can take you home."

"I'm not going back to you, Ben."

"But he's a liar!"

"Out. Out. Out. All of you."

Jacob headed for the door. Conversation in the living room came to a hush when the group emerged from the kitchen, but Celia couldn't worry about strangers now. Jacob threw open the door, and Chris barged in.

"Did she drop her little bomb?" Chris asked, pointing at Emily.

"Yes," Celia said. "Now they're leaving. All of them."

"Bet Jacob didn't tell you the whole story."

"Chris," Jacob said. "Let it be."

"I won't. Elizabeth Tanner took the ring," Chris said. He looked around as if expecting a gasp.

"We got that far," Jacob said.

"She also offered your father money to get out of town."

Celia froze. "She what?"

"Enough money to put you through your first year of college."

"Why?"

"Because she's always been jealous of you. She didn't want you marrying Jacob, spending the rest of your life in Hampton Beach."

Celia turned to Jacob. "That still doesn't explain your part. Why did you let her do that, Jacob? Did you change your mind? Did you not want to marry me?"

"No, God, no. Of course not."

"Then why?"

"Tell her, Jacob, or I will," Chris said.

"Your father asked me to," Jacob said.

"No. No. He wouldn't do that."

"He didn't like you hanging around Emily. Or me. He hated Elizabeth, too. He wanted to get you out of the whole mess. When I told him that Elizabeth stole the ring and tried to bribe me into breaking up with you, he went to confront her. That's when she offered *him* money."

"My father wouldn't do that. He wouldn't take a bribe from her."

"It was enough money to send you to college for the first year, Seal."

"Oh my God," Celia said. His new job. A bonus. That was a little white lie.

"He knew you wouldn't leave voluntarily, so he concocted the whole 'Hampton Burglar' thing. He knew you wouldn't leave unless it was to protect him."

"I don't believe you," Celia said. But part of her did.

"He was even the one who made the flier," Jacob said.

"Oh my God." Celia turned to Elizabeth. "How could you? How could you manipulate our lives like that?"

"You went to college, didn't you?"

"We were never the same." Celia turned back to Jacob. "You thought I wouldn't go to college if I stayed here and married you?"

"I didn't know what to do. But I knew you were smart. Your dad said you deserved a good education. He asked me to do this for you. He said if I loved you enough, I'd let you go, and if we loved each other enough, that you'd come back to Hampton Beach after college." He left the rest hanging. Celia hadn't come back.

"Please," Celia said. "Everyone out. I need to be alone."

"Everyone out?" Ben said. "Everyone?" He made a beeline for the kitchen. Celia couldn't believe she was spending fifty percent of her time following people around her own house. And by now, the guests were too curious to even pretend to be polite. Half of them followed Ben into the kitchen. Once there, with everyone watching, Ben lunged at the counter. What was he doing—taking leftovers? Ben held a can of Chock Full O'Nuts aloft.

"Ben," Celia said.

"Guess what's in here, folks? Pete Jensen. That's right. I'm holding the remains of Pete Jensen."

Anna Beth was in the kitchen. She looked at Celia. "Was that what was left of him after the shark?"

"That's just coffee, Ben," Celia said.

"Just coffee. Just coffee. You want to make me look like the idiot, Celia? You want to force me to show them?" He jostled the can as he talked. He brought his hand to the lid.

"Don't—" Celia said as Ben pried it open. Bits of ground coffee flew straight up in the air and then rained down on Ben's face.

"Coffee!" Ben said.

"I told you," Celia said.

"Where's your dad?"

"I sprinkled him in the ocean this morning."

"You did?" Jacob said.

"I did."

"I would have gone with you," Jacob said.

"It was something I had to do alone." She turned back to Ben. "Unless you're going to make a fresh pot, I still would like all of you to leave. The party is over."

CHAPTER 11

Celia sat on the beach. It didn't take long before the waves calmed her. This was exactly why she needed to follow through with her dream. There was no better gift than giving someone a place where they could decompress, rejuvenate. Put everything into proper perspective. Was she really going to hold a grudge from twenty years ago? Could she say she was sorry about going to college? If she hadn't, she wouldn't be in the position she was in now, would never be able to open Ocean House to families. And as far as her father and Jacob were concerned, they had done what they did out of love. Misguided, perhaps. But certainly not selfish.

Celia took the Chock Full O'Nuts can out of her bag. Of course she'd lied to Ben. She hadn't released her father, but she had kept her father's tin out of the kitchen. But it was time now. And just as she stood, she saw a familiar figure making his way to her.

"I got your message," Jacob said. "Are we too late?" Celia had told Jacob she was having a little memorial and going to release the ashes. She had said he'd be welcome to join her.

"We?" Celia said. Jacob held his hand out behind him.

Celia couldn't believe it. A small group was making their way toward them, each holding a candle in one hand and a scuba flipper in the other.

"What's going on?"

"These are all the people still here from back then. They all know the truth about your father. They want to pay their respects. Is that okay?"

Celia nodded; she was too choked up to speak. The group gathered on the beach with their flippers and candles. Chris was there with his wife and kids, along with the older woman from the open house, Anna Beth, and several others whom she didn't know. It didn't matter. They were family now as far as she was concerned. Celia set the coffee can in one of the flippers, laid it on the beach, and within a few minutes, a wave took it in its foamy mouth and began the process of carrying it out to sea. "Bye, Dad," Celia said.

Jacob had brought a bottle of scotch, her father's favorite, and they took turns drinking and passing it around, as each person had some kind of Pete story to tell. Finally, when they were almost finished, Celia pulled a red rose out of her bag, kissed it, and tossed it to the waves. Jacob took her hand and squeezed. One by one, the crowd made their way back home.

"Do you want to be alone?" Jacob said.

"Never," Celia said.

"Thank heavens," Jacob said. "If you had said yes, you would have had to toss me out to sea as well." As they walked along the beach, Jacob picked up a large stick. As Celia watched he drew a heart in the sand.

"That's sweet," she said.

"I'm not finished. Close your eyes." Celia did. She could hear the stick scratching in the sand. "Open them." Celia opened her eyes. Jacob was kneeling next to the heart. In the center he had written a message. MARRY ME.

"Yes," Celia said. "Yes." She shamelessly threw herself at him, and they shared a long, deep kiss. Jacob pulled away first.

"I have a proposal," he said.

"But I just said yes."

Jacob laughed. "Another one."

"I'm listening."

"I want to sell my mother's ring and use that money for the travel fund for the families."

"I love the idea."

"I just don't want you to look at that ring and have any bad memories. We'll pick out something better."

"I totally agree. And I don't need anything fancy."

"In that case," Jacob said. He reached into his pocket and pulled out a little shell ring, the kind they sold on the boardwalk for three dollars. Celia laughed and held out her hand. Tears came to her eyes as he slipped it on.

"I love it," she said.

"Next year I'll replace it with coral," Jacob joked.

"I can't wait until we get to the starfish anniversary," Celia said. Hand in hand they began walking the beach. A little ways down, Jacob stopped.

"Recognize where we are?"

Of course she did. Celia followed his gaze up to the boardwalk, and then to that special spot underneath it.

"Want to repeat history?" Celia said.

"I thought you'd never ask."

"But first." Jacob pulled her into him and kissed her deeply. Celia felt the sound of the ocean waves crashing onto the shore as she passionately kissed him back. Then the two ran for the spot where they had first made love, where Jacob would have proposed the first time, where they had been left wondering what happened to their love and why. Everything had come full circle. She was back. She was where she was always meant to be. Only this time she wasn't just a summer girl, and Jacob wasn't just a summer love. Celia Jensen was filled with a spirit of abandon, and love, but most of all, hope. Soul-lifting, rejuvenating, unconditional hope.

HIS BRIDE TO BE

Lisa Jackson

CHAPTER 1

"Damn it, Leigh, I was counting on you!" Hale Donovan swore loudly, not caring that the door to his office was ajar and his secretary could hear his every word. He stretched the telephone cord tight, pacing across thick fawn-colored carpet and wishing he could ring Leigh Carmichael's beautiful neck. As he glared out the window of his office, twenty stories above the crowded streets of San Francisco, he clenched his fingers tightly around the receiver. Outside, the lofty spires of the city's skyscrapers rose against the vibrant California-blue sky.

Hale barely noticed—he was too furious.

All he could see was the entire deal with Stowell Investments going down the proverbial drain. He'd been a fool to trust Leigh; she was cut from the same cold cloth as his mother, Jenna Donovan, a woman he could barely remember.

"Hale, you still there, darling?" Leigh's husky voice sounded over the wires, and she chuckled softly.

"Of course I'm still here," he snapped back.

"Good. Then you understand."

"What I understand is that you're reneging. Why?" he asked, knowing Leigh was trying to manipulate him. Again.

"I'm not interested in pretending," she said sulkily.

He could almost hear the wheels turning in her mind half a world away.

"I can't see ruining my vacation in Marseilles just to save your neck."

"You picked one helluva time to tell me! The cruise starts Friday!"

"Well, then, if you want me to go so badly, maybe you should make the engagement official," she suggested, her voice sultry and suggestive.

"What're you trying to do, Leigh? You know the whole thing's an act."

"Not to me. The only way I'll come back to San Francisco and pose as your fiancée is if you really want me to be your wife!"

Shoving one hand through his hair in frustration, Hale dropped to the corner of his desk. His eyes narrowed thoughtfully as he conjured up her face—a gorgeous face—with high cheekbones, pouty lips, and ice-cold jade-green eyes. "Just what is it you want, Leigh? A ring?"

"Not just any ring, Hale. A diamond ring with at least three sparkling carats, and a promise that we'll walk down the aisle within the next two months."

He laughed. She was joking. She had to be! Their affair had ended six months before and they were both happier without the entanglements of a relationship. He yanked off his tie and slung it over the back of his chair. "Look, Leigh, I don't have time for games."

"This isn't a game."

For the first time he heard the undercurrents in her voice—the thread of steel running through her words. "I don't want marriage, Leigh. I'm not cut out for it. Neither are you."

"That's where you're wrong," she wheedled. "I think I'd be perfectly content to become Mrs. Hale Donovan."

"Damn it, Leigh—"

"Call me back if you change your mind."

The receiver on her end of the line clicked loudly in his ear.

Muttering, Hale slammed the receiver back into its cradle. In a way he was relieved. Two weeks of pretending to be in love with Leigh would have been hell. However, he needed a woman to pose as his wife-to-be before he set sail on William Stowell's yacht on Friday. Only a fiancée would prevent Stowell's daughter, Regina, from throwing herself at him.

Frowning, he strode to the bar and splashed brandy into a short crystal glass. He wanted to buy out William Stowell so badly he could taste it, but he wasn't willing to marry William's daughter, Regina, just to clinch the deal. Unfortunately she was scheduled on the cruise, as well.

Twenty years old, spoiled and sullen, Regina had continually pursued Hale for the past six months. Hale wasn't interested. Not in Regina, and especially not in marriage.

As far as he was concerned, marriage was a trap. What he needed was a woman—a woman he didn't know—a woman who would agree to pose as his intended for two weeks, then conveniently drop out of sight once he'd bought out William Stowell's shares of Stowell Investment Company. Hale's lips compressed into a cold grimace as he sipped his brandy. He would call Paul Hastings in Personnel and tell Paul to find him a woman who had beauty, brains, charm and, most important of all, a vast, unsatiated greed!

Valerie Pryce shifted uneasily in her chair and waited. Across an expansive mahogany desk, the personnel director of Donovan Enterprises studied her résumé as if it were the Emancipation Proclamation.

A short man with a neatly cropped red beard, stiff white shirt and expensive pin-striped suit, Paul Hastings fingered his collar. "You graduated from UCLA in business two years ago."

"That's right." Valerie managed a smile that felt forced. She couldn't let Hastings know how much she needed a job—any job.

"And while you went to school you supported yourself by modeling and acting?"

"Just a few commercials and a small role on a soap opera." What did that have to do with anything? she wondered. Smoothing her skirt and hoping she didn't look as nervous as she felt, she met his gaze evenly.

"But you didn't want an acting career?"

"The jobs dried up."

"Oh." He scanned the first page. "You're single."

Valerie bristled a little, but reminded herself that she needed this job. "Yes."

"Never been married?"

"No."

"What about boyfriends?"

"I don't think that's any of your business," she said, clamping her hands over the arms of her chair.

He lifted a palm. "You're right, of course. Just asking." Paul tilted his chair back and stared at her, his eyes narrowing behind thick glasses as he took in her features. "I'd like you to meet Hale Donovan."

"The president of the company?" she repeated, stunned. Good Lord, why?

Stuffing her résumé into a file, Paul chuckled. "Around here we refer to him as God . . . or Lucifer. Depending on his mood."

"Sounds charming," Valerie observed.

"He can be." Paul dialed the phone, spoke quickly into the receiver, then shoved back his chair and led Valerie through a maze of hallways to a private elevator. He punched out the number for the twentieth floor, and the doors slid shut.

"Is it normal for anyone applying for a job as an administrative assistant to meet Mr. Donovan?" she asked as the elevator groaned and started to climb.

"It is when they're applying to become Mr. Donovan's personal assistant."

Valerie nearly gasped. Personal assistant to Hale Donovan? "That's the job?"

Paul slanted her a nervous glance. "It just opened up yesterday afternoon. Ah, here we are." He waited for her to exit, waved at a tiny gray-haired receptionist behind a spacious desk and smiled. "He's expecting us, Madge."

Without missing a beat at her computer keyboard, Madge nodded and Paul shoved open one of two gleaming cherry-wood doors.

Valerie drew in a deep breath. Since she'd first set foot inside Donovan Enterprises less than an hour before, she'd been shuffled from one office to another, spoken with several assistants in Personnel and finally landed here, in front of Hale Donovan's office, reading his name engraved in brass as she was bustled inside. She braced herself. She hadn't expected an interview with God himself.

Hale heard the door open and wished Paul Hastings would just go away. Since the previous afternoon, when he'd called and demanded to meet a woman to pose as his bride-to-be, he'd interviewed nearly forty would-be Mrs. Hale Donovans. Forty of the most self-centered, vain and nervous women he'd ever seen. None had come even close. He couldn't imagine spending two hours cooped up with any of them, and the thought of two weeks aboard a yacht as he pretended to care about one of those shallow, self-directed women turned his stomach.

He was beginning to think his plan wasn't worth the effort.

Paul cleared his throat.

Rubbing the back of his neck, Hale turned, uninterested until his gaze collided with the serious eyes of a tall, slender woman who held herself with a bearing that could only be described as regal. Her hair was honey blond, highlighted with pale streaks and swept away from her face in a French braid. Wearing a magenta blouse and black skirt that matched her jacket, she crossed the room.

Large, intelligent hazel eyes rimmed in curling dark lashes peered at him, and the tilt of her chin was bold, nearly defiant. Her cheekbones were high, tinged pink, and her lips were curved into a wary smile. "Funny," she said, staring boldly at Hale, "I never pictured God wearing blue jeans."

Paul inhaled swiftly and looked as if he'd just swallowed something much too large for his throat. Choking, he shot the woman a warning glance and made hasty introductions. "Hale Donovan, this is—"

"Valerie Pryce," she said, extending her hand.

Hale clasped her slim fingers, and was surprised at the strength in her grip.

"Ms. Pryce brought her résumé in this afternoon. She's looking for a job with the company."

"She's not from an agency?" Hale was surprised—he'd pegged Valerie for a model, a sophisticated New York type.

Paul shook his head. "No, she's a walk-in, but I think she'll work out," he said, eyeing Valerie curiously. "Her résumé's in here." He placed the file folder on the corner of Hale's desk. "Keep me posted."

"I will."

Paul exited, closing the door behind him.

"I think you made him nervous," Hale said, amusement flickering in his gaze.

"I didn't mean to."

Hale twisted his thin lips. "He's had a long day."

"So I gathered." She watched this man cautiously. He simply wasn't a typical executive, at least not in her opinion. Dressed in faded jeans and a blue cambric shirt with its sleeves shoved over his forearms, he looked as though he belonged on a ranch, or in the back lot of a movie studio, working as a stuntman on a B-grade western, not in a chrome-and-glass office decorated with metal objets d'art and tan leather.

His hair needed to be trimmed; black locks curled over his collar and his jaw was dark with a day's growth of beard. His features, all angles and blades, fitted into a face that was too rugged to be called Hollywood handsome. A long nose separated hollow cheeks and stopped just short of a thin, almost cruel mouth. His looks might have been classified as severe, had it not been for his eyes. Steel gray and deep set, guarded by thick, black brows and long, straight lashes, they were lit by an inner spark, a flicker of humor.

He picked up her résumé, scanning it as he crossed an expanse of thick carpet to an overstuffed leather chair.

She noticed how easily his legs and buttocks moved beneath the denim—fluidly, gracefully, though she sensed a restlessness in him. He seemed to have the coiled energy of a caged animal.

"You worked for Liddell International?"

"Two years."

He nodded thoughtfully. "Why'd you quit?"

"It was time," she said.

"It *is* my business, you know."

"Only if you hire me."

Sighing, he dropped onto the arm of the contemporary chair. His gaze never left hers. "What happened? Liddell is a great company."

There was no reason to lie. He'd find out soon enough. "My boss and I had a . . . disagreement."

"About?"

Her lips twisted cynically. "Personal rights."

"Meaning?"

"Meaning he came on to me, okay?" she shot back angrily. "We were working late, he made a pass, I didn't respond and my career at Liddell died." There was more to it, of course.

But she didn't think the fact that Brian Liddell Jr. had expected her to sleep with him was any of Donovan's business.

Hale was staring at her. "That's sexual harassment," he said softly.

"I know."

"You could sue."

Drawing in a deep breath, she whispered, "I decided I'd just rather forget it. Besides, I don't have time for a lawsuit. I need to make a living."

Hale tried to ignore the compassion that moved him. He hadn't misinterpreted the flicker of pain in her eyes. Whatever had happened at Liddell had been more than just a simple come-on. Her hands shook a little as she tucked them into the pockets of her jacket. "Would you like a drink?" Standing, he crossed to the bar.

"No, thanks."

"You're sure?"

"I think I'll wait until after the interview." She seemed to draw from an inner strength, and though she had paled, she was facing him squarely again, having regained her composure.

"Did Paul tell you about the job?" Hale asked, opening louvered doors to the bar. Crystal stemware and shiny bottles sparkled from the soft recessed lights hidden above the mirrored backdrop.

"He didn't get that far. In fact, he was a little vague about the particulars," she said, deciding to get to the point. "All he told me is that I'm interviewing to become your personal assistant."

Hale's brows quirked as he reached for an opened bottle of brandy and a glass. "That's one way of putting it."

"Give me another."

He didn't turn around, but his gray gaze caught hers in the reflection of the mirror. "What I'm looking for, Ms. Pryce, is a woman who will pose as my fiancée for the next two weeks."

"Your fiancée?" she repeated.

He saw her catch her breath. A shadow of disappointment clouded her eyes, and she actually blushed.

"But I thought . . ."

"Paul should have been straight with you."

"It would have helped!" she snapped, her cheeks flaming. "What is this?"

"A simple business proposition," he replied, bemused at her outrage. At least he'd shocked her out of whatever secret was tormenting her.

"I don't like the sound of it."

"Just listen," he suggested, striding back to his desk and leaning a jean-clad hip against it. "I'm trying to buy out William Stowell of Stowell Investments. He and I are planning to hammer out a deal next week aboard his yacht. We'll be sailing up the coast to Canada. Unfortunately his daughter, Regina, is coming along, and William thinks I should marry her. Regina seems to agree." The corners of his mouth tightened. "I don't."

"So why don't you tell her so?"

Hale smiled faintly. "I have. More times than I want to count. She doesn't believe me. Neither does her father."

"You expect me to believe this?"

"It's true." Taking a long swallow of scotch, he studied her before placing the empty glass on his desk.

"It's crazy."

"A little," he agreed, shrugging. "But why would I make it up?"

Good point!

"Besides, it ensures me the company of a beautiful woman," he added, his eyes glinting.

"Does it?" She drew an outraged breath, slinging the strap of her purse over her shoulder with more aggression than necessary.

"The job is yours if you want it."

"No way."

"It could be interesting."

Was he serious? "What I need is a *real* job, Mr. Donovan. Not some insane scheme where I pose as your mistress. I didn't go to night school for three years to be paid to fawn all over you for two weeks. I think you'd better find someone else."

"There isn't time."

"Isn't time? Give me a break! I'm sure if you looked hard enough you could find any number of women who'd want to play house with you on a cruise. I just don't happen to be one of them."

"I'll make it worth your while."

"I guess you didn't hear me, Mr. Donovan. I'm not interested." She turned on her heel and marched through the double doors, sweeping past Madge in a cloud of indignation. How could she have been so stupid? Assistant to the president! Ha! The problem with anything that looks too good to be true is that it usually is!

Slamming her palm against the elevator call button, she fumed, waiting impatiently. From the corner of her eye she saw Hale Donovan, his jaw set as he strode toward her.

"Don't you want to hear me out?" he asked.

"No!"

"We haven't even talked about money."

"We don't need to."

A soft bell rang, and the elevator's doors parted. Gratefully Valerie stepped inside.

Hale followed, blocking the doors with his shoulder. "Give me five minutes. I'll bet I can convince you."

The nerve of the man! Narrowing her eyes, she hissed, "I don't have a price tag."

"Everyone does."

Ignoring him, she slapped the button for the first floor. The elevator didn't move.

"Think about it," he suggested.

"Oh, I will," she assured him, raising her chin a fraction, leveling her gaze at his arrogant face. "And I'll laugh."

Before he could stop himself, he reached forward, grabbing her arm quickly. The elevator lurched and the doors started to close before he stopped them with his foot. "I'll call you."

"Don't bother."

Madge appeared in the open door. Her anxious brown eyes flicked from Hale to Valerie and back again. "Paul's on the line. He wants to know how things worked out. There's another woman—"

"We don't need another woman," Hale said quietly, his eyes fixed on Valerie.

For a heart-stopping second, he clenched steely fingers over her arm.

"Tell Paul I've found the one I want."

CHAPTER 2

Who was Valerie Pryce?

Hale stood at the glass wall behind his desk and watched the traffic and pedestrians swarming through Union Square.

The intercom buzzed, and Madge's raspy voice sounded. "Paul's on two."

"Got it." Hale picked up his receiver. "Donovan."

"I have a couple more women you might want to interview," Paul suggested, his voice sounding tired.

"Not interested."

"But—"

"Didn't Madge make it clear? I want Valerie Pryce." Hale paced from one end of his office to the other. The telephone cord stretched, then recoiled as he strode away from his desk, then back past it.

"Did you hire her?" Hastings asked, sounding mildly surprised.

"Not exactly." Hale waved impatiently. "She didn't sign a contract, but it's just a matter of time," he said, glancing nervously at his watch.

"Then she agreed?"

"Not in so many words—"

"I thought you wanted someone today."

"I do." Hale clenched his teeth. He knew he was being stubborn and unrealistic. The woman just plain didn't want the job. But he couldn't forget her. With the razor-edged intuition that had guided him over the years, he believed that Valerie Pryce was the woman who could pull this off. The challenge in her intriguing hazel eyes, her regal bearing and her quick, irreverent humor gave her the right combination of charm and class.

Paul brought him back to the conversation. "Well, if she's not working out, there are four women from the Jewell Woods Agency down here. Any one of them—"

"You're not listening, Paul," Hale cut in, picking up Valerie's résumé and scanning the two sheets of paper as if they held some clue to his fascination with her. "My fiancée for the next two weeks is going to be Valerie Pryce."

"You might tell her about it," Paul suggested, his voice tinged with more than a little sarcasm.

"I will. I'm on my way over there now."

"She might not agree."

"I'll convince her."

"How?"

"Come on, Hastings. Money talks." Hale reached for his leather jacket and swung it over one shoulder. "Call Kendrick in the legal department. Tell him what I want. A contract for two weeks—leave the amount of compensation blank. And give the name of personal assistant to the position."

"If I were you . . ."

Hale waited, listening, his fingers tight around the receiver. He heard Paul sigh in disgust.

"If I were you, I'd just be straight with William Stowell and forget all this phony engagement business."

"I tried that," Hale reminded him, his gut twisting as he remembered his last meeting with Stowell. William had hinted he'd like nothing better than to call Hale his son-in-law.

Obviously Regina had agreed. Behind her father's back, she'd come up with her own plan to trap Hale.

After six hours of heavy business negotiations and several drinks with Stowell, Hale had unlocked his hotel room door and found Regina, wrapped in nothing but pink silk sheets, lying across his bed. A bottle of champagne had been chilling in an ice bucket near the headboard. Regina had smiled coyly up at him, a dimpled come-hither grin pursing her lips, as he'd leaned heavily against the door frame.

"I've been waiting for you," she whispered in a clumsy attempt at seduction.

"How'd you get in?"

She smiled. "The desk clerk doesn't ask too many questions."

"I think you'd better leave," Hale muttered, angry she was there. He was tired, and all he wanted was a hot shower and a warm bed—a bed without Stowell's daughter.

"Not yet," she murmured.

"Now."

"We could have fun—"

"Your father would kill me, and I'd hate to think what he'd do to you."

"What Daddy doesn't know won't hurt him," she said, brows lifting as she sank her teeth into her lower lip.

"Forget it, Regina. I'm not interested."

"Why not?" she complained, holding the sheet around her and looking so young it had made his skin crawl.

"Look, it won't work," he said, and when he'd finally realized she wasn't about to budge, he'd left her, still wrapped in silk, her cheeks scorching red at his rejection.

Hale sighed in exasperation at the memory. Though he knew William wasn't behind Regina's advances, Hale didn't need a replay of that awkward scene. He also knew he couldn't spend the next two weeks with her—not unless he appeared to be off-limits.

On the other end of the line, Paul cleared his throat. "You're sure about this?"

"Positive. Send the models home and tell Kendrick to get everything in writing."

Valerie knocked once on the door of her mother's small apartment, then unlocked the dead bolt. "Mom?" she said softly as she entered. The shades were drawn, the air heavy and still.

Footsteps approached as Valerie closed the door behind her.

"She's resting," Belinda whispered, cocking her head toward the bedroom.

"Is she all right?"

"Better every day," Belinda said with a smile. A stocky woman with black hair pulled into a tight bun at the base of her skull, Belinda was a godsend. Since the accident in which her mother had been hit by a speeding car, Belinda, a private nurse who worked at a nearby hospital, had lived here, helping with Anna Pryce's care and recovery. "Your mother's a strong woman."

Valerie smiled. "She's had to be."

"I think she's awake."

"Good." Valerie walked down a short hall and shoved open the bedroom door.

Anna, thin and wan, was lying on her back, a sheet drawn to her chin. The only light in the room flickered from the television set. A hand-knit afghan was folded at the foot of the old double bed, and magazines and books littered every available surface of the bureau, night table and bookcase.

Valerie smothered a grin as she recognized the characters from her mother's favorite soap opera, *Life's Golden Sands,* the same daytime drama on which Valerie had once played a small role.

"So you're here, are you?" her mother murmured, struggling into a sitting position.

"I thought I'd stop by."

"How'd the interview go?"

Valerie tilted her hand in the air. "Not great. I think I'd better keep looking."

Anna, tucking a wayward lock of fine, brown hair behind her ear, studied her daughter. "You had your heart set on Donovan Enterprises."

"There are other companies."

"But you've always said you liked the way Hale Donovan did business."

Valerie wrinkled her nose. "I've changed my mind. Besides, there wasn't a position open."

"But you saw it in the paper . . ." her mother protested, waving at a stack of newspapers near the bed.

"It had already been filled. But it doesn't matter. I've got callbacks at a couple other places."

"Well, if you ask me, whoever's in charge at Donovan Enterprises made a big mistake not hiring you!"

"I'll tell him the next time I see him," she replied with a grim smile. There were a lot of things she'd like to tell Mr. Donovan, but of course, she'd never get the chance. And that was probably a blessing, she reminded herself.

"Ask Belinda to make some coffee," her mother suggested. "And draw open the blinds—I swear, this place is like a tomb!"

Grinning, Valerie snapped open the shade. "I'll make the coffee. Belinda's got to get to the hospital."

Her mother skewered her with a knowing glance. "Then use the real coffee. I don't need any of that phony caffeine-free stuff."

"But your doctor—"

"Doesn't know a thing about coffee." Her mother grinned. "And don't waste any time. I think Lance is trying to kill

Meredith!" her mother said, mentioning two long-running characters on *Life's Golden Sands.*

"He'll never get away with it," Valerie called over her shoulder as she started the coffeemaker.

"Oh, what do you know?" her mother sang out, laughing quietly.

Belinda followed Valerie into the kitchen. "She's better today."

"I think so, too."

"But, then, I didn't show her these." Belinda reached into her purse and pulled out several small envelopes.

"Don't tell me—bills," Valerie guessed.

"Just six."

Valerie's stomach tightened. Not just six—six more.

Belinda chewed on her lower lip. "Look, I didn't want to tell you, but—"

Valerie waved her apology aside and managed a cheery smile. "Don't worry, I can handle it." She took the bills, stuffed them into her purse and waited as the coffee drizzled into a glass carafe.

"So how did the interview go?"

"Like gangbusters," Valerie muttered sarcastically as she poured two cups of hot coffee. "But I didn't get the job." She saw the lines knotting Belinda's smooth forehead and amended, "Well, actually, I could've taken one job, but it isn't the one I wanted." Thinking of Hale Donovan's outrageous proposal, she gritted her teeth. "Don't worry, there are lots of jobs. I'll find one this week."

"Sure you will." Belinda snagged her favorite navy-blue sweater from a hook near the door. "I'd better run. I'll see you tomorrow."

With a wave, Belinda left, and Valerie, carrying both steaming mugs to the back bedroom, ignored the little voice in the back of her mind that kept reminding her that she was running out of time and that, if she'd used her head, she should have at least heard Hale Donovan out.

"Forget it," she mumbled.

"Forget what?" her mother asked.

"Nothing. Now tell me—what's going on?" She handed her mother a cup and pretended interest in the program. "Lance won't kill Meredith," she predicted.

"Oh, and why not?"

"I just read that the actress has renegotiated her contract."

Her mother rolled her eyes. "You really know how to take the fun out of this, don't you?" But she chuckled and made a face as she took an experimental sip of coffee.

"Maybe Meredith will kill Lance," Valerie suggested.

"And she should, too," her mother agreed. "The way he's treated her . . ."

Two hours later Valerie climbed the triple flight of stairs to her apartment. She was still trying to push thoughts of Hale Donovan aside. Though she'd attempted to concentrate on anything but her interview with him, she could still hear his voice, see the image of his angular face, feel the mockery in his cold gray eyes. Fumbling with her key, she finally jammed it into the lock. "Bastard," she muttered.

She shoved the door open, and her gray tabby cat, Shamus, zipped out the door and onto the landing. "Miss me?" Valerie asked, bending down to pet his soft, striped head. Purring loudly, he rubbed against her legs.

"I bet you're hungry, aren't you? Well, come on in, let's see what we've got."

Black-ringed tail aloft, Shamus trotted after her, then hopped onto a window ledge.

Valerie tossed her coat over the back of her daybed and kicked her shoes into the closet. Her apartment, which she fondly called the crow's nest, was little more than an attic loft tucked high in the gables of an old renovated row house

in the Haight-Ashbury district. The ceilings sloped dramati-
cally, the floors were polished oak, and aside from a walk-in
closet, bathroom alcove and kitchen tucked behind folding
doors, her entire living space consisted of this one room.

"And it's a great room," she told herself as she opened the
folding doors to the kitchen, flipped on a burner and placed
a kettle of water on the stove. She'd lived here since moving
to San Francisco two years before and felt lucky to have an
apartment with a view of the bay.

Pouring cat food into Shamus's dish, she called to him.
"Well, come on." He hopped off the sill and landed not two
feet from the bowl, sniffed disdainfully at the dry kiblets and
cocked his head toward her as if he expected something
more elegant.

"Sorry, boy, that's all we've got."

The kettle whistled shrilly. "My turn," she told the cat as
she gave him one last pet, then scrounged in her cupboards
for a tea bag of orange spice. She found one last bag, dunked
it in the steaming water and soon the room was filled with
the scents of oranges, cinnamon and cloves. Tomorrow, she
thought, testing the tea, tomorrow she would look for another job. Not just any job, but a bona fide job that would
pay enough to cover the bills and help support her mother.
The kind of job she had hoped to find at Donovan Enterprises.

"Cross that one off the list," she murmured, conjuring
Hale Donovan's image. His features swam before her eyes,
and she frowned thoughtfully as she sipped the hot tea.
Handsome? Yes. Arrogant? Definitely. Intriguing? No . . .
well, yes.

She wished she'd never laid eyes on him. Yanking the
pins from her hair, she leaned back, cradled the warm cup in
her hands and sighed. Shamus leaped onto the couch and
curled next to her.

With an effort, she closed her mind to Hale Donovan and
concentrated on the next few days. She had to find a job and

fast. Tomorrow she'd send out more copies of her résumé,
call a couple of leads and— A loud rap on the door startled
her, and Hale Donovan's voice boomed through the panels.
"Valerie?"

Her heart did a peculiar flip, and she jumped, nearly
spilling her tea. *Donovan? Here? Now?*

"Valerie? Are you in there?" He pounded loudly again.

Startled, Shamus flew off the couch and slunk behind a
potted palm. "Chicken," Valerie muttered, though her own
heart was hammering wildly.

"Valerie?" Hale called again.

"I'm coming, I'm coming," she said. She set her near-
empty cup on a table, drew in a deep breath, then padded to
the door in stocking feet. Peering through the peephole, she
saw him, big as life, on the landing. Wearing a dark leather
jacket and a grim expression, he leaned against the scarred
mahogany railing. She'd hoped that his appearance had
changed a little, that he wasn't as handsome as she'd recalled,
but she'd been wrong. Hale Donovan in person was downright overwhelming. His arms were crossed over his chest,
his eyes fastened on her door, his thin lips pursed impatiently.

"It's now or never," she whispered, steeling herself as she
yanked open the door. Her stomach knotted as she stood
squarely on the threshold. "What're you doing here?"

"I wasn't finished making you an offer."

"And I told you I wasn't interested."

"I know, I know, but I thought that by now you might
have calmed down a little." He raked stiff fingers through
his wavy, coal-black hair. "I didn't mean to offend you."

"No?" she mocked, wishing her insides would quit shaking and that she didn't find him so attractive and could simply listen to what he had to say.

"You didn't hear me out."

"Believe me, I heard enough."

His crooked smile caused her heart to trip.

"I suppose I did come on a little strong," he said.

"More than a little."

"Just give me a few minutes to explain," he suggested. "What've you got to lose?"

Everything, she thought wildly. This man distracted her far too much. His restless energy infected her. His glances cut deep, as if he were looking for something in her eyes—something elusive. Swallowing hard, she swung the door open and stepped aside. "You're wasting your breath."

"Mine to waste."

"Okay. Five minutes." Glancing pointedly at her watch, she closed the door behind him and stood, arms folded beneath her breasts, her back against the cool panels of the door, and waited.

Surveying the eclectic blend of art-deco paintings, antique tables and mismatched furniture, Hale said, "I want to offer you a job—a legitimate job." She started to protest, and he lifted a hand, silencing her. "Just hear me out. The title will be personal assistant, but, of course, you'll be more than that. You'll pretend to be my fiancée. Just for two weeks. Then the charade will be over. Think of it as an acting assignment."

"It's deception."

He nodded. "For a good cause."

"To thwart Regina Stowell's interest in you—I know. But she's your problem—not mine."

"And you could be the solution."

"I already told you I don't want the job. Deal with Regina Stowell yourself."

Jamming his fists into his pockets, he muttered, "Regina's twenty, spoiled and very stubborn."

"And you don't want to offend her father." She tossed her hair over her shoulder. "So you've cooked up this crazy scheme and expect me to run interference for you!"

"As I said, it's temporary."

"I'm still not interested."

Hale studied her. A captivating woman, Valerie Pryce. With wavy, uncombed blond hair framing a small, near perfect face, her eyes shifting from gray to green, her brows puckered in frustration, she touched him in a way he hadn't been touched in a long, long while. It worried him a little, but not enough to convince him she wasn't the right woman. "I'm willing to pay twenty-five thousand dollars."

Valerie sucked in a surprised breath. Her eyes widened, and she stared at him as if he truly had gone mad. "Twenty-five thousand?" she repeated.

"Plus expenses."

She raised her chin a fraction, but he sensed she was wavering.

"I'm not for sale, Mr. Donovan."

"Think of it as rent."

Her eyebrows pulled together. "Rent? That's worse!"

But he could hear the hesitation in her voice, knew she was mulling over his offer. He felt a twinge of disappointment. So she did have a price, after all. "Look, you need a job, and I need you."

"Not me—any woman."

He shook his head. "A woman who will be believable as my fiancée. Neither Stowell nor his daughter would believe I'd just linked up with anyone."

"If you're trying to flatter me—"

"I am. And you should be. I've looked at women from every agency in town. None of them fit the bill. In order for someone to pose as my bride-to-be, she's got to be everything I'd want in a wife. She has to be more than beautiful, Valerie. She has to be smart, savvy and have a sense of humor."

"You don't know the first thing about me!"

A muscle worked in his jaw. "Twenty-five thousand is a helluva lot of money for two weeks' work, which I should remind you is simply cruising up the Pacific coast on a private yacht, docking at Portland, Seattle, Victoria and anywhere else we want to! All you have to do is pretend to like me a little."

"That might be impossible," she shot back. What arrogance! "I think I'd have to put in three years at some Hollywood drama school before I could pull off an act like that."

He grinned—that irreverent slash of white that took her breath away.

"I'll make it easy on you," he said. "I'll try my best to be irresistible."

"You just don't know when to give up, do you?"

"I know what I want." He pierced her with his narrowed eyes.

Valerie swallowed against a suddenly dry throat. "And you think that whatever it is can be bought."

"Can't it?" he goaded.

Her temper, already strung tight, snapped. She crossed the small room in three swift strides and positioned herself squarely in front of Hale. "I came to Donovan Enterprises for a job, a real job! I can audit your books or program your computers. I've had experience working with attorneys as well as the IRS and I've even made coffee for the boss when I worked in the secretarial pool. But I've never, *never* been asked to pretend to be the boss's mistress!"

She was so close he could feel the heat radiating from her, see fire sparking in her eyes. "I didn't ask you to be my mistress," he said succinctly.

"Yet—"

"I don't intend to."

Pursing her lips, she said tautly, "I sincerely hope not, Mr. Donovan. Just because I didn't file a complaint against my boss at Liddell doesn't mean I'll go along with anything as cheap as—"

He caught her by the hand. "Twenty-five grand isn't cheap," he said quickly, gripping her wrist. His nostrils flared, and his eyes sparked. "And don't get the wrong impression about me. If I wanted to sleep with you, I wouldn't go about it this way."

She wanted to slap him, but the fingers curling over her wrist clenched so tightly she barely dared to breathe. There was a power running through him as charged as an electric current, leashed by the thin hold he was keeping on his patience. And yet, she couldn't help bait him. "No?" she goaded, tilting her head back. "And just how would you go about seducing me?"

"You want a demonstration?" He slid his jaw to one side. His gaze, as fierce and bright as a silvery moon, delved into hers, then shifted pointedly to her mouth.

Valerie's breath lodged deep in her throat. Unconsciously she licked her lips. Hale stiffened, his gaze moving lazily from her lips to her eyes and back to the corner of her mouth.

She watched as his Adam's apple worked. For a breathless second she was sure he was going to kiss her. Her knees went weak at the thought that she'd pushed him too far. "I don't think a demonstration would be such a good idea," she whispered.

"Neither do I," he agreed, his mouth a thin line, his voice raw. Dropping her wrist, he stepped back a few paces, leaning his back against the wall and ramming his hands into the pockets of his jeans. "What I'm offering you, Ms. Pryce, is the chance to live the life of a princess for two weeks. And I'm willing to pay you very well for the opportunity. Most women—"

"I'm *not* like most women."

His head snapped up, and he impaled her with his sharp, magnetic gaze again. "I know. That's why I want you."

Her heart began to pound so crazily she thought he could surely hear it.

"Do we have a deal?"

If she had any pride at all, she thought, she would tell him to get out, to take his bloody offer and shove it. But she wasn't stupid, and unfortunately she needed the money. Twenty-five thousand dollars would go a long way to pay off her loan from college, help pay her mother's bills and leave enough of a nest egg to tide her over until she could find another job.

But what kind of strings were attached? She didn't know him, and couldn't let herself trust him. Why did she feel he was holding something back?

From the corner of her eye, she noticed Shamus sneaking toward the drapes. Valerie stalled. "Maybe I should talk this over with my roommate," she said.

"Your roommate?" He glanced around the room, and Valerie realized he was looking for any trace of a man.

Shamus ducked behind her rolltop desk. "Yes, uh, he and I discuss everything."

"He?" he repeated, turning back so his eyes could bore into hers. "But I thought—"

"Oh, it's nothing like that," she said hastily, enjoying her joke. "Very platonic . . ."

Hale glanced meaningfully down at the daybed. "Platonic." His jaw tightened, and at that moment Shamus poked his head from under the desk and sauntered over to Valerie, who reached down to pick him up.

"Meet Shamus," she said with a bright smile. "My roommate."

Hale wasn't amused. His eyes grew dark. Glancing pointedly at his watch, he muttered, "Our five minutes are over. So what's it going to be, Ms. Pryce?"

Valerie dropped the cat on the couch. She swallowed hard, trying to find her voice. "Okay," she finally agreed, trying to think rationally while her thoughts were spinning out of control. If she were going along with his crazy plan, she wanted some concessions—big concessions. "I'll do it. On . . . one—make that two—conditions."

"Name them."

"One—I don't sleep with you."

He twisted his lips into a lazy, disarming smile that caught her completely off guard.

"Agreed."

"Two—I want a contract that spells out the terms of my employment. And I want to work for you not just for two weeks, but for six months."

He clenched his jaw. "No way—"

"Oh, yes!" she insisted. "I want to prove to you that I can make it at Donovan Enterprises, and not just as a bimbo strutting around in a bikini, batting my eyelashes at you while we're sailing the seven seas!"

"Just one ocean," he corrected her.

"Look, Mr. Donovan—"

"Hale. We're engaged. Remember?"

" 'Hale,' " she repeated, "I've worked long and hard to get where I have. Just give me a chance. After the initial two weeks, I'll work for the same salary I was getting at Liddell."

"And how will we explain that we're no longer engaged?"

"Those things happen all the time."

"Not to me."

"This scheme was your idea," she reminded him. "It's got to be easier to break a phony betrothal than to pretend it exists."

"It would make more sense if we never saw each other again."

"Maybe so," she said, gambling. "But it's the only way I'll go along with it."

Hale hesitated as he reined in his temper. He shoved one hand through his hair in frustration. "You drive a hard bargain, Valerie."

"So do you."

Reaching into the pocket of his jacket, he withdrew an employment contract. "Got a pen?"

She found one in her purse and handed it to him.

Before he signed, he eyed her. "You are single, aren't you?" he asked.

"Very."

"Is there anything else that would prevent you from becoming my wife?"

She smiled at that. "You mean besides common sense? No."

"Good." Hesitating only a second, he pulled off the cap of the pen with his teeth, read the document, made a few quick slashes and scrawled an additional paragraph. After signing, he handed the contract to her.

She read it slowly, paragraph by straightforward paragraph. Hale had scratched in an additional clause, which lengthened the term of her employment from two weeks to six months and allowed her a salary of five hundred dollars more per month than she'd earned at Liddell. All in all, her employment with Donovan Enterprises was almost too good to be true.

Her stomach fluttered and her palms began to sweat.

"Satisfied?" he asked.

Nodding, she shoved aside all her nagging doubts, took the pen from his outstretched hand, then signed her name quickly on the line next to his. "There you go," she said, handing him back the single sheet. "When do I start?"

With a grin, he said, "Right now."

"Now—but I can't!"

Hale's eyes narrowed angrily. "We have less than forty-eight hours to get to know each other. I think we'd better get started."

"But—"

"Listen, Valerie," he said coldly. "You just signed on—the meter's running." He flopped onto the couch and leaned back as if he were incredibly weary. "Start at the beginning. Where you were born, if your parents are living and where. Tell me about your brothers and sisters—and if you've been married before."

The magnitude of what she'd just done hit her full force. There were a lot of things she'd rather keep secret from Hale Donovan—a private side of her she'd like to remain that way. "Just how much do you want to know about me?" she asked boldly, already regretting that she'd signed his damned contract.

"Everything."

She cleared her throat. "There are some things that are private—I don't share them with anyone."

He sighed, and some of his toughness seemed to disappear.

Closing his eyes, he leaned his head against the back of the sofa and said, "Everyone is entitled to privacy. I'm not trying to turn you inside out. I just need to know that I'm not in for any surprises."

"Such as?"

"Such as a husband or boyfriend who'll want to start throwing punches the next time he sees me."

"I already told you I wasn't married."

"No boyfriends at all?"

"Not currently."

He relaxed a bit. The lines around his mouth vanished. "Good. Another man would be hard to explain."

"You don't have to worry about that," she said, thinking fleetingly of Luke. She wondered if she should mention him, but decided against it. Luke was long gone—somewhere in Montana by now—and Valerie didn't want to think about him. Ever.

"Let's get started," Hale said, straightening. "Where did we meet? In Union Square? The Caribbean? At the office?"

"I don't know," she replied, already resenting her part in this deception. "I'll leave the lies to you."

"I'm not very good at lying."

"Then you should have come up with another idea."

"It's too late now," he said, his voice stone-cold. "I already had our engagement announced in the papers."

"You *what*?"

"It'll be in the next edition."

"But you didn't even know I'd agree!" she gasped, outraged. She thought of her mother and the stack of newspapers at her bedside. Surely she would read the news!

"Of course I did. Everyone has a price."

Valerie wanted to argue the fact, but couldn't. He'd bought her, hadn't he? She shuddered inside. The ink on her employment agreement wasn't even dry and she was already second-guessing herself, wondering if she'd just made a deal with the devil himself.

CHAPTER 3

"Okay," Hale said, studying Shamus with a wary eye. "Other than what's written on your résumé and that you live here with this friendly guy"—he tried to pet the tabby's striped head, but Shamus backed away, hissed loudly, then streaked across the room to the French doors—"what else should I know about you?" He turned his attention from the cat to Valerie.

"You want to know my background," she murmured, feeling stripped bare under Hale's steady gaze. For something to do, she opened the doors to the balcony, and as the cat slunk out, a warm, moist breeze invaded the room.

"Right. All the high points. You can tell me on the way to dinner."

"Dinner?"

"And shopping," he said, starting for the door.

Things were moving much too quickly. "Shopping—for what?"

"An engagement ring, for starters."

"No way! I'm not going to—"

"Sure you are," Hale cut in. "This has got to look convincing. And as far as the rest, you'll need clothes for the cruise."

"I have clothes."

He cast a glance toward her ridiculously small closet. "The Stowells dress for dinner every night—and I'm not talking about cutoff jeans and flip-flops. I mean they dress in formal attire. You'll need at least ten designer dresses—some evening gowns to start with—"

"Slow down," Valerie said. "I agreed to pretend to be your fiancée, but I didn't say I'd change anything about me."

"You'll have to fit in or Stowell will know something's up."

"Fit in?" she threw back at him. "I thought I was the perfect woman—the only one who would do."

"You are."

"Then you'll have to take me as I am, which is not, by the way, anything close to uppercrust. I'm just a working girl trying to make something of myself, and you and William Stowell and the rest of the world will have to accept it!"

Hale frowned, his brows forming a thick, single line across his forehead.

"You wanted the facts—well, you're going to get them," she went on, warming to her subject. "I was born in Phoenix, Arizona. My folks moved to L.A. when I was five and we stayed there until I was thirteen, when my father died of a heart attack. I don't have any brothers or sisters and I've never been married. I put myself through UCLA by taking small acting parts—mainly commercials—and modeling assignments. I graduated and landed a job at Liddell, but you know all about that—"

"Not all," he reminded her.

A blush, starting at the top of her shoulders, climbed up her neck and tinged her cheeks. Ignoring him, she said, "My mother's name is Anna Pryce. She lives here in San Francisco and is recovering from an accident in which some idiot plowed into her car with a huge pickup, then took off. He's never been found."

"Hit-and-run?"

"Yes," she said, cringing inside. "Fortunately she's recovering, but she's got a lot of time on her hands and she just happens to read the newspaper from the front page through the automobile ads. I doubt if she'll miss our engagement announcement."

"We can explain that."

"Can we? I just came from her apartment, where I told her that I didn't get the job at Donovan Enterprises. Her comment was that the guy that interviewed me wasn't too smart."

A crooked smile crept across his jaw. "I think I'd like to meet your mother."

"Don't worry, you'll get your chance." Angry with herself, she walked onto the balcony, where Shamus was perched on the rail, eyeing gray-and-white seagulls that swooped and floated on the wind overhead.

Hearing Hale's footsteps behind her, she turned, squinting against the late-afternoon sunshine. "You know, Donovan, if we're going to play this game, we'd better do it right. Otherwise your web of lies might start untangling. Just think what might happen if my mother called the editor at the *Times,* told him he'd got his facts wrong and demanded an apology—in the paper?"

"She wouldn't."

"You don't know my mother." She tossed her hair over her shoulder. "And you don't know that William Stowell, or any of his family, doesn't read the society news. If the Stowells see a retraction, instigated by my mother—"

"You've made your point." He clamped his mouth shut.

"Good." Feeling the warm breeze tangle her hair and brush her cheeks, Valerie stared once again at the view. The noise of the city sounded distant, and the fragrant scent of roses from the planters on the deck wafted in the air. She thought about her mother—how hurt she would be that Valerie hadn't confided in her. "I think we'd better straighten things out with Mom, and fast."

"I already said I'd meet her."

"And charm the socks off her, right?"

"For starters."

Valerie didn't want to think about her mother's reaction to Hale. The way Valerie's luck was running, Anna Pryce would probably like the arrogant son of a gun and welcome him as her future son-in-law! What a disaster that could be! "Listen, Hale, I don't want to lie to Mom."

"What's this—a latent sense of conscience?"

"She'll have to be told the truth," Valerie said, thinking aloud. Her mother deserved to know she had no intention of marrying a man like Hale Donovan.

"No way," he said, his smile fading. "I can't take the chance."

"Just my mother—no one else has to know."

His smile collapsed. "Do you think I'd go to all this trouble, then sabotage myself? It's only for a couple of weeks. Then, once the papers with Stowell are signed and we're back on land, you can tell her anything you want."

Valerie's eyes narrowed. "You really are a bastard. You know that, don't you?"

All kindness left his features. He jutted his jaw forward, and his eyes snapped with an inner fire. "Don't ever," he warned, his voice the barest of whispers, "call me that again." He strode swiftly back into the apartment and reached for her jacket, hanging on the coat tree near the door, then flung it at her as she followed him inside. "Let's go."

She caught her jacket on the fly. "I'm sorry if I—"

"Forget it."

Realizing she'd touched a raw nerve, she slipped into her shoes. "I didn't mean to offend you."

"You didn't," he shot back, waiting until she crossed the threshold, then closing the door firmly behind her.

"But—"

"Let's just pretend it didn't happen. Okay?"

Valerie tilted her chin up and met his angry gaze with her own. "It's forgotten, Hale," she said slowly, "but the next time I try to apologize, let me."

"Hopefully there won't be any reason to."

As she stood alone with him on the landing, the magnitude of what she'd agreed to do hit her full force. This man was handsome and powerful, and used to giving out orders that were instantly obeyed—no questions asked.

Mentally Valerie crossed her fingers. They'd only been together half an hour and already they were at each other's throats. How could they possibly spend two weeks cooped up on a boat together?

His car was parked three streets away, a sleek black Jaguar glinting beneath the late-afternoon sun. "My mother will never believe we're a couple," Valerie said, eyeing the car as he unlocked the door for her.

"Why not?"

"I took a solemn oath never to date a guy with an expensive car."

His dark expression lightened as he slid behind the wheel. "Strange vow, isn't it?"

"Call it self-preservation."

With a flick of his wrist, the powerful engine thrummed to life. "Why?"

"Most of the boys in college who drove around in flashy cars turned out to be self-centered, egotistical jerks."

"That's a pretty broad statement."

She shrugged slightly as he eased into traffic. "I suppose."

"And prejudiced." He shifted, putting the Jag through its paces. Fresh air, filled with the salty scent of the sea, blew in through a partially opened window. "Where did you learn to be so cynical?"

"Seems like a natural progression," she said, staring out

the window and trying to block out the image of Luke that invariably came to mind. Luke, blond and tanned by the Southern California sun, with an all American face and roving eye. Proud owner of a flashy red Porsche and a surfer's body honed to perfection. The quintessential boy who refused to grow up—the only man Valerie had ever come close to loving.

She felt the weight of Hale's gaze upon her and forced a smile. "So—what are we going to tell my mother?"

"I've been working on that," he said, cranking on the wheel. As they drove down the hilly streets, Valerie could see the sparkling waters of the bay, dark blue and shimmering. Seagulls flew overhead, and boats sliced through the water, leaving frothy wakes.

Hale parked near Ghiradelli Square, a former chocolate factory, which was positioned on the hill overlooking the bay. The series of brick-faced buildings had been renovated and now housed a maze of shops and restaurants.

He helped her from the car, then took her hand and guided her up a flight of exterior stairs. Olive trees, flower beds and benches were interspersed between buildings with such names as Mustard Building, Power House or Cocoa Building. Shoppers and sightseers browsed through the alleys. Birds chirped and flitted from the shrubs to the walkways.

"This isn't the way to my mother's, you know," Valerie said as they passed a mermaid fountain.

"Isn't it?"

"What're we doing here?"

He opened the double oak-and-glass doors of an Irish restaurant tucked into a shaded corner of the square. "This is my favorite place in the city," he explained.

The smells of spices and smoke filled a cozy restaurant with bare, glossy tables, glass-encased candles and a long bar of dark wood inlaid with brass. The bar had no stools, and patrons bellied up to it and rested their feet on a genuine brass rail. Behind the polished wood, mirrors rose to a fifteen-foot ceiling. Green, brown and clear bottles were reflected in the glass.

The sounds of laughter and whispered conversation drifted over the hum of lazy paddle fans mounted high overhead. Hale didn't wait to be seated, but tugged on Valerie's hand and led her to a corner booth with a view of the street below.

"You're a regular," she guessed.

"You could say that."

A waiter appeared as they sat, and brought two frosted glasses of hearty Irish ale.

"I don't get a choice?" Valerie asked as the waiter disappeared between the closely packed tables.

Hale grinned across his mug. "Consider it an initiation rite."

"One that all your fiancées go through?"

Winking broadly, he settled back in his chair and eyed her over the frosted lip of his mug. "I've never been engaged before."

"What happened? Didn't you offer enough money?"

He lifted one corner of his mouth. "I guess not—until now."

"So who else have you initiated?"

"Most of the women I've dated have been here at one time or another."

"Oh." She couldn't hide the disappointment in her voice and wondered why it was there. What did it matter if Hale had brought dozens of other women in here? This was all just an act—nothing more. To hide her feelings, she picked up the menu. "Do I get to choose my own meal?"

"I'll work on it, but it might be tough. The guy who owns this place, Tim Buchanan, is an old fraternity brother of mine. When he hears that we're here, he'll probably"—Hale glanced over her shoulder, and his grin widened—"well, speak of the devil."

"About time you showed your ugly mug around here, Donovan!" Tim Buchanan moved lithely between the tables. Over six feet tall, crowned with a thatch of blazing red hair that matched his neatly clipped beard, he wore a crisp white shirt, black slacks and bow tie. His face was dusted with freckles, and small, blue eyes peered fondly at Hale. He reached across the table and clasped Hale's hand in a grip that looked positively punishing. "And who's this?" he asked, turning his attention to Valerie.

"Valerie Pryce . . . Tim Buchanan. Valerie's my fiancée."

Tim's smile froze. He turned his head abruptly, and his gaze landed back on Hale. "The devil, you say! You? Married?" He turned back to Valerie, and a small smile played beneath his red beard. "Well, you've got yourself a handful, that you do, Ms. Pryce. If this guy ever gets out of line, you call on me!"

"Oh, I won't need any help, but thank you very much," she said with a heartfelt sigh. "Hale's just an angel. Anything I want and"— she shrugged her slim shoulders and lifted a palm—"there it is!" With what she hoped was an adoring expression on her face, she turned to Hale. "Isn't that right, darling?"

"An angel?" Tim hooted, and the back of Hale's neck burned scarlet. "Donovan? Wait till I tell Father O'Flannery!"

"Who's he?" Valerie asked innocently, though she could sense Hale squirming in his chair.

"Who's he? The man who personally acquainted Hale with the wrath of God." Laughing loudly, Tim turned, signaled to the bartender and said, "A round on the house—my best friend is getting married!"

The men at the bar cheered, and Hale sank lower in his seat. Tim wasn't finished. "Dinner's on me—the house specialty!"

"Hey, you don't have to—"

Tim cut off Hale's protest with an impatient wave. "It's

not every day you walk in here and announce you're getting married. I'll be back in a minute."

Still chuckling, he headed through swinging doors that Valerie assumed led to the kitchen.

"What the hell was that all about?" Hale demanded, the skin on his face stretched taut. " 'Angel,' my eye!"

"I just thought you should know what we're going to be in for," she replied, enjoying herself. It was time he found out this charade wasn't going to be a bed of roses. "The next couple of weeks aren't going to be easy on either of us."

"What does it matter? You're being paid—and very well."

"Then you'll want me to continue to play the part of adoring wife-to-be, right?"

Hale frowned. "Just don't overdo it."

"Wouldn't dream of it, darling," she replied, her hazel eyes twinkling mischievously as Tim brought back two steaming platters of crawfish smothered in a spicy brown sauce, spinach salads with lemon and bacon and a bottle of champagne.

"May as well do this right," Tim said as he uncorked the bottle. The cork popped, frothy champagne slid down the long neck of the bottle, and Tim poured three glasses, holding his aloft. "To the years ahead," he said solemnly, "life, love, happiness and fertility!"

Hale nearly choked.

Valerie laughed out loud.

And Tim, smirking, winked at his friend, then gulped his drink. "About time you took the plunge," he said before slapping Hale on the shoulder and heading back to the kitchen.

"I thought you weren't going to overdo it," Hale reminded her, jabbing at his salad with his fork.

"I'm trying not to, believe me," she said, but felt the cat-who-ate-the-canary grin spreading across her face.

"Just don't push me," he warned.

"Wouldn't dream of it, 'darling.'" She touched the rim of her glass to his. "Here's to the next two weeks."

"May they pass quickly," he muttered.

"Amen!" She sipped from her glass, enjoying the feel of the champagne as it bubbled in her throat. Hale refilled her glass several times, but she didn't care. The tip of her nose grew numb, and she felt the unlikely urge to smile giddily. And most unnerving of all, she couldn't take her eyes off Hale. What would it be like to really be in love with him? she wondered as she studied his strong chin, his thin, sensual lips, his deep-set and brooding eyes.

"Irish coffee?" Tim asked when he returned for their empty plates.

"And dessert—chocolate mousse?" Hale suggested, glancing at her for approval.

"I couldn't—I'm stuffed," she whispered.

Tim lifted one brawny shoulder. "Then I'll bring one serving with two spoons."

"Just like in a 1950s soda shop," Valerie said with a giggle.

Hale shot a murderous glance in her direction.

"Right—for lovebirds," Tim agreed, chuckling.

A muscle worked in Hale's jaw. Valerie thought he might explode and tell his friend the engagement was all an act, but instead, to her mortification, he reached across the table and grabbed her hand, stroking the back of her fingers with one thumb. "Then again, maybe we don't have time for dessert or coffee," he said huskily, his gray eyes smoldering with unspoken desire. "We've got better things to do."

Valerie blushed and felt her mouth turn to cotton. Licking suddenly dry lips, she jerked back her hand.

"Well, don't let me hold you up," Tim said, sending Hale a knowing look as he was called back to the bar.

"That was unnecessary!" Valerie hissed as Hale, taking her elbow in a proprietary grip, propelled her out of the restaurant.

"You asked for it."

"I did no such—"

"Oh, come on, you were really working me over in front of Tim. And you enjoyed every minute of it!"

She couldn't argue. She had felt a perverse satisfaction at making him squirm. There was something about knocking Hale Donovan down a peg that she couldn't resist. "Okay, okay," she agreed as he elbowed open the door, "maybe we should start over—with a truce."

He raised a cynical dark brow, and his hand never left her arm as he guided her through the crowds in the square, around a corner and up a short flight of steps. "A truce—you think that's possible?"

"Probably not, but it's the only way we're going to survive the next two weeks."

"Agreed." He offered her a roguish smile that caused her heart to trip unexpectedly. "Now before the store closes . . ." Still holding her arm, he shoved open the door of a jewelry shop. A small bell tinkled as they crossed the threshold.

"Mr. Donovan!" A reed-thin woman with thick, dark hair pinned away from her face glanced up, smiled and quickly closed the glass case where she'd been arranging bracelets. She hurried across the small shop to greet Hale. In heels, she was nearly as tall as Hale, and her suit, a rich red silk, rustled as she stretched out a slender hand. "What can I do for you today?"

"We need a ring—a diamond."

The woman raised her finely arched eyebrows a fraction. "A cocktail ring?"

"Engagement."

"Oh." She sounded vaguely disappointed as she moved over to a glass case where diamonds of every description were displayed in open, velvet-lined boxes.

"This is my fiancée, Valerie Pryce."

"My best wishes," the woman murmured.

"Thank you," Valerie ground out.

"Now what kind of diamond would you like?"

"Nothing too flashy, just a nice stone without a lot of frills." Hale glanced at Valerie. "That okay with you?"

"It doesn't really matter to me, remember? I'm not all that crazy about being here in the first place."

The saleslady did her best to keep her expression bland, but Valerie could read the questions in her eyes—a million of them.

Hale shot Valerie a warning look, then asked to see the ring.

"Any special cut?" the saleslady asked. "Square? Pear-shaped?"

"How about that one?" Hale pointed to a ring near the front of the case, and Valerie had to bite her tongue. The setting and stone were gorgeous.

With great care, the woman pulled out a platinum ring crowned by a winking marquis-cut stone and slipped it on Valerie's ring finger. The diamond looked huge—not gawdy, by any means, but still it felt like a deadweight on her hand.

"It'll need to be adjusted—just a little, but I can have that done while you wait—"

"Fine," Hale said. "Charge it to my account."

"Will do."

Valerie handed the ring back to the saleslady, who walked crisply to the back of the store. "Don't you think you're pushing this too far? What're you going to do with that ring when this is all over?"

"I haven't thought that far ahead."

"I don't believe you. I think you've thought this all out very carefully." She studied him through narrowed eyes. "But you really don't have to buy that ring. Can't you just rent one or buy an imitation?"

"And have you appear cheap to the Stowells?" he mocked. "No way. This has got to be the real thing."

"You must want Stowell's company very badly."

"I do."

"And it doesn't matter what it costs or that you have to lie in order to get it?"

"It's worth it."

"So it all comes down to money, right?"

"Doesn't everything?" he asked.

Valerie wanted to ask him about love and happiness, but she bit her tongue. The man was obviously jaded. He thought money could buy him everything he wanted or needed in life, and maybe it could. It had bought her, hadn't it?

As she watched him move impatiently from one glass case to the next, she realized he was a man who didn't believe in love and didn't have time for it. He was too busy amassing his next million to get involved in anything as complicated as love.

Within minutes the saleslady reappeared, wearing a satisfied smile. "Here we go—let's see if this is any better." She tried the ring on Valerie again and it fitted perfectly, the bright stone catching the light.

"Great," Hale said.

"It's a beautiful ring," the saleswoman agreed as she motioned to another case. "Could I interest you in a necklace or earrings—"

"No!" Valerie said quickly.

Hale grinned wickedly. "Not right now, but we'll think about them."

"Do." The saleslady pressed a card into his hand. "Just give me a call. And congratulations."

Valerie didn't say a word all the way back to the car. This engagement thing was getting totally out of hand.

"You don't like the ring," Hale said as he slipped the Jaguar into the tangle of early-evening traffic.

She slid a glance in his direction and noticed the smile toying at his lips. Damn the man, he was enjoying this. "The ring's beautiful. It's the sentiment that bothers me."

"Don't worry about it."

"I'll try not to. All part of the deal, right?"

"Right." He grimaced tightly as he shifted down. "Okay, so where does your mother live?"

Valerie rattled off the address, and Hale turned south. "Have you come up with a plausible story yet?" she wondered aloud. "Mom will ask a ton of questions."

"How about the truth? You fell hopelessly in love with me and threw yourself at my feet."

Valerie smothered a smile. "Oh, that'll work."

"Or maybe you're after my money—that's closer to the truth."

"You're pushing it, Donovan."

"'Honey,' remember? From now on it's 'honey.'"

"Oh, right." Good Lord, what had she gotten herself into? "Well, 'honey,' you'd better come up with a good story, because Mom will expect one."

"By all means."

She settled back in the Jaguar and watched him from the corner of her eye. A handsome, intelligent man, he showed a spark of humor, which softened the hard edge of his arrogance.

"How about we met at the beach a few weeks ago, but we kept our affair—"

"No affair. This is my *mother,* remember?"

He slid a questioning glance in her direction. "This isn't the Victorian era."

Valerie stared straight ahead. "Not to you, maybe, but my mother and I *don't* discuss my sex life. Let's keep it that way."

"Whatever you say."

"Good. Now, what's our story?" She cringed inside. This was getting more complicated by the minute. Sighing, she leaned back in her seat. Maybe after the first lie, it would get easier.

"How about this," Hale suggested. "We kept the fact that we were in love a secret because we wanted to be sure of our feelings before we told the world we'd found each other."

Rolling her eyes, Valerie muttered, "This sounds like a story line for *Life's Golden Sands.*"

At that he looked perplexed.

"It's a soap opera, the one on which I played a minor part for six months—a fact you'd better remember if you want to pull this off. I was Tess, the tortured stepdaughter of rich Trevor Billings, whose natural son was always coming on to me—"

"Enough! Spare me all the grisly details," Hale growled. "I get the idea."

He found a parking space within two blocks of the apartment building, and before Valerie could catch her breath, she was letting herself into her mother's second-story unit.

"Val? That you?" her mother called.

"Yep! And I brought a . . . friend." She closed the door behind Hale and saw her mother seated on the living room couch, an open book on her lap. Valerie took a deep breath. "Mom, I'd like you to meet Hale Donovan."

"The man who . . . ?"

Stuffing her hands into her pockets, Valerie said, "The man who wouldn't hire me. And there's a reason for that—"

"I'm in love with your daughter, Mrs. Pryce," Hale said, stepping forward and placing his arm possessively across Valerie's shoulders. "And we have a strict policy at Donovan Enterprises. We don't allow close relatives to work together. That goes for the boss, too."

"But . . . ? Val?" her mother asked, confused.

Valerie felt horrid. "I think I should explain—"

Hale cut her off. "I've asked your daughter to be my wife and she's accepted," he said to her mother. The words sounded so sincere Valerie nearly believed him.

Anna Pryce's mouth dropped open. "You're getting married?" Her gaze, clouded with suspicion, flicked from Valerie to Hale and back again.

"Yes."

"When?" she asked, stunned.

"Soon," Hale said vaguely.

"Now wait a minute." Anna shoved her book aside and pinned her daughter with her unconvinced stare. "Why is this the first I've heard of it?"

"It, uh, is sudden," Valerie offered lamely.

"That's the understatement of the century." Anna's eyes snapped. "Now let's start all over. At the beginning. And don't tell me the beginning happened between this afternoon and this evening, because I just won't believe it. What's going on here?"

Valerie swallowed hard. She'd always been a lousy liar. "Look, Mom," she said, sitting on the couch and touching her mother's arm. "I should have told you all about this sooner, I guess, but we just decided to make our engagement official this afternoon."

"After you left here," her mother clarified.

"Right. And I know it's kind of a shock."

"A big shock."

"Right—I know, but I just want you to trust me on this, okay?" She took her mother's hands between her own.

"Marriage is a big step."

"Mom, I'm twenty-four."

"And you almost made a mistake once before, remember?"

From the corner of her eye, Valerie saw Hale's muscles stiffen. "That was a long time ago."

"So now two years is a long time—"

"Mom, please. Believe me, I know what I want."

Anna sighed tiredly and pinched her eyebrows into a suspicious frown. "I guess I don't have much choice, do I? You've always been a stubborn thing."

"Amen," Hale whispered.

"We won't rush into anything," Valerie promised, shooting him a warning glance.

"Good," her mother replied.

There was more she wanted to say—a lot more. Valerie could sense it.

Feeling guilty, Valerie said, "I do have one favor to ask you. Hale and I are going on a cruise—just up the coast with some friends and business associates of his." To her surprise, her mother didn't bat an eye. She was probably still in shock. "Would you mind taking care of Shamus for a couple of weeks?"

"That beast? He hates me."

"And you adore him."

Anna glanced at Valerie's left hand, where the diamond glittered mockingly. "Of course I will," she said gently, though her forehead was still creased. "But when you get back, let's talk. I mean, really talk."

"We will," Valerie promised, wondering how she could tell her mother that everything she'd said was a bald-faced lie.

CHAPTER 4

"Did I pass inspection?" Hale asked once they were back in his car. He slid the Jaguar into gear and pulled into traffic. The sun, leaving a blaze of gold and magenta in its wake, had settled into the Pacific.

Valerie shook her head. "If you're asking if my mom bought our story, I think the answer is no. But she's going along with it just to humor me. And that's the point, isn't it?"

"Exactly."

Valerie leaned back in her seat, and as dusk settled, the interior of the car seemed smaller still—more intimate. Hale's carved features were shadowed with the coming night. His jaw appeared even stronger, his eyes more deep set, his lips thin, nearly cruel.

She noticed his hands on the steering wheel, large and strong. And his legs, with the fabric of his jeans pulling taut over his thighs, were dangerously close to hers. Swallowing uncomfortably, she fidgeted with the strap of her purse and shifted away from him, pressing her right side against the passenger door to assure her as much space as possible between his body and hers, then forced her gaze to the windshield.

She wasn't usually uncomfortable around men, but Hale had a way of making her restless; his sidelong glances were unnerving, his innate sexuality impossible to ignore.

He found a parking space not far from her apartment house and walked with her to the front door.

"You don't have to come up," she said as she twisted her key in the lock and felt the dead bolt give way.

"No," he drawled, "I suppose I don't." Leaning one shoulder against the door, he studied her for several heart-stopping seconds. "But we still have a lot of work to do. Your mother was just the first hurdle, you know."

"But a biggie."

Hale smiled, and in the night his flash of white teeth seemed genuine. It touched a spot in her heart she had thought no longer existed—a spot Luke had destroyed.

Suddenly she wanted to know all about Hale. "What about your family? Won't you have to tell them anything?"

His smile faded as quickly as it had appeared. "I don't have any family."

"None?" she said.

"My folks are both dead."

"I'm sorry—"

"It happened a long time ago. I don't really remember them. There's nothing for you to be sorry about," he clipped.

"But don't you have any brothers or sisters or cousins?"

"None." Under the twin bulbs mounted over the doors, his black hair gleamed and his eyes turned stone-cold.

"I didn't mean to pry," Valerie said quickly, embarrassed, "but I think I should know a little about you, too. If the Stowells are going to believe I'm engaged to you, it would only make sense that I know your history—at least part of it."

He took a few seconds to answer. "I suppose you're right."

"Well, I'd look pretty stupid if I showed up on the yacht and all I knew about the man I intended to spend the rest of my life with was that he owned an investment company."

He shrugged and held the door open for her. "You're right. I'll fill you in tomorrow morning."

"What're we doing tomorrow?"

He laughed, and started down the steps. "You'll find out then," he said, his voice filled with amusement as she shut the door behind him and turned the key.

Climbing the three steep flights, she wondered if she'd made a colossal mistake linking up with someone as unpredictable as Hale Donovan. Surprisingly, she felt lighthearted at the prospect of seeing him again, and that bothered her. It bothered her a lot.

The next morning Valerie yanked every garment she owned from her closet and tossed each piece onto her open daybed. She had small piles of skirts, dresses, blouses, jackets, sweaters and slacks, all very tailored and nice enough, though nothing extravagant or particularly expensive.

"So who cares?" she muttered, staring at an even more dismal stack of jeans, shorts and T-shirts. Shamus hopped onto the bed and settled between two of the piles. "Thank you, but I don't think I need cat hair all over my wardrobe." Gently she lifted the fat tabby and stroked his silky head. "So what d'ya think? Will I pass as the illustrious Hale Donovan's bride?"

Shamus yawned, scrambled out of her arms and flopped on the floor where the sunlight filtered through the window to warm the old oak boards.

"Yeah, a lot of help you are," she mumbled, realizing as she sorted through her clothes and came up with a few suitable outfits that Hale had been right. She didn't have much in the way of yachting attire—and she didn't really care.

She packed two sundresses, a couple of pairs of slacks and matching sweaters, then tossed her favorite pair of jeans and her only decent shorts into her suitcase. As an afterthought she found her one silk blouse, added it to the case and sorted through her shoes. After organizing her meager wardrobe, she flipped on the coffeemaker.

Ten minutes later the doorbell rang, and Shamus, a streak of greased lightning, made a beeline for the open French doors.

Valerie checked the peephole, saw Hale's handsome face and braced herself. Dealing with Hale reminded her of going into battle. Unlatching the door, she asked, "Are you always this prompt?"

"A habit I can't break." He strode into the room, slapped a newspaper onto the table, then smiling, surveyed the mess on the bed. "Packing?"

"If you can call it that."

He motioned to the suitcase. "Need anything?"

"Nothing I can't buy myself."

"You're sure about that?" To her mortification, he walked over to her open case and took stock. "Where's the rest?"

"The rest of what?"

"Your other bags."

"I don't have any other bags. I thought I'd pick up a few more things and that would be it."

"This isn't an overnight camp-out on the beach, you know."

Valerie bristled. "And *you* know that I'm not going to pretend I'm some kind of rich debutante. I don't have that kind of money and I think I'm a few years too old. I'm a working girl, I come from middle-class roots, and if William Stowell doesn't like it, he can damn well lump it!"

Hale's mouth twitched.

"I don't think he'll care where I came from as long as you convince him that you're involved with me and that you're not interested in his daughter or her money."

His head snapped up. He dropped her clothes. "Her money?"

"That is what this is all about, isn't it? You've got to prove

I've got the money behind me to keep you interested. Otherwise Stowell won't believe that Hale Donovan, who worships the almighty dollar above all else, is seriously going to marry me!"

"That wasn't the reason."

"No—then what was?" she demanded, crossing the room to stand so close to him she could smell his cologne, see the flecks of blue in his steel-gray eyes.

"I just wanted you to feel like you fitted in."

"Don't worry about me. I'll be fine."

"If you say so."

"I'm positive," she said, angling her face up to his defiantly. "You chose me, Donovan, so I expect you to take me as I am."

"It's 'honey,' not 'Donovan,' remember?" A twinge of a smile tugged at his lips.

"This is all a big joke to you, isn't it?"

"I don't joke when business is involved," he said, "but I think we may as well enjoy ourselves as much as possible. We can spend the next couple of weeks pretending to like each other in front of everyone and lunging for each other's throats when we're alone, or we can try to get along. I think you were the one who suggested a 'truce.' "

"Call me an idealist," she mocked, but smiled in spite of herself.

"Let me pour you a cup of coffee," he suggested, opening first one cupboard, then the next, until he found two ceramic mugs labeled UCLA. "From college?"

"Umm." Not only from college, but from Luke. The first gift he'd ever given her. She felt her face drain of color, but accepted a cup and sipped gratefully.

"We made page one of the society section," Hale announced, then poured another cup for himself.

Valerie's stomach dropped as she flipped open the newspaper he'd brought in with him. On the first page of the society section in bold black letters, the headline read: DONOVAN TO WED.

"Oh, great," she whispered, scanning the article, which listed her name, that she was a graduate of UCLA and a resident of San Francisco. Other than that, she was fairly anonymous. The article stated that no date had been picked for the wedding, then went on to sketch out a little of Hale's success in business. "It's not too bad," she admitted.

"A little on the vague side," he said, "but it covers all the bases."

"Don't you mean it covers your backside—as far as Stowell is concerned."

"That, too." Hale took a swallow and gulped, nearly sputtering. "What *is* this stuff?"

Valerie wasn't in the mood to be razzed about her coffee. With a sweet smile she didn't feel, she said, "It's a mild decaffeinated Colombian blend mixed with Viennese mocha."

"Well, it's horrible."

"Thanks a lot—it's my special brew."

"Yeah, well, it needs work—like a complete overhaul."

She lifted her brows innocently. "Then it's a good thing we're not really getting married, or you'd have to live with it."

"Nope. I'd make the coffee. Come on, I'll take you out for a real breakfast."

She should have been angry, she supposed. His high-handedness was uncalled for. But the dimple in his cheek and the glint in his eyes convinced her he'd only been teasing. "Breakfast and then what?" she asked, locking Shamus inside.

"Whatever the day brings."

"Is this the surprise you told me about?"

"The first of many," he said with a laugh.

Outside, the morning fog was beginning to burn off. Wisps still hung over the water, but most of the hilly city was exposed to the August sun's warm rays.

Hale drove down the steep streets to the waterfront, where they took a ferry north across San Francisco Bay to Tiburon. There they left the Jaguar and stood on the upper deck of the boat, near the prow. Salt spray filled Valerie's nostrils with the scent of the sea, and the wind was strong enough to burn her cheeks. The water was clear and smooth, and she had to shout to Hale to be heard over the heavy drone of the ferry's huge engines.

Hale didn't touch her, but stood close, the breeze ruffling his hair as they passed Alcatraz, stopped at Angel Island, headed north again and finally docked at Tiburon.

Hale drove into the town and parked in a parking lot near the waterfront.

Valerie slipped out of the car, and felt warm rays of the sun beat against her crown. Hale took her hand, and though she was surprised, she didn't protest, but followed as he guided her along a cement walkway to the docks and a tiny café perched over the water.

His fingers felt strong and warm, and despite the fact that his touch wasn't the least bit intimate, Valerie felt her pulse accelerate.

He shoved open the door, and a small bell tinkled. Spying Hale, a plump waitress with freckles and short-cropped brown hair snatched a couple of menus and smiled broadly. "Well, Mr. Donovan," she said with a grin. "Long time no see."

"Hi, Rose. It has been a while."

"Well, don't make yourself such a stranger." Her bright gaze rested on Valerie, and as they walked through a back door to a covered patio, Hale made introductions.

"I read where you were finally tying the big one," Rose said. "High time."

"Mmm," Hale replied noncommittally.

Rose handed Valerie a menu. "You're a lucky lady," she

said, pouring water for each of them as the doorbell chimed again. "I'll be back for your order in a minute."

"Another fraternity brother?" Valerie asked once Rose was out of sight.

"Very funny."

"Why did we come all the way over here for breakfast?" she asked.

"Atmosphere, for one thing."

The small café had plenty of that. The few tables scattered over the flagstones were shaded by a trellis over which fragrant lilacs blossomed in purple clusters. Beyond the porch was a path leading to the dock and an open view to the bay, where gleaming yachts plowed through the blue water.

"Tomorrow we'll be boarding *The Regina*—"

"The what?"

"Stowell named his boat after his daughter."

"Oh."

"I thought you'd like a sneak preview. After breakfast we'll go down to the dock and I'll point her out to you."

A cold knot tightened in Valerie's stomach. Until that moment she hadn't really thought about sailing away with Hale—or what fourteen days cooped up with him could do to her. In just twenty-four hours he'd managed to unnerve her. What would happen in two weeks?

"Have you decided?" Rose asked, breezing back to the patio, notepad poised and ready.

"Oh, uh, sure . . ." Valerie scanned the menu quickly. "A Belgian waffle with strawberries."

"I'll have the seafood omelet," Hale said, then winked at Valerie. Her heart did a ridiculous somersault. "And a cup of coffee. Real coffee."

An hour later they walked to the dock and watched several magnificent white vessels sail through the water. Huge yachts raced against smaller sleek sailboats.

"Stowell's boat is moored at the yacht club, one of the closest berths." Squinting against the sun, Hale stood behind Valerie and pointed, resting his arm lightly on her shoulder. "It's one of the largest—see."

"They're all large," she said, slipping sunglasses onto her nose and following the extended path of his finger. Shining white vessels, their masts and rigging outlined against the blue horizon, swayed gently on the water. Smaller sloops were moored next to larger cutters, ketches and schooners.

"I could take you over and introduce you today."

"I'd just as soon wait until tomorrow."

He slanted her a lazy smile and linked his arm through hers. "Chicken."

"That's me," she said with a laugh.

"I think you'll like the Stowells."

"Will I?" she asked, then shrugged. "I like most people."

"I thought maybe I'd scared you off—all the talk about their money—and their daughter."

"I won't hold it against them that they're rich, if that's what you mean."

His smile widened. "You know, Ms. Pryce, if we try, we might just enjoy ourselves on this trip."

She doubted it. Two weeks cooped up with Hale while he was trying to negotiate a business deal? What would she do? Chitchat with Regina—a woman with whom she had nothing in common? Nothing, that was, except for Hale Donovan. Yep, it sounded like a rip-roaring good time already. She could hardly wait.

Lost in thought, Valerie slid into the sunbaked interior of Hale's Jaguar. She watched as Hale tossed his jacket behind the front seat and shoved his shirtsleeves over his tanned forearms. An interesting man, Hale Donovan, she thought as they drove through a dusty parking lot and turned toward Highway 101.

Small drops of perspiration collected at her hairline, and she rested her arm on the open window, surprised at how at ease she felt with a man she barely knew. He reached into the glove compartment, found a pair of mirrored aviator sunglasses and shoved them onto his nose.

"You promised to tell me something about yourself," she finally said.

"What do you want to know?"

"Everything, I suppose."

"I graduated from Berkeley ten years ago, worked for someone else for a while and saved some money. I bought a company that was going bankrupt, for a song, turned it around, made a profit, bought another company the next year and just kept buying and expanding."

"The man with the Midas touch."

"I wish," he muttered, adjusting his glasses.

"What about your personal life?"

"I don't have time for one."

"But there have been women," she hinted.

"Not many."

"No?" Men as wealthy and handsome as Donovan usually had women crawling all over them.

"If there were women—or at least one woman—I wouldn't have had to find a stranger to pull off this charade, now would I?" he asked flippantly, his jaw clenched.

"What about your friends?"

"You met Tim. I have a few others. Most of them work for me."

"Your *friends* are your employees?"

"Some of them. Some of the people who work for me don't like me much." He cranked hard on the wheel and turned south, toward San Francisco. "Anything else you want to know?"

"Where did you go to high school?"

Was it her imagination, or did he flinch? She couldn't see his eyes, hidden as they were behind his glasses, but she felt a sudden coldness invade the car's interior. "I went to a private school in Oakland. It's not important. Stowell won't expect you to know anything about it."

"But if the subject comes up—"

"Change it!"

"Aye, aye, Captain," she shot back, irritated at his dictatorial tone. "Since we obviously can't talk about your personal life," she went on, unable to hold her tongue, "why don't you tell me about your business? Good ol' Donovan Enterprises. Weren't you in trouble with the IRS a couple of years ago?"

Now he really did flinch. "A couple accounting errors. We cleared them up."

"Then there was that takeover of some oil leases—"

"That was straightened out by the attorneys. What's the point, Valerie?"

"I just want a feel for the company I'm going to be working for."

"A little late for that, isn't it?"

"Maybe not. There've been rumors that Donovan Enterprises walks a thin line with the law."

"Is that why you wanted a job with us?" he mocked.

"Look, I needed a job. It's that simple. You pay well and offer a good chance for advancement."

He twisted his mouth in a sarcastic grin. "So to hell with our ethics, is that it? You know, Ms. Pryce, if I didn't know better, I'd think you might be an opportunist."

"Me? Oh, come on!"

"If the shoe fits—"

"Enough with the clichés," she muttered, but couldn't help grinning.

"Then I'm to assume you're through assassinating my character?"

"For the time being." She stared through the windshield. The Golden Gate Bridge loomed ahead, spanning the neck of the bay and leading across clear, sun-dappled water to the city. Hale drove straight to Fisherman's Wharf, searched for a parking spot and settled for a place several blocks away.

"Come on," he said, climbing out of the car.

"What're we doing here?"

"Consider it part of your training." He drew his lips into a smug smile, and though she couldn't see his eyes behind those sunglasses, she guessed he was laughing at her.

They spent several hours wandering through the docks, eyeing fresh produce and seafood, trinkets and souvenirs. They walked slowly with the tourists crowding the sidewalk. The sounds of voices and automobile engines and the pungent scents of fresh fish and salt air, all mingled in the warm afternoon.

Hale stopped at several spots, buying cooked crab and smoked salmon at one fish market, a loaf of crusty French bread and scones at a small bakery and two bottles of Chianti from a tiny shop that specialized in local wines.

"Now what?" Valerie asked, laughing as they walked up the few blocks to the Jaguar.

"Now we go to my place."

"Your place?" she repeated, her smile falling from her face and her confidence slipping.

"Scared?"

Yes! "Of course not, but I don't see why—"

"Because to make our story believable you'll have to know where and how I live, right?"

"There's no reason—"

"The Stowells have been to my house. All of them. Come on. I won't bite. I promise."

She racked her brain for a logical excuse. Though she knew it was childish, she wasn't ready to be alone with him in the privacy of his home—not yet. "I have to finish packing tonight."

"We won't be late."

"I guess I don't have much of a choice."

"Just consider it part of the job."

And the job was making her more uneasy by the minute, Valerie thought ruefully.

Once they were inside the car, he drove southwest and up the steep, winding tree-lined streets of Pacific Heights.

Hale's house was an old renovated Victorian. With a brick facade and four full stories, the narrow house was taller than the maple trees in the small front yard.

Inside, wood floors gleamed with a warm patina and thick Oriental carpets in shades of earth tones lay in each downstairs room. The furniture was arranged strategically, and watercolors, largely of seascapes, adorned the walls.

The original carved woodwork had been restored, and a travertine fireplace comprised an entire wall in both the living and the dining room. Chandeliers hung from the ceilings, and antique tables were placed around expensive, modern pieces.

"Eclectic," Valerie murmured.

"Interior by Elaine," he said, eyeing the rooms clinically as he led her to the back of the house. "She's a decorator a friend recommended to me."

In the kitchen were gleaming granite counters and sleek, stainless-steel appliances. Large enough for a chef, a huge gas range was set into a long island.

"A gourmet's dream."

He acted as if he didn't care, as if he barely noticed his own kitchen. Setting his bags on the counter, he glanced around, pulled off his sunglasses and grinned a little sheepishly. "I'm hardly ever here. I have an apartment at the office. So when I work late . . ." He shrugged. "Doesn't seem to make much sense to drive all the way over here."

He showed her the rest of the house, a weight room, bath and study on the third floor and on the fourth a loft that housed the master bedroom. Complete with sloped ceilings and skylights, the bedroom stretched from the front of the house to the back. Another fireplace was nestled between cherrywood bookcases, and a cluster of burgundy-colored chairs filled one corner, while a massive, king-sized bed dominated the room.

"Don't tell me," Valerie said, eyeing the color-coordinated pieces and artfully arranged potted plants. "Elaine again."

"Bingo." Hale laughed, and the sound echoed against the high ceilings overhead.

"Does she put your suits and ties together, too?"

"That I handle on my own."

"I'm relieved to hear it."

"Are you?" he asked, and his gray eyes glinted suggestively.

"Of course I am," she said, refusing to lick her lips, though she suddenly felt nervous. "It's nice to know a thirty-year-old man can do a few things for himself."

"More than a few." His voice had lowered an octave.

"I'd hope so." Her skin tingled a little.

Leaning a hip against the rail surrounding the stairs, he crossed his arms over his chest. The fabric of his shirt was stretched tight, pulling at the seams. "You really do push it, don't you?"

"Push what?"

"Me, for one thing. But I suspect that you push and push and just keep pushing in everything you do."

"Not a bad attribute for an employee."

"But a decided fault in a wife."

"I'm not going to be your wife. Remember?"

"Just be careful—around the Stowells."

"On my best behavior," she mocked, lifting her hand. "Scout's honor."

Before she could react, he reached forward and clasped his fingers around her wrist. "This Stowell deal is important to me."

"So you've said."

"Don't blow it."

"Oh, I won't, 'sugar,'" she replied tartly, and saw him wince at the sarcastic tone of her endearment, "because it's important to me, as well."

He didn't release her, just stared straight into her eyes. Though she wanted to shrink away, she met his gaze with all the willpower she possessed. She thought she felt a change in the room temperature as he pressed his fingertips against the sensitive skin inside her wrist. Her pulse fairly fluttered and her heart was slamming against the inside of her ribs, but she managed to keep her hands steady.

"Just so we understand each other," he whispered, his voice husky and raw.

"Oh, I'm sure we do." She inched her chin up mutinously. "Now if the tour's over, maybe we should end this for tonight. I'll call a cab."

"Before dinner?"

"I didn't know I was staying."

"Consider it part of the job."

"Are you trying to make this unpleasant?" she asked, wishing she could think of a way to get out of staying longer. Lingering in his bedroom was just plain crazy! Conflicting emotions tore at her, and she knew it was dangerous to prolong any intimacy whatsoever. His touch made her blood race; his gaze made it hard to breathe.

"Relax, Valerie. We have a lot of work to do." He slid his fingers against her skin as she yanked her hand back. "And we still have things to talk about."

"Then let's get it over with." Trembling inside, she marched down the stairs with all the bravado she could pull together.

Once in the kitchen again, she relaxed a little. While he cracked the crab, she cut French bread and slathered it with garlic butter, then concocted a red cocktail sauce from lemon juice, herbs, catsup and Worcestershire sauce.

They ate outside on a balcony off the kitchen, with a

view of the bay. The water was dark under the night sky; the winking lights of the city glowed like fireflies on the hills sloping down to the water.

Half lying on a chaise longue, Valerie sipped wine from a stemmed glass and snacked on crab, salmon and bread. The sounds of the city floated through the air.

Hale propped his shoulder against the railing. "I think we should tell the Stowells we're not sure when we plan to be married, but probably around the first of the year."

"For fiscal reasons?"

He ignored her jab. "We'll tell them that when we get back to San Francisco, you plan to start working for me, as my assistant, to learn as much as you can about the business—just in case anything happens to me. You, of course, will be my sole beneficiary."

"You think he'll believe that?"

"Who cares? It's plausible. That's all that matters."

"What about children?"

"What about them?" he asked, his voice gruff, his eyes growing dark.

"People always ask. Even if you're not married."

"We haven't discussed it. We'll say we're taking one step at a time, that sort of thing."

"Okay." She leaned back, letting the wine slide down her throat, forgetting that this was all just an elaborate deception. With the help of the wine, she pretended that this fantasy of becoming Hale's wife was real. What would she do if she were really Mrs. Hale Donovan? How would her life change? Studying him from beneath the sweep of dark lashes, she smiled. Above his head a slice of silvery moon hung low in the sky, and the leaves from the trees in the tiny front yard rustled in the moist wind from the bay. "I suppose we're going to live here—after we're married?"

"You're the bride—you decide."

"Let's make it easy. We'll stay here. What about the honeymoon—it should be somewhere exotic, don't you think?"

"The Bahamas?"

She shook her head. "How about a couple of weeks on the Riviera and then another week in the Alps?"

"Stowell won't believe I'd take that much time away from business."

Smiling lazily, she said, "Well, I guess you'll have to find a way to convince him. After all, a sophisticated woman with my expensive tastes wouldn't be satisfied with a weekend at the beach."

"You're a working woman, remember?"

"But I'm marrying the boss. I expect to be treated like a princess."

"Touché, Ms. Pryce." His gaze, bright with amusement, touched hers. "You're learning quickly."

"Must be because I have such a great teacher."

"Must be."

Hale studied her thoughtfully. Her face, radiant in the moon's silvery glow, was turned up toward him, her smile flashed gently, and though she seemed slightly nervous, she never let up—always kept him guessing. That was what he liked about her best, he decided as he leaned his elbows back against the rail. And liking her was dangerous. He didn't want to feel anything for her—not friendship, not compatibility, not affection. She was just someone who worked for him—someone he had to put up with for six months. Someone who could help him fend off Regina Stowell's attentions while he went about his business.

"Maybe I should call a cab."

He felt a wayward urge to ask her to stay. Though he knew the notion was foolish, he wanted to prolong their time alone together. "I'll drive you." Seeing the protest forming on her lips, he added, "It's no bother, really."

"If you're sure."

"Just let me get my keys."

All too soon they were speeding through the city in his car, the scent of her perfume wafting to him, her leg only

inches from his. For the first time he realized just how difficult spending the next two weeks alone with her might be.
She had a way of touching his emotions—making him laugh
or igniting his temper with one little comment.

At her apartment, he walked her to the front door and
wished he could come up with a reason to stay. "I'll see you
in the morning—about ten thirty."

"I'll be ready," she said with a smile that quivered a little
as she unlocked the door and hurried inside. "But ready for
what?" she wondered aloud as she trudged up the stairs.

Only time would tell.

CHAPTER 5

"The last thing we need is that cat," Belinda grumbled as Valerie set a rather grumpy Shamus on the floor of her mother's apartment.

Valerie chuckled. "You'll love him. Besides, he'll liven things up around here and keep the rodent population under control."

"We don't have a rodent problem," Belinda said, but reached forward to pet the cat's head. Shamus ducked away from Belinda's hand and hid behind the couch. "Friendly as always, I see."

"He'll calm down," Valerie predicted as Belinda snagged her jacket out of the closet and waved good-bye.

"He'd better," her mother said. She was sitting in her favorite rocker, a beat-up antique she'd owned for as long as Valerie could remember. "So—you're taking off this morning?"

"Yes." Valerie sketched out what she knew of the trip.

"I've been reading up on your fiancée, you know," Anna replied, pointing to a stack of magazines on the table. "He's quite a man."

"Isn't he?" Unable to resist, Valerie picked up a copy of *San Francisco Today,* turned to a dog-eared page and found a glossy black-and-white photo of Hale staring up at her. The article was entitled "The Master Mind behind Donovan Enterprises."

Anna sighed. "All I learned is that the man's a workaholic. It sounds like he spends twenty out of twenty-four hours at the office or wheeling and dealing."

"That's about right," Valerie agreed.

"There's not one word about his family."

"He's a very private person."

"So now he needs a wife?" Anna asked skeptically.

"You know how it is—"

"No, I don't. Why don't you tell me?"

"I know this is kind of sudden."

"Kind of?" her mother repeated, rolling her eyes. "Kind of, she says! I knew your father for ten years before I started dating him. A year later we were engaged and we waited until he'd finished college before we got married."

"Not everyone grows up in the same small town," Valerie retorted, hearing a defensive note creep into her voice and hating it. This lying had to end!

"I just hope this isn't a reaction to Luke," her mother went on. "A rebound thing."

"Hale Donovan is a far cry from Luke Walters."

"I know, but . . ." Her mother threw up her hands. "As you so succinctly put it, this marriage business is happening so fast I can barely believe it."

"We haven't eloped, have we?"

"Not yet." Anna narrowed her eyes thoughtfully. "But I wouldn't put it past you."

Valerie laughed. "Believe me, that's something you don't have to worry about."

"Don't ship captains have the authority?"

"This is a private yacht, Mom, not an ocean liner. Really, you don't have to worry."

"That's what mothers do best."

"Then worry about yourself. Just try to get better so you can get back on your feet."

"I'm doing my best," Anna replied a little testily.

"I know you are." Valerie squeezed her mother's frail shoulders. "Now, I promise I'll call and e-mail, and the minute I get home I'll race over here with tons of useless souvenirs you won't possibly ever need or want."

Anna Pryce laughed and looked directly into her daughter's eyes. "Just be happy, Val," she said as Valerie walked back to the door. "That's all that matters."

"I will, Mom. *Ciao*." She breezed out of her mother's apartment and tried to shake off the uneasy feeling that this trip with Hale would prove to be anything but happy.

Hale arrived promptly at ten thirty. She half expected to see him in a blue, double-breasted jacket, white slacks and jaunty sailing cap, but was pleased to find him dressed in faded Levi's, an unbleached cotton, cable-knit sweater and leather jacket.

"Casual, aren't we?" she teased as he reached for her large suitcase.

His lips twitched. "I didn't want you to feel under-dressed."

"I wouldn't have, believe me." She'd thought about her outfit long and hard and decided upon layering clothes she could peel off if the temperature climbed: khaki slacks, a striped T-shirt, peach sweater and three-quarter-length coat. Not exactly yachting apparel, but simple, practical and comfortable. Besides, Valerie figured, she'd leave the fashion statements to Regina.

He loaded her two suitcases into the Jaguar, and Valerie tossed her coat behind the seat. Hale gunned the engine. With a roar, the powerful car took off through the steep hills of the city and across the bay, to Tiburon.

The morning was clear and bright, the rays from a brilliant sun streaming from the sky to fleck the water and warm the air. Wearing sunglasses and feeling the wind catch in her hair, Valerie felt an exhilaration she hadn't expected. This trip, no matter how it turned out, would be an adventure she wouldn't forget for the rest of her life.

She purloined a glance at Hale and nearly laughed. His face was relaxed and one arm was resting on the open window. His shirtsleeves had been thrust up over his elbows, and his aviator sunglasses covered his eyes. Handsome, confident, a little on the arrogant side, Hale Donovan was a very interesting man and this trip was bound to be memorable. She only hoped it wouldn't end up a fiasco.

They rounded a final turn and drove through tall, wrought-iron gates, which were now wide open. "There's Stowell," he said, his features tensing perceptibly.

A small group of people were clustered on the deck of one of the largest boats moored in the yacht club. William Stowell, a short, rotund man dressed in full yachting regalia, held up his hand when he noticed Hale's car. A slender, gorgeous girl grinned widely and began waving frantically.

"Regina?" Valerie guessed.

"Regina."

"Enthusiastic," she said dryly.

"Very."

Regina was dressed in a fuchsia-colored tube top and white slacks. A broad-brimmed hat covered her head. She flicked one disinterested glance at Valerie before turning all her attention to Hale.

Valerie clamped her back teeth together. This might not go as well as she and Hale had planned. What if Regina didn't know about the engagement? Worse yet, what if she didn't care? With a confidence she didn't feel, Valerie climbed out of the car and helped Hale with her bags. "I assume you brought a change of clothes?" she asked.

"I sent my bags earlier. Come on, it's now or never."

Together, with the eyes of father and daughter Stowell watching, they made their way aboard *The Regina*. The deck, polished teak, gleamed under the sun's warm rays. Built-in lounges and chairs surrounded a table laden with fruit, croissants, champagne and coffee.

William Stowell, a short, puffy-faced man with wiry gray hair surrounding a bald pate, greeted them. "Just in time for breakfast," he said, smiling warmly at Hale and pumping his hand. Spying a deckhand nearby, he said, "Here—let me get someone to take your bags below . . . Jim, see to Mr. Donovan's bags, would you?"

"They belong to Valerie," Hale said, but handed the bags to the shipmate, anyway.

"Oh, yes, Ms. Pryce . . ." William Stowell turned warm eyes on Valerie. "I've been reading about you."

"My fiancée," Hale said, making quick introductions.

Regina paled visibly. Her tanned skin whitened, and she blinked rapidly. "Glad to meet you," she said, forcing a trembling smile.

"You, too," Valerie said.

Regina shot a killing glance at her father. "You *knew* Hale was engaged?"

"Just read about it yesterday."

"It would have been nice if you'd said something."

"Hale!"

Valerie turned, squinting against the sun. A tall, stately woman with a cloud of white hair was walking briskly toward them, her arms extended.

Hale clasped both the older woman's hands in his. "How're you, Beth?"

She smothered a smile and proclaimed, "Absolutely wretched! I planned what I thought would be a nice vacation and that damned husband of mine has turned it into a business meeting!"

"You knew it all along," William protested, chuckling. He glanced at Valerie and winked. "She's always grumpy before she's had her first cup of coffee."

"That's ridiculous!"

William's eyes twinkled. "Quit griping and meet Hale's future bride."

"Bride?" Beth's smile wavered a bit, and she turned interested gold-colored eyes on Valerie. "Well, well, well . . . we knew he was bringing a friend, of course, but a fiancée?" Taking Val's hand in hers, she stage-whispered, "It's about time someone hog-tied this one."

"Oh, Mother," Regina moaned.

"Forgive my wife," William said, "she can't let me forget she grew up on a ranch in Montana."

Beth's lips twitched. "After thirty years he's still trying to make a lady out of me."

"And failing miserably," William confided, but Beth didn't seem to notice. She poured a cup of coffee from the service. "Well, William is right about one thing—"

"Only one?" her husband inquired.

Beth ignored him. "I'm not really awake until I've had my second cup. How about you?" She offered the cup to Valerie.

"Thank you." Valerie took a sip and, above the rim, caught Hale's gaze. Amusement danced in his eyes, and he had trouble hiding a smile.

"Let's have some breakfast, then I'll show you to your rooms. Maybe by then Stewart will have deigned to join us." Beth motioned everyone to the small, shaded table on deck.

"Stewart's joining us?" Hale asked.

"So he says, but he's late," Beth replied.

"Again," William agreed. "I swear that boy is always a day late and a dollar short."

"More like a hundred dollars," Regina said coldly, then turned to Valerie. "Wait until you meet my brother, then you'll know what we're all talking about."

"Well, let's change the subject," Beth decreed. "I'm sure

Hale's fiancée isn't the least bit interested in our family squabbles."

Hale sat next to Valerie, where they made small talk and brunched on fresh strawberries, flaky croissants and pastries.

Drawing her finely arched brows into a petulant frown, Regina sat across from Valerie and Hale as she poured herself a glass of champagne. "So when's the wedding?" she asked as Valerie pushed her plate aside.

To Valerie's surprise, Hale linked his fingers through hers. "After the first of the year," he said easily.

"Why wait?" Beth asked.

Valerie's throat went dry. "We, uh, thought we should give it a little time. We haven't known each other all that long . . ."

"So? I knew the minute I set eyes on William that I was going to marry him."

William grinned. "I guess I didn't have a chance."

"Best thing that ever happened to you," Beth insisted.

Valerie had to suppress a giggle.

"Some people like to take their time," Regina said, brightening a little and flashing a beautiful smile in Hale's direction.

"Not like you, though, is it, Donovan?" Stowell muttered. He poured himself a second cup of coffee and added a thin stream of cream. "You seem the type to see what you want and go after it—the way you did with my company."

"Marriage is a little different," Hale responded. Casually he draped his arm over the back of Valerie's chair. His sweater sleeve touched her hair, but she didn't move as he went on, "Marriage is a lifetime commitment."

Regina seemed amused. "Is it? Not according to Stewart!"

Beth sighed and shot Regina a killing look, before explaining, "Our son has had a few . . . problems . . settling down."

"The black sheep of the family," Regina added, obviously

enjoying the turn of the conversation as she fingered her long-stemmed glass and sipped champagne.

"He's just a little misguided right now." Beth set down her cup to end the conversation and turned her attention to Valerie. "If you're ready, I'll show you your rooms."

"I'll do it," Regina offered sweetly. Standing, she held on to her hat as a stiff breeze caught the broad brim. "This way."

She motioned with her free hand and led them down a short flight of stairs to the main salon. Though not particularly spacious, the room was well planned. A television, radio, computer, and audio system were mounted in a gleaming bookcase. Lavish built-in settees lined three walls, and a few movable chairs and tables were clustered throughout the room. The cream-colored carpet was thick but durable, and contrasted with the leather chairs and tucked upholstery. "Through here," Regina said, waving them into a short hallway toward the stern.

She shoved open a small door. "This is your stateroom," she said to Valerie. "Hale is right next door—unless you two would prefer to bunk together."

Hale slid his arm around Valerie's waist. "Maybe—"

"This will be fine," Valerie cut in before Hale could say anything else. Sleeping in the room next to Hale's would be bad enough, but she shuddered to think what would happen if they were housed in the same stateroom. Though she didn't consider herself the least bit prudish, she knew danger when she saw it. And being close to Hale both day and night was bound to spell trouble.

Regina smiled knowingly. "Then I'll see you topside later." Her gaze lingered on Hale for a second before she disappeared.

When Regina was out of earshot, Valerie pulled away from Hale. "I don't think she believes us."

"She would have if you hadn't acted like such a nineteenth-century prig, for crying out loud!"

"I didn't!"

"Oh, no? The way I saw it, you nearly came apart when she suggested we sleep together. You couldn't wait to set her straight." He grabbed her arm, propelled her into her room and slammed the door tightly shut behind him. "Now listen to me, Pryce. You don't have anything to worry about from me. Your precious virtue isn't in any danger. But I expect you to *act* like you want me. We're supposed to be getting married, for God's sake, so don't play up this frightened little virgin act. It won't wash with the Stowells and it doesn't wash with me!"

"I'm not a frightened, little anything! And as for the sleeping arrangements, even people who sleep together sometimes keep separate rooms for appearances' sake!" she fumed.

"Only those with something to hide!"

"Like us?" she asked, eyes narrowing. "Now, are you finished ranting and raving like a lunatic?"

"I was just pointing out your mistake."

"It's not a mistake. I agreed to pretend to be in love with you and enjoy your company, but I don't remember signing anything that stated I should act like some hot-to-trot coed plotting ways to jump into your bed!"

"Just don't play up the ice-maiden bit!"

She drew back her arm and felt her hands curl into fists. "Ice maiden—"

There was a sharp rap on the door. Before she knew what was happening, Hale stepped forward, wrapped his arms around her and ground his lips on hers with such a fury she couldn't speak. Her pulse jumped as he splayed his hands possessively on her back. He shifted then, pressing tight, instinctively molding her against him. The world seemed to spin . . .

The door to the cabin was prodded open gently, and Beth, blushing to the roots of her snow-white hair, peeked inside. "Oh, I'm sorry—"

Hale snapped his head up, and he grinned wickedly, looking for all the world like a devilish boy caught with his hand in the cookie jar. "Don't be."

"I was just seeing that all your things were in the right rooms—well, you can let me know later."

"No, really, it's all right," Valerie sputtered. Dear Lord, was that her heart slamming against her ribs?

Beth shut the door discreetly behind her.

Hale let her go, and Valerie whirled on him. "What was that all about?"

"I was just undoing some of the damage you caused."

"By mortifying me?" she challenged, ready to do battle.

"By showing my affection, my undying love," he mocked.

"Oh, save it, Donovan!" Dropping onto the edge of her bed and catching sight of her reflection in a mirror over the built-in dresser, she felt totally ashamed. Her eyes were wide and luminous, her cheeks flushed, her lips swollen, her hair falling around her face in loose, unruly curls. She looked wanton and willing and ready. Groaning, she shoved her hair out of her face, then skewered him with an angry glare. "We're alone now, you don't have an audience to play to. You don't have to pretend to be smitten."

"Just remember our contract," he suggested, his expression grave, his skin whiter than it had been.

Raising her chin a fraction, she surveyed him through narrowed, furious eyes. "How could I forget it?"

His jaw worked a second, and he seemed about to lash out at her. Bracing herself, she waited, ready for the next attack, which, thankfully, didn't come. He yanked open the door and strode through, letting it slam behind him.

"Thank God," she whispered, sighing and lying back on her bed. This was worse than she'd ever imagined! His kiss had turned her legs to jelly. Never would she have expected her reaction to be so soul jarring, so violent. Her heart was still hammering out of control!

Slowly she drew in several deep, calming breaths, then

propped herself on one elbow and studied her room for the first time. It was compact but comfortable. The raised bed was tucked into the outside wall, and beneath it were three large drawers. There was a small closet near the foot of the bed, a built-in bureau and lamps mounted overhead near the bed and center of the room.

Were the situation different, Valerie knew she would easily be able to enjoy herself here. She stripped off her sweater, found her two bags, placed her clothes in the drawers beneath her bed, then opened a door to what she assumed would be a bathroom. However, as the door swung inward, she realized she was staring into another stateroom—Hale's.

The room was identical to hers, except that the furniture arrangement was reversed.

"Great," she muttered, noting three large suitcases and two trunks propped against the bed. "He must be moving in permanently."

Rather than take a chance on being caught in Hale's room, Valerie hurried back through the door, turned the lock, then spent the next few minutes locating the bathroom and linen closets.

"Find everything?" Beth asked her as she reentered the salon.

"I think so."

"Well, now that you're settled, let me give you the grand tour. William and Hale are already talking business—can you believe it?"

"Oh, yes," Valerie replied. Nothing, but nothing, was more important to Hale than his precious company—or, in this case, Stowell's company.

Beth walked toward the bow, showing her a dining salon, the galley, two more staterooms similar to hers, and the owner's quarters, larger than the others with a double bed, two closets, built-in desks, television set and separate bath. Through another door a small study was tucked against the hull.

"It's beautiful," Valerie said as they climbed to the top deck, where Hale and William were deep in discussion, sipping drinks, laughing and talking. Regina, having changed into a pink bikini, was stretched out on a chaise, sunglasses covering her eyes.

"I hope you're not all waiting on me!" A handsome man, cocky grin steadfastly in place, climbed on board.

"We were about to set sail without you!" Beth snapped, though her eyes grew warm.

This, Valerie guessed, must be Stewart. With coffee-brown hair and tawny eyes, strong, square jaw and deep tan, he grinned warmly as he saw her. "You didn't tell me we were going to have a special guest," he said, ignoring his mother's waspish tone. Shoving his hands into his pockets, he sauntered up to Valerie. "I'm Stewart."

"Valerie Pryce."

"Hale's fiancée," Beth clarified.

"Fiancée? Well, how about that?" Stewart, not the least bit ruffled, slid a glance at his sister. "So someone's managed to tame the wild Donovan beast."

At that moment Valerie felt a proprietary hand slip around her waist. Hale had disengaged himself from William and was standing behind her, linking his fingers possessively over her abdomen. He made it visible to everyone aboard the yacht that she was his. Through the cotton of her slacks, his fingertips pressed hot and hard against her skin. She could feel their bold impression as if there were no barrier keeping her flesh from his. Her pulse reacted crazily, and it was all she could do to keep her mind on the conversation.

"I guess congratulations are in order!" Stewart said heartily. "Let's toast the bride and groom." With a flourish, he swept a linen napkin from the table, covered the neck of a champagne bottle chilling in the bucket and struggled with the cork. It popped. Frothy bubbles foamed out of the bottle, and Stewart, without missing a beat, poured several glasses.

"Regina . . . ?" Beth asked, and mulishly Regina took a glass.

Stewart held one out to Hale, another to Valerie, then lifted his glass high into the air. "To the future Mrs. Donovan," he said, ignoring his sister's black look. "May she always be happy and as beautiful as she is today."

"Here, here!" William agreed.

"To love," Beth chimed in, her eyes glowing.

Valerie forced a sad smile. She felt a fraud. Already she liked Beth and William Stowell, and she hated lying to them.

"And to a safe trip," William interjected.

They all lifted their glasses to their lips.

Hale tightened his fingers around Valerie's waist. "And a prosperous one," he added.

Valerie's spirits sank to the bottom of the bay. Even in the merriment and celebration of their "engagement," Hale's mind was on his deal with William Stowell and the money he would make from it.

Strangely she felt let down. Her disappointment was ludicrous, of course; Hale's mind was always on business—she'd known that from the first time she'd met him. She wasn't going to change him, and she shouldn't even want to. Yet the warm fingers on her waist coupled with a giddy champagne-induced glow caused her heart to beat a little faster. What if? she wondered, leaning back against Hale and feeling the hard wall of his chest against her shoulder blades. What if, during the course of their voyage . . . Hale's priorities reversed and money wasn't his all-consuming need?

Impossible! Or was it?

"More?" Stewart lifted the half-empty bottle from its silver bucket and cocked his head in Valerie's direction.

"I don't think I should," Valerie replied.

"Live a little," Hale suggested, his breath light against her ear. Delicious tingles skittered down her spine.

"My motto exactly," Stewart said, ignoring his father's dark glare. "We may as well enjoy ourselves since we're stuck with one another for the next couple of weeks!" He grabbed the neck of the opened bottle and poured more champagne into Valerie's glass.

The yacht's engines rumbled loudly. "About time," Hale said under his breath.

"Anxious?" she murmured.

"Aren't you?"

Turning, she planted a playful kiss on his cheek and whispered, "The sooner this is over, the better."

"Amen," Hale agreed, his eyes growing dark. He slipped his sunglasses onto his nose and finished his drink, but kept one arm closed around her, and no one on board could miss the implication. Valerie was his. And she was, she realized, bought and paid for like a slab of beef.

Uncomfortable, Valerie slipped away from him and moved to the side of the deck, where she leaned over the rail and watched the smaller boats and the marina disappear. Ahead, the dark waters of the bay beckoned. Sunlight sparkled on the surface, and sloops, their colorful sails billowing with the wind, sailed by.

Seagulls floated on the breeze as *The Regina* knifed through the bay, turning westward to the open waters of the Pacific Ocean, where she would spend the next two weeks.

Valerie experienced an unfamiliar weakness in her knees. As she watched the harbor recede, she realized that for the next two weeks there was no turning back.

CHAPTER 6

To Valerie's surprise, her sea legs didn't fail her. She hadn't been aboard a boat since she was twelve, the summer before her father had died, and she'd expected to experience a little bit of seasickness, but she didn't. In fact, the salt sea air and gentle rumble of the ship's engines agreed with her.

That first afternoon she didn't see Hale for more than fifteen minutes. He and William Stowell locked themselves into Stowell's den and didn't so much as poke their heads out on deck. Beth was busy going over meal plans with the cook, so Valerie spent a couple of hours sunbathing not far from Regina. Several times she tried to draw the younger woman into conversation, but was met with only monosyllabic responses.

She sipped iced tea and read until she couldn't stand it any longer. "So," she finally said, closing her mystery novel and looking over at Regina, "where do you live?"

Regina, lying supine on a mattress, didn't so much as blink. "The city."

"An apartment?"

"Umm."

"Where?"

With a sigh, Regina lifted her sunglasses. Her expression bored, she asked, "What's it to you?"

"Nothing—I was just making conversation."

"Okay—well, I live in a two-bedroom condo near the Presidio. I had a roommate, we didn't get along, so she moved out. For the time being, I'm alone."

"Oh."

With a frown, Regina turned onto her stomach, untied the back of her bikini and lay motionless, her oiled body glistening a deep bronze color. "Anything else you want to know? You know, like where I work, if I'm dating, that kind of thing?"

"I guess not," Valerie said, sticking her nose back into the worn paperback she'd found in her cabin. She didn't expect Regina to continue the conversation, but the younger woman slid her sunglasses to the tip of her nose and observed Valerie over the rims. "So what gives?"

"What do you mean?"

"With you and Hale." Regina didn't so much as blink her dark brown eyes.

"We're going to be married."

"Oh, right," Regina said. "But you have separate rooms."

Valerie smiled. "We're not married yet."

"Seriously? How . . . old-school." Regina rubbed some coconut oil onto her shoulder. "Sorry. That sounded a little nasty. I didn't mean it. I just think that it's kind of weird that you're not sharing a cabin."

Valerie smiled coolly. "I guess I'm old-fashioned."

"And Hale?" Regina's dark eyes narrowed.

"Deep down he's very conservative."

"Sure he is," Regina replied. "That's why he's considered a rebel in the investment world. The man is known for taking risks—big risks. I don't think 'conservative' is in his vocabulary."

Lifting a shoulder, Valerie turned her attention back to

her book and pretended interest in the dogged attempts of detective Matt Connery to solve a murder in Detroit.

"You know, we were expecting Hale to bring along a 'friend.' In fact, I was sure Leigh Carmichael might be joining us."

"Who?"

"You don't know who Leigh Carmichael is?" Regina's teeth flashed in the sun.

"I've never heard of her." But Valerie felt every muscle in her body tighten. There was a studied casualness in Regina's tone—a cool disinterest that contrasted with the gleam in her dark eyes.

"Just how well do you know Hale Donovan?"

Valerie shifted uneasily in her chair. "Hale and I only met a few weeks ago."

"And he never told you about Leigh?"

"Not a word," Valerie admitted, her temper starting to flare.

"Well, at one time she thought she was going to be Mrs. Hale Donovan. I guess she was wrong."

"I guess," Valerie said, turning back to her book, as if she couldn't care in the least about Leigh Carmichael or any other woman in Hale's past.

Regina wasn't about to give up. "I heard she was coming back to San Francisco—she's been in Europe all summer—and the rumor was that she intended to settle down with Hale." She twisted on the cap of her tanning oil and readjusted herself on the chaise longue.

Valerie sighed patiently, but didn't comment.

"I just wish I could see her face when she reads that Hale's going to be married. Unless I miss my guess, she'll cut her trip short and come storming back to San Francisco."

By that time the deception would be over, Valerie thought, feeling an unlikely twinge of sadness. Then it wouldn't matter if Hale and Leigh resumed whatever relationship they'd had.

Though she tried to concentrate on the plot of the mystery, Valerie's thoughts kept straying to Hale and Leigh and Regina. Frowning, she was reading the same paragraph for possibly the twentieth time when Beth stormed onto the deck, poured herself a tall glass of iced tea, plopped onto a deck chair and held the cold glass against her perspiring forehead. "I tell you, that man is a moron!" she said with a sigh.

"What man?" Regina asked, eyeing her mother.

"The chef your father hired! I swear he doesn't know a frappé from a flambé!"

"Do you?" Regina asked, smiling.

"Well, no, not really," her mother admitted. "But it's not my job to know!" She took a long sip from her glass and sank back in the chair. "You know how your father wants his meals."

Regina glanced at Valerie. "On board, dinner isn't a meal, it's an event."

"It would serve him right if I took over the galley," Beth said fervently. "Wouldn't he be surprised if I handed him a leather-tough steak, corn bread and chuckwagon beans?"

Regina giggled. "You wouldn't."

"Oh, yes, I would. If Hans—can you believe that? A French chef named Hans—gets too uppity, watch out!"

Three hours later, Valerie changed into a white skirt and silk blouse. She wore her one pair of diamond earrings and clamped a wide gold chain around her throat. Eyeing her reflection, she touched up her lipstick and caught one side of her hair over her ear. "Good enough," she muttered as a soft knock sounded on the door that separated her room from Hale's.

"Val?" he asked quietly.

Her pulse jumped a little as she quickly flipped the lock. Hale stood on the other side, freshly shaven, his hair combed neatly. He wore a stiff white shirt, crimson tie and black dinner jacket. "You didn't need to lock me out," he said, smiling.

"Maybe I was locking myself in."

"Maybe you're afraid of me." Rubbing his chin, he let his gaze drift slowly down her body, then up again.

Valerie's heart went wild. Pumping crazily, it thundered in her chest. To hide her reaction, she slipped a bracelet over her wrist and laughed. "Don't flatter yourself, Donovan."

"I won't—just as long as you don't kid yourself."

"Wouldn't dream of it," she retorted, but noticed the amusement lingering in his eyes. Arrogant bastard! she thought, ready to engage in verbal battle again but managing somehow to hold her tongue. There wasn't any reason to antagonize him. Yet.

Together they walked through the main salon to the dining area, where fresh flowers and glass-encased candles adorned a linen-clad dining table.

"Oh, there you are!" Beth cried.

Valerie's heart sank. Hale hadn't been kidding when he'd told her the Stowells dressed for dinner. Beth had on a shimmering, floor-length white gown. Emeralds encircled her throat, and her hair was pinned away from her face.

As for Regina, who entered seconds after Hale and Valerie, she was dressed to the teeth in red chiffon that draped over one shoulder and swirled to her knees. Her long hair was swept away from her face and pulled into an elegant French braid. She rained a positively dazzling smile on Valerie, who felt dull in comparison.

Chin up, she silently told herself, refusing to feel low class just because her skirt and blouse weren't designer originals.

"Drinks?" William asked, opening a small mirrored bar on the sideboard.

"Just white wine," Valerie replied.

"Manhattan for me," Stewart announced as he swept into the room in a wine-colored dinner jacket and charcoal-gray slacks.

William mixed the drinks, and Beth insisted everyone find his place at the table.

"Right here, honey," Hale said, patting the chair next to his.

Valerie swallowed back a hot retort. Instead she smiled demurely and pretended she didn't in the least feel uncomfortable, though her stomach was in knots and a thin layer of perspiration covered her skin.

"No sign of seasickness?" William asked.

"Not yet," she said. "My father used to take me sailing."

"Did he?" Stewart leaned forward, interested.

"It was a long time ago."

As the chef-cum-waiter ladled bouillabaisse into their bowls from a tureen, William said, "I'm just glad you're used to the sea. Unfortunately we might be in for some bad weather."

"But today was beautiful!" Regina argued.

"I know, but according to the weather service and Coast Guard, there's a storm brewing off the coast of Oregon."

"Great," Regina grumbled.

"Well, no use worrying about it until it breaks," her father said. "Maybe we'll get lucky."

As the dinner progressed, Valerie listened to the conversation and observed the members of this voyage.

Hale was absolutely charming throughout the meal. From the spicy fish stew and crisp salad through dessert, he kept the conversation rolling and even took the time to compliment the chef for the main course—succulent prawns cooked in wine. He seemed oblivious to Regina and Stewart, both of whom watched him throughout the meal. Regina tried her best to be carefree and witty, smiling at Hale's jokes and never once making eye contact with Valerie. On the other hand, Stewart's gaze moved restlessly around the table and he seemed uncomfortable, yanking at his collar, frowning into his drink, his gold eyes wary and suspicious.

Valerie, nervous, picked at her meal. She barely tasted her soup, salad, shrimp or dessert of strawberry mousse.

"Let's have coffee in the main salon," Beth suggested.

"Good idea." William winked at Valerie. "Maybe we could interest Hale and Valerie in a quick game of bridge."

Chuckling, Hale walked with Valerie to the salon. "Don't let these two con you," he warned, his eyes dancing. "They'll play for quarters and by the end of the evening you'll be broke."

"Sounds like the voice of experience talking," she murmured.

"It is."

"Come on, Donovan, you're a gambler," Stewart cut in, his eyes narrowing as he poured himself an after-dinner brandy. "At least, that's what I've heard."

"Not when the cards are stacked against me."

"Only bet on sure things?" Stewart goaded.

"I try." Hale offered Stewart a lazy smile, but his jaw was clenched.

Valerie, to diffuse the tension crackling between the two men, said, "I'd love to play bridge, but I don't know how."

Beth waved away her excuses. "Time you learned."

"I'll be glad to show her how to play," Stewart offered amiably.

"Good idea!" William boomed, already settling in at a small table in the corner. "While Stewart's coaching Valerie, the rest of us can play. Regina, you and I'll take on your mother and Donovan." He settled his eyes on Hale. "How about a small wager?"

One of Hale's brows arched. "How small?"

"A hundred?"

"You're on."

For the next hour Stewart explained the game to her, showing her different hands, bids and cues. Valerie tried to keep her attention on the game, but her gaze wandered often across the room to the table of four. Hale's eyes gleamed.

Caught in a fast-paced game, he loosened his tie, unbuttoned his collar and cuffs and rolled his sleeves up over his elbows.

Regina's laugh tinkled through the salon, and Valerie felt a stab of jealousy.

"So, you and Donovan are getting married," Stewart said, shuffling the cards again.

"Umm."

"That'll be the day."

"What?" Valerie turned back to Stewart.

"I said I don't believe it."

Valerie's throat went dry. "Why not?"

"I've heard rumors before."

Just like Regina.

"No woman's ever managed to get him to walk down the aisle." He leaned back and surveyed her through lowered lids. "What makes you think you've changed him?"

"I wouldn't dream of changing him," Valerie purred, goaded nonetheless.

"Then you won't be getting married."

"Only time will tell, won't it?"

Still studying her, Stewart set the cards on the table, then rubbed the back of his neck. "I may as well be honest with you."

"By all means."

"I don't trust Donovan."

"Why not?" Valerie asked, knowing she should defend the man she was to marry and yet unable to muster the right amount of self-righteousness. Unfortunately she didn't trust Hale, either.

"I've heard about him. Some of the takeovers he's attempted have been a little"—he flattened out one hand and tipped it side to side—"unethical."

"I don't think so."

Stewart shrugged one shoulder. "I know, *technically* he stays within the law, but some of his methods are questionable—ethically and morally."

"And no one's ever won a lawsuit against him," Valerie reminded him, inching up her chin.

"Only because of healthy out-of-court settlements." He glanced over to the other table. "Oh, Donovan's careful, all right, but in my opinion he's a little on the shifty side."

"Well, I guess we're *all* entitled to our opinions," she said crisply, surprised at the defensive tone in her voice, "but next time you might keep them to yourself."

"I'm just trying to warn you, that's all."

"Warn me of what?"

"That Donovan might not be completely honest with you."

"Why would you care?" Valerie asked.

"Because you're different from the other women I've seen Donovan with."

"I hope so."

"What I mean is that you're more—now don't be offended"—he glanced down at her white skirt and simple blouse—"but you seem more naive."

"Naive?" she repeated, remembering how Luke had deserted her and how her boss at Liddell had expected sexual favors for her advancement. "I'm afraid you're wrong, Stewart."

"I just don't want you to get hurt."

"By Hale?" she asked, shaking her head. "Don't worry about it."

"All he's interested in is money, you know. Women are a dime a dozen."

"Are they? Well, thanks for the advice, but I know what I'm doing."

"People in love rarely do," Stewart said cynically.

"But I'm not . . ." She cleared her throat. "Look, it's really none of your business. Hale and I are in love and we're getting married." Before Stewart could guess that she was lying, she stood and leaned across the table. "Thanks for the lessons—and the advice, but, really, I'm a big girl. I know what I'm doing." With a forced smile, she shoved her hair from her eyes and hurried up the stairs to the deck.

This trip was going to be torture. If she wasn't arguing with Hale, then she was defending herself to Regina or Stewart! Fourteen days—and this was just the first! How would she ever survive?

"This is crazy, just plain, downright crazy," she muttered, striding across the deck. Winds from the west had kicked up the sluggish, sultry air. Clouds scudded across the sky. The smell of the sea was tangy and wet as it filled her nostrils. The engines of *The Regina* didn't miss a beat, throbbing evenly, driving the craft northward in the hot August night.

Valerie raked her fingers through her hair and felt the sheen of perspiration on her brow. Between the temperature and the tension in the salon below, she'd begun to perspire.

She heard footsteps on the stairs and glanced over her shoulder to see Hale, his jacket discarded, his shirt unbuttoned, climb topside. "Problems?" Hale asked.

"I just needed some fresh air!"

"It was a little stuffy down below."

She didn't answer, but turned away from the ocean long enough to see him lean his hips against the rail. His gaze held hers for a second before she looked away again, staring out at the ink-black water.

"Stewart can be a real pain," he said slowly.

"So I noticed."

"What happened? Did he come on to you?"

"No." Wrapping her arms around her middle, she contemplated telling him about Stewart's attitude toward him, but decided it didn't matter. Why stir up any more trouble? She just had to get through the next couple of weeks. Then she was out of this mess and out of Hale's life except as his employee, which was all she'd ever wanted to be.

A nagging voice in the back of her mind accused her of lying to herself, but she didn't listen.

She shrugged dismissively. "I'd had enough bridge lessons for the day."

"And enough of Stewart?"

She chuckled. "He's just worried about me."

Hale snorted. "Is he? I wouldn't bet on it. The only reason he's on this cruise is to try to put a monkey wrench into my deal with Stowell. He's not too thrilled with me buying his father's company."

"So I gathered."

"I guess it's not all that hard to understand," Hale admitted thoughtfully, his gaze touching hers. In the moonlight, shadows from the shifting sea drifted over his face.

Valerie's stomach twisted. Why did he seem so handsome and mysterious? His eyes had darkened to the color of the sea, and the stiff breeze caused a thick thatch of his hair to fall over his eyes in fetching disarray.

"I guess I can't blame him, really," Hale said. "Stewart grew up thinking the investment company would be his someday. Then I came along and tried to ruin everything by convincing Stowell to sell to me."

"So it's a matter of inheritance?"

"Or right of possession. Stewart's worked for his father for years—ever since he graduated from college. He just expected to run the show when William retired. Now, if I get my way, he won't have that chance."

"But even if you bought Stowell out, couldn't Stewart still work for you?"

Hale's teeth flashed in the darkness. "Now there's an interesting thought—Stewart working for me. How do you think that would turn out?"

"Not the best," Valerie admitted, finding the scenario amusing.

"That's an understatement if I ever heard one."

"Stewart doesn't believe we're going to get married."

"He will," Hale predicted. "Besides, it's not him I'm worried about."

"I know, but—oh!"

Hale suddenly grabbed her wrist, spun her against him and lowered his head quickly to cover her mouth with his own. Her lips were parted, and he took advantage of the small space between her teeth to thrust his tongue into her mouth, eagerly moving his lips against hers, twining one hand in the strands of her hair.

Valerie's mind went blank. She pressed her hands to his chest, but didn't push away. Nor did she respond. She just let the kiss happen.

"Valerie . . . ?" Stewart's voice reached her ears, and her heart sank.

Hale lifted his head, and his eyes seemed glazed as they focused on Stewart.

Valerie, too, felt light-headed.

"I didn't mean to interrupt," Stewart muttered, his color rising as he mounted the final steps to the deck.

"It—it's all right," Valerie said quickly. Her voice sounded breathless, and she nervously combed the tangled strands of her hair.

"I just thought I'd say good night."

"Good night," Hale said. He kept one hand firmly around Valerie's waist.

"See you tomorrow," Valerie added.

"Right." Scowling slightly, Stewart disappeared below the deck.

"Maybe that convinced him we're serious," Hale said, a cocky smile curving his lips as he released her.

"I hope so." Good Lord, why was her voice so low and raspy? Hoping to clear her head as well as her throat, she took in a deep, stinging breath of salt air.

Hale, stepping away from her, shoved his hair from his face. Was it her imagination, or did his hand shake a little? "Didn't you enjoy the show?"

"I don't 'enjoy' deceiving people."

"Well, you'd better get used to it."

"I don't think I can. Ever."

He turned then, his nostrils flaring slightly, and clamped his hands over her shoulders. "Just remember it's for a good cause—your pocketbook."

"And yours!"

He hesitated a second, his eyes luminous with the moonlight. "Especially mine." For a split second his gaze drifted to her already swollen lips.

Valerie was sure he was going to kiss her again. Her breath caught in her throat. Her pulse thundered over the muted hum of the boat's powerful engines. Sweat dampened her skin. But he dropped his hands, turned on his heel and, muttering angrily between clenched teeth, disappeared down the stairs.

She let her breath out in a rush and sagged against the railing. Without exception, Hale Donovan was the most aggravating man she'd ever met in her life! How in the world was she going to pretend to be head over heels in love with him for the remainder of the cruise?

"You can do it, Val," she assured herself, though deep inside she was shaking. "He's just a man—that's all. Just one damned, arrogant, opinionated male!"

And a man, who, with just one kiss, could rock her to her very soul! Somehow she'd have to put a lid on her emotions. She didn't dare let Hale think, even for a split second, that she felt anything for him. If he had a glimmer of how he affected her, the game would be over. Because, like it or not, it wasn't Hale she didn't trust.

With a sinking desperation she realized she couldn't trust herself!

Hale tossed back the last of his brandy. He heard the rain lash at the deck overhead. In the span of three short hours, the weather had turned from calm and muggy to turbulent.

The boat, still heading northward, pitched and swayed beneath his feet.

Aside from the crew, everyone on board *The Regina* had retired for the night, but Hale knew that sleep wouldn't come easily. Though negotiations with Stowell were progressing, he felt restless and annoyed.

For the first time since they'd set sail, Hale second-guessed himself. He'd thought that bringing along a woman posing as his fiancée would make things easier, but he'd been wrong. Dead wrong. Fending off Regina's advances would have been child's play compared to dealing with the gamut of unfamiliar emotions that toyed with him.

In less than twenty-four hours, he'd felt everything from elation to jealousy. Worse yet, he'd had trouble keeping his mind on business. Frowning so hard his jaw hurt, he snapped off the lights in the salon and walked down the short hallway to his stateroom.

Once there he yanked off his tie, kicked off his shoes, flopped on the bed and stared at the connecting door between his cabin and hers. Was she asleep, or as restless as he?

God help him, he thought, feeling the boat roll and pitch, but he had to remember that his interest in Valerie Pryce was all just part of their bargain. It didn't matter that she was the most intelligent and innately beautiful woman he'd ever met in his life. And it sure as hell didn't matter that she had the sharpest tongue he'd ever encountered. She was off-limits. Period. And all their touches and smiles, winks and kisses were part of the deal, nothing more.

Valerie Pryce was an actress, and apparently a damned good one, because just for a moment when he'd kissed her, he had thought she'd responded. But that wasn't possible. Or was it?

"Cut it out!" he muttered angrily at himself while squeezing his eyes shut. Soon it would be over. He'd own William Stowell's company and Valerie would leave.

He hadn't forgotten that she had six months to work with him, but he'd already planned to make her life miserable at work, pay her off and be done with her. He couldn't have an ex-fiancée hanging around the office, could he?

A sharp jab of conscience stung him, but he ignored it. Valerie Pryce was a woman, and unfortunately, like most others, money was the only thing she understood. Oh, she could talk about a lot of things—like life and love and happiness—but when push had come to shove, Valerie had shown her true colors. She had a price just like everyone else.

CHAPTER 7

"Miserable weather!" Regina grumbled, tossing her cell phone aside. She snapped off the television and stalked to the window, glaring at the rain beating against the glass.

"It's supposed to break up tomorrow." Beth, sipping from a ceramic mug, thumbed through the latest issue of an interior design magazine.

"Tomorrow?" Regina groaned. "You mean we have another day cooped up in here?"

"You'll survive," Beth predicted.

"I doubt it!"

Valerie, who had spent the day finishing her book, read the last page and tossed the mystery aside. Regina was right. The day had been long. William and Hale had spent every waking minute locked in the den, working out the details of the sale. To Valerie's disappointment, they hadn't even joined the rest of the entourage for lunch.

Frowning, Regina announced, "I may as well get dressed for dinner!"

Beth didn't look up, just flipped through the slick pages of her magazine. "It's still two hours away."

"Well, there's nothing else to do!"

Valerie stood and stretched. She wasn't about to sit around and listen to Regina rant. "If it's okay, I'd like to see the galley."

Beth grinned. "It's okay by me—but remember, the galley is Hans's sacred turf."

"He doesn't like anyone butting in," Regina said.

"I don't blame him," Valerie replied with a cheery smile, "but I think I'll take my chances nonetheless, and I swear I won't 'butt in.'"

"It's your life," Regina muttered, but she offered Valerie the first genuine smile of the day.

The galley, located down a short flight of stairs, was a small, compact room equipped with all the comforts of home compressed into a much smaller space. Several pots simmered on a two-burner stove, and the tangy odors of garlic and onion permeated the air, wafting deliciously.

Hans, a portly man with thin, blond hair, meat hooks for hands and a dour expression, was furiously chopping vegetables on the counter while muttering to himself. Diced mushrooms and scallions were already piled in small bowls near a stainless-steel sink.

"Need any help?" Valerie offered, poking her head into the tiny room.

"No!"

"Are you sure?"

"It's a wonder I can cook at all," he grouched, glancing over his shoulder at Valerie, though he didn't turn to face her. "No gas, so few burners, and this room—so hot!"

Valerie thought the galley was a vast improvement over her own pantry-size kitchen in San Francisco. Complete with coffeemaker, refrigerator, freezer, microwave, butcher-block counter and stove, *The Regina*'s galley was clean and well equipped. Cupboards and a pantry filled one wall, and overhead, fluorescent bulbs offered bright, if artificial, light.

"What's for dinner tonight?"

"Coq au vin."

"Sounds wonderful."

"If it is, it will be a miracle," he vowed, though the spicy fragrances wafting through the room belied his grumbling.

"You know, I'd really be glad to lend a hand."

Turning at last, he folded his plump arms over his chest. *"You* are a guest."

"That doesn't mean I can't chop vegetables or wash dishes or boil water."

"Did Mrs. Stowell send you down here?" he asked, narrowing his eyes suspiciously.

"Of course not. In fact, she and Regina warned me you wouldn't be too thrilled if I tried to step foot on your 'turf.' "

"Did they?" He laughed heartily. "Well, they were right. Thank you, but no, I can manage very well. There's not enough room for two."

"If you say so."

"But you're welcome to watch."

And watch she did. For the next hour and a half. Surprised at the big man's agility in the kitchen, Valerie found a stool and, like a schoolgirl learning her lessons, observed him adding seasoning and vegetables to his stock, never once taking the time to measure. While the stew simmered, he washed and tore spinach into individual salads, tossed on bits of bacon and water chestnuts and whipped up salad dressing in a blender.

He spoke little, but did take the time to explain what he was concocting. "Now there will be no surprise at dinner," he said when he finally stopped to wipe his hands on his apron.

"That's all right. Believe me, I've had enough surprises in the past few days to last me a lifetime."

He chuckled. "Then perhaps you should get dressed?" Valerie glanced at her watch and cringed. Only fifteen minutes until Hans began serving. After last night's meal, she wasn't too enthused about dining formally. "You're right. Thanks for the lessons."

"Anytime," he said with a lift of one big shoulder.

Valerie hurried to her stateroom, yanked off her clothes, then stared glumly at her closet. If tonight's meal was anything like the previous night's dinner, she again would be underdressed. "Too bad," she mumbled, pulling out a simple black dress and her favorite magenta jacket. The fabric wasn't elegant by any means and the tailored dress was perfect for the office, but definitely too demure for the dinner party. Unfortunately she had no choice.

She wore black stockings and heels, and brushed her hair until it crackled, letting it fall in loose waves around her face. Then, after a touch of lipstick and mascara, she eyed her reflection and sighed.

"Valerie?" Hale's voice called through the connecting door. "You ready?"

"As ready as I'll ever be," she said under her breath. She opened the door and found him as sophisticated and handsome as the night before. Dressed in a gray dinner jacket, black slacks, crisp white shirt and tie, his hair neatly combed, he would fit right in with the dinner crowd. Even if his date didn't.

Valerie forced a smile and cheered herself with the thought that Hale's gaze was warm and friendly as he offered her his arm. Her heart tripped, and for a second she couldn't find her voice. She hooked her hand through the crook of his elbow and smelled the woodsy scent of his aftershave. Dear Lord, he was handsome. She hadn't seen him since breakfast, and in that short time she'd forgotten just how imposing and overwhelming he could be.

The Stowells were already in the dining salon when Valerie and Hale arrived, arms linked. Regina, wearing an emerald-colored gown and diamond necklace, glanced at Valerie's outfit and looked away, compressing her lips to cover a smile.

Stewart wasn't so obvious, yet there was something akin to pity in his eyes when he hoisted his glass and said, "Valerie, lovely as always."

An embarrassing blush crept over Valerie's face. Beside

her, Hale stiffened, the muscles in his arm becoming rigid as he helped her into her chair.

William poured drinks and settled into the captain's chair at the head of the table. He winked at Valerie. "Your man here drives a hard bargain."

"Oh, I know," Valerie replied as the salad was served.

"Doesn't miss a trick. I swear, if I didn't know better, I'd think he was trying to wrest this company away from me just so he could sell it to someone else at a higher price."

I wouldn't put it past him, Valerie thought, but sipped her wine instead.

"Now that's an interesting concept," Stewart cut in, waving his fork in his father's direction. "If that's the case, why don't you just cut out the middleman and sell directly to Donovan's buyer?"

"I'm not planning to sell Stowell Investments," Hale said.

Stewart persisted. "You have a history of buying cash-poor companies, turning them around and selling them for a profit."

"Your father's company isn't cash poor."

"No, but still—"

Hale's gaze landed full force on Stewart. "Yes, you're right. I could. *If* I had a buyer and *if* I wasn't personally interested in keeping the investment firm as part of Donovan Enterprises. Once I buy the company from your father I can do anything I damn well please with it."

Tension fairly crackled in the air. Valerie laid a staying hand on Hale's arm, but he didn't notice.

Stewart, rebuked, attacked his salad with a vengeance, while Beth tried to steer the conversation to safer territory. "Let's not talk business," she said. "It's all so boring, and really, I'd think you two would just about be talked out."

"Never," her husband replied, but added, "Miserable weather, isn't it?"

"The worst!" Regina rolled her eyes. "I told you we should have headed south."

"Your father and I wanted to see something different this year," Beth said pointedly, "though I don't know that it matters whether it rains or shines when you're cooped up in a den discussinging business."

"These things take time," William assured her as the salad plates were whisked away and the main course served.

Beth poured more wine into her glass. "Yes, I'm sure they do, but I know they won't interfere with going ashore when we dock."

"Of course not," William replied, his round face brightening. "After all, this is a vacation."

"Some vacation," Regina grumbled under her breath. "This trip is about as exciting as a case of poison oak."

Beth clamped her mouth shut, and for the rest of the meal conversation lagged.

After dinner they again took coffee in the main salon, but William and Beth retired early. "Have to be on my toes tomorrow, you know," William said with a broad wink as he drained his cup. "I don't want Donovan to pull any fast ones."

Hale shrugged.

"Oh, William, come on," Beth said, wrapping one arm around her husband's. "You and I both know Hale Donovan's as honest as the day is long."

Stewart snorted in disbelief.

Valerie felt Hale bristle, but he held his tongue.

After quick good-nights, Beth dragged William down the hall toward their stateroom.

Stewart poured himself another brandy. "Anyone else?" he asked, his gaze meeting Valerie's in the mirror over the bar. His eyes were friendly, and he lifted his mouth into an inviting smile. "Valerie?"

"No, thanks."

"How about you, Donovan?"

"Not tonight."

"I'll have one later," Regina put in.

"Well, I hate to drink alone, but when pressed . . ." Stewart grinned widely and shrugged.

Regina closed the bar. "You drink too much."

Stewart raised his brows. "Probably," he agreed amiably.

"Don't you even care?" Regina snapped.

"Do you?"

"No," Regina said. "I guess it doesn't matter to me if you drink yourself to an early grave."

"And does it matter to you that our father intends to sell his business to Donovan here?"

Regina shook her head, then ran her fingers through her lustrous dark mane. "I couldn't care less." She slid a knowing glance in Hale's direction, and a small, secret smile touched the corners of her mouth.

A stab of envy cut through Valerie—not that there was anything about which to be envious, she reminded herself. But that smile, intimating that Regina and Hale shared a private memory, wounded her nonetheless. *You're being childish,* she silently told herself, but she felt a hot stab of jealousy just the same.

"I think I'll turn in, too," Valerie said.

"And ruin the party?" Stewart was astounded. "It's early."

"It's been a long day."

"Correction—a boring day!" Regina said, pouting.

Hale smothered a smile, and taking Valerie's hand in his, said, "Maybe tomorrow'll be better." His gaze held hers for a breathless second, and she saw his pupils dilate suggestively. Her throat closed, and she heard her heartbeat thunder in her ears.

Regina poured herself a drink and cast Valerie a scathing glare. "We can only hope," she said.

"Come on, it's time for bed," Hale whispered loud enough

that Stewart and Regina couldn't help but overhear. Tugging on Valerie's hand, he flashed her a positively indecent smile.

Valerie, despite the drumming of her heart, was consumed with an overwhelming urge to slap that crooked grin off his handsome face.

"I can find the way myself," she said evenly.

"I'm sure you can," he taunted.

Fists clenched, Valerie turned on her heel, then marched stiffly out of the room. The nerve of the man! Acting as if all he had to do was say the word and she'd throw herself at his feet and plead with him to make love to her. What ego!

He caught up with her at the door to her stateroom.

"Good night, Hale!"

"Good night, Valerie," he whispered, then took her into his arms and kissed her long and hard, closing his arms around her.

"Hey . . ." she whispered, drawing back.

He ducked past her into *her* cabin! "What do you think you're doing?" she demanded. "Get out!"

"I will."

"Now!"

"In a minute." To her annoyance, he locked the door behind him and grinned like a Cheshire cat.

"I thought you were leaving."

"I am. Don't worry." He cast her an amused glance. "Do I bother you that much?"

"You bother me a lot."

He smiled crookedly. "Then you must be starting to like me."

"Is that it? And all this time I was sure I loathed you!"

His grin widened. "You didn't loathe me last night."

"Last night?"

"On the deck. Remember?"

How could she forget? "I was acting."

"Like hell."

Feeling cornered, she crossed her arms under her breasts.

"I'm a very good actress, Hale. Just ask the producers of *Life's Golden Sands,* or better yet, the actor who played my lover!"

He eyed her thoughtfully and tugged at his tie, loosening the tight knot. "Oh, I don't doubt that you can act," he drawled, "but give me some credit, will you?" Though he didn't move closer, his gaze locked with hers and his smile all but disappeared. His eyes darkened a shade, and he rubbed his chin thoughtfully. "Valerie, I *know* when a woman is pretending and when she's responding. There's something about the glaze in her eyes, the way her knees sag and her weight falls against me that tips it off."

"I'm not going to argue with you," she said, ignoring the accelerated rate of her pulse. "Believe what you want. If you insist on deluding yourself that I'm half in love with you, go right ahead! If it eases your conscience to think that I really would want to marry you, that's your prerogative. But if you're interested in the facts, Mr. Donovan, then believe me, kissing you has no effect on me whatsoever." She was lying through her teeth—what was it about him that made her pride cover her true emotions? And why did she yearn to knock him down a couple of pegs? Pretending interest in her fingernails, she added, "You're just a man, Hale. My employer, nothing more. And by the way, last night—and just now—those kisses? They weren't so great."

"Oh, no?"

"No."

"Then maybe I'd better try to improve."

Chuckling, he kissed her again, and it took all her willpower not to respond to the quick, wet flicks of his tongue, the pressure of his hands on her back, the persuasion of his parted mouth against hers.

When he lifted his head, he quirked one side of his mouth. "Face it, Valerie. You're beginning to fall for me."

She nearly choked. "You have the biggest male ego I've ever seen," she challenged, wishing she didn't feel the tell-tale flush on her skin. "And I would never, *never* come close to caring for a man like you!"

"And what kind of a man is that?"

"A man who wants gold for his mistress!" she said, unable to hold back the words. "You have a heart of stone. All you care about is money!"

His nostrils flared indignantly, and the cords in his neck stretched tight. He flexed his fingers for several heart-stopping seconds, and she knew instinctively that she'd pushed him too far. Good. He deserved it. She wasn't about to back down.

But his voice when he spoke was amazingly calm. "And you, Ms. Pryce, are a liar."

"Pardon me?"

"Just who's kidding whom here?" he wondered aloud, a small, wicked smile toying with his thin lips. Lightning quick, he snatched her wrist and with a quick tug slammed her body against his. She nearly fell, but he caught her and in the blink of an eye lowered his head and captured her lips with his in a kiss that was as punishing as it was passionate.

She tried to pull back, but he held her close. As his fury gave way to pleasure, he moved his mouth gently over hers and splayed his hands possessively against her back.

No! she thought, forcing herself not to respond. This was her chance to prove he had no effect on her whatsoever. But her traitorous body didn't heed her head. Her breath started coming in shallow bursts, and a wondrous warm sensation swirled deep inside her, heating her in gentle, pulsing waves.

She closed her eyes and pressed her palms against the smooth fabric of his jacket. Gradually she wrapped her fingers around the back of his neck. The feel of the hairs of his nape, the heat of his skin against her fingertips—it seemed as though she couldn't get enough of him.

Hale finally lifted his head, and to Valerie's humiliation, his eyes were as clear as crystal. He hadn't felt a thing! *He* had been acting! "I guess that proves my point," he said.

"Or mine," she responded. Thankfully her voice was as

steady as his. Though her fingers shook slightly, she brushed back the unruly strands of her hair and smiled confidently. "Now, I think you know what you can do with all your chauvinistic philosophy on lovemaking. Good night, Mr. Donovan."

With a superior smile, she unlatched the connecting door and held it open, hoping beyond hope that Hale couldn't see her pulse twitching violently in her throat.

"Good night," he said, pausing at the threshold and saying again, "You don't fool me, you know," then slamming the door shut behind him.

A second later she heard the lock slide into place—from his side of the door! As if he expected her to try to get to him! Of all the egotistical, arrogant nerve! Closing her eyes, she let out the breath she'd been holding and wished she could scream or kick or slap the infuriating man. Instead she satisfied herself by kicking off her shoes and muttering a list of oaths a mile long about the particular lack of sensitivity in the male of the species!

CHAPTER 8

Rain continued to pound *The Regina*'s teak deck for nearly three days. Valerie barely saw Hale, and when she did, he seemed distant and brooding. Regina pouted, Stewart grew sullen and even Beth was cranky.

"Some vacation this has turned out to be," Regina growled, eyeing her reflection in the mirrored bar and adjusting the collar of her sweater. She turned her head side to side, and lines formed over her eyebrows. "My tan's fading!" She pulled her mouth together as if it had drawstrings attached to it.

"You'll survive," Stewart predicted.

Valerie, who had read three books, visited Hans before every meal and worked out to an exercise tape each morning, glanced out the window. Streaks of sunlight pierced through thick gray clouds. The sea, though still choppy, was calmer than it had been. "At least the rain's stopped."

"But for how long?" Regina wanted to know. "I've heard that it rains all the time in Oregon!"

"Not all the time," her mother corrected. .

Restless, Valerie made her way up to the deck, which,

though still damp, was no longer slick with rain. Fresh air misted against her cheeks, and the breeze tangled her hair. The Oregon shoreline was visible. Craggy, fir-laden cliffs jutted upward from an angry storm-ravaged sea.

She heard someone on the stairs, and her breath caught in her throat at the thought that Hale might join her. He hadn't so much as said ten sentences to her since their argument the other night, and she looked forward to the chance to clear the air. Though she hadn't been in the wrong, she hadn't been honest, either. Hale Donovan and his damned kisses affected her as nothing ever had.

"Is it safe?" Stewart asked, smiling as he climbed the stairs and crossed the deck. The wind caught his shirttail, and it flapped noisily.

"Safe from what?" she asked. Disappointed that Stewart, not Hale, had decided to join her, she rubbed the chill from her arms and forced a smile she didn't really feel.

"Wind and rain for starters, or worse yet, abject idleness and the chance for boredom to set in."

"I've heard it said that boredom is a state of mind."

"Don't tell Regina."

"I wouldn't."

He stood next to her at the rail, his shoulder touching hers as he squinted toward the shore. For a few minutes he didn't say a word. The silence was companionable, the scent of moist salt air bracing. Valerie relaxed until he said, "God, this is a slow cruise. So, how're you and Donovan getting along?"

"As well as can be expected."

"You haven't seen much of him."

"He's been busy."

"So I gathered." Stewart cocked his head and stared at her. "You know, if you were my fiancée . . ." He let his voice trail off and offered her a shy smile.

"You'd do things differently?" she asked.

"Very differently." He covered her hand with his, pressing

her palm into the railing as he linked his fingers between hers.

"How?" Hale asked loudly as he mounted the stairs. Valerie stiffened. She tried to pull back her hand, but Stewart's grip was firm.

Hale approached. His brow was furrowed, his lips drawn into a tight line as he skewered Stewart with his angry glare. "Tell me, how would *you* do things differently?"

Stewart shrugged, but still claimed her hand. "Well, for starters, I wouldn't ignore her."

Hale turned to Valerie. "Have you been ignored?"

Valerie swallowed hard. She felt cornered. "Not really."

"I didn't think so." Hale glanced at Valerie's hand, her diamond visible through the gap between Stewart's fingers.

Valerie wanted to drop right through the deck, but Stewart seemed to gain strength in the confrontation.

"Give me a break, Donovan. You and Dad have been holed up in that study ever since we set sail! Valerie's had to entertain herself."

"Except when you decided to step in and help out," Hale said slowly, his gaze positively glacial.

"Someone should show her a good time."

"A 'good time'?" Hale fumed.

"Right. Some people take time to enjoy life, Donovan. Whether you know it or not, there's more to being alive than buying and selling stock and preparing financial statements or beefing up annual reports or whatever it is you do."

The wind rushed over the deck, jangling chains, causing Stewart's shirt to billow, blowing Hale's raven-black hair over his forehead. The cold sea air felt charged with electricity, but not from the storm. "If I've been neglecting Valerie," Hale said calmly, "I'll make it up to her. Starting today."

Valerie couldn't stand the tension a moment longer. "You don't have to do anything—"

"Sure I do. Stewart has a point, doesn't he? We did take

this cruise to celebrate our engagement." He leaned a hip against the rail, and the dimple in his cheek was visible. "Besides, most of the business is concluded. Aside for a few loose ends, the deal's done."

Stewart blanched and dropped his hand to his side. "What do you mean? He actually sold to you?"

"We'll have the lawyers draw up the papers when we get back to San Francisco."

"Then there's still time to talk him out of it!"

"I don't think so."

Shirt flapping behind him, Stewart strode to the stairs and disappeared from sight.

"You didn't have to bait him," Valerie accused.

"I didn't."

"Sure."

"Look, Valerie, Stewart seems to think I'm out to get him by stealing his father's company. That's not the way it is. I'm offering Stowell a fair price. If he wants to sell to me, it's his business—not Stewart's."

"Stewart doesn't see it that way."

"Unfortunately Stewart's a fool. He wants everything for nothing. William would have liked nothing better than to increase his only son's responsibility, groom him for running the investment firm someday, but Stewart wasn't interested in hard work. Nor was Regina." Hale studied the mutinous tilt of Valerie's chin. "So now you and Stewart are friends?" he asked, disgusted with the dark turn of his thoughts. But jealousy stung him. He'd noticed Stewart looking at Valerie in the mirror over the bar last night and had seen his hand resting on hers just a few minutes ago.

"Does it bother you?"

"Of course not," he lied, "but, then, I'm not really in love with you, am I?" To his surprise she paled a little. "Because if I were, make no mistake. I'd be mad as hell—and ready to tear him limb from limb. Whether you know it or not, he was coming on to you."

"He was just being friendly."

"Ha!"

"I *know* when a man is 'coming on' to me, Donovan," she said, thinking with a roiling stomach of her experience at Liddell. Her boss had been coming on to her and strong. Shuddering slightly, she said, "Stewart isn't interested in me."

"Do you really believe that? He was all over you!"

"He touched my hand, for God's sake. Big deal!"

"We're supposed to be engaged!"

"I know, I know," she said, exasperation tingeing her cheeks pink. "But I told you he didn't buy our story."

"Then we'll just have to try to be more convincing, won't we?" Seeing Stewart touching Valerie, laughing with her, gnawed at him.

"How?"

"Let's start right now!"

Tugging on her hand, he led her back down the stairs to the main salon. Beth and Regina were watching television, but looked up as Hale and Valerie entered. To Valerie's horror, Hale plastered a devilish grin to his face and winked at them before half dragging Valerie into his stateroom.

"You're driving me crazy," he said loud enough to be overheard. "Let's move up the wedding day—or at least the wedding night!"

"What?" she croaked out.

"I just don't know if I can wait!" He kicked the door shut with his heel.

"Have you lost your mind?" she challenged, whirling on him. Eyes bright with fury, she advanced on him.

"Already gone. The day I signed a contract with you!"

He dropped her hand, and she reached for the connecting door, only to find it locked—from her side!

Leaning over a large trunk, he glanced over his shoulder and laughed. "Now you know how it feels!"

"Is that what this is all about—me locking you out?"

"No."

"Then it must be that you enjoy humiliating me."

"Not humiliating you—but paying you back. And, yes—guilty as charged."

"You . . ." She wanted to call him a bastard, but she remembered his reaction before and snapped her mouth shut. "You try another stunt like hauling me in here, and I swear I'll break the contract with you and tell the Stowells everything!"

"You'd lose a lot of money," he reminded her.

"The satisfaction would be worth it!"

A small, amused smile played across his lips, and it was all she could do not to slap him.

She took several deep breaths before saying, "Now if you're done mortifying me for the evening, I'm going to leave."

"Not yet."

"And why not?"

"Because I have something for you."

Oh, no, now what? She watched as he pulled a trunk from the corner, snapped open the locks and threw back the lid.

Valerie gasped as she saw dresses, over a dozen of them, neatly folded away. Green, white, red, blue, every color she could imagine—a veritable rainbow of expensive clothes. "What have you done?"

"I went shopping—well, actually Madge went shopping."

"Madge?"

"My secretary."

"I know who she is. But wait. Let me get this straight," Valerie whispered, dumbfounded. "Your secretary went shopping *for me*?"

"Yes, for you. I'm sure as hell not going to wear them!"

"Funny. Very funny."

He chuckled.

"You've had them since the beginning of the trip and you're giving them to me now?"

"If I remember correctly, you weren't in the mood for gifts," he reminded her. "I felt lucky that you wore the ring.

Now if you'll go into your room and unlock this damned door, we can put them in your closet."

"You're not serious." Shaking her head, she forced her eyes away from the gowns and back to his face.

Signs of impatience strained his features. "Why not?"

"But I can't accept these—"

"Consider it part of your employee benefit package."

"But—"

"No 'buts,' just go unlock the door. And don't worry about the size, they should all fit."

"How do you know?"

"I checked the labels of your clothes the day before we left San Francisco."

Her anger, still simmering, heated to a rapid boil. "You didn't." But she knew he had. A man like Donovan wouldn't leave anything to chance—not even a simple dress size. She remembered him pawing through her suitcase in her apartment. "You had no right—"

"I had every right. I agreed to pay you to pose as my fiancée, now, come on. There's only a little time before dinner."

"I'm not wearing any of these."

"Don't be so damned proud!"

"I'll stop—the minute you stop being so damned overbearing!"

He laughed then, and a tenderness shone in his eyes. "God, you're stubborn."

She wanted to argue, but she knew that he was right.

"Look, Valerie, maybe this isn't all very proper—at least according to your antiquated code of ethics, but bend a little, will you? We don't exactly have a conventional work arrangement, and I only bought these dresses to save you some embarrassment. I've seen how Regina and Stewart look at you. Beth and William, too. Unless you like their pity—"

"They don't pity me! And as for Regina, she's thrilled that I can't compete with her!"

Hale clucked his tongue and wagged his head. "Oh, you compete all right," he said, leaning back on his heels and staring up at her. "And you know what? She always comes up short."

Valerie's throat thickened. Was he really complimenting her? She searched his face and found his eyes, as gray as a Pacific storm, serious and intense. "Then . . . uh . . . I guess I don't need new clothes."

"I want you to have them."

"Why?" she wondered aloud, hating the horrid turn of her thoughts but unable to hold her tongue. "Maybe you're not worried about my embarrassment at all."

"No?"

"Maybe you're the one who's ashamed."

"Of you?"

She stared down at him and got lost in those eyes. "It's just possible you're embarrassed because I haven't molded myself into the image you seem to think you need for a wife—a woman who wears fancy gowns, expensive jewels and who doesn't give a damn about animal rights and has two or three fur coats tucked in her closet!"

Hale sighed. "You haven't embarrassed me yet," he said softly. "And no matter what you may think, I wouldn't judge you by your taste in clothes or the value of your wardrobe."

"Well, that's a relief," she mocked, hoping to break the tension slowly building between them. "I feel *so* much better already. Mr. Anything-for-a-buck does have a set of values that he claims isn't totally controlled by the value of the dollar!"

Hale shook his head, his dark hair gleaming in the soft light of the cabin. "You know, Valerie, you are without a single doubt the most irritating woman I've ever met."

"That must be why you chose me," she tossed back, but could feel her anger fading as quickly as an eagle taking flight.

"Must be," he growled.

Valerie walked through the door to the hall and into her

room before she unlocked the connecting door separating their cabins. With a grunt, Hale hauled the trunk into her stateroom and dropped it on her bed. "Wear something special tonight," he suggested.

"Any particular reason?"

He paused at the door and stared at her. "I just want to show you off," he said, then disappeared. The lock clicked softly behind him.

Valerie was left with her heart in her throat. Was he sincere? Or just mocking her again?

"Oh, it doesn't matter," she told herself as she hung up the dresses one by one. Madge, bless her, had exquisite taste. Though Valerie felt more of a fraud than ever, to appease Hale she stepped into a strapless blue dress. With a pinched waist, fitted skirt and sequined bodice, the dress sparkled and shimmered when she walked.

Valerie couldn't help the rush of excitement that coursed through her blood. Of course she knew she was being childish—a new dress, or trunkful of them for that matter, didn't change things. In fact, if she were thinking properly, she'd probably realize that dressing to please Hale was a mistake, one more thread in his web of lies. But she couldn't resist. For just this one night she wanted to play the part of his bride-to-be as if she meant it!

She French-braided her hair, twisting it away from her face, and applied her makeup with more care than usual.

A soft rap sounded on the connecting door, and Valerie glanced up just as it swung open.

Hale poked his head into her room, and his eyes turned the color of quicksilver when he saw her. "Madge has great taste," he murmured.

"Remind me to thank her when we get back."

"I will—believe me." His Adam's apple bobbed, and he stuck two fingers into his collar, as if it were suddenly too tight. "I guess I should've had the trunk delivered to your room on the first night. Would you have accepted the dresses?"

"No—"

"Then I made the right decision."

"You *knew* I'd take them now?"

Chuckling, he shook his head. "Oh, no, Ms. Pryce, I can't begin to imagine how you'll react to the things I do."

"But you thought you could convince me."

"I *hoped.*"

She shrugged. "Well, it's only for one night."

"We'll see."

Slightly irritated, she grabbed her clutch purse. "We're already late for dinner."

"Just one more minute." He ducked back into his room and reappeared with a long, slim jeweler's case.

Valerie's heart nearly stopped. *Now what?*

"I think we'd better complete the transition, don't you?"

"Transition?"

"Right. From working girl to—"

"Don't say 'debutante.'"

"I was going to say—"

"And not 'princess.' I can't stand all that stuff."

"From working girl to doted-upon fiancée of one of the West Coast's most eligible bachelors."

"That's worse!" she said, but laughed despite herself.

"Oh, relax and enjoy yourself," he chided, opening the case and withdrawing a necklace and bracelet of clear stones.

"Oh, no, Hale, I couldn't—"

"They're crystals, not diamonds," he said quickly.

"Don't tell me—even you have to budget," she teased.

He cocked one dark brow, but didn't say a word, just looped the necklace around her throat, while she adjusted the bracelet. The crystal beads felt as cool as ice against her skin. With hot fingers he brushed her nape, and a small tingle darted up her spine. As for the necklace, the shimmering glass caught in the soft lights and reflected against her skin. She adjusted the strands, then looked into the mirror to find Hale's reflection staring back at her.

The intensity of his gaze seemed to burn through the glass. Valerie's mouth went cotton dry as her gaze touched his for a pulsing second; then she turned quickly away and fumbled for her purse. What was it about him that made her feel as foolishly naive as a schoolgirl? She was a grown woman, for God's sake, and though not worldly-wise, she wasn't as innocent as a child.

"Valerie." Behind her, his voice was a whisper, and he clamped his hands over the bare skin of her upper arms. His breath fanned the skin at the base of her skull, and her skin flushed warm. "I just want you to know—"

Tap. Tap. Tap. "Valerie? You in there? Hans is ready to serve." It was Stewart's voice on the other side of the door.

Startled, Valerie stepped away from Hale, from his intense eyes, warm fingertips and erotic touch.

She opened the door. Stewart was waiting, drink in hand. He took one slow look at her before letting out a long, low whistle. "Look at you," he whispered, nearly awestruck, before he caught sight of Hale.

"We're on our way," Hale growled.

Valerie swallowed a smile. "Be nice, honey," she reprimanded primly, laying a hand on Hale's arm and linking her free hand through Stewart's.

Hale tensed. He narrowed his eyes, but Valerie pretended not to notice as they entered the dining salon.

At the sight of Valerie, Regina's mouth dropped open, but she recovered, motioning to the bar. "Can I get you something?"

"Nothing for me," Valerie replied.

Hale didn't bother responding, but walked to the bar and splashed a healthy shot of scotch into a tumbler. He felt Regina's interested gaze on him, knew his knuckles were white around the glass, but didn't care. His other hand, tucked in the pocket of his slacks, was curled into a fist. The simple fact was that given the least bit of provocation, he'd like to smash that fist into the smug smile glued onto Stewart Stowell's dimpled chin!

Jealousy, hot and venomous, swept through him, and a burning possessiveness of Valerie pounded in his temples. *You're a fool,* he told himself. Jealousy and this overpowering need to possess were the trademarks of an idiot—the kind of emotion that he'd always scoffed at.

To his surprise he heard Regina mumble, "Nice dress," to Valerie. The younger woman looked over the expensive fabric, and the mocking glint so often resting in her eyes was missing.

"Thanks." Valerie glanced his way. "It was a gift from Hale."

"It's . . . gorgeous," Regina admitted, studying the delicate layers.

"Well, come on now, let's eat," Beth said, entering the room in a swirl of peach silk. Her gaze swept the dining salon, landed on Valerie, and she smiled, not saying a word as Hans served scallops in a cream sauce.

Conversation was lighter tonight. The break in the weather seemed to lift everyone's spirits. Stewart laughed and joked and flirted outrageously with her, and Valerie enjoyed his seductive glances and remarks. Hale, the consummate actor, played his part of the jealous husband-to-be to the hilt. He grew even more silent and brooding as the salad, soup, and main course followed one after another.

"So tell me, where did you and Hale meet?" Stewart asked as coffee was served.

Surprised at the question, Valerie, who had talked her way through dinner, was suddenly tongue-tied. She glanced at Hale for help, but was met with a cold stare. The second their gazes touched, she knew he wasn't about to help her out. "I—it was a couple of months ago."

Regina fingered the gold rope at her neck. "But where? At a party? One of those fund-raising benefits?"

"No . . ." Valerie glanced pleadingly at Hale, but he just sipped his coffee. Apparently he was going to let her hang them both. Well, damn him, two could play at this game.

"What then?"

"Actually, we met when I interviewed for a job at his company."

Regina's mouth rounded into a tiny little "o."

Stewart, who had reached for the bottle of wine, hesitated before taking hold of the neck of the bottle.

And Hale—his cold eyes grew instantly hot.

"Really?" Stewart asked.

"Well, that was just the start, of course," Valerie went blithely on, though she felt Hale touch her leg under the table, warning her not to tread too far. Smiling, she tilted her head to one side and stared innocently at him, though the hand on her leg was positively burning through her skirt. "Since then, well, things have progressed."

"Did you hire her?" Stewart asked, amusement flickering across his face.

Hale forced a lazy smile. "Not until I convinced her to marry me."

William and Beth both chuckled, but Valerie felt as if her throat was welded shut. No sound escaped. The grin Hale sent her was absolutely wicked.

"Well, that's a novel proposal," Regina offered, still thoughtfully rubbing her necklace.

"To say the least." Stewart poured himself a generous portion of wine, and Valerie realized in that instant that he was a true snob—shocked that Hale would date anyone who worked for him.

As they finished their coffee and conversation dwindled, Valerie felt the strain in the room. Though Beth didn't seem the least concerned, her announcement that she'd applied to work for Hale caused speculative glances from the two younger Stowells.

Excusing herself before she said anything else that might cause further scrutiny on her engagement to Hale, she hurried upstairs to the deck.

A stiff breeze blew from the west. Lavender-shaded water stretched to the horizon to meet a pink-tinged sky. A few thin clouds obscured the lowering sun, and to the north lay a group of small islands, green with fir trees.

Bracing her hands on the rail, Valerie studied the ocean and watched a seagull circle and dip. The first week was nearly over, she thought to herself. All she had to do now was just hang in there. Some of the rigging groaned in the wind, and as always, the throb of the engines hummed in the coming night.

She didn't know Hale had joined her until she noticed a large male hand gripping the rail not an inch from her fingers. Glancing up, she saw the tight line of Hale's jaw, the compressed anger in the white brackets surrounding his mouth. "Why the hell did you spout off about meeting me in an interview?" he growled.

"You could have fielded that question yourself," she reminded him. "But oh, no, you weren't interested, were you?"

"I was interested all right—interested in why my fiancée was throwing herself at another man."

"Me?" She couldn't help but laugh. "Throwing myself at . . . oh, no, you don't think I'm interested in Stewart." She giggled again, and the back of his neck turned scarlet. "That's rich, Hale. Very rich. Stewart and *me*?" Her stomach quivered and laughter bubbled up from her throat.

He yanked roughly at his tie. "Looked that way to me."

"Stewart was flirting, yes, but—"

"And you were leading him on!"

"Never."

"Come on, you enjoyed every minute of it."

"Don't you think you're carrying this jealous-lover bit a

little too far?" she asked, shaking her head. "No one's here to overhear you, so you're just wasting your breath!"

"It doesn't matter if someone overhears us or not!" he muttered between clenched teeth.

Dear Lord, he was really playing this to the hilt! If Valerie didn't know better, she'd swear he was actually jealous! Of Stewart! She tried to swallow her laughter, but couldn't. The idea was so preposterous that she giggled again. "For your information, Stewart is *not* my type."

"And who is?"

"What does it matter?"

"Look, we had an agreement," he said, his eyes snapping as he turned and faced her, clamping one hand over her fingers. "And that agreement states that for every single hour of the day *and night,* you play your part. You don't flirt with other men, you dote on me, you act as if the very core of your existence depends on the fact that we're in love."

Valerie's laughter died in her throat. "You're kidding, right?"

"No way!"

"But no one in today's world acts like that."

"My future wife would!"

"Then I'm afraid, Mr. Donovan, you're going to spend the rest of your life a very lonely man. Because no sane woman in this day and age is going to bow and serve and grovel—"

"I don't expect groveling."

"Well, praise the Lord!" she said sarcastically.

"Look, Valerie, we're doing this *my* way."

"Oh, yes, sir!" she snapped. "Wouldn't think of doing it any other way, sir!"

His nostrils flared, his eyes grew dark, and he started for the stairs.

"And by the way, Mr. Donovan, sir," she challenged, reaching the stairs before he did. "You can take all your dresses and jewelry and throw them overboard for all I care, because I won't be wearing them!" Shaking with anger, she reached behind her neck and fumbled with the clasp of her necklace, intending to hurl the damn crystal beads in his face. But one finger caught in her hair and she succeeded in loosening only a couple of pins. A thick curl tumbled freely to her shoulders.

"The dresses stay," he insisted, but his eyes had darkened and his gaze was fastened on the lock of hair hanging against her skin.

"Like hell!"

He swore, muttering under his breath as if he were trying to fight a rising tide of desire. But despite his efforts, he gave in, seeming unable to fight a force stronger than his own will. With one quick movement he encircled her in his arms and yanked her against him so hard, the breath expelled from her lungs in a rush. Valerie gasped just as he lowered his lips to hers with an intensity that caused her knees to turn to liquid. Her heart went wild, her pulse thundered, and she wound her arms around his neck, not because she thought someone was watching, but because she had to steady herself.

His lips were warm and wet and sensual. Closing her eyes, she was lost in the scent of his aftershave, the cool breath of the sea, the lull of the rocking boat. He moved his hands over her bare back and delicately invaded the intimate cavern of her mouth as if he were tasting some delirious, forbidden fruit.

"Oh, Valerie," he whispered, dragging his mouth from hers and running shaking fingers through his wind-tossed hair. "This—this was a mistake."

Heart still quivering, she glanced around, wondering where the audience was. But the deck was empty. She looked into his eyes again and noticed the passion—hot and unbridled—lingering in his gaze.

"Why did you kiss me?" she asked. "No one's here."

He clamped his jaw tight and turned from her, staring instead at *The Regina*'s frothy wake. "I wish I knew," he said so softly the words were nearly lost to her. He jammed his hands into his pockets, and the tails of his jacket flapped in the breeze. "I wish to God I knew!"

CHAPTER 9

"We're stopping in Portland," William announced the very next morning.

"What on earth for?" Stewart asked lazily. Flopped on one of the striped chaise longues on the deck, he winced as he spoke, shading his eyes as if even sunlight were painful.

Valerie, after a horrid night's sleep, was glad for a chance to get off the close quarters of *The Regina*. The tension between herself and Hale was too thick, and she needed a break.

"Astoria's closer," Stewart grumbled.

"I know, I know, but your sister wants to go shopping, and Portland's a larger city."

"And a long way inland. Can't she shop when we get back to San Francisco? Now, that's a bigger city."

"The rest of the trip won't change. In fact, we'll be in Victoria when we planned," William replied.

"Whoop-de-do," Stewart muttered.

Beth joined them and scowled affectionately at her son. "Oh, quit whining, Stewart. If you let yourself, you might just enjoy this trip. What's your hurry anyway?"

"Good point," Stewart agreed with a glower. "If Dad's

really selling out to Donovan, I don't have a job to race back to, do I?"

Beth wasn't in the mood to pamper her son. "I guess you'll have to find yourself a new one."

At that remark, Stewart lowered the brim of his captain's hat, crossed his arms over his chest and closed his eyes.

Valerie pretended interest in a magazine, though the antics of the Stowells amused her to no end. How a down-to-earth woman like Beth and a stalwart businessman such as William could have raised such spoiled children was beyond her.

As for Hale and William, they were once again holed up in the den, hammering out the smaller details of the buy-out, and Valerie was grateful. She needed time away from Hale. Thinking about last night's kiss had kept her awake all night. What had he meant? Was it possible he was actually falling for her? She couldn't believe it—wouldn't delude herself into thinking for one minute that he cared the least little bit for her.

The Regina sailed inland through the mouth of the Columbia River, a huge expanse of gray-green water that divided Oregon from Washington. On either side, forested hills rose from the water, and Valerie was happy at the thought of giving up her sea legs for dry land.

Sunlight washed the hills and glinted on the river. Valerie leaned against a mast and tried not to dwell on the fact that Hale Donovan was the most charming, witty, handsome and downright infuriating man she'd ever met. His humor appealed to her, except, of course, when it was at her expense, and his unconventionality intrigued her. Were the situation different, she decided ruefully, she could fall in love with a man like Donovan. "Good thing it's all a charade," she muttered to herself, scuffing the toe of her sandal against the deck and feeling the wind catch in her hair.

As the captain guided the boat from the Columbia into the deep channel of the Willamette River, Valerie tossed her hair out of her eyes and squinted at the changing shoreline. But as she did, she caught a glimpse of Hale standing not ten feet from her.

He was resting his jean-clad hips on the rail and staring at her from behind his mirrored sunglasses. "Mornin'," he drawled with a grin.

"Good morning," she replied briskly, self-conscious that he'd been watching her. "How long have you been here?"

"Only a couple of minutes." Slowly rubbing his freshly shaved jaw, he said, "While we're alone, I think we'd better get a few things straight."

Here it comes—another royal edict, she thought ungratefully. "Such as?"

"I'm serious about you not flirting with Stewart—"

She started to protest, but he held up his hand to cut her off. "Just for the future, okay? I know I came on like Attila the Hun last night and I shouldn't have, but I just don't want to blow this deal with Stowell."

"I know, I know." She tried to keep her eyes off the thin, seductive line of his lips, but her gaze seemed drawn to his face and his rough-hewn features. "Let's just forget about last night."

As if I could, he thought wryly. That kiss had all but twisted his guts inside out. He'd lain awake most of the night filled with a craving he couldn't begin to trust. "That might be easier said than done."

"We don't have much longer."

And it was sure to be torture—sheer torture. Just being here with her, seeing her slim, tanned legs move easily beneath the hem of her shorts, watching as the wind tangled and snatched at her hair, observing the tiny span of her waist, was more than he could take. She was getting to him, and his willpower was being slowly eroded day by day, minute by precious minute. Sooner or later something would have to give.

They cruised into Portland under a web of bridges spanning the Willamette. Skyscrapers in brick and mortar, concrete and steel, glass and marble, lined the banks. On the west side, a park, lush, green and resplendent with fountains, stretched along a seawall, beyond which the skyscrapers gave way to sharp, verdant hills. To the east and beyond the city, the spine of the smoky-blue Cascade Mountains provided a rugged horizon.

Valerie couldn't wait to go ashore. After promising to meet Hale and Stewart in a courtyard restaurant, she and Regina disembarked and set out to explore the stores near the waterfront. She mailed a quick postcard to her mother, then followed Regina, who apparently knew the shopping district.

Regina was definitely in her element. They passed through one towering department store to the next. "Well, they're not as elaborate as the stores in San Francisco or L.A.," she said, pausing to sniff a fragrance at a perfume counter, "but some of them are quaint and unusual."

Valerie agreed when Regina discovered a tiny, but well-stocked boutique on 23rd Avenue, after they explored an area known as the Pearl district. The store boasted two floors of the most exotic and expensive clothes in Portland. Regina managed to find two hats, three pairs of shoes, some skinny designer jeans, two pairs of earrings and yet another drop-dead black dress. She handed the salesclerk her charge card, then, as the sale was rung up, turned to Valerie. "This is fabulous," she proclaimed, regenerated. "Aren't you going to try anything on?"

Valerie thought guiltily of her overflowing closet aboard *The Regina*. The last thing she needed, at least for the present, was more clothes. "Not today," she said evasively, helping Regina with her packages.

"Come again," the clerk said, a pleased grin stretching from one side of her pert face to the other.

Regina flashed her a thousand-watt smile and promised, "Next time I'm in town."

Overloaded with packages, they took a cab to the waterfront, then wandered along the seawall, watching sailboats, barges and tugs move upstream against the Willamette's current. Trees shaded the walk, and a dry easterly wind rustled through the leaves.

The restaurant, a narrow brick building with a walled-in courtyard, overlooked the river. Planters filled with colorful petunias, impatiens and ivy were interspersed between the tables. Hale and Stewart were seated at a table shaded by a striped umbrella. They sipped from tall glasses and, surprisingly, seemed congenial.

"Buy out the town?" Stewart asked, eyeing his sister's bags and packages.

"Not yet." Refreshed from the excursion, Regina plopped into a vacant chair and ordered a drink. "But just give me a couple of days!"

"Ah," Stewart joked, "the great American buy-out!"

Valerie chuckled, and even Hale laughed. As a foursome they lunched on crab salads and hot rolls, and for the first time since the cruise began, Valerie felt a camaraderie within the group. Even Hale was on his best behavior, laughing and teasing, winking at Valerie and clasping her hand as if he really did love her.

Later, while Regina and Stewart headed back to the yacht, Hale and Valerie strolled along the waterfront, not touching, but only inches from each other. A jazz band was playing in the park, and they stopped to listen. Couples with children, and lots of single people, were stretched out on blankets in the thick grass, listening to the intricate melodies. The sky turned from blue to amber to a dusky shade of rose.

Hale spread his jacket on the ground, and they sat together, listening, not saying a word, shoulders touching, enjoying the calm summer evening. Slowly, as if by magic, the street lamps lit the ever-darkening night. Skyscrapers became grids of illumination, their squares of light reflected in the Willamette's black depths. Jets of water in fountains sprayed skyward, bathed in the colorful beams of concealed lamps.

Valerie leaned against Hale, resting her head in the crook of his neck. He looped his arm around her shoulders.

"I guess Regina was wrong about the rain in Oregon," she said, staring up at a clear midnight-blue sky. "It doesn't pour all the time."

He chuckled and plucked at a piece of grass as the music continued. "I've been here two or three times a year for the past ten or twelve. I've only seen it rain once."

"So it's just a myth."

"Or I've been lucky." He stared into her eyes for a second, then glanced past the band to the river.

Valerie stared at the column of his throat, so close, so masculine. The shadow of his beard darkened his chin, and the smell of him, musky and male, was ever present. She tried to ignore his masculinity, but the erratic beat of her heart wouldn't quit and her eyes were drawn to the curve of his neck and the dark hair peeking from beneath his collar. Oh, he was male, all right, very male!

As the music stopped and the band packed their instruments, Hale said, "I guess we'd better go."

"I guess." She stood and brushed the dust from her shorts.

A breeze swept over the water, catching his hair and bringing the heavy scent of the river with it. Valerie rubbed her bare arms, and without asking, Hale dropped his jacket over her shoulders. "You're cold?"

"No—not really." But the warmth of his jacket filled with the scent of him felt natural and right. She glanced up at him and found his face relaxed and thoughtful.

"This has been an . . . interesting day," he said.

"Hasn't it?" *I wish it would never end,* she thought ruefully. Why couldn't this sense of closeness, this tenderness be with them always? Why did they continually go for each other's throats?

They walked to the marina together, and Hale helped her onto *The Regina* as the craft rocked gently. Downstairs, in the main salon, Beth and William were involved in a cut-throat game of cribbage.

"Well, there you are!" Beth said, beaming as she won and her husband tossed down his cards in disgust. "You missed dinner, you know."

"I'm sorry—"

Beth waved Valerie's apology aside. "Don't worry about it." Her eyes twinkled. "I'm just glad you two finally spent some time alone together."

Hale squeezed her waist and cast her an adoring glance. Real or fake? True emotions or part of the charade? Valerie couldn't tell. She wound her arm around his and returned his smile with a radiant grin of her own. "We did have a good time," she admitted softly.

"Wonderful! William and I spent the day shopping for supplies and sightseeing. Then we decided to play some cards—"

"Which was a big mistake," William cut in, grumbling good-naturedly.

Beth rolled her eyes and continued, "William wants our next stop to be Victoria. Then on the return trip we'll cruise through the San Juan Islands to Vancouver, British Columbia, down into Puget Sound to Seattle before finally returning to San Francisco."

"It sounds like heaven," Valerie said, thinking ahead. If she could keep her relationship with Hale on an even keel, and if Regina's good mood continued, the rest of the journey would be wonderful—if, of course, she didn't do anything as foolish as let herself fall in love with Hale Donovan.

"Never," she vowed in a whisper, removing her arm from Hale's. This trip was just a preliminary test. When they finally returned to San Francisco, she'd begin her real job and then she could prove to Hale just how trustworthy and efficient and valuable an employee she really was.

* * *

The next three days were the happiest of Valerie's life. The weather was perfect, Regina charming, Stewart subdued and Hale the most attentive and charming fiancé a woman could hope for. He stayed at her side, and they talked for hours about business, world politics, the economy, sailing, horseback riding and anything else that came up. The only subject that seemed off-limits was his past. Never once did he mention his childhood, nor did he have an anecdote about his teens. Though Valerie learned a lot about Regina and Stewart, she knew no more of Hale Donovan's childhood than she had on the first day of the cruise.

The following day the wind shifted and with it, everyone's good mood. The air turned breathless and sultry, and tempers flared. Regina was sullen again, her tone with Valerie sharp throughout the day.

Stewart, who had given up drinking before dinner, began mixing martinis again that afternoon. And Hale grew strangely quiet. Valerie felt his gaze on her, but instead of a twinkle in his eyes, she saw something else in those gray depths—something dangerous and brooding. He didn't smile once that day. He drew his brows together, and though he was polite, he never once initiated a conversation.

At dinner Regina was peevish, poking at her poached salmon and complaining bitterly to Hans. "It's not done enough," she said, pronging a flaky piece of lemon-drizzled fish. "If I'd wanted sushi, I would have asked for it!"

There was, of course, nothing wrong with the salmon steak, and Hans, his face bright orange, brought her another piece, at which she wrinkled her nose but mashed it all over her plate.

"I'm sick of fish," she said churlishly.

"Well, you'd better get used to it, because it's about all we brought along for this leg of the journey," her mother snapped. She narrowed her eyes on her daughter. "And don't you ever, I repeat *ever,* treat Hans that way again!"

Regina's cheeks burned bright, but she tossed her head and shoved her plate aside.

Beth sighed and seemed about to say something else . . . when William, to diffuse the tense conversation, suggested they go into the salon for coffee and bridge.

Regina pouted and turned her attention to her cell phone and Stewart seemed more interested in the bar than cards, which left Hale and Valerie to take on Beth and William.

They lost the first hand and the next, and Hale barely said a word. Valerie's stomach knotted, but she played as cleverly as she could, considering the fact she'd only had a few lessons. More than once she caught Hale staring at her, his eyes thoughtful, his mouth stern—as if she'd done something to deserve his disapproval.

The game progressed much too slowly for Valerie. She couldn't wait to either escape from Hale's scrutiny or haul him into a private corner and demand to know what was wrong. However, with everyone watching, she held on to her patience and played cards as if her life depended on it.

"We'll dock in Victoria in the morning," William announced. He slapped a card on the table and took the trick.

Valerie was starting to understand bridge, though when William and Beth started their rapid-fire bidding, she was sometimes at a loss and occasionally misplayed.

"How long will we stay there?" Regina asked in a flat tone.

"Just one day and night."

"Good."

"Bored, are we?" Stewart asked.

Regina slid a glance at Hale and sighed. "*We* have important things to do back in the city," she said. "Well, at least one of us does."

"Ouch," Stewart muttered, glowering into his half-full glass of scotch.

"Prickly tonight, aren't they?" William whispered out of the side of his mouth.

Nodding, Beth pursed her lips, laid down a trump card and proceeded to take the remaining tricks, winning the hand.

This was her chance to escape. "That's it for me," Valerie said, stretching. "Maybe someone else would like—"

"I'd love to!" Regina piped up, instantly losing interest in her phone. "Hale, you will be my partner, won't you?"

Valerie was stunned. She'd expected Stewart and Regina *both* to take their turns at the bridge table. All night she'd planned for a little time alone with Hale, intending to find out just what she'd done or said to put him in such a foul mood. But now Regina's eyes were shining, her rosebud lips drawn into an expectant smile.

Hale glanced quickly at William, seemed about to decline, then said, "Of course I will, unless Stewart wants to play."

Stewart rolled his eyes. "I don't feel like being massacred tonight, thank you. Mom and Dad are much too bloodthirsty."

"Then I guess you're stuck with me!" Regina remarked, her dark eyes twinkling as she stared at Hale. She fairly flew across the room to land in Valerie's recently vacated chair.

"Stewart, really, you could play in my place," his father offered.

"With Mom?" Stewart shook his head, but lifted one side of his mouth in a sly grin. "I might misplay a card and she'd ground me—or worse!"

"I *never* grounded you!" Beth responded with an amused laugh. "Not that you didn't deserve it just about every day of your life!"

Valerie left them bickering happily. Pretending she didn't see the furious glint in Hale's eyes, she abandoned him to Regina, who was practically drooling to be his partner. Valerie had hoped that Regina had given up on Hale, as the past few days had been so carefree, but obviously, from Regina's sullenness tonight and the girl's absolute elation with becoming his partner in bridge, Valerie had been wrong. And she'd been wrong about something else—her reaction. Regina's flirting with Hale cut to the quick. A sharp pang of jealousy pierced her. Stupidly she wished she'd never left the table— never given Regina a chance.

"Don't be an idiot," she muttered to herself as she closed the door of her cabin shut behind her. "You don't care about him! You don't!"

She threw herself on her bed, reached for the book she'd put off reading for over two years, only to discover the paperback spy thriller missing. Searching nightstand, table and bookcase, she came up empty. "That's odd," she thought aloud, but wasn't about to go back to the main salon and check again. No doubt, Hale was still angry with her, and she had learned that sometimes it was better to avoid him until his black mood passed, which usually wasn't too long.

She heard the tinkle of Regina's laughter and Hale's hearty chuckle. Her heart twisted. "It doesn't matter," she insisted, but as she unzipped her dress, she caught sight of her reflection. Her lips were turned down, and deep creases lined her forehead.

The dress, a pale peach confection provided by the president of Donovan Investments, slid to the floor. Valerie dropped onto the stool near her bureau. Her heart ached. She cupped her chin in one hand and stared at her mirror image. "You've got it bad, girl," she told herself, recognizing the unthinkable.

Bending her head, she pulled the pins from her hair and felt the weight of her braid fall past her shoulders. She unclasped her necklace and dropped it into her open jewelry case. Snapping it shut, she saw the diamond on her hand— that horribly beautiful stone that reminded her that her engagement, this cruise and the attentions of Hale Donovan were all a farce.

Her cheeks grew hot, and she closed her eyes against the

truth. Because, whether she liked it or not, she was falling in love with Hale Donovan.

"Dear God," she whispered, the thought striking her like a thunderbolt. She threw on an oversized T-shirt and lay atop the bed, not bothering with the covers. The night was hot, the cabin stuffy. Snapping off the lights, she listened to the noise from the salon. She glanced at the bedside clock every ten minutes. The neon numbers seemed to mock her, and she tossed and turned, waiting for the sound of Hale's footsteps in the hallway, hoping that he might knock on her door. For the first time since their journey had begun, she'd left the bolt on the connecting doors unlatched.

She wanted to talk to him . . . alone. Never before had she been afraid of her feelings, but never before had her feelings betrayed her. *Except with Luke.* Ah, yes, Luke, the reason she'd decided never to fall in love again.

An hour passed before she heard Hale in the hallway outside. His footsteps paused at her door. Her heart went straight to her throat.

But he didn't knock, and she heard him open and shut his cabin door. Straining, she listened as he rustled about in his room and imagined him stripping off his jacket and tie, unbuttoning his shirt, pulling the tails from the waistband of his slacks . . .

Clamping her teeth together and clenching her fists around the thin blanket covering her bed, she willed herself to stay in her room, because if she made the first move, opened the door that was not only a physical barrier but the symbol of all that was between them, what would he say? What would she do? How could she stop herself from fulfilling the erotic fantasy of falling into bed with him?

She heard him sigh, and her heart stirred. Squeezing her eyes shut, she tried to sleep, only to stare at the clock and watch the minutes slip slowly by.

"Sleep—sleep," she told herself.

She must have dozed, because the next time she looked at the clock the neon numbers flashed two thirty. The cabin was hot and stuffy, her skin damp with sweat.

With a groan, she tossed back the sheet she must have pulled over her and sat up, feet dangling from the bed. She glanced at the connecting door, and her pulse leaped. She loved him. It was that simple.

Angry with herself, she shoved her hair out of her eyes. How could she have fallen for a man like Hale Donovan, a man who valued a dollar more than anything, a man who seemed to have no past, a man willing to hire a woman to pretend to be his fiancée in order to deceive a friend and businessman?

Her head began to throb. *And are you any better? William and Beth Stowell have done nothing but kind things for you and yet you continue to lie to them—go along with this cheap facade.*

Knowing that sleep was impossible, she found her slippers and made her way through the darkened craft to the deck. She needed fresh air and space and time to think.

Once on deck she felt better. Moonlight cast a silvery path on the dark water, and stars blinked back at themselves on the inky surface. There wasn't a breath of wind, and the ship, aside from the churning engines, was still and quiet.

Taking several deep breaths, Valerie walked to the side of the boat and rested her elbows on the rail, staring into the black water.

Sweat collected on her forehead. She closed her eyes for a second and experienced the uncanny sensation that someone was watching her every move. The hairs on the back of her neck bristled.

"What's the matter—couldn't sleep?" Hale's voice cut through the stillness.

Valerie nearly jumped out of her skin. As she whirled, she caught sight of him, stripped naked to his waist, the muscles of his chest and arms visible in the half-light. Her eyes were drawn to the dark mat of hair covering hard pectoral muscles and the washboard of his abdomen. "I—I didn't know you were here."

He didn't answer her, just regarded her with wary eyes.

"But I'm glad you are," she forged on.

"Are you?"

What was this new game he was playing?

"Why?"

"I thought we needed to talk."

He lifted a dark brow, and hooking his thumbs into the belt loops of his jeans said, "So talk."

"Something's wrong."

"What?"

"That's what I'd like to know. Ever since you came up on deck this morning, you've been moody."

"Have I?"

He was baiting her. She knew it. Yet she couldn't help but rise like a trout striking at a fisherman's lure. "Haven't you?"

He lifted one shoulder; the muscles flexed for a brief second. Valerie's chest tightened.

"What is it, Hale? What's wrong?"

His eyes darkened. He stared at her and said, "You lied to me."

The accusation hung suspended between them. What was he talking about? "Lied?" Shaking her head, she turned one hand palm up. "I never lied about any—"

"No?" he cut in angrily, his lips twisting into a sardonic grin.

"No."

"You're sure?"

"Positive!"

"Then tell me," he said slowly, his nostrils flaring. "Who's Luke?"

CHAPTER 10

"How do you know about Luke?" she asked, shaken.

"This . . ." He tossed a paperback book into the air and caught it deftly. Even in the darkness she recognized the cover of the novel she'd misplaced earlier in the evening.

"Where'd you get that?"

"You left it in the salon. I picked it up to give it to you, and it fell open to the first page."

He didn't have to say another word. Luke had given her the book two years before. She knew the inscription by heart. "For now and always—my heart will remain in your hands. I love you, Luke." It had been an anniversary gift—given her on the one-year anniversary of the day she'd met Luke in her political science class. He'd left her one week after giving her the book.

Striding across the deck, he handed her the paperback. "I thought there wasn't anyone else."

"There isn't."

"So why bring the book with you? As a reminder?"

"No . . ." She flipped through the pages, then tossed the paperback onto a nearby table. With a frown she admitted, "It's taken this long to get over him."

In the shadowy moonlight, Hale's face appeared rugged, his anger clear in his angular features. "How long?"

"Two years."

"And there's no chance of the two of you getting back together?"

"No!" she snapped, then bit her tongue and tried vainly to control her rapidly escalating temper. "And what business is it of yours anyway?"

"I just don't want him showing up and becoming the fly in the ointment, so to speak. You said there were no boyfriends or jealous lovers that I'd have to worry about."

"There aren't."

"Except for Luke."

"Except for Luke," she repeated, goaded and wishing to knock Hale down a couple of pegs. He had no right to make her feel guilty about loving someone before she'd met him and she intended to let him know it. "Nowhere in our agreement did it say I wasn't allowed to have a past. What happened two years ago can't possibly matter."

"Maybe."

She couldn't stop herself. His high-handedness brought out the worst in her. Shaking, she pushed herself upright and tilted her face upward, her eyes blazing into his. "Well, at least I *have* a past. I have friends and family and yearbooks and memories of my life for the past twenty-four years, but you"—she gestured wildly with her hands—"as far as I know, you didn't exist until you entered college. You have nothing, not one single thing to prove you were even alive!"

Sucking in a swift breath, he surrounded both her wrists with steel-strong fingers. "Enough!"

"What is it, Hale? What are you hiding?"

"Nothing, damn it!"

"Well, neither am I!" She yanked her hands back and started for the stairs, but he caught up with her.

As quick as a cat, he caught one hand in his and whipped her around. "What happened to our truce?"

"You abused it—by prying!" She held up the paperback and wagged it in his face.

"And you abused it by lying."

"I never lied."

"Just left out some important details."

"But not my whole life, Hale," she said, letting out her breath. "I didn't hide my whole damned life from you. You met my mother, saw where I lived, asked questions and I answered. But me, I'm faced with a brick wall."

"Maybe I don't have a past," he said softly.

"That's crazy—"

"It's very sane. Believe me." He relaxed his grip, but kept his fingers around her wrist. In the half-light she noticed a sadness steal across his features, gentling the hard angles of his face.

What had he been like as a boy? she wondered, and ached inside that she hadn't known him then. Had he always been so jaded, so callous—or had his past shaped him into the hard-edged businessman he'd become?

He lowered his eyes to her lips and swallowed. Gently, he moved his fingertips along the insides of her wrist. Slowly he tugged, pulling her forward, bending his head and suspending his mouth above hers, his breath fanning her chin. "Oh, Valerie," he murmured on a sigh as soft as the night. "Sweet Valerie . . ." He touched his lips to hers, tasting and feeling.

Valerie's pulse leaped to life as his kiss, starting so chaste, deepened with a passion that flowed from his body to hers. Her heart clamored. She pressed her body to his, her soft flesh molding perfectly against his thighs, hips and chest.

Taking her hands within his, he surrounded her, wrapping his arms so tightly around her that her breasts were thrust against him. Covered only by the thin T-shirt, her nipples were pressed intimately against his rock-hard chest. Responding to the nearness of him, smelling the musky scent of his maleness, tasting the salt on his lips, she pressed closer, opening her mouth, feeling her nipples harden and ache. *Love me,* she silently begged.

"What am I going to do with you?" he murmured into her open mouth. His tongue penetrated her mouth just then, causing a quicksilver flame to shoot through her blood, stirring a response so deep within her she quivered to her very soul.

Pulling her wrists free, she wrapped her arms willingly around his neck and returned his kisses with the fire of her own. What was there about this complex man that brought her close to tears one second, fired her with fury the next, then within a split second consumed her with a longing so intense she could only think of making love to him?

She was warm inside—with need and want. Warm with secret fires that no other man had ever stoked. *Please, Hale, love me,* her mind screamed silently, while she battled that very love herself.

He lifted his head, his eyes silver with passion, his hands shaking as he placed them on each side of her face. "This—this can't happen," he rasped, trying and failing to control his breathing. "Not yet."

"Not ever," she agreed.

"Oh, God." He ground his teeth and released her, clearing his throat and shoving his hair from his face. "I should never have hired you. I should've known the first time I laid eyes on you that this would be a mistake!" *But instead I persisted—hounding you—nearly forcing you because deep inside I wanted this moment, I wanted to feel you tremble in my arms. Damn it, from the first moment I saw you, I wanted to make love to you.*

Hale walked backward until his buttocks thumped against a mast. His blood thundered, his head pounded and his heart was thudding like a sledgehammer. Mouth dry, he slammed his eyes shut against the seductive vision she created. With moonlight in her hair, her eyes glazed with desire, he could barely control himself. He clenched his fists behind his back and pressed the back of his hands hard against the mast. "I think we'd better call it a night, Valerie."

Before he did anything foolish like kissing her again, he forced his eyes open and strode to the stairs. His steps were lightning quick as he headed straight to the cabin. Damn, but his hands were shaking and the fire in his loins wouldn't quit. Just the thought of her, warm and pliant in his arms, was enough to turn him inside out.

He threw himself on the hard bed. Then moaning, he rolled over and squeezed his eyelids shut, knowing he'd never fall asleep and trying to block out all thoughts of her.

But he heard her on the stairs, shuddered as her door clicked open and closed again, and wished to God he'd never set eyes on her!

The Regina plowed through the Strait of Juan de Fuca to moor in Victoria the next morning. Valerie told herself to forget the past night, but the moment she saw Hale, she knew their meeting the night before wouldn't soon be forgotten. His gaze shifted away from hers, and the corners of his mouth were pulled downward.

Valerie pretended interest in the view, but she knew the instant his gaze returned with a sizzling intensity that cut her to the bone. Her fingers whitened around the railing, but she kept her gaze glued to the sea as *The Regina* slowed in the harbor.

Sailboats, cabin cruisers and every other boat imaginable vied for position in the marina. Tall masts and rigging swayed in the breeze, and the boats rocked with the lapping water. White hulls sparkled in the morning light.

Beyond the array of vessels, the waterfront of Victoria, a walkway and street were bustling with morning activity. Already tourists strolled near the water, and cars and buses buzzed past. Beyond the street, Valerie saw a wide expanse of manicured lawn and shrubbery in full bloom—the grounds of a copper-domed building that looked like a cross between an English castle and a Muslim mosque. High overhead, white birds—probably pigeons and seagulls—circled against a flawless blue sky, and a red-and-white Canadian flag snapped in the wind.

"This is one of my favorite cities," Beth proclaimed as she joined Hale and Valerie on deck. "So much culture! So much life!" With a smile, she stared at the view and tucked a few strands of white hair under a wide-brimmed hat, then pushed a pair of sunglasses onto her nose. "I can't wait to go shopping. All those interesting shops and English pubs. And high tea—be sure to take high tea."

"Oh, we will," Hale agreed easily, to Valerie's surprise. After last night, she'd expected him to keep his distance. "As a matter of fact, we'll take breakfast ashore."

"What a marvelous idea! I think we will, too. I'll give Hans the word not to bother this morning." She disappeared down the stairs, leaving Hale and Valerie alone.

"Come on," Hale suggested, grabbing her hand, "let's leave now, before we get stuck with Regina and Stewart again."

Valerie linked her fingers with his and cocked her head to glance up at him. "Are you sure this is a good idea?"

"No, as a matter of fact it's probably one of the worst I've had in a while."

"Worse than a phony engagement?"

He groaned. "Even I'm beginning to regret that!" But his eyes crinkled at the corners, and he whispered, "It's working, isn't it?"

"You tell me."

He squeezed her hand. "Too well, I'm afraid." Together they strolled along the docks, then wended their way through the narrow streets, where horse-drawn carriages competed with cars and trucks. Bookstores, china shops, art galleries and authentic English pubs were clustered together in brick squares where baskets of flowers hung from old-fashioned lampposts.

Hale and Valerie ate Belgian waffles and cheese blintzes in a tiny café overlooking the square. He didn't mention their chance moonlight meeting on the deck, and neither did she, though when she caught him staring at her over the rim of his cup, his eyes were penetrating and dark.

He's trying to pretend last night didn't exist, too, she realized. *But it will always be there.*

Her stomach began to churn, and she shoved the remains of her breakfast aside. Twirling the cup nervously in her hands, she said, "What do you want to see next?"

"It doesn't matter."

"The gardens? Museum? Shops?"

"You choose," he suggested, then grabbed one of her hands with his own. "But first, tell me about Luke."

"There's nothing to tell."

He didn't believe her. His eyes as much as called her a liar. "There must have been something."

"Once, maybe," she said with a shrug. Withdrawing her hand, she cradled her coffee and settled back in her chair. "I met him in college. He was brilliant, but more into surfing than school. He didn't have to work at studying much. The first year we were together everything was fine, but after that . . ." She stared into her cup, as if she could find some answers to questions that had flitted through her mind for two years. "He decided he had to find himself. So he gave up everything—a scholarship to grad school, his Porsche, his surfboard and me—to trek around Montana."

"What's in Montana?"

"I wish I knew. Or maybe I don't."

"Another woman?"

She swallowed against a knot in her throat. "I don't know," she admitted, sipping from her now-cold cup. "He was pretty vague. He knew some guy who had a cabin in the mountains and he thought he'd spend the summer there. That was two years ago, and I haven't heard from him since."

"You loved him?"

She'd asked herself that same question a thousand times. "I thought I did."

"And now?"

"Now I've convinced myself it couldn't have been love. Otherwise it wouldn't have ended."

Hale's lips twitched. "You—a romantic? I never would have guessed. I thought you were a pragmatist."

"I am . . . usually."

"But you think real love endures forever."

"Don't you?"

She expected him to say that real love didn't exist. Instead he frowned. "I don't know." His gaze touched hers for a magical split second. "I just don't know."

The waiter came with the check, and as they left, Valerie linked her arm through his and pushed all thoughts of Luke and their dead-end relationship aside. No, she'd never really loved Luke, and now it didn't matter. Luke was part of her past. Hale, she hoped, was her future.

Hale insisted upon a carriage ride, signaling a driver in a black top hat and paying the fare. They climbed into the back of the open spring buggy, and at the crack of a whip, the horse, a heavy-haunched gray gelding, clopped noisily, slowly down the street.

Slinging his arm around Valerie's shoulders, Hale held her close as the driver-cum-tour-guide pointed out spots of interest. The sky was vibrant and blue, the air filled with the scent of blossoms, sea and horse. Feeling the romance of their adventure together, Valerie sighed contentedly and snuggled close to Hale.

"Happy?" he asked, stroking her hair.

"Mmm."

She could hear the steady beat of his heart over the sharp click of metal horseshoes as they rode through an ornate gate guarded by two hand-carved lions.

Nestled in Hale's arms, Valerie watched the bustle of the city and wished the day would never end.

They had high tea in a fabulous glass-encased structure that was alive with lush indoor gardens. The building smelled of rich soil and exotic plants, and the sound of birds twittering reverberated against the panes.

Valerie and Hale sat at a small table, sipped tea and munched on finger sandwiches. Hale was charming and relaxed, his gray eyes warm, his smile contagious.

"Beth was right, this is a beautiful city," Valerie finally said as conversation waned.

"Maybe we should spend the night."

She nearly choked on a swallow of tea. "Here—together?"

He glanced around the room at the glossy vines and trees. "Not here—I thought you'd prefer a quaint Victorian inn."

"I think we'd better stay on the yacht."

"In separate cabins?"

She raised her chin an inch. "What are you suggesting?" Though she tried to sound indignant, her voice betrayed her and she could feel her eyes sparkling.

Setting his cup down, he stared straight into her eyes. "We've ignored what happened last night long enough, don't you think?"

"I thought you wanted to forget about it."

"I tried. It's impossible."

She couldn't argue that point. She sipped from her cup again and discovered that her hands were shaking. "I'm not interested in an affair," she said bluntly, her cheeks burning. "I told you that at the beginning."

"I know, Valerie," he said softly. "And I wasn't, either. At least, I didn't think so. But you've made me change my mind."

She shoved back her chair, its legs scraping on the floor. "I think we'd better go—"

He caught her wrist. "You can deny it all you want, you know, but there's something between us—something more than friendship."

"I don't think we're friends."

"But we could be lovers."

Dear God, was that her heart pounding so loudly? "What we are is business associates. Nothing more."

"You're kidding yourself."

"I don't think so." Rather than continue the argument, which was quickly escalating into one of their volatile battles, Valerie strode outside and started walking toward the marina.

Hale caught up with her, matching her furious strides with his own. "Don't try to make me believe you don't know what's happening," he said, "because you felt it, too."

A lie formed on her tongue, but he shook his head, holding one finger to her lips and shushing her as they walked.

"And don't expect me to believe that you were only acting last night. We were alone and you responded, and whether you want to believe it or not, Valerie"—he took one long stride and planted himself in front of her—"we're falling in love!"

Love? She stopped short. Was he serious? *Love?* "I think you're confusing love with lust."

"Not me. I know both."

"Do you? And who were you in love with? Leigh what's-her-name?"

He laughed then, throwing back his head at the thought. "No, not Leigh. And her name's Carmichael. She'd be devastated that you didn't know who she was."

"Sorry—" She tried to brush past him, but he caught her shoulders, holding her squarely in front of him on the sidewalk while other pedestrians had to file around them. "This looks ridiculous," she ground out.

"Leigh never meant anything to me."

"She was your lover."

Hale sighed. "That was a long time ago."

"Not according to Regina."

"Since when do you believe her?" he asked, his eyes twinkling with amusement. "Don't worry about Leigh. She's out of my life. Come on." As if the conversation had ever existed, as if they'd never said one cross word, he grabbed her hand, dashed across the street and started walking.

"Where are we going?"

"To an authentic English pub."

"We just ate."

He flashed her his lazy grin. "I know, but we've only got so much time and I'd like to take you on in a game of darts."

"Darts?" *Was he out of his mind?* But she didn't argue, and after wandering through a couple of antique stores and a candy shop, he guided her to a small, dark pub where they served fish-and-chips, kidney pie and dark ale.

Valerie relaxed, ate as much batter-dipped cod as she could stand, then surprised Hale by beating him once at darts. In the next two games, she lost.

By the time they headed back to *The Regina,* the sky was dark, the air cool. Lights blazed in the surrounding buildings as they walked along the waterfront.

Hale draped his arm around her shoulder, and she didn't object. This day had been too perfect, she didn't want to spoil it, and his hand on her arm, so possessive and warm, felt right.

Moonlight ribboned across the dark water near the marina and the sea breeze lifted Valerie's hair. She glanced at Hale, and her heart tripped at the sight of his strong profile. Dear Lord, how she loved him. She'd known him less than two weeks, and he was the one man with whom she couldn't fall in love. Nonetheless she had. Despite all her vows and self-made promises, she'd fallen for him.

Inside, the boat was still and quiet—and warm from the hot summer's day. The Stowells weren't yet aboard, and apparently the captain and crew had gone ashore to sample the nightlife. She and Hale were alone. Completely alone on the gently rocking boat. They both knew it, though neither mentioned the obvious.

"It's late," she said.

"What about a nightcap?"

"I don't think so." The last thing she needed was a drink! Staring into Hale's erotic gray eyes, seeing the taut angle of his jaw, the sheen of perspiration on his skin, the cords of his neck, the muscles of his back moving fluidly as he strode about the salon, she decided she had to be careful. "I'd better say good night."

"We don't have to, you know."

"Of course we do."

"This could go on and on forever."

He was so close, his breath fanned her face. The heat from his body radiated to hers. "I don't think so."

"Always the proper lady, eh?" With one finger he traced the curve of her jaw, then inched up her chin to touch her lips.

"Proper? No. A lady? Sometimes. But I try my best to be a smart woman." Valerie's insides quivered, but she forced herself to stand perfectly still. She couldn't let him know what a powerful effect he had on her—already he guessed how she felt.

His finger trailed down her neck to rest at the tiny circle of bones at her throat. He outlined them slowly, watching in fascination the trembling pulse encased within. "Let go, Valerie," he suggested, wrapping his strong arms around her. "For once in your life, trust your instincts."

Lowering his head, he brushed his lips slowly over hers. Her blood caught fire, heating her from the inside out as his lips grew harder, more insistent.

She tried to fight the overpowering urge to surrender, but her eyes closed and she leaned against him, opening her lips to the sweet, wet embrace of his tongue, feeling his hands tangle in her hair.

Her head lolled back, and she moaned as Hale kissed the curve of her throat, and lower as he trailed his tongue against her skin to skim the neckline of her dress and ignite fires of desire on the skin beneath.

Her breasts ached, and willful thoughts invaded her mind. *What would it hurt? He said he loved you, didn't he? Believe him—trust him. For once in your life, Valerie, take some happiness.*

When he lifted her off of her feet, she didn't protest, but clung to him, her hair spilling over his arm, her eyes watching his face beneath lowered lids. He kissed her at the door to their cabins, and she returned his kiss with ardor, running her fingers over the coarse hair at his nape.

She closed her ears to the nagging doubts crowding her mind, thought only of the feel of his lips and hands, the warmth seeping through her.

"Will you stay with me?" he murmured against her ear, and his very breath fanned the flames of already-rampant desire.

She could barely breathe as he kissed her and carried her into his cabin. Somewhere in the back of her mind she knew she was making an irrevocable mistake, but she couldn't stop returning his kisses. She loved him. And that was all that mattered.

He splayed his hands across her back, and the smell of him was everywhere as he laid her across the bed, falling gently over her and stroking her rib cage with the flat of his hand.

"Valerie, sweet, sweet Valerie," he rasped, his breath short and swift. Placing one hand between her breasts, he felt the pounding of her heart. "Let me love you."

He moved his hand then, cupping a breast through the soft cotton fabric. Her nipple hardened, and she sucked in a swift breath, realizing just what was happening. The heat swelling deep inside was burning with a want she knew only he could fill.

He moved, stroking her breast before she gasped for quick gulps of air and rolled away. "N-no," she cried, choking on the horrid word. Her body begged for more of his sweet, gentle touch, but she forced herself to think beyond this one glorious night.

"I love you."

Weakening, she saw desire burning bright in his eyes and knew that lust was talking. "P-please, don't—"

"Marry me, Valerie."

Marriage? "Don't say . . . You don't have to—"

"This isn't an obligation!" he ground out, his teeth flashing in the darkness as she scrambled to her feet.

Anger and confusion clouded his eyes, and she remembered the last time she'd been in this position, when her boss at Liddell had forced his hard, heaving body on hers and begged her to let him make love to her. Fortunately she'd escaped—and she'd wanted to. But this was worse. She longed to stay with him—her body screamed to join with his.

Stupidly she reached forward, touching the curve of his jaw.

He groaned, then gently shoved her hand aside. "You'd better leave now," he said, clenching his teeth. "No—don't," he said when she took a step forward. "I'm warning you, Valerie. I can only take so much."

"But—"

"Just leave! And lock the damned door."

Her chest so tight she couldn't speak, she turned and strode to her room. She closed the door separating them, but didn't throw the bolt. If he came to her, she wouldn't stop him. She couldn't. She loved him too much.

She flung herself on the bed, trying to reason, trying to tell herself that loving him was the biggest mistake of her life.

Think, Valerie! she told herself. And she did. All night long. And what she decided during those long, dark hours was that she should take a chance. A man like Hale Donovan came along once in a lifetime, and she should trust him. Not tonight, but maybe tomorrow, and if things turned out as she'd hoped, for the rest of her life.

He'd asked her to marry him, hadn't he? Tomorrow she intended to find out if the offer still held.

She loved him, and that was that. Now she had the chance to be his bride.

Thoughts of love and marriage, of bearing Hale Donovan's children, flitted through her mind as she dozed fitfully. Yes, she loved him, and yes, she could trust him.

As the gray streaks of dawn filtered through her small window, she dozed, smiling to herself.

Yes, she'd accept Hale's marriage proposal. Yes, she'd throw off the chains of this charade. And yes, she'd make love to him. Everything would be perfect, she thought, finally drifting into a trouble-free sleep.

CHAPTER 11

The next morning, while William and Beth were spending a few final hours in Victoria, the most beautiful, statuesque woman Valerie had ever set eyes on strolled onto *The Regina*. With flashing jade-green eyes, lustrous black hair, creamy white skin and pouty lips, she boarded as if she owned the yacht.

"Leigh!" Regina gasped, shooting Valerie a questioning glance.

Leigh? As in Leigh Carmichael?

"This *is* a surprise!" Regina gushed.

Leigh laughed throatily. "I thought you were expecting me." Before saying anything else, she leaned over the deck rail and called to the dock. "Could you bring the bags up?"

Stunned, Valerie watched as a cabbie, his car still idling on the dock, hauled several oversized bags onto the deck. Leigh paid him, then flopped onto a chaise and slipped her hat from her head. "Where is Hale?"

"Oh, he's on board somewhere," Regina replied, glancing anxiously at Valerie.

Leigh grinned. "Won't he be surprised? He wanted me to join him in San Francisco, but I couldn't get away. I was in

Europe, you know." She sighed and, holding her straw hat by
the crown, fanned herself. "Lord, it's warm!" Spying a pitcher
of iced tea, she asked, "Do you mind?"

"Help yourself," Regina answered.

Valerie's stomach twisted. So Hale had asked Leigh to
pose as his fiancée and she'd had the pride to decline. Now
what? And why had he lied? He'd sworn his affair with
Leigh was long over. If so, how did she know where to find
him? Valerie twisted her hands in the folds of her skirt.

"Where is everybody?" Leigh poured herself a full glass
of tea from the glass pitcher and held the glass to her forehead, emitting a contented sigh.

"Mom and Dad are in town. They'll be back soon. Stewart's with Hale, and Valerie and I were just up here talking."

Leigh swung her gaze to Valerie as if seeing her for the
first time. "You're a friend of Regina's?"

Valerie felt perspiration dot her back, and it took all her
willpower to keep her gaze steady with Leigh's. "We've become friends on the cruise," she said, hoping to sound non-
committal . . . when her world was actually falling apart.
Obviously Hale's relationship with Leigh was far from over.

Regina, looking uncomfortable, made hasty, vague introductions. Where once Regina might have been amused at the
awkward situation, now she actually seemed unnerved. "This
is Valerie Pryce. Leigh Carmichael."

Valerie forced a smile onto her frozen face. "I've heard a
lot about you," she offered lamely.

Leigh drew her perfect dark brows together. "You must
know Stewart." She glanced at the ring on Valerie's left hand
and began to smile. Her green eyes twinkled merrily. "Don't
tell me—you're going to marry him!" Leigh cried, throwing
her head back and laughing. "I can't believe it. Someone's
actually tying down the elusive Stewart Stowell!"

Collecting herself, Valerie shook her head. "No, actually,
I've only known him a short while."

"But the ring—I thought . . ." Leigh stopped herself. Her beautiful face washed of color.

There was no reason to lie. Valerie was backed into a corner. "I'm here with Hale," she admitted as calmly as possible.

To her credit, Leigh composed herself and sipped her tea. "Hale?"

"Yes."

Studying the ice cubes in her glass, she said, "So that's how you've heard of me." Sighing, she asked, "Did Hale bother to mention we're engaged?"

Valerie felt as if she'd been kicked in the stomach.

"No, I don't suppose he did," Leigh decided with a dismissive wave of her hand.

Regina glanced at Valerie. "But that's impossible—"

"Just because we haven't been together for a few weeks?" Leigh asked coyly, though she seemed more nervous than when she'd first boarded. "Okay, I'll admit that when Hale called and invited me to join him, I was a little uncomfortable. We hadn't announced our engagement, not officially, but what better place than this?" She gestured to the teak deck, rigging, flapping sails and sun-dappled water.

"Yes, what better place?" Valerie whispered, her throat burning. All those lies. Last night. All those vows of love. How often had he said them? To how many women? In her heart she wanted to believe that she was the only one—that he wouldn't lie to her, but he had.

Regina frowned. "I don't understand. Valerie and Hale—"

"Work together," Valerie cut in, shooting Regina a look that could kill. The less said here, the better. She didn't know what Leigh's game was, but Valerie thought she'd better hear her out before she made any rash statements about being engaged to Hale herself. After all, her engagement was a phony. Maybe Leigh was lying, but maybe not.

"I'm a little embarrassed to admit this," Leigh went on as she poured herself another glass of tea. "But Hale called while I was in Marseilles, and we had this stupid little argument. I even told him I didn't want to show up and announce that we were engaged when it hadn't been in any of the papers." She caught the eye of one of the crew members. "Oh, Jim, would you see to my bags, please?" she asked, pointing to the mountain of matching luggage near the main sail.

"Leigh?" Hale's voice cut through the warm morning air.

Valerie froze, but saw him from the corner of her eye.

His expression murderous, his hands planted firmly on his hips, he stood near the stairs. He flicked his gaze to Leigh before focusing squarely on Valerie.

Leigh's features relaxed, and her eyes sparkled. "Oh, there you are!" she cried, crossing the deck quickly and wrapping her arms around his neck. "I thought for a minute I'd gotten on the wrong boat!"

No, that's my mistake, Valerie thought anxiously.

"You've met Valerie," he said.

"Just!"

Hale didn't move. His face was carved in granite. "What are you doing here?" he asked, peeling her arms away from him.

"Oh, please," she cooed, "don't tell me you're still angry! I'm sorry I didn't meet you in San Francisco, but it was just so inconvenient. And you surprised me."

"*I* surprised *you*?" he asked, glancing at Valerie. Dear God, what was Leigh doing here? Had she heard about his engagement? And Valerie—he watched her lower herself weakly down in one of the deck chairs.

Leigh fingered his collar. "Most people aren't proposed to long distance—"

"I don't remember proposing to you," he said calmly.

Leigh waved her hand against his argument. "Oh, come

on! You called me in Marseilles and asked me to marry you. This trip was supposed to be a celebration of our engagement."

"I think you misunderstood," he said through tight lips as he peeled her fingers from his shirt.

"But—"

Moving away from Leigh, Hale dropped a proprietary hand on Valerie's shoulder. The minute his skin touched hers, he felt her shaking. "You said you already met Valerie."

Leigh nodded.

"Good. Because *she's* the woman I intend to marry."

"Marry? *Her?*" Leigh moved her lips in protest. "Pardon me?"

"It's all right," Valerie said, standing quickly despite the clench of Hale's fingers over her shoulder. There wasn't any reason to drag this out. Regina already knew something was very wrong, and Beth and William Stowell, chatting together, arms linked, were boarding.

Hale's deception was over.

William looked up, caught site of Leigh and ground to a stop. Beth, too, saw the unlikely group. "Oh, my," she whispered.

A frown as deep as the Grand Canyon crossed William Stowell's round face. "Well, Leigh," he finally said when the silence stretched long. "I didn't expect to see you here."

"Obviously," she said dryly, shooting Hale a pouty glance.

Valerie's stomach flip-flopped, and she wished there were some way of escaping, but Hale clamped his hand more firmly over her shoulder. "There's been a mix-up, that's all," he said. "I did call Leigh in Marseilles," he said slowly, narrowing his eyes on the gorgeous woman, "and we did discuss marriage and this trip."

Valerie sagged a little.

"But she wasn't interested in cutting short her vacation. In the meantime I met Valerie. She came into the office on an interview and I knew then that she was the woman I wanted to spend the rest of my life with."

"Her?" Leigh cried, disbelieving.

"Leigh, I'd like you to meet my fiancée," Hale said as Valerie slowly rose.

Valerie just wanted to escape, but Hale dropped his arm to her waist and held her firmly against him with strong fingers. Unless she wanted to cause more of a scene, she didn't dare move.

"I think there's been a mistake," Valerie said.

"A big one," Leigh agreed vehemently. "I just flew halfway around the world!" She turned her sparking green eyes on Hale and wagged a furious finger in his face. "You! You asked me to meet you—sent me the itinerary! How could you find someone else to pretend to fall in love with you in so short a time?"

"This isn't an act," Hale insisted.

"Oh, come on, Hale. Get real!" Leigh gestured to the Stowells. "How dumb do you think they are?"

Valerie gasped.

"That's enough," Beth insisted.

But Leigh couldn't stop. "You don't expect them to believe that you, a confirmed bachelor, are going to marry a woman you barely know!" She glanced at the rest of the group, as if hoping to confirm what was so obviously apparent to her.

"I think this has gone on long enough," Valerie said. "Hale can explain. Now if you'll excuse me a minute—"

"You're not going anywhere," Hale said.

"Watch me."

"Valerie, please—"

But she couldn't stand to hear another lie. "We'll talk later," she said, tears burning the back of her eyes. Now she was the one who was lying. She had no intention, if she ever got off this damned boat, of seeing him again. "If you'll excuse me," she said to the group in general as she shrugged off Hale's arm and headed to the stairs.

"I love you," he shouted, and all other sounds seemed to disappear.

Valerie stumbled. If only she could believe him! She glanced back, saw the crowd and realized he was still playing his role. Swallowing the thick, hot lump in her throat, she groped for the rail to the stairs. She wouldn't break down. Not now. But her eyes burned. Fighting blinding tears, she ran to her room.

Why had she ever agreed to this crazy scheme? In the past few days she'd begun to care for the Stowells, and now they'd know her only as a phony and a fake, a woman who had intentionally deceived them, made them look like fools!

Feeling about one inch tall, she threw open the doors of her closet and hauled out her two small bags. There had to be some way she could talk to Beth and explain. Or could she? And what about Hale? Dear God, how would she ever forget him?

Fingers shaking, she snapped open the bags and began tossing her clothes, not the elegant dresses he'd bought for her, but her very own clothes, into suitcases.

"You don't have to leave." Hale's voice, though barely a whisper, echoed loudly through the room.

Turning, she found him filling the doorway, just as he'd filled her life for the past two weeks. "Of course I do," she returned shakily, hating the fact that he would see her so close to tears.

"If you'd just listen to me—"

"No, Hale, this time you listen to me," she said, her eyes burning, her chin quaking as she thrust it forward. "The game is over. Over! I don't know what you're going to tell William Stowell, or if it matters anymore. Leigh's here, so she can keep Regina at bay. Now all you have to do is convince William you made a mistake with your women—but that you're still interested in his company."

"It's not that simple."

"It's as simple as you make it!"

She reached for the smaller bag, but he shut the door behind him and locked it. Her knees sagged, but she forced herself to remain upright.

"Hear me out, Valerie," he insisted, his back to the door. His face looked drawn, and his hands actually trembled when he lifted them to shove his hair from his face. "Just stay long enough to let me convince you I love you."

"We're alone, Hale. You don't have to pretend."

"I'm not pretending, damn it! I love you, Valerie. You have to believe me."

His cocky smile had disappeared, and even his anger seemed to have faded. His face was lined and his eyes sincere.

Oh, dear God, she wanted to trust him. But all she had to do was think about Leigh Carmichael, think about the lies, the deception of William Stowell, her part in the scheme, and realize what a consummate actor Hale Donovan was. Hadn't he proved his chameleon-like ability to change roles time and time again in the past few weeks?

Her throat was so dry she could barely speak. When she did, her voice was the barest of whispers. "Please . . . Leave. Before we say or do something we'll regret."

"Too late for that," he said. "I regret not being honest with you from the first. The reason I chose you, Valerie, was that from the first time I set eyes on you I knew you were a woman I could love."

"No . . ." she choked out. *Don't believe him! He's lied all his life to get what he wanted! No one knows that better than you!*

"I want you to marry me," he said slowly, his voice even, his eyes flinty. He didn't move one step closer, just stood at the door, quietly insisting.

Valerie felt herself breaking inside. "I have to leave, Hale."

"Not until you say you'll marry me."

"And then what, Hale?" she snapped. "We'll go back to San Francisco and then what?"

"We'll get married."

"You're not serious!"

"More serious than I've been about anything in my life," he said solemnly.

He seemed sincere, but then, he was a natural actor, a man with a purpose, a man who had bought and sold her just to buy another man's company. "Good-bye, Hale," she said, holding her bags, waiting for him to move, praying she'd find the strength to escape.

He took one step closer. "Trust me, Valerie."

"Hale?" Leigh's voice floated down the short hall, followed by her quick footsteps.

Valerie grabbed the door handle. "She's looking for you."

"She means nothing to me."

Valerie tightened her fingers on the door handle. "Well, someone had better tell her."

"I will."

She yanked open the door, only to have him slam it shut with his shoulder. "Please, Valerie."

She blinked hard. "I want to believe you, Hale, but I can't. You told me from the beginning that this was only a temporary position, an act, all part of our agreement. You can't expect me to believe that now, after everything you've said and done, that you're in love with me."

His smile was sad. "I do love you. And I think you're in love with me, as well. You're just too stubborn to admit it."

"Stubborn?" she repeated.

"As a mule."

"Hale?" Leigh's voice was impatient. "Will someone kindly tell me what's going on?"

"That's your cue," Valerie said as Leigh pounded on Hale's stateroom door.

"Wait for me," he said as he slipped into the hallway.

Valerie didn't move. Not until she was sure Hale had sequestered Leigh. Then, before she did anything as stupid as listen to her foolish heart, she pulled the diamond ring from her finger, set it in a dish near her bed and silently crept down the hall. With any luck she'd be able to say hasty goodbyes to the Stowells, grab a cab and take the first flight out of Victoria.

CHAPTER 12

"I just don't understand," Valerie's mother said after Valerie's lengthy explanation. "It was all an act?"

Standing at the door of her mother's apartment, Valerie shifted from one foot to the other. "That's right. Hale and I never intended to get married."

"So you lied. To me."

"Yes, Mom, I lied," Valerie admitted, feeling like a schoolgirl again.

"Too bad." Anna sighed. "You know, I kind of liked him."

"Donovan? You about went through the roof when I told you we were planning to get married."

Anna grinned. "It was a shock, I'll grant you that. But you know I want nothing more than for you to get married and be happy."

"With Hale Donovan?" Valerie shook her head. "The man's impossible."

"Besides," Anna said wistfully, "it's time I had some grandchildren to spoil."

"Mom!" Valerie gasped. "What are you saying? You're still not recovered—"

"But I'm getting there." Anna laughed. "And grandkids might just be the medicine I need."

Valerie rolled her eyes. "Save me," she whispered.

"Well, maybe things will change," Anna decided. "You *are* working for Donovan Enterprises, right?" She handed Shamus, stuffed unhappily in his cat carrier, to her daughter.

"Not anymore."

"But you had a contract."

"I think I blew it," Valerie said with a sigh. She'd only been back in San Francisco four hours and it seemed like an eternity since she'd left Hale.

Shamus meowed loudly.

"I know, I know," Valerie said to the cat. "Look, Mom, I'll call you tomorrow. I just wanted you to know the truth before it hit the papers."

"And when will that be?"

"I have no idea," Valerie admitted as she closed the door behind her.

Outside, she climbed back into her car and headed home. The day had passed in a whirlwind of planes and cabs. She'd stopped by her apartment only long enough to jump in her car, drive straight to her mother's apartment and collect Shamus.

"And now what do we do?" she asked the tabby as dusk settled over the city, draping the hills in a cloak of purple light. "Back to square one?"

Shamus didn't deign to answer.

Valerie parked in her usual spot. Balancing the cat carrier and two suitcases, she trudged up the three flights to her apartment, jabbed her key into the lock and kicked open the door.

"About time you showed up," Hale drawled.

Valerie stopped dead in her tracks. Shamus hissed. She dropped one suitcase, and Hale, blast the man, had the audacity to smile. Draped insolently on her couch, the heels of his Nikes propped on a chair, he flashed her that heart-stopping grin she found so irresistible. His jaw was dark with the shadow of a beard, his mouth framed by deep lines, his eyes as warm and erotic as ever. Dressed in worn jeans and a beat-up leather jacket, he looked as if he belonged here.

Just the sight of him nearly broke her heart. Why couldn't she force herself to hate him?

"Close the door, Val."

"Wh-what are you doing here?"

"I think we have some unfinished business."

"But . . . how?" She glanced around the room. "How did you get in?"

"You left an extra set of keys in that." He pointed to a beach bag she'd obviously forgotten while escaping *The Regina*.

She leaned against the wall. "And you couldn't resist breaking and entering."

"I didn't break—just entered."

Though her heart was galloping a thousand miles a minute, Valerie tried to keep some rein on her thoughts. She shrugged out of her coat and let Shamus free. The cat made a beeline to the French doors. "What about the Stowells?"

Hale cocked one dark brow. "What about them?"

"Where are they?"

"Still yachting up north, I guess."

"You don't know?"

"Nope." Stretching, he climbed off her couch, walked forward and closed the door she'd left open. "And I don't care."

"Give me a break—"

"You've had your break," he said evenly, though his smile faded a little. Standing so close she could see his pupils dilate, he said softly, "I told William Stowell I wasn't interested in his company." He fingered a wayward strand of her hair, and his touch sent tingles sliding down her spine.

"Stewart's ecstatic about the turn of events. William's mad, and Beth—she told me I'd better chase after you."

"So that's why you're here?"

"Nope."

His breath fanned her face and his fingers were playing havoc with her senses. Valerie swallowed. "Then why?"

"Guess."

"I couldn't."

"Because of you."

Her heart leaped. Her fingers clenched. *Don't believe him, Valerie. He wants something!* "Me? But why?"

"Because this afternoon you walked out on twenty-five thousand dollars and the best job you'll ever find in this city. If you read the contract you signed with me carefully, you'll realize you signed a noncompete agreement."

She winced a little, remembering the contract. "You'd hold me to it?"

"Of course I would."

She narrowed her eyes. "But why?"

"Because you're supposed to work for me for the next six months. Your idea, remember?"

"But not as your fiancée."

"No. As my assistant. And my wife."

The words stunned her. "Your wife?"

"Marry me, Val."

Was he serious? Her palms began to sweat. "I don't think we can convince William Stowell we're still engaged."

"This has nothing to do with Stowell."

"No? Then what?"

"You and me," he drawled.

It was all she could do to stand her ground. Her heart hammered, and she licked her lips nervously. "Don't you think this has gone on long enough?"

"A lifetime isn't enough."

Valerie stared at him. She wanted to believe him—dear God, if only she could! But just this morning another woman had showed up as her replacement—a woman who had known all about the cruise, a woman ready to pose as Hale's fiancée.

"Look, I don't know why you're here, or who you're trying to convince you have all the right intentions, but it doesn't matter. And if you really intend to uphold the noncompete clause, I'll find another job. In another field."

Hale shook his head. "You wanted to work for me, didn't you? You wanted to prove you could be my assistant?"

"Yes."

"And now I'm giving you the chance to be my wife."

Slowly he reached into his jacket pocket and withdrew his handkerchief. "You forgot something besides your bag on the yacht." Opening the cloth, he held out the diamond ring he'd bought her less than two weeks before.

She shook her head, fighting the crazy urge to throw her arms around him and tell him that she'd love to marry him, that she'd willingly spend the rest of her life with him, that in her wildest fantasies she dreamed of only him.

Instead she kept her voice reasonably calm. "We don't even know each other."

"I know all I have to."

Her head was spinning, her throat constricting. Things were moving too fast. Though she knew she should yank her hand back as he placed the ring on her finger, she didn't.

"Come on." Taking her hand in his, he unlocked the French doors and stepped onto her deck.

Shamus darted behind the planter. The sounds of the city seemed far in the distance, the lights winking on the bay reflections of the stars.

"So," Hale said as a breeze teased his hair, "what do you want to know about me?"

"How about your family for starters?"

He grimaced, his eyes becoming as dark as the night. Seconds stretched to minutes. "All right," he finally said. "I never knew my father. He left before I was born."

"And your mother?" she asked, seeing a pain in his eyes.

"My mother." His expression hardened. "My mother gave me up when I was two. I don't remember her. Other than from one picture I had. But I threw it out after I realized she never wanted to see me again."

"When you were two?" she whispered, her heart nearly stopping.

"I was in the way. You see, she found herself a wealthy man, a man who wasn't interested in raising someone else's kid."

"Oh, Hale, no . . ." Valerie whispered, the tears she'd battled all day filling her eyes. "But your grandparents . . . ?"

"Were dead. I grew up in foster homes. Some were okay. Others . . ." He shrugged, frowning and stuffing his hands into his pockets. "Well, it all worked out, I guess. I've never seen my mother since the day she left me." His voice was emotionless, but Valerie had to struggle against her own tears. She ached for the little unloved boy he'd once been. No wonder he thought money was so important—that he could buy whatever he wanted. His mother had abandoned him in pursuit of the almighty dollar.

"I'm sorry."

"It wasn't your fault." He offered her a weary smile. "Anything else you want to know about me?"

"Everything," she admitted.

"Everything." He let out a long breath. "That might take a while."

"I've got the time," she whispered, trusting him at last.

Moonlight caught in his eyes. "Do you?"

"If forever's long enough."

He blinked, as if astounded. Then a smile spread slowly

from one side of his face to the other. "Why, Ms. Pryce, are you proposing to me?"

Valerie laughed. "Or propositioning you. Whatever you want."

"Oh, no. This time we tie the knot. Before you have a chance to escape." With that he wrapped strong arms around her and held her tight. His lips hovered over hers.

Her pulse thundered, and a warmth, liquid and soft, stirred deep inside. She wound her arms around his neck and held him close. There was so much to learn about him—so much to love. And she had the rest of her life.

When he finally lifted his head, he rested his chin on her crown. "I love you, you know."

"And I love you."

"Lake Tahoe is only a few hours away," he said, glancing at his watch. "We could be married by midnight."

"Tonight?" she gasped.

"Tonight."

"But what about Shamus?"

"We'll be back tomorrow."

"And my mother—"

"Can read about it in the newspapers."

Valerie laughed, thinking of her mother's response. "You know, she just might like that."

"I love you, Valerie Pryce."

"And I love you." She gazed up at him and couldn't help smiling. "But this won't get you out of that contract. I still intend to work for Donovan Enterprises and prove that I can handle the job as your personal assistant."

Hale laughed. "You already have."

"Don't think you can weasel out of it."

"Wouldn't dream of it," he countered. "In fact, I think we should draw up a new agreement. One that states exactly what your duties will be as my wife, what will be expected of you, how you'll spend your days."

"Not on your life, Donovan. This time the only piece of paper we need is the marriage license."

"Amen," he whispered, kissing her again, drawing her into the circle of his arms and holding her as if he never would let her go. "Stay with me forever."

"I will," she vowed, and she meant it.

Epilogue

Lake Tahoe

Valerie stood on the edge of the dock, squinting against the lowering sun. The sky was on fire, boats knifing through the clear water, the beach littered with dozens of people.

So where was Hale?

A large yacht slid into a berth in a nearby marina, and for a second, Valerie was reminded of *The Regina* and the two weeks she'd spent aboard the gleaming vessel and how she'd fallen in love with Hale. That had been nearly three years earlier. She rubbed her arms with the coming night as the sun settled behind the ridge of forested mountains to the west.

"Hey!" Hale's voice reached her, and her heart did that same little flip it always did at the sound of his voice.

She turned and found him walking up the planks of the dock, their two-year-old son, Nate, balanced upon his shoulders. The boy, with dark hair and big eyes, grinned widely when he spied his mother. "Mommy, look! I'm big."

"Yes, you are, buddy," she said as she walked barefoot

toward them. She grinned up at her son, his chubby legs caught beneath Hale's wide shoulders.

"Bigger than you!" Nate chortled, looking down at her, and Hale had to laugh.

Her throat still caught at the sight of her husband, and when he placed one hand over her shoulders and trapped his son's ankles with the other, she felt that same little thrill at his touch. She wondered if it would ever go away and vowed not to let it. The three years had been the best of her life.

She fell into step with Hale, he in faded jeans and a T-shirt, she in a short skirt and gauzy blouse. They walked through the sand and tall stands of pine to the private house they owned on the lake's shoreline.

Her life had changed after accepting Hale's proposal. Theirs had been a small, private wedding on this very shoreline a bare four weeks from the fateful day she'd first walked into his office and applied for a job.

Her mother had attended and surprisingly was thrilled with the match. To her credit, Anna, too, much improved and now walking with a cane, was dating, though she confided to Valerie that she was "taking it slow, or at least slower than you did! Which shouldn't be too hard, considering that you got married faster than Kim Cochran on *Life's Golden Sands.*"

Valerie had gotten pregnant soon after the wedding, and she'd worked as Hale's assistant until the moment her water broke in the office. Since then she'd been staying at home with their son in their penthouse apartment with its magnificent views of San Francisco Bay. On the weekends, they came here to a house that Hale had bought years before. Small and rustic, the cabin had been built a hundred years earlier on the shoreline. Surrounded by pine trees, with an incredible view of the deep blue waters of the lake, this little cabin was more than their "home away from home"; it was their retreat. Here, Hale could decompress and spend uninterrupted hours with his family. It was perfect.

Hale, once he'd become a father, had made a concentrated effort to cut back his once all-consuming interest in the next deal.

"Guess who I heard from today?" he asked as they walked up two steps to the broad front porch where an old swing swayed slightly in the breeze.

"I couldn't."

"Stewart Stowell."

"Really?"

"Yep." He held the screen door open for her, then said, "Watch your head, Nate," as he ducked down and followed her inside the two-bedroom cottage that was about as different from their sleek penthouse as night to day. Cozy furniture was placed around a freestanding fireplace, and hundred-year-old windows opened to the lake and forest. The galley kitchen was small, but efficient, and the two bedrooms could have fit into their spacious master bedroom in the city.

God, how she loved it here.

"So what did Stewart want?"

"Me to invest in the company."

"What?"

"Yeah, isn't that something?" He swung his son onto the floor, and Nate's little legs, already in motion, propelled him to a toy box that Valerie had just filled after picking up the toys. In three seconds Nate had dumped the box and plopped into the middle of a pile of plastic trucks, train pieces, and sturdy books.

"Daddy, come play!" he insisted.

"I will, bud. Just give me a minute."

For once, Nate didn't protest, but started trying to link magnetic train cars.

Valerie asked, "What did you say when he made you the offer?"

" 'Thanks, but no thanks.' " Hale shook his head. "Stewart got what he wanted, so he can deal with it. I bet his old man is having a heart attack. You know what they say about getting what you wish for . . . well, Stewart got it—in spades." Hale added, "Oh, and guess what?"

"I couldn't."

"Regina got married."

"Really? To whom?"

"Some Italian shipping tycoon who's twice her age and has racked up three ex-wives, along with half a dozen kids. According to Stewart, William's livid, but it's a done deal." Hale walked to the kitchen, and she heard the sound of the refrigerator door opening and closing.

"Are we invited to the wedding reception?"

He laughed. "Want to go?"

"No!"

Again he laughed, that deep sound that was now familiar and always warmed her. From the kitchen he called, "Can I get you something? Beer? Wine? Soda?"

"Thanks, but not right now."

Returning to the room, Hale twisted off the cap from a long-necked bottle, took a sip, then stretched out on the faded rug and began helping Nate put tracks together. Valerie lowered herself onto the floor as well and wondered how she could have ever been so lucky as to find this man she absolutely adored and have a son who was the very essence of her being. Life was good.

"So," Hale said, sending her a look over his shoulder. "Nate and I went into town and found this." He dug into his pocket and retrieved a small jeweler's box.

"What? Oh."

"You didn't think I'd forget our anniversary, did you?"

"Our anniversary is next week."

"Yeah, well, maybe we decided to jump the gun, hey, buddy? Right?"

Nate didn't respond; he was so into playing with a train car. Even when Hale ruffled his dark curls, the boy kept trying to fit one car into the next.

Hale handed her the box, and her heart swelled. "What's this? A cotton ball? Or a tiny spool of thread. Isn't that the tradition on the second anniversary? Cotton."

"Old-school. Now, it's something like china, I think."

"Like you would know."

"I know more than you think."

"Amen." She plucked the tiny box from his outstretched hand, opened it, and spied a set of earrings, perfectly matched to the ring he'd given her two years ago, the one she wore, the once "fake" engagement ring that had become the real thing. "Oh," she whispered, eyeing the glittering diamonds. "They . . . they're stunning. Thank you," she whispered, genuinely touched. "But, come on, you did *not* get them at the local store."

"Guilty as charged. I actually ordered these myself from the jeweler who made the ring."

"You did . . ."

"Good."

"Beyond good. They're beautiful," she said, and let him help her put them on, then kiss the nape of her neck before letting her hair fall over her shoulder again. "Well, since we're doing this early, I have something for you, too."

"Really?" One dark eyebrow rose expectantly, and he slid a hopeful glance toward their open bedroom door.

"Hmmm. Maybe that, too . . . later." She gave him a sexy little smile and added, "But, no, that's not the surprise."

"What?"

"You'll see." Winking, she climbed to her feet, then hurried into the bathroom while he looked after her, holding a beer in one hand and a piece of toy train track in the other.

"Can't wait," he called after her.

She retrieved her present from a drawer, then returned

to the living area to sit on the floor next to him. "You'll have to."

"Wait? Why? What are you talking about?"

"It's only for a little while."

"How little?" he asked, intrigued, but a light was beginning to dawn in his eyes.

"About eight months, I'd guess—maybe seven and a half," she said, handing him the stick from the pregnancy test she'd taken earlier.

"Wait a second. Are you telling me . . . ?" He glanced down at the test stick.

"Uh-huh, you, Hale Donovan, are going to be a father again, and our Nathan will have to learn to share, as he'll be a big brother."

"Seriously?" A smile stretched over Hale's lips. Before she could answer, he swept her into his arms, pulling her against him and kissing her hard on the mouth.

"Hey!" she said, laughing and gasping for breath. Good Lord, she was the happiest woman on earth at this minute.

Hale placed a hand over her flat abdomen. "Another one?" Tears glistened in his eyes. "You know, you and Nathan and this new little one, you're the only family I've ever known, all I've ever wanted. I . . . I—"

"You're the best dad ever," she said as her throat closed and she felt the sting of tears against her eyelids.

"God, I love you."

"And I love you."

"I never thought . . ." His voice trailed off.

"We'll be together forever," she promised.

He laughed. "I'm going to hold you to that." He kissed her again, then swiped at his eyes. "From the first moment you walked into my office, I knew you were the one, but I had no idea that we would have all this and—"

"Daddy! You play trains with me!" Nate demanded, looking over his shoulder, impatience pulling his little features into a knot. Then, before he was prompted, he added a quick "Please?"

"You got it, bud!" Clearing his throat, Hale gave Valerie another quick kiss, then turned his attention to his son. "You got it."

Romantic Suspense from
Lisa Jackson

Absolute Fear	0-8217-7936-2	$7.99US/$9.99CAN
Afraid to Die	1-4201-1850-1	$7.99US/$9.99CAN
Almost Dead	0-8217-7579-0	$7.99US/$10.99CAN
Born to Die	1-4201-0278-8	$7.99US/$9.99CAN
Chosen to Die	1-4201-0277-X	$7.99US/$10.99CAN
Cold Blooded	1-4201-2581-8	$7.99US/$8.99CAN
Deep Freeze	0-8217-7296-1	$7.99US/$10.99CAN
Devious	1-4201-0275-3	$7.99US/$9.99CAN
Fatal Burn	0-8217-7577-4	$7.99US/$10.99CAN
Final Scream	0-8217-7712-2	$7.99US/$10.99CAN
Hot Blooded	1-4201-0678-3	$7.99US/$9.49CAN
If She Only Knew	1-4201-3241-5	$7.99US/$9.99CAN
Left to Die	1-4201-0276-1	$7.99US/$10.99CAN
Lost Souls	0-8217-7938-9	$7.99US/$10.99CAN
Malice	0-8217-7940-0	$7.99US/$10.99CAN
The Morning After	1-4201-3370-5	$7.99US/$9.99CAN
The Night Before	1-4201-3371-3	$7.99US/$9.99CAN
Ready to Die	1-4201-1851-X	$7.99US/$9.99CAN
Running Scared	1-4201-0182-X	$7.99US/$10.99CAN
See How She Dies	1-4201-2584-2	$7.99US/$8.99CAN
Shiver	0-8217-7578-2	$7.99US/$10.99CAN
Tell Me	1-4201-1854-4	$7.99US/$9.99CAN
Twice Kissed	0-8217-7944-3	$7.99US/$9.99CAN
Unspoken	1-4201-0093-9	$7.99US/$9.99CAN
Whispers	1-4201-5158-4	$7.99US/$9.99CAN
Wicked Game	1-4201-0338-5	$7.99US/$9.99CAN
Wicked Lies	1-4201-0339-3	$7.99US/$9.99CAN
Without Mercy	1-4201-0274-5	$7.99US/$10.99CAN
You Don't Want to Know	1-4201-1853-6	$7.99US/$9.99CAN

Available Wherever Books Are Sold!
Visit our website at **www.kensingtonbooks.com**

Books by Bestselling Author
Fern Michaels

___The Jury	0-8217-7878-1	$6.99US/$9.99CAN
___Sweet Revenge	0-8217-7879-X	$6.99US/$9.99CAN
___Lethal Justice	0-8217-7880-3	$6.99US/$9.99CAN
___Free Fall	0-8217-7881-1	$6.99US/$9.99CAN
___Fool Me Once	0-8217-8071-9	$7.99US/$10.99CAN
___Vegas Rich	0-8217-8112-X	$7.99US/$10.99CAN
___Hide and Seek	1-4201-0184-6	$6.99US/$9.99CAN
___Hokus Pokus	1-4201-0185-4	$6.99US/$9.99CAN
___Fast Track	1-4201-0186-2	$6.99US/$9.99CAN
___Collateral Damage	1-4201-0187-0	$6.99US/$9.99CAN
___Final Justice	1-4201-0188-9	$6.99US/$9.99CAN
___Up Close and Personal	0-8217-7956-7	$7.99US/$9.99CAN
___Under the Radar	1-4201-0683-X	$6.99US/$9.99CAN
___Razor Sharp	1-4201-0684-8	$7.99US/$10.99CAN
___Yesterday	1-4201-1494-8	$5.99US/$6.99CAN
___Vanishing Act	1-4201-0685-6	$7.99US/$10.99CAN
___Sara's Song	1-4201-1493-X	$5.99US/$6.99CAN
___Deadly Deals	1-4201-0686-4	$7.99US/$10.99CAN
___Game Over	1-4201-0687-2	$7.99US/$10.99CAN
___Sins of Omission	1-4201-1153-1	$7.99US/$10.99CAN
___Sins of the Flesh	1-4201-1154-X	$7.99US/$10.99CAN
___Cross Roads	1-4201-1192-2	$7.99US/$10.99CAN

Available Wherever Books Are Sold!
Check out our website at **www.kensingtonbooks.com**